The Bac

Phoebe Luckhurst was born in London and brought up in Glasgow. She is a Senior Commissioning Editor at *The Sunday Times Magazine*, and has written features and interviews for the *Guardian, Sunday Times Style, Elle, ES Magazine, Grazia,* the *Telegraph* and *Vogue*. Phoebe has had the theme tune to *The OC* stuck in her head since 2003 and once almost spent her student loan on a micro-pig. She no longer shops online when drunk. *The Lock In* was her debut novel.

By the same author

The Lock In

The Back Up Man

PHOEBE LUCKHURST

PENGUIN BOOKS

PENGUIN BOOKS

UK | USA | Canada | Ireland | Australia
India | New Zealand | South Africa

Penguin Books is part of the Penguin Random House group of companies
whose addresses can be found at global.penguinrandomhouse.com

First published by Penguin Books 2023
001

Set in 12.5/14.75pt Garamond MT Std
Typeset by Jouve (UK), Milton Keynes
Printed and bound in Great Britain by Clays Ltd, Elcograf S.p.A.

The authorized representative in the EEA is Penguin Random House Ireland,
Morrison Chambers, 32 Nassau Street, Dublin D02 YH68

A CIP catalogue record for this book is available from the British Library

ISBN: 978-1-405-94950-7

www.greenpenguin.co.uk

To Sam, always

I

Connor had many good qualities – height, intelligence, a maestro's appreciation of *Gogglebox* – but Anya had to admit, in the four years they'd been together, a sense of poetry had never been one of them.

Year in, year out, anniversaries, birthdays and Valentine's Days had been marked with a box of Lindor balls and a jaunty, all-caps text ('TWO YEARS OF US!' marked passion of a sort, she supposed). The first time he told her he loved her – on the sofa, while they were eating spaghetti bolognese – he caveated it with a hasty, 'I think.' At the time, she'd decided he was simply overcome by the occasion.

So, in many ways, she ought not to have been surprised that were he to dump her, he'd do it in the parking bay of a Shell garage on their way home from Sunday lunch at his mother's.

'I'm sorry, OK. Really,' Connor had said weakly, as the tears started to crystallize on Anya's eyelashes. It was dark outside, and the spectral lighting and nauseous, petroleum odour of the Shell garage made everything feel even more nightmarish. 'It's been on my mind for a while, and I woke up this morning and decided I couldn't put it off any longer, but we were going to my mum's. I knew she'd be annoyed if we cancelled, and that she'd have bought enough food for both of us . . . so I had to wait until after that. I couldn't do that to her.'

'To her?!' Anya had whispered incredulously, but Connor hadn't seemed to notice.

And so she had watched the rain drip slowly down the windscreen as Connor drove them home to the flat to thrash out the miserable details. As soon as he turned the key in the lock it had begun: the whys (I just don't want this anymore), the whens (I don't know – a while I suppose) and the hows (well, no – we can't both stay here). Anya asked them each over and over: voice small, robotic and disbelieving, until Connor's wretched, whispered answers finally silenced her. Eventually, she just stopped dumb, chewing her thumbnail as she watched him pack a suitcase – the expensive one, with the built-in phone charger that they'd always shared on trips away.

'I'll go to Duncan's.' He was rolling his clothes neatly – like he always did – and the orderly, space-efficient way in which he was leaving her stung.

'How—'

'I'm so sorry, I really am.' He didn't look up but sounded so uncomfortable that she felt fleetingly sorry for him. 'I didn't mean . . . well, I've . . .'

He gave up and slid a roll-on deodorant inside his Asics trainers, then continued to fold his boxers, neck reddening in the awkward silence. Sooner than she'd hoped, he was standing in the doorway of the flat, suitcase beside him.

'When will you—'

'I'll give you a few days.' He seemed determined to avoid a real conversation – a back and forth with any consequences or conclusions – although her face must have said something that resonated, because he relented. 'A week, then. To get yourself sorted.' His eyes were watery, and he was fidgeting with his stubble, and she felt a pressure in her chest.

'Connor—'

'If you . . . if you could just let me know as soon as you've found somewhere to stay. Well, that would be great.' The flat was his, and he'd soon be reclaiming it. 'Oh, and Anya . . .' her heart crumpled now at the sound of him saying her name, 'I think we should . . . well, I don't think we should text. For a little while. Unless it's about where you're staying, of course.' He was staring at a space about half a metre to the left of her. 'I just think it would be easier for both of us.'

Nothing felt easy now, but he was already turning clumsily on his heel, running the suitcase over his toes in his panic to make his getaway. He paused on the top step.

'I'm sorry, Anya.'

And then Connor was away, suitcase wheels grinding on the staircase, avoiding her gaze so carefully that persisting in watching him leave her seemed pointless. She closed the door weakly, slumped against it and slid towards the floor, tears welling in her eyes.

When she heard the sound of footsteps, her breath caught and at an insistent knock, she scrambled to her feet. But it was only Georgie, her arms outstretched. Her sister's hair was pulled up into a low bun and her eyebrows looked as perfect as they always did.

'Sorry, I was too quick,' she mumbled into Anya's cheek, 'I bumped into him at the bottom of the stairwell.'

Anya leapt out of their embrace like she'd been electrocuted. 'What did you say?' It had been minutes and she was already desperate for news.

'Well, I couldn't pretend I didn't know, but we didn't stand there for ages talking about it,' Georgie mumbled, as she settled on the sofa in the living room, which felt empty and echoey, even though Connor had only taken the PS4. 'I told him there were plenty more fish in the sea.'

A pause.

'That's what you're supposed to say to me, Georgie.' Anya wrapped her arms around her knees. She was sitting on the floor but felt like she had vertigo.

'Ah, shit. Right. Yes.'

Mercifully, her sister had brought gin and, inexplicably, a multi-plug extension socket.

'I panicked.' Georgie pulled it out of her bag and placed it on the coffee table where they both stared at it for a moment. 'It was on display near the checkout and then I thought maybe he'd have taken all the plugs.'

'Why would he do that. *How* would he do that?' Anya could tell she was about to cry properly. Georgie was cool-headed and practical; if Connor's departure had sent her into a tailspin, what could it do to Anya? What might *she* buy at the supermarket? Thousands of batteries? A life's supply of bayonet lightbulbs?

'I don't know why – he always brought the adaptors when we went on holiday – look, just have it, OK?' Georgie pressed the multi-plug into Anya's palms. 'And let's get a gin down you.'

Her sister had summoned the cavalry. Anya was several shots deep when Paddy arrived bearing his own supplies: three oven pizzas and a bottle of tequila. Georgie buzzed him in as Anya, on a break from sobbing, was staring at the wall and muttering, 'I just can't believe he's done this.'

4

When Paddy appeared in the doorway, he clocked the Gordon's and shook his head gravely.

'I knew we'd end up with too many spirits.'

Tossing his grey coat on the back of the squishy armchair – Paddy always looked put together, even in a crisis – he placed the tequila on the table, then helped himself to a gulp of Georgie's drink. She opened her mouth in outrage.

'All right, all right, I'll get myself one' – he placed the glass back on the table in front of her and headed towards the kitchen – 'then I want the whole story.' He waved the pizza. 'I got one ham and pineapple and two pepperonis, by the way.'

Anya tried to say thank you, but it came out as a croak, and Georgie squeezed her hand. When Paddy reappeared a few minutes later, he was holding a slender plastic cup on which was printed the name of the recruitment firm where Anya worked, the office where she and Connor had met four and a half years ago. At least he now worked somewhere else, so she wouldn't have to see him in the office, doing an edgy two-step in the tiny kitchenette ('Do you mind if I just—?') and waiting while the other one finished up with the milk, although this was of limited comfort.

'Did he take all the glasses?'

Paddy sounded off-hand, but Anya blinked with alarm. 'What?'

'There are only a few in the cupboard . . .'

Anya sensed Paddy and Georgie exchange a glance as she stood up and – feeling the gin swilling in her legs – pitched out of the room and into the kitchen. A quick examination confirmed all their glasses and, more importantly, all of her cookbooks were accounted for. Relieved, she returned to the others.

'He didn't take any of the glasses,' – she was breathing heavily – 'I think we just don't have very many.'

'Well,' Paddy started, with another meaningful look at Georgie, 'I'm glad we've cleared that up.' He was sitting in the armchair now and Anya picked her way unsteadily back towards the sofa, where she wrapped her arms around her legs again and felt another lurch of the stomach at all the Connor-less life stretching out ahead of her.

'So, tell us then' – Paddy took a swig of his gin, then leaned forward, palms pressed in prayer, voice low – 'what happened?'

Haltingly, Anya filled them in on the details, stopping a few times to press her palms to her face to catch the dribbly tears, and Paddy and Georgie made noises in the right places. As she reached the end of the tale, she rubbed her eyes with the sleeve of her jumper. It was wool and made them itch.

'He's been acting a bit weird recently. Quiet and grumpier than usual.' She thought she caught a ghost of an expression on Paddy's face. 'But I thought it was just work. I know he hates his new boss . . .' she trailed off with a defeated shrug.

'Is there someone else?' Georgie asked gingerly, and Anya wished that the theatrics of break-ups did not come with their own clichéd script.

'I don't know,' her voice was thick with snot. 'I asked, but if there is he didn't admit to it. Maybe?' She bit her thumbnail and watched them both from behind swimming eyes.

'Oh, Anya.' Paddy crunched down on a piece of ice and grimaced.

'Who dumps someone like that after four years?' Georgie started indignantly. 'Four months maybe, but four years—' She stopped abruptly when she clocked Paddy's hard stare. There was a brief silence until he crunched on some more ice and winced again.

'Ouch. Sorry. Hit a filling that time.'

Anya felt a tear roll down her cheek, and Georgie squeezed her hand again. Paddy gave her a sad smile.

'Well, this settles it. They can call a substitute English teacher tomorrow. I'll pull a sickie.'

'Really?' She blinked gratefully at him. Paddy was an English teacher at the school where he and Anya had met, which still felt ludicrous to her, although he was now two years into the job.

'Of course.' He took a sip. 'You call in sick too. We can watch Attenborough all day.'

She managed a weak smile and Paddy nodded, satisfied.

'*And* I need to find somewhere to live.'

Anya turned her head again in Paddy's direction – it felt heavy – and asked, despite knowing the answer: 'Can you boot Ivy out?'

Ivy was Paddy's housemate, a loud Australian girl who cut her toenails at the kitchen table and used the word 'funsies'. Despite these steep odds, Paddy was enormously fond of her.

'No, I can't, Anya,' he said gently. 'I like Ivy. And she signed a lease. We are betrothed.'

Anya slumped an inch further into the sofa, while

7

Georgie stroked her soggy, woolly forearm. 'How long has he given you to get things sorted?'

'He said a few days, a week, maybe.' She closed her eyes to steady herself. 'He can't stay at Duncan's for long. He doesn't even have a spare room.'

Anya was certain that they were all, at that moment, remembering the housewarming at Duncan's that she'd dragged them to last year. Every spare surface of the flat had been covered with one of the following: an electric guitar; Rangers' memorabilia; beer paraphernalia; and by the end of the evening, a sticky layer of beer itself. They didn't remember much about his sofa – apart from the bit when a leery, beery bloke passed out on it, snoring wetly – but they couldn't imagine it was comfortable for Connor.

'I'll ask around.' Paddy frowned at his phone screen industriously. 'I'm sure someone has a room you can move into until you get things sorted.'

Anya hugged her knees even tighter at the thought of someone's bare, spare room being her new home.

'I know where you could go' – Georgie said flatly – 'but you might not like it.'

'Where?' Paddy stopped jabbing at his phone screen.

'Claire's. She's down on Hamilton Drive now – a big place, she earns enough. And she definitely has a spare room; she showed me last time I was round there.' Georgie sounded apologetic about Claire's abundance of square footage. 'I'm sure she'd give it to you for mates' rates, Anya.'

At this, Paddy snorted and Georgie shot him a glower. 'What's so funny?'

'Sorry. It's just the idea of Claire having mates.'

Georgie ignored this. 'Anya?'

With a long, steadying breath, Anya drew herself up in what she hoped – despite the snot and the soggy knitwear and the general emotional decay – was a dignified manner.

'Georgie, I am *not* going to live with Claire. Frankly, I'd rather move back to Renfrew Street.'

Renfrew Street was where she, Paddy and their friend Tasha had lived in their third year of university, in a flat that had infestations of mice, slugs *and* black mould (the holy trinity!). The building had later been condemned.

'Right,' Georgie said, soothingly. 'Of course not. Ignore me.'

They stayed in the living room for hours. After Anya entered a sort of catatonia, Paddy stuck the telly on and he and Georgie had pantomimed enthusiasm for a trashy reality TV show about people who worked on cruise ships, while Anya blinked bewilderedly at the liveried staff and their high-seas dramas. At around 11 p.m., Georgie clapped her hands together with an air of finality.

'Shall we go to bed? I have to be up for work.'

Anya had forgotten it was a Sunday. Things like this – dramatic, life-altering things – weren't meant to happen on a Sunday. Sundays were for gentle, non-threatening emotions and familiarity, and considering leaving the house until you realize that would involve putting on a bra and a shoe with a proper sole.

'Shotgun!' Paddy.

'What for?' Georgie petted Anya's head.

'The bed. Obviously.'

'Fine.' Georgie rolled her eyes. 'I'll take the sofa.' She had already produced an overnight bag and, from it, pyjamas, cleanser, moisturizer and a sleep mask, which she began to lay out on the sofa.

Wobbling slightly, Paddy gripped the top of the arm-chair. 'God, I'm more pissed than I thought.' He stretched out a hand towards Anya. 'Come on, you.'

Anya raised a weak arm and Paddy rolled his eyes.

'Oh, get up. You're too heavy for me to lift anyway.'

After using her toothbrush – 'You don't mind, do you?' he'd asked, once it was already hanging out of his mouth – Paddy had fallen asleep straight away. As he snuffled lightly, Anya stared at the ceiling, gripping the mattress with one hand as the memories came back in furious, disordered snapshots.

Last Saturday, pushing a trolley through the aisles, bickering cheerfully over what to have for dinner; a long, searching kiss last Hogmanay; their most recent holiday to Tuscany, in the spring, holding hands over a candlelit table then walking back to the hotel, gripping one another, unsteady from the wine and the cobbled stone paths. They never even fought, not really, not like she knew plenty of other couples did. There was the odd huff, the odd snappy word, but mostly they saw eye to eye on everything. Had there been signs, and had she simply ignored them? She supposed they hadn't spent as much time together recently; there had been a few Fridays and Saturdays when he'd made his excuses, and she'd ended up going out with Paddy instead. But that was normal, wasn't it? After four years, wasn't that the point? You were comfortable, settled, liberated to see your friends, safe in the knowledge that your relationship would carry on, untroubled.

Clearly not. 'It's been on my mind for a while,' was what he'd said, gravely, staring through the windscreen as he turned the world on its axis. Anya wondered if he'd spent disquieted nights like this, staring at the ceiling while she slept unwittingly.

Paddy issued a firecracker of a snore and rolled on to his side, tugging most of the duvet with him and she came to, turned on to her side and stared miserably at the wall until dawn.

2

It had been humiliating having to text her cousin Claire and beg to move into her spare room. Or it would have been, so Anya had made Georgie do it.

Claire was a last resort, although she was disappointed at how quickly she had reached that point, just forty-eight hours after Connor had dragged the good suitcase out of the door. But of course, most of her friends had long since arranged themselves into couples sharing one-bedroom flats, with no room for a spare part. Some of them had even moved to the suburbs, talking about primary schools and green space and low crime rates (at least a few of them had the good grace to look abashed as they did so). Meanwhile, Paddy had Ivy, and Anya's other best friend Tasha was in Vancouver, more than 4,000 miles away, which she hated but could not do anything about. Georgie, meanwhile, lived with Elspeth, a yoga teacher and nutritional therapist who, regrettably for the world at large, also had her own podcast. There had been a hopeful moment when Paddy remembered that his colleague Francesca's nan was looking for a lodger at her place in Milngavie, but sadly, the nan in question had already found someone. And so Cold Claire was her only option.

'I could ask one of my friends?' Georgie suggested, as she spooned spinach on to Anya's plate (or was it Connor's? She wondered if there were rules for how they'd divide the crockery). It was a sign of how bad things were that Anya had surrendered the cooking to Georgie.

'I'm not moving in with one of my *little sister's friends,*' Anya mumbled from inside the hoodie in which she'd cocooned herself as soon as she got home. It was a minor miracle she'd made it into work – even if said minor miracle was mainly thanks to Georgie, who had buzzed on the doorbell at 7 a.m. bearing a perfectly ripe banana, which she pressed into Anya's hands by way of greeting ('for energy') and then frogmarched her into the shower, declaring that Anya definitely looked like she needed a leave-in conditioner. 'That would be tragic. They'll all remember me from school as your cool, older sister.' Georgie's face remained impassive, so Anya continued, 'I can't just turn up on their doorstep with boxes of my stuff, spinning a tragic tale about Connor leaving me.' This hurt too much, so she added quickly, snippily: 'Also, don't they all live in eight-person house shares designed for five?'

'Anya, I'm twenty-seven. So are most of my friends. Most of us live in quite civilized flats now.' She finished doling out six potatoes on to Anya's plate.

'Well, anyway, I don't really like many of your friends, no offence.' Anya was pulling on the drawstring of the hoodie. One end was too short now.

'Thanks. What about SpareRoom?' Georgie sat down opposite her.

'I don't want to move in with a stranger. Especially not when I'm in this state.'

Georgie looked like she was trying very hard not to roll her eyes.

'OK, fine.' She picked up her fork. 'But you know what I'm going to say now.'

Anya did know.

'I don't want to have to ask her myself. She'll laugh.'

'No, she won't, Anya. She's nice—'

'Can't *you* just text her?'

Georgie had always got on much better with Claire who, despite being only twenty-nine, already owned a fairly large Victorian terraced house in the West End of Glasgow on account of her job as a solicitor at a city law firm. She was also already engaged to Richard, although he worked in IT, and had a funereal bearing, receding hairline and poor grasp of rudimentary social niceties. That Claire didn't *quite* have it all had been of some poisonous solace to Anya.

They'd all grown up together in Hillhead and attended the same school, each a year apart (Anya eldest, then Claire, then Georgie). Even as a teenager, Claire had been – as far as Anya was concerned – very cold and severe, lacking in charisma and unburdened by anything approaching a sense of humour. Her mother, Auntie Sal – who was thankfully warmer than her daughter – had worked as a midwife up at the Queen Mum's before it closed, and so Claire would often end up at theirs after school, though she'd refuse to watch telly with Anya and Georgie. Instead, she'd do homework at the kitchen table, marking her worksheets in precise handwriting that looked uncannily like a computer font. She always left her potato smileys, much to the delight of Anya and Georgie's father who'd hoover them up when he walked in the door at 6.30 p.m.

It was no secret that Claire and Paddy shared a mutual

hostility, which could be traced back to a long weekend in Fort William in their teens, when they clashed so strongly over the best way to erect a four-man tent that Georgie had had to physically separate them. As adults, they still struggled to make civil conversation; Anya, frankly, could sympathize with Paddy. But Claire and Georgie had stayed close whilst at university, and often had lunch in town, which made Anya feel hot and jealous. In Georgie's company, Claire had even been known to smile, and she had asked Georgie to be a bridesmaid at her wedding next year. Anya had been invited to show people to their seats, an offer she had tried to decline but Georgie wouldn't let her.

It didn't help that Anya didn't like Richard; indeed, even Georgie, who liked everyone, found Richard 'difficult'. He was pompous and self-satisfied, the sort of man who claimed expertise in any and every topic, and delivered it in an impatient, condescending tone that made Anya press her fingernails into her palm in frustration until he finally stopped talking. He was eleven years older than Claire and although Anya always liked to consider herself liberal and open-minded, she somehow could not help finding this a little odd. What she also found creepy was that for his fortieth birthday party, he'd made guests – including Georgie but not Anya – visit an escape room in a business park near Motherwell. Whichever way you looked at it, there was something discomfiting about collecting your friends, locking them in a small room that smelled of feet and watching as they scrambled to escape.

Georgie sighed now and picked up her phone.

'Fine. I'll text her. But when she says yes, you have to be grateful.'

Anya took a mouthful of mushy spinach and grimaced.

'And' – Georgie had seen her face and Anya felt a prickly guilt – 'if you don't like it, you can cook instead.'

'Sorry.' Anya could feel the lump of spinach in the back of her throat but managed a half-smile. 'It's delicious.'

She had barely been in the kitchen since Connor left; last Saturday evening – when she'd prepared her sweet potato and coconut stew with lashings of Greek yoghurt and pumpkin seeds – felt like another lifetime, and the pair of them like two entirely different people. Anya's food had been a centrepiece of their relationship, and Connor had been an enthusiastic guinea pig for every dish she prepared for @anyaeatstoomuch, the hobbyist Instagram account she had created a few years ago.

At university, Anya had run a restaurant blog, where she'd earnestly delivered her verdict on local greasy spoons and branches of Pret a Manger. A few years ago, she and Tasha had found it and spent an afternoon in hysterics reading her plummy posts, but Anya had also remembered how much she'd loved the project at the time and hadn't been able to stop thinking about it; until one afternoon, stomach squirming, she had created @anyaeatstoomuch, though she didn't tell Tasha (or Connor, or anyone) until she had several months' worth of pictures of meals she'd made with knowing, self-conscious captions and hashtags (#thesecretingredientisbutter #thenmorebutter). Tasha, Georgie and Paddy promptly started liking every post, and – in spite of her instinctive self-deprecation – Anya was proud of the account, which felt like a grown-up evolution of that earnest, overwritten blog she'd loved so dearly.

She had an initially (very) modest following, although it

had been growing steadily ever since (thanks, mainly, to the hours Anya spent studying other masters of the art) and had once been featured in an influential local food blog, in an article entitled 'Six West End foodies you need to follow now'. They called her 'unpretentious and adventurous', which she liked.

But the thought of making something to eat alone – of laying the table for one, no eager audience for the tasting notes she delivered in her silly Michelin-star voice – hurt too much to contemplate.

'How was work?' Georgie tried to spear another potato but it bounced off her plate and skittered along the table. She popped it into her mouth with her fingers.

'It was OK,' Anya replied. 'I just kept my head down.'

For almost six years, Anya had worked in recruitment at a smart office on Hanover Street. It often struck her as dispiriting that she had made a career of finding brilliant jobs for other people. She hated recruitment. She hated its smug buzzwords and the little headsets they wore in the office, and she hated the shiny suits and the whiteboard where their manager – a hyperactive sleazeball called Marc di Marco, who had the confidence of a far more remarkable man and the biggest headset of them all – salivated as he wrote up their names in order from best to worst performer. She hated that she was quite good at it, that she'd started out as an office temp, and that her role had now started to assume the menacing shape of a proper career.

Despite the money, the only good thing she'd ever got out of it was Connor. They'd snogged at one of Berners Bilton's after-work pub sessions following weeks of feverish email flirting and had started dating almost immediately.

Connor had left Berners Bilton two years ago to join a rival, better firm, and since then Anya had toyed with the notion of leaving – especially on Sundays, as another week loomed and she would spend hours in the kitchen cooking in order to distract herself – but the job was never bad enough to justify it. It was merely unsatisfying, which was possibly worse.

'Well, it's good you went in at all.' Georgie's bar for Anya was clearly very low. 'And it's Tuesday! It'll be the weekend before you know it.'

Anya hated that since Connor had left her, she and Georgie hadn't had any real conversations – just what felt like the sort of scripted small talk you'd have with a very new colleague you weren't mad about. She knew she was terrible company and that her sister was doing her best, but for some reason this made Anya angrier.

'Great.' She rolled her eyes. 'I can't wait.'

Georgie gave her a look, but before she could offer anything else, her iPhone lit up and she pounced, fingers flying across the screen. Anya had seen from across the table that it was Claire and felt an instant hot-cold sensation in her stomach.

'OK.' Georgie was grinning. 'You're on!'

'What did she say?'

'She says of course you can stay. Family is family.' Georgie sounded satisfied. 'But you have to help with the cleaning and things.'

'Obviously, I would do that.'

Georgie ignored the petulant tone and replied to Claire.

'There we go.' She nodded purposefully. 'She says why

don't you come by and see the room on Saturday. And then you can move in on the Sunday if you like it.'

'OK,' she managed eventually. The speed at which her life had upended itself was dizzying.

'And thank you, Georgie, for being such a brilliant sister and sorting my whole life out.'

'Sorry.' Anya bit her thumbnail and shot Georgie an apologetic look. 'Thank you, Georgie' – she reached across the table for her sister's hand and squeezed it – 'for being such a brilliant sister and sorting my whole life out.'

'Any time.' Her sister squeezed it back. 'I can come on Saturday. To see the room, if you like?'

It was kind, but Anya suspected that watching her cousin and sister's easy patter would make her feel worse about moving in there.

'No, it's OK. But thank you.' She paused. 'And some help moving in would be nice. If you don't mind.'

Georgie smiled.

'Of course I don't.'

The rest of Anya's week passed in the monochrome blur of routine: coffees; phone calls; all-staff meetings in which she contributed nothing; her days bookended by standing on the Subway platform, feeling the hot whoosh of Bakelite air, wondering quite how she'd got there. On Friday evening, freedom at last; she had rerouted via the small Italian deli near Connor's flat, where she'd bought the expensive ingredients for a simple truffle pasta.

Bracing herself, she had tiptoed into the kitchen and then, within minutes of beginning to cook, had found herself lulled by the routine, the sound and smell of the bubbling garlic, the tickle of spices in her nose. This was small but important progress; as she curled tagliatelle around a fork, she felt closer to normal than she had done all week, even if it only lasted the ten to twelve minutes the pasta was boiling for.

When Saturday came around, she felt like she was about to sit an exam. Anya had agreed that she'd be at Claire's at 10 a.m., and on the walk over, she clenched and unclenched her fists. As she reached the right house, she almost kept walking, until she remembered she had no alternatives. Her cousin's front door was tall and white, with coloured glass windows and a sign on the letterbox that said 'NO JUNK MAIL' that Anya knew was in Richard's handwriting. With a sigh and a hard swallow, she pressed the doorbell and heard a chime deep from within.

After a few moments, her cousin opened the door.

'Anya,' she stated.

'Hi Claire.' Her voice had a note of forced jollity.

'Come in.'

The house had a strange smell, like someone had burned a bath bomb, or left a bunch of lilies festering on a radiator.

'How have you been?' Anya tried, brushing her shoes vigorously on the hairy welcome mat.

'Good, thank you.' Claire closed the door behind her and glanced Anya up and down. 'Can I take your coat?'

Gallingly, Claire had always been long and slender, with cheekbones that could cut glass. Her long, straight dark blonde hair hung down her back, and she always wore the sort of plain clothes with architectural cuts that only the very thin could pull off. While there was undeniably a facial resemblance between the three of them (as children, Claire had been mistaken for a sister), Anya was shorter, darker and a little stockier, and Georgie was somewhere in between them both: taller than Anya, less ethereal than Claire, prettier than both of them, with her huge brown eyes and slightly wonky smile.

'Oh, um, thanks.' Anya shrugged out of her coat and passed it to Claire, who hung it on a stand in the hall. For a second, they both stood facing one another and Anya tried to remember when they'd last been together. Georgie's birthday? That was in February; it was September now.

'Shall I show you the room, then?' Claire had turned without waiting for Anya's response, and started heading up a looping staircase, Anya following in her wake. On the landing, they stopped in front of a closed door and she felt a shiver of unease.

'Recently, Richard's been using it as a glorified filing cabinet' – Claire sniffed to indicate her disapproval – 'but I'll obviously have him take his papers to his office before you move in.'

Anya imagined having both a spare room and an office.

'So' – Claire opened the door – 'what do you think?'

The room was empty, besides three big boxes of documents, a desk and a small lamp. There was a sash window framed by some heavy green velvet curtains, which looked on to the street below. The carpet – also green – was thick and bobbly. Anya couldn't imagine waking up here, although she could imagine staring at the ceiling as the witching hours inched past, wondering what had gone wrong.

'Is there a . . . bed?'

'No. You'll have to get one.' Claire examined one corner of the room and waved dismissively. 'I'm sure a single would fit in that corner.'

A single bed for a single Anya.

'We can do you £300 a month.' Claire was standing in the doorway now and Anya took her cue to hurry out. 'And I'm sure Richard could drive you to IKEA to get the bed.'

Anya imagined a drive, alone, with Richard and felt clammy.

'Oh God, no, no – I couldn't ask him to do that. He must be so busy. I'll get Paddy to take me – he loves IKEA.'

Claire pursed her lips, possibly at the utterance of Paddy's name. 'All right then.' She closed the door. 'You can move in tomorrow, if you'd like. Georgie mentioned it was urgent. You've seen the rest of the house, haven't you?'

Anya had not seen the rest of the house but sensed that to point this out would draw attention to the fact that she and Claire didn't spend a lot of time together.

'Aye – yeah, a few times. Lovely place.' She'd work it out when she moved in.

'Thank you,' Claire said, crisply.

They were descending the curving staircase now, and Anya had a strange, creeping feeling. Of course: Richard was standing at the foot of the stairway, in the front hall. His hair had receded further since she'd seen him last, although he was cultivating a stringy beard.

'Hi, housemate!' Anya tried gamely.

'Claire, we need to get the broadband looked at. It's been terrible this morning.' A flicker of weary recognition. 'Good morning, Anya.'

Richard was from Edinburgh, which – besides everything else – she'd always held against him, although Anya had to concede she hadn't made the best first impression either. On their first encounter, a Sunday lunch round Auntie Sal's, he had spent rather a lot of time lecturing her mother about the importance of changing her passwords regularly and had later overheard Anya commiserating with her mother about 'being stuck with that bore all afternoon'.

'I was just showing Anya the room.' Claire extended a cheek to Richard, who gave it a cold, dutiful peck. Anya assumed they had silent, clinical sex, which at least meant she probably wouldn't hear it from her new bedroom.

'Ah, yes.' Richard flared his nostrils.

'Thanks so much for having me,' she mumbled.

'It wasn't my idea.'

'Right.' She tried a smile, but he didn't respond in kind.

Claire, ignoring this exchange, had walked down the hallway, towards the front door with its stained-glass panels.

'Let me know what time you'll be coming, will you?' She opened the door. 'I'll have to get you a key cut.'

Anya swallowed at the prospect of packing everything she owned into boxes. It felt like it could take forever.

'Would – um – two p.m. work?'

'Yes. Don't be early though. I'm going to yoga and won't be back until one thirty.'

'No problem. Two p.m. it is.' Anya had got the arms muddled on her coat and felt silly. 'Thanks, Claire.'

'It's fine.' Her cousin smiled without her eyes. 'I'll see you tomorrow.'

And then Anya was on the step, the front door pulled abruptly behind her. Certain they were watching her through the door's glass, she walked to the end of the path and took a few confident strides to the right, until she was in front of the neighbouring house, at which point she pulled her phone out. Two WhatsApps and her breath caught; true to his word, Connor had not been in touch since last Sunday, but perhaps – in the universe's kismet way – now that she'd sorted something out, he'd texted to say everything was a mistake, and he was on his way back from Duncan's now. She delayed reading the texts for a few moments in order to hold on to this feeling of possibility.

Of course, it was only Georgie and Paddy. She opened Georgie's message first.

How did it go with Claire?
Please say you were nice

Automatically Anya started typing.

I was!!!

She stopped and – spatters of drizzle hitting the screen – deleted this, and instead read Paddy's message.

How was the house of horrors
When do you move in
Am going to Oran Mor with Ash and Mark this
afternoon if you need a drink

Anya made a face. Ash, Paddy's sole friend from primary school, was the sort of woman who used the word 'wedmin'; her fiancé Mark's interests were limited to Ash, craft beer and explaining the specific buses he had taken in order to arrive at his destination. Still, beggars couldn't be choosers, even if she didn't really have time for the pub because she needed to put her life with Connor into boxes.

> Sounds good
> I definitely need a drink
> What time
> ?
> Also, will you take me to IKEA to buy a bed
> I'll cook you dinner if you do

She was still standing on the street and, with a shiver, felt the creep of eyes on her. Richard was staring out the first-floor window of her new bedroom. Even from a distance, she could tell he was glaring at her. Gamely, she tried a wave. He closed the curtains.

She pulled her coat lapels around her and started walking back to Connor's. Paddy had replied.

> Yes of course
> Tomorrow?
> And we're meeting at 2pm
> Come join!

She tapped out a response.

> Great
> See you later x

The flat was cold when she returned to it – key sticking in the lock as it always did – and Anya kept her coat on to sit in the living room, hands writhing in her pockets. The curtains were half-drawn and through the gap she could see chimney tops and spidery aerials, urban turrets silhouetted against the cloudy sky. She would never see this view again, probably, not unless she and Connor somehow managed to achieve an impossible friendship.

Now it was official, she needed to tell him she was going. She'd been putting it off because doing so allowed her to believe he might change his mind but delaying the text could not, unfortunately, deny the reality, much as she might wish it to.

For thirty minutes she painstakingly drafted a Whats-App. Her phone was running out of battery and the screen had automatically dimmed, which added to the sense of doom.

Eventually, she had something.

> Hi, I hope you're doing OK.
>
> I'm just texting to tell you that I'm leaving the flat tomorrow and moving in with Claire. I'll pack up everything that's mine but if there's anything I leave then please let me know and perhaps I can arrange to pick it up. Or you can send it to me. X

She wanted to add something else – 'I miss you' maybe or 'Love, Anya' – but she knew she wasn't supposed to.

Anya had visited her WhatsApp thread with Connor too many times this week, reading and re-reading their last few months, looking for ghosts and clues and red flags, but hadn't been able to locate anything sinister, which had made everything feel even more unreal and unreasonable. It felt like there should at least have been a single message she could point to, one with such an explicit subtext that she'd have no one to blame but herself for missing the neon signpost. But there was nothing – if anything, he'd told her he loved her more in the weeks before he left. Anya had counted.

Before she could stop herself, she sent the message, watching the two ticks appear but not turn blue. For a few moments she stared at the screen again, willing Connor to appear, but he didn't and so she gave up and placed the phone face down on the table. It was just after eleven, which meant Anya could get almost three hours of packing done before going to meet Paddy and Ash.

She'd moved in three years ago after they'd agreed that, since she was spending most of her time here anyway, she might as well become a permanent fixture. She had immediately set about adding brightness and character, Connor marvelling at her efforts. 'It feels like a proper place now,' he'd said one afternoon, watching her straighten the poster they'd bought at GoMA, and which Anya had had professionally framed. She remembered the thrill of feeling important and useful and permanent.

Of course, it turned out she wasn't permanent, and her importance and usefulness were only temporary too. In fact, Anya could be boxed up and put in suitcases and it would be almost like she'd never been there.

Her clothes were easy: she cleared the rails and tipped her drawers into a suitcase and then sat on the top in order to pull the zipper shut. She flung shoes into canvas tote bags, and toiletries too. The bathroom looked empty without her shampoo and half-finished shower gels and self-tan moisturizers and washbags full of holiday-sized travel essentials. She hoped that Connor would feel as sad as she did when he saw the vacant spaces, although suspected this was unlikely.

She was grateful when it approached 2 p.m., and she could stop for a while. Perspiration beading on her forehead from the effort of loading boxes and bags for life, she fled the flat without a backwards glance and quick-marched the fifteen minutes to the pub where Paddy and Ash and Mark were already waiting.

'How are you doing?'

Her face already hurt from fake smiling.

'Fine!'

She knew he didn't believe her, but Paddy kept himself to a meaningful nod, passed her an empty wine glass and started pouring from the bottle of red.

Mercifully, she'd had two large glasses when Connor replied.

> Hi Anya, I hope you're doing OK. Thanks for letting me know.
> Glad you can go to Claire's.
> If you could leave the keys on the table when you go that would be brilliant. Thanks so much. Hope moving goes OK. X

She felt like her heart was breaking but didn't say any-thing to Paddy. Instead, she asked for another glass of red immediately, enjoying the feeling of it slipping down her throat, warm and anaesthetizing. She mostly let their con-versation wash over her, responding a few beats too late to every quip, her register a little off-kilter. At one point, Paddy squeezed her hand under the table.

Just after 6 p.m., bright-eyed and a little wobbly, she decided she must go.

'I have to finish packing!' As she was putting her coat on she toppled the bottle of red with a jerky arm. Paddy caught the bottle and avoided her eyes.

'Are you going on holiday?' Ash looked delighted.

'No – I'm . . . I'm moving.'

28

'Oh!'

Anya felt too hot in her coat.

'Which movers are you using?' Mark asked.

'I'm helping her.' Paddy smiled firmly. 'I'll see you tomorrow, Anya.'

She nodded too many times, flashing Paddy a grateful look, and then with a last flailing wave, made for the door, almost stepping on a small dog in her haste to escape. Outside, the evening was dusky, the clouds gone now, the horizon aflame, and Anya couldn't recall ever feeling as miserable at the sight of a sunset.

The flat was still cold and the boxes in the hallway looked unfriendly. She picked up an empty one and entered the living room.

Connor didn't read as much as her so the shelves in there looked naked and dusty when she'd removed her books and placed them in a box. All the games – Scrabble, Cluedo, Monopoly, Risk – were his, and she contemplated sabotage, taking a single piece from each game (perhaps the Monopoly card that declared a bank error in the player's favour), and then realized this was the sort of behaviour people told others about at dinner parties. She left the framed picture of them on the mantlepiece but placed it on its front so you couldn't see their grinning faces pressed together. Moments later, she returned to put it upright again. She hoped it might hurt more.

She'd left the kitchen until last: it felt like the setting of their relationship. All those meals she'd cooked there, carving celeriac and butternut squash; blending and blitzing and roasting; hair frizzy from standing over the hob, browning garlic and onions and spices. But she couldn't put it off forever. Skin prickling, she started to place the utensils reverently into a box, and carefully wrapped her casserole dish, weighing scales and crystal glasses.

Plates and mugs she was less sure about, so she simply divided the collection down the middle, ensuring Connor got the bowl with the chip. She placed her cookbooks in another box, pausing to flip through her scrapbook of curling recipes, cut out from weekend supplements, its heft feeling like ballast against disaster.

By midnight, she was exhausted and had a headache from the daytime wine, so she curled up on the sofa because she couldn't handle a last night in their bed and slept fitfully again.

Morning came, as it always did, and she spent the last few hours in her old life drifting into and out of rooms like a maudlin ghost, occasionally spotting something – a pen, or a receipt – which she'd toss into one of her bags. Just after midday, Paddy and Georgie arrived and together they squished all of her stuff into Paddy's small car, which smelled like Polos and Marlboro Lights.

After they'd loaded up, they both smiled hopefully at her and she tried not to cry.

'I just need to go leave the keys.' She disappeared up the stairs to the building alone before one of them could follow her.

The flat already felt like it had turned on her, its energy somehow hostile. She left the keyring – a sombrero – still attached on the chain, with a vague, fanciful fantasy that he would see this memento and be compelled to change his mind, then locked up for the last time, posting the key through the letterbox. And then they were off, Georgie squeezed into the back, Anya up front with Paddy.

When they turned up at Claire's ten minutes later, Anya felt winded.

'Ready?' Paddy squeezed her shoulder.

'Not really' – she worried at her lips with her teeth – 'but let's get it over with.'

'Good girl.'

The house still smelled of festering lilies. Claire was delighted to see Georgie, neutral on Anya and sniffy with Paddy, though she'd shown willing, carrying a suitcase up to Anya's new room, while Richard stood on the landing, stroking his stomach with long, bony fingers.

Claire had moved all of the papers out of the room, which made it feel even more soulless, and things weren't improved much by the boxes and suitcases of Anya's things. In fact, the chaos made everything feel like a bad dream, and she wanted to leave as soon as she'd deposited the last canvas bag of magazines and tangled cables on the green bobbly carpet. Paddy and Georgie had pre-empted this.

'Let's go to Cooper's.' They'd appeared on either side of her. 'You can unpack later.'

Much later, tiredness gnawing at her, feeling full and unhappy from the plate of nachos she, Georgie and Paddy had shared, Anya reflected that at least she'd got there: lying alone on a slowly deflating blow-up mattress in Claire's spare room had to represent some sort of rock bottom.

3

To: tasha.kelner@penandpencil.com
From: anyamackie@gmail.com
Re: S-O-fucking-S

Well. Remember last time I emailed I said I had 'nothing to report' and that 'everything was pretty same old here' and 'I miss you though'? Well, now only one of those things is true. Can you guess which one?

*****guessing space*****

Obviously, it's the bit about missing you.

So, Connor left me. Last weekend. We'd been at his mum's house, a whole afternoon perched on her horrid florid sofa drinking stewed tea and grinning every time she talked again about our 'coddled generation'. Then in the car on the way home, he says, 'I can't do this anymore,' and all that other clichéd bullshit and my whole world fell apart. So, guess where I've ended up.

*****more guessing space*****

Bloody Cold Claire's. Obviously, she has a massive, lovely house – although creepily decorated – but I'm in her spare room sleeping on an air mattress and wondering where it all went wrong. Claire is fine, if totally charmless, but her 'partner'

Richard is the sort of person who makes my skin itch to look at him. He's growing this weird beard and I keep finding these stringy hairs in the sink that are definitely not mine or Claire's. Also, he wears Crocs. Like out of the house, not just as a house shoe.

But obviously, the main problem is Connor. It all feels like a horrible nightmare. Sometimes I forget it's happened, and then I remember and it feels painful again. Paddy and Georgie have been brilliant but they're not you.

Maybe you could move home and then we could live together again, and relive the glory days of the Renfrew Street cesspit, but without the mice, slugs and black mould? I know Vancouver is great, but is it *that* great?

Sorry I've talked about myself for this whole email. Anyway: how are you, how is work and how is the hot Loic the Frenchman? I checked our horoscopes and it says that today I will feel 'torn between stubbornness and a desire for harmony', which probably means I'll have another weird stand-off with Richard over how to load the dishwasher. It says that you have 'a deeper capacity for empathy right now', which is how I knew my instinct to email you was right. I look forward to your wisdom.

Miss you very VERY much xxx

PS I did look and there is a flat on Renfrew Street available, two-bed, kind of perfect – it's even above a chippy, which I'm sure means it smells amazing 24/7. Think about it next time you're on a hike or doing something else wholesome and pure and Vancouver-ish.

According to the clock in the corner of Anya's laptop screen it was 8 p.m., which meant that it was only midday in Vancouver. Maybe Tasha would read the email straight away and respond, ideally with the news that she'd left her impressive job in advertising, signed the lease on the Renfrew Street flat and was booked on to the next flight home. She hit send and then pressed her fingers over her eyelids. Her eyes burned.

It was Wednesday evening, the fourth day of life under Claire and Richard's roof, and she'd sleep-walked through three more days of work, arriving home that evening to the sound of Richard giving a telephone operator from Scottish Power a brusque dressing down. Downstairs right now, her new housemates were watching an iPlayer-ed episode of *University Challenge*, each speaking over the other in their haste to prove they were more clever. Having listened to two starter questions to show willing, Anya had backed out of the living room wordlessly and climbed the stairs to email Tasha.

Unlike Anya, Tasha had always known what she wanted to do, and had gone out and done it. She'd started her advertising career on a grad scheme in the Glasgow office of a major global agency; two years ago, she'd been offered a role as a Senior Project Manager in their Vancouver outpost. Anya had felt winded at the news.

'But I want to go,' Tasha pointed out. She never sugar-coated anything. 'You can come visit.'

'But it's 4,000 miles away!' Anya had googled this pre-emptively.

'They have these things called aeroplanes, Anya.' Tasha grinned. 'And we can always email. And FaceTime.'

Tasha had always been braver than her too. They'd met properly in their second semester at Glasgow University, in the kitchen at their halls in Murano Street. Anya had come in to make a coffee, while Tasha was fishing a crumpet out of the toaster with a fork.

'Wait – sorry – it's just, you should turn the toaster off first.'

Tasha spun around, dropping the fork on the counter.

'Shit, you gave me such a fright!'

Anya had clocked Tasha before – she was loud, bleach blonde and boldly dressed (today, a bright pink boilersuit). She was a Londoner, which Anya – who was attending university in the same postcode in which she'd grown up – found to be impossibly worldly. Her voice sounded posh to Anya, but all English people sounded kind of posh to her.

'Sorry,' Anya mumbled. 'It's just you might get electrocuted.'

Tasha raised an eyebrow and for a second Anya thought she was going to laugh at her, but then she switched the toaster off at the wall and resumed fishing with the fork. Finally, she retrieved the crumpet and held it aloft.

'And I didn't get electrocuted!' She switched the toaster back on. 'Want one?'

Anya was meant to be writing an essay.

'Yes please.'

Their friendship was a slow burn, chats in the kitchen turning into wine from mugs in their respective rooms, turning into birthday invites and mixing their friendship groups (Tasha's was more glamorous, of course). She was gregarious and generous and Paddy – who had also stayed in Glasgow for university – adored her, sometimes to the

35

extent that Anya occasionally felt a little small and jealous and boring.

But they became a successful three. In second year, she and Paddy had lived in a huge house with five others; in third year, she, Tasha and Paddy had moved into the mouldering Renfrew Street flat and shared hangovers and heartbreaks. Anya cooked every night (she was in a Thai phase that year), and they'd had countless parties, people squeezed into every inch of the grotty property, drizzling fizzy supermarket mixers into the prickly brown carpet.

After university, Tasha had moved to a big shiny flat near the river that befitted her big shiny new job, and Anya had eventually moved in with Connor after a few years of living with her parents. She and Anya had merrily Whats-Apped all day, all week, always, but since Tasha moved to Vancouver, they'd preferred email: the longer, considered updates a more satisfying way to keep up with each other's lives than the short, sharp WhatsApp bulletins. They told each other everything, although Anya knew it had taken her a week to email Tasha because there was a part of her that felt pathetic and embarrassed about having to admit what had happened. It felt like a reflection on Anya. Someone like Tasha would never get dumped at a petrol station and have to move in with a boring cousin. In fact, Tasha didn't even have any boring cousins; her sprawling, bohemian family only appeared to breed artists, executives, architects, and one poet (Tasha's little brother, Finn).

Anya was getting maudlin and frowned. She would not let another evening descend into stagnant self-pity. With effort, she dragged herself into the bathroom and stood under the shower, feeling restored until she noticed a long, stringy hair plastered to the shower wall.

At least Thursdays were still good days: she had a standing appointment to eat savoury pasties in George Square with Georgie, who worked in a junior comms role for a small Scottish education charity based twenty minutes from Anya's office. Unless the weather was really terrible, there they met, and it was always Anya's favourite part of the working week, except for the bit when she switched off her desktop and walked out of the door for the weekend.

All she needed to do was get through the morning.

'Anyaaaaaa!' came a bellow from somewhere in the centre of the office.

She tried to slink into her cubicle quietly, her pulse quickening as she took the final steps from the kitchenette to her desk, but Marc di Marco had spied her and appeared beside her desk. As ever, he smelled like Toilet Duck and metallic sweat or, as Anya and her colleagues put it, 'eau de c***'. She wondered, nervously, what she'd done to attract Marc's attention this morning.

Clenching her fists under the table, Anya forced herself to look at him.

'Hi, Marc.'

He was leaning on one of the filing cabinets that bookended Anya's bank of desks, the other arm propped on a skinny hip, and appeared to be vibrating lightly. Anya's colleague Callum swore that he had once discovered a mostly empty blister pack of Modafinil on the desk in Marc di Marco's office.

'Heard it on the grapevine,' he whined in his nasal twang.

Anya noticed that his face was screwed into an expression of exaggerated sympathy and felt a sudden, leaden fear.

'Heard what?' she asked mechanically, fearing that she already knew the answer.

'You and C boy.' A predatory simper. 'I heard that he' – Marc glanced around to ensure his audience were paying attention, which Anya knew they were – 'left you.' He said the last bit at a near yell.

Immediately, Anya felt like she had swallowed something live and kicking. The only person she'd told about Connor was Mhairi, her closest work friend, and only because Mhairi had heard her crying in the loos. They were close for colleagues but hardly real friends; still, Anya felt instantly betrayed.

'Yes. Well.' She could feel the dreaded colour rising in her cheeks and her hands start to shake. She was glad she couldn't see Mhairi from her desk. 'I don't think it's appropriate for you to talk about my relationships at work.'

This was a long shot, and she knew it.

'Give it up, darling.' She hated the way he curled the 'r'. 'I heard it from Kenneth McLeish over at Bird and Briggs.' Marc di Marco crossed his arms in satisfaction.

So, it wasn't Mhairi's fault. The Glasgow recruitment consultants' world was small, and Anya supposed it had only been a matter of time. Still, she wished it hadn't been Marc di Marco with the scoop. He'd shuffled further from her desk to ensure he could be seen the length and breadth of the office now, and had both hands on his skinny hips, tapping a foot.

'Four years, was it?' Marc di Marco was examining her face carefully and she didn't trust herself to respond. 'So, tell us' – he grinned a slobbery smile and Anya's blood ran hot and cold – 'is it true he chucked you in a car park on the way back from his mum's house . . .'

'SHUT UP!!'

Anya stood up so fast her office chair spun and she found herself in Marc di Marco's face, shoulders squared, so close she could see the blackheads on his nose. Her breathing was ragged.

He stepped back a pace and raised both palms in surrender.

'I was just messing around. Don't get your knickers in a twist . . .'

'I said shut up, you skeezy little weasel—'

But her voice was squeaky and tremulous, and she'd already run out of steam. Had Connor told everyone it had happened in the Shell garage? Feeling the office pitching, she took a wobbly step backwards and observed Marc di Marco. He had an eyebrow cocked.

'That's no way to speak to your boss, Anya.' He sounded delighted.

'Well – that's all right since actually you can stick your fucking job.' She'd yelled the last part.

Before he could interject, she grabbed her handbag from under her desk – hands trembling – and stood up. The office was so quiet now you could hear the buzz of the huge strip lights.

He stepped forward and she flinched.

'You're making a big mistake, darling.'

'Go take a shower, Marc.'

She stepped past him and walked the three or so metres away from her ex-desk to the double doors of the office,

39

knuckles whitening on her handbag's strap. She kept her eyes trained on the floor, avoiding the gapes of her colleagues, trying to pretend she couldn't hear their murmurs, the glee at a scandal disguised as concern.

When she reached the doors, she fumbled with the big green button and virtually fell through them in her haste to escape. Waiting until she was around the corner and in the stairwell, she breathed again, gulping and gulping until she thought she was going to be sick. But after a few moments, she grew convinced that someone would pursue her and panicked, stumbling down three flights of stairs, gripping the banister all the way. When she made it to the building's entrance hall, her pulse was roaring in her temples, and Anya carried on out of the main doors.

Outside, the city was oblivious: taxis glided around corners; buses lurched into their stops; people paced and milled and queued in the Leon across the road. It felt strange that everything was so normal when Anya had just made a colossal, explosive decision. She stepped out of the path of a bespectacled man whose eyes were glued to his phone.

It was barely 9.30 a.m. and Georgie wouldn't be at their meeting bench in George Square for hours, but on a Thursday morning, Anya couldn't think of anywhere else to go. She couldn't go back to Hamilton Drive; Richard was working there, jabbing at his keyboard in the gloom of his office, and she couldn't bear to have to explain to him what had happened, what she'd done, why she was home barely two hours since she'd left for work. And so she walked to George Square, where she had her pick of the benches. At that hour, only one was occupied by a benevolent drunk who tipped his Tennent's Special lager in her direction. She nodded politely back, heart still in her throat.

She needed to speak to someone. Mhairi had already called twice, but she didn't want to speak to her, didn't want to imagine Marc di Marco lurking in the background, listening, salivating. Paddy would be at school and Georgie would only panic, plus Anya could tell her in person in a few hours anyway.

Her hand shook as her fingers flew across the screen.

To: tasha.kelner@penandpencil.com
From: anyamackie@gmail.com
Re: S-O-fucking-S

Tasha, I think I've literally lost it. I just screamed at my boss, quit my job and then ran out of my office. Obviously, this is a moment I have dreamed of for many years because I hated it but OH GOD WHAT HAVE I DONE.

Sorry, you're getting me very much in the aftermath here. I am sitting on a bench in George Square near a really nice drunk man.

Fuck. First Connor, then Claire's house, now unemployment. Please help.

Sorry about all the capitals, I know you hate when I do that.

Xxx

After sending it she felt a little better; at least her heart was no longer catapulting up her gullet. She tried sitting still for a few minutes, but it was a nippy late September day and soon she was fidgety with cold. Pulling her coat around her and stuffing both hands in her pockets, she set off again, this time towards the Buchanan Galleries shopping centre, feeling like a hunted truant.

The mannequins in their trench coats and party outfits depressed her, as did the soundtrack of bubblegum pop piped from every store, and so she holed up in the food court on the top floor, reading a discarded *Metro* and nursing an Americano. Her mood veered between dread and a fidgety exhilaration – a sense of possibility, in spite of everything – although maybe she was just hungry.

When it was time to meet Georgie, she sloped back towards George Square, though the man with the Tennent's had disappeared and Anya felt oddly bereft. As she whipped around, indecisive about which bench to home in on, she almost collided with her sister, who was bearing two greasy Greggs bags.

'Hi, hi! Perfect timing.' Georgie handed one pastry to Anya, then tossed her tote bag on to the nearest bench, and sat down. 'I got you a fake steak bake because I thought we should try being vegetarian. I was just reading an article about Greta Thunberg and felt both awe and crushing guilt.'

'Thanks, Georgie.' Anya lowered herself slowly on to the seat. She wasn't sure how to start.

'I reckon I wouldn't even know this isn't meat, you know.' Georgie had already started, nodding at the paper bag that was warming Anya's knees. 'Try it.'

Anya took a deep breath.

'I did something really stupid and I have to tell you about it.'

Her sister promptly put her pastry down and rearranged her face into a neutral expression.

'Connor.'

Anya shook her head. She felt sick.

'More stupid than that.'

'OK.' Georgie frowned. 'What?'

'I just quit my job. I yelled at Marc di Marco and then I ran out.' She swallowed. 'I've been mooching around Buchanan Galleries all morning.'

This came out in a rush; Georgie pressed her lips together. She looked like their mother when she did this, and Anya felt a trickle of cold fear.

'Why?' she asked eventually.

'He was teasing me about Connor and I snapped. I didn't know I was doing it until I started doing it.' She risked a look at Georgie, but her expression was too crest-fallen now and it stung, so Anya resumed staring into the middle of the square, where a ragged flock of pigeons was congregating around a discarded carton of takeaway chips. 'I'm sorry.'

'Can you get it back?' Georgie's eyes were big. 'Go into the office and grovel and—' she trailed off, and Anya imagined going back to Marc di Marco with her tail between her legs and felt vaguely nauseated.

'No,' she said. 'I can't. I don't think it would work, any-way.' She was certain this was true.

'But what are you going to do for money?'

'I don't know.' The thought of her life free-falling gave her that sense of vertigo again. 'I haven't really thought about it. I didn't mean to do it' – she was blinking fast – 'obviously I hated that job for a long time, but—'

'But you don't have another one.'

'I *know*, Georgie.'

Anya regretted snapping immediately.

'Sorry,' she added quickly. 'I'm just panicking a little.'

'It's OK.' Georgie patted her hand absent-mindedly. 'We're going to sort it out, OK? You'll find something new and amazing. It's all going to be fine.'

'Do you think?'

'Definitely. I mean, you found jobs for people for years. You must have some clue how to do it.'

Anya didn't have the heart to tell Georgie that this wasn't really how recruitment worked. Instead, she tried a bite of her fake steak bake. Georgie was watching her carefully.

'This tastes nothing like meat.'

'I thought you'd say that.' Georgie shrugged. 'I like it.'

Anya tried another nibble to show willing. It tasted like eating a hot, salty sponge.

'What a sham. I bet I could do a way better veggie steak bake than this.'

Georgie rolled her eyes.

'What are you going to do this afternoon?'

The thought of the afternoon stretching ahead of her was a little terrifying.

'Go home, I suppose. Well. Claire's.'

Georgie looked anxious now.

'Want me to come round later?'

Anya shook her head.

'No. It's OK. I sort of feel like being by myself.'

'Promise you won't just lie in bed all evening, moping?'

'Oh, Georgie.' She balled her hands, put them in her pockets and tried a game smile. 'I just can't make those kinds of promises right now.'

4

At 6 p.m., Berners Bilton's battle-axe of an HR woman, Pam McKechnie, had emailed Anya to confirm what she had already known: her outburst had been taken as a verbal confirmation that she wished to leave her role and, 'in the circumstances', they were waiving the notice period. She was out, with immediate effect. Anya would receive her last salary and any outstanding holiday pay at the end of the month. Pam wished her all the best, although Anya was fairly certain she didn't.

She'd read the email in the Tesco Metro near Claire's house, feeling her stomach plummet into her shoes. Despite the message's threat of imminent financial doom, she had continued to load her basket with ingredients. When she'd got back – tiptoeing past Richard's study, where she could hear him giving a nasal monologue about phishing emails, and instantly pitying the person on the other end of the phone – she'd prepared a spinach and seaweed soup, frying an onion, adding the stock, then adding the seaweed and tofu, and eventually handfuls of dark green spinach. She'd served it with crusty sourdough croutons and plenty of turmeric and cumin, and paused to take a picture of it for @anyaeatstoomuch, liking how it looked on Claire's presumably expensive Scandinavian crockery. Once it was up, Anya had gulped a bowl at the kitchen table, the broth warming and salty and soothing her soul.

Then she'd crawled into bed, checking Instagram too often, and feeling too gratified by the sight of the little red bubble saying another person had liked her broth.

She'd forgotten to un-set her alarm, and it had trilled at 6.50 a.m., a rude and insistent reminder that Anya had nowhere to be and no one to see. At least she'd already been awake, replaying the moment with Marc di Marco on repeat, remembering the way the pores on his nose looked at close range, while her chest pounded with adrenaline and her fingers fizzed with nervous energy.

She could hear Claire and Richard moving around, starting the morning relay of showers and toothbrushing to a soundtrack of Radio 4. Eventually, around 8.30 a.m., she heard the front door slam – Claire – and then a little while later, the study door click shut – Richard – and Anya finally unfurled herself from the foetal position and reached for her iPhone. Tasha had replied.

To: anyamackie@gmail.com
From: tasha.kelner@penandpencil.com
Re: S-O-fucking-S

ANYA!!!! I'm so sorry and fucking hell. Are you OK? Obviously not. Imagine I'm with you right now. I would be giving you a bear hug so tight that you might break a bone.

I'm speechless about Connor. I mean, obviously, I can say all the things about how the relationship can't have been right if he did this, how he didn't deserve you, but I imagine you don't want to hear any of that bullshit right now because you are deep in heartbreak and probably listening to the xx's first album all day and night. My top tip would be not to do this. Do you want to tell me more? Or would you rather not talk about it?

Claire's house sounds like a weird social experiment. Did I meet Richard? He sounds like he should be on some sort of register of creeps. Can you cut his beard off when he's sleeping? We need to get you out of there. Can't Paddy get rid of that dippy Australian and move you in?

Now, the job. This is the only bit that to me kind of seems like it could be a backhanded gift from the universe. Anya, you've hated that job for years. This is your chance to do something else. Turn Anya Eats Too Much into something proper! As I have always said you should, because you are the best chef I know and you know it too.

Also, I can lend you some money if you need. Just let me know.

Vancouver is great. But it's getting cold, even colder than Glasgow the Renfrew Street year where all the radiators were broken. I tried ice hockey the other week! I fell over loads but it was pretty fun, kind of like being in an American high school movie. Or a Canadian one. I don't think they have as many classic ones though. Loic is good. I don't really know what he's saying half the time but we don't talk all that much. Nudge, nudge etc.

I miss you too. Please email me back ASAP with updates. And don't jump off a bridge. Paddy and I would only fight about who will do the speech at the funeral.

Shall we FaceTime soon? I know the time difference melts my mind a bit but maybe we could do a weekend?

Love you, T xxxx

Anya re-read the email twice, imagining it read in Tasha's English accent, peppered with 'like' and 'so', and her funny long vowels that Anya and Paddy, with their identikit Weegie accents, sometimes teased her about. She would reply later to inform Tasha that she had not yet listened to a single song by the xx; truthfully, she was too worried to listen to anything in case soaring chords triggered total emotional implosion. On the other hand, it was only 9 a.m. and she was already in the foetal position, although at least Anya now had a real mattress to have a breakdown on. Paddy had taken her to IKEA but after seeing a poster in the aisles of a single person building the single bed frame, she had opted only for the (single) mattress. For some reason it felt less depressing.

'I'll buy you a bed, Anya,' Paddy said flatly. She had lied and said the frame was too expensive.

'No!' A pause. 'I don't want a single bed anyway. It's like accepting I'm a single person.'

Paddy had made a pointed expression.

'I'll be fine with just the mattress. Can you help me lift it into the trolley, please?'

For a while, Anya tried lying on her side and ignoring her roaring thoughts, listening to the creaks and groans of a house at rest. Eventually, she conceded – with a grumble – that Tasha's words had got to her.

She was right, of course. About everything, usually, but especially about work. Recruitment was never what Anya had wanted to do. If she squinted, leaving Berners Bilton was virtually good news – especially by recent standards – as long as she ignored the fairly urgent need to find a new source of income.

She unfurled herself and sat up. This was not quite as momentous as she'd hoped: her single mattress was rather thin and she could feel her bum nudging the floor. Nonetheless, she struggled to her feet, and stepped towards the boxes of cookbooks in the corner. Anya Eats Too Much: could she really turn it into something bigger? The thought made her feel both thrilled and slightly irritated. Bloody Tasha, making the world feel open and possible.

She took several books from the top of the box and then sat down on the floor, rifling through the first at random, a rustic Tuscan tome spattered with oil and tomato paste, and her own scribbled notes in the margin ('use passata instead!!'; 'good with conchiglie – holds sauce well').

Anya had never done any formal training (unless you counted a Standard Grade in Home Economics), but she'd studied her craft, in her own informal, unorthodox way. Food had always been a big part of her life at home, when friends, neighbours, waifs and strays would gather at their big wooden kitchen table for bountiful meals from her mother's fairly conventional repertoire (meat, sauces, potatoes and bakes, always with a side salad and always followed by a dessert). Anya knew even then that food held power: the power to soothe and settle quarrels, to make life a little more cheerful, even temporarily – especially if something frothy like tiramisu was involved. When Paddy's parents had been getting divorced, he'd come for dinner almost every evening for six months and although they never talked about it, Anya knew that these meals had helped. But it wasn't until she was sixteen and had started working weekend shifts as a waitress doing silver service at plush events held on glass-plated office

49

floors and in secret rooms of museums and galleries, ferrying plate after plate of perfect food to waiting tables, that she had become obsessed with the artistry of cooking.

This food was unlike anything she'd seen before. It was fascinating; silly and frilly with garnish; and looked insubstantial in the middle of huge dinner plates that made Anya's arms ache as she snaked between the tables. Sometimes she'd have to pour a sauce on to a starter and she'd try to do this with a flourish, like the chef had shown her. When she collected the plates, she examined which meals had gone down the best, and which ones people had ignored or picked at, and she wondered if he minded. (As an adult amateur chef, Anya always did – she couldn't help it.)

She started reading cookbooks in her spare time, beginning with her mother's ones – traditional *Good Housekeeping* volumes and Delia Smiths – and then graduating on to more exciting ones bought from bookshops with her waitressing earnings. In Glasgow in the late noughties, exciting cuisine mainly meant anything that wasn't centred on a carbohydrate, and she'd study these thrilling dishes, with their endless steps, and imagine serving them up on one of the huge white dinner plates she carried at work.

At the weekends, Anya started to attempt recipes, bribing Georgie to be her sous-chef with the promise that she could eat what they made. When Anya had made her first roast lamb with homemade mint sauce, Georgie had insisted their mother take a picture of it using the family camera usually reserved for sports days and Christmas (mortifyingly, this picture was still stuck to the fridge in her parents' house in Balfron. The years had not been kind to it). When Anya went to university, people in her halls watched in awe as she managed to conjure proper meals – soupy ramens and salmon gravlax and lemony pasta – using the rudimentary kitchen facilities. Anya spent any cash she wasn't spending on nights out on more cookbooks and flashy utensils, and often, in between lectures, she'd mooch up Byres Road and go to a gift shop whose ground floor was devoted to expensive kitchenware, which is where she discovered the existence of Le Creuset. She asked for and received one of the big casserole dishes for Christmas in her second year and when it wasn't in use, she kept it wrapped up inside two woollen jumpers in her wardrobe and checked on it regularly.

In her twenties, as Glasgow's food scene underwent a transformation, she treated trips to new restaurants as recon missions, often flagging down a harried waiter or waitress to ask about herbs and ingredients. 'Are you allergic?' asked one horrified waitress, when she asked what was in the risotto. 'No, she's just being a geek,' Connor replied, cautioning Anya with a look.

So, she'd had a training of sorts. And she really could cook everything – from the traditional to the elaborate to the experimental. Anya wasn't very brilliant at anything, but she was good at food.

Could she spin Anya Eats Too Much into a living? A proper food blog or a catering company . . . or something? The idea seemed ambitious and complicated and nebulous, and it would need work and strategy and money. And possibly a FaceTime with Tasha, and several good nights of deep, unbroken sleep. But it was possible – or certainly not impossible.

She reached for her phone. The seaweed and spinach

soup had clocked up 3,456 likes. Before that, the last post had been a lemony, paprika-y paella, smoky yet sweet thanks to the plump red bell peppers she'd bought from the market stall near the Subway (run by a leathery charmer who'd been there since the mid-eighties; the stall was a bit of a locals' cult favourite). The picture – like most of them – had been taken in Connor's kitchen, but she tried to focus on the food, not the gnarled wooden kitchen table they'd sat at almost every day for so many years. Scroll, scroll: there was the miso-roasted squash she'd made on a dispiritingly chilly day in July, a portion shot in her prized shallow turquoise bowl (2,032 likes), Connor grumbling to eat as she dithered over getting the picture right. She scrolled to the gooey brownies that she hadn't got quite right, not quite enough salt; and the baked cod that – try as she had – hadn't been very photogenic, but had tasted perfect: flaky and lemony, the cayenne pepper adding just the right amount of spice.

There was something reassuring about seeing all these dishes; they made her feel anchored to something, and a little peckish. Although he'd loved eating the food, Connor had always found the account a little silly. 'Wow, just like Gordon Ramsay,' had been his assessment after she hit 5k followers. She'd laughed it off – it was silly – but it had stung a little. Perhaps – just perhaps – she could show him.

But she would have to hold this thought because her mother was ringing.

Anya's mother had in fact already called – four times last night – but Anya had felt too raw to face the inevitable inquisition about what precisely had happened at

Berners Bilton. There had also been a number of texts, which had started gentle ('Are you OK? Please call') but evolved quickly to snippy ('Anya. Call us please') and shrill ('Anya????'). Anya had not replied to a single one of these either. Inevitably, there had also been messages of 'concern' ferried via Georgie, who had WhatsApped just as Anya had finished cleaning up after dinner (the only sanctuary in the whole of Claire's place was the kitchen, which had windows and shiny surfaces and every appliance Anya could dream of).

Georgie
Anya I'm sorry but please can you call Mum??
She won't stop messaging me
She's doing my head in

Anya blinked fast, feeling immediately hunted.

Anya
I'll call them when I'm ready
Also: thanks for telling her I'd quit my job
!!

Georgie
Sorry
I was worried!
And now Mum's worried you're having a breakdown

Anya
Well I am

She was, probably.

Georgie
You aren't

Just give them a ring

Please

They just want to check you're OK xx

Anya

FINE

I'll do it tomorrow

Despite Georgie's assurances, Anya was very worried about what they'd say. Their parents were practical, west of Scotland stock – the Calvinist sort who didn't believe in fripperies like 'gap years' or 'dream jobs' – who had, until their partial retirement two years ago, been in gainful employment since their early teens. Anya's mother's first job was as a Saturday cashier at a dry cleaners in Clydebank ('and don't think it was fun, Anya,' she'd said, more than once. 'Don't think being around all those coats was some sort of *treat*'). Anya's rash decision to quit, with no plan, flew in the face of the life they'd made and the type of life they believed in.

But she could only run for so long, and her mother was no quitter. Frankly, there was a good chance that she was already on her way over to Claire's, grinding her teeth like she always did when she drove. Heart sinking, Anya picked up the phone.

'Hi Mum.'

'Anya! *Finally!* You're alive!'

'Of course I'm alive, Mum—'

'Now bear with me one second, I'm just parked up outside the post office and I'm trying to fiddle with that little handle on the seat. Your father always has it pushed so far back from the wheel.'

There was some kerfuffle in the background and Anya heard her mother utter an 'ooft'.

'OK, that's better. I could barely reach the pedals.'

'Mum, you shouldn't be on the phone while you're driving, especially if you can't reach the pedals—'

'Now listen here.' Her mother's tone was business-like now. 'I've been trying to get hold of you and you know it. What's all this about you quitting your job?'

'It was time for a change,' Anya attempted stiffly. 'You know I hated that job.'

She was sitting cross-legged on the floor, still surrounded by the cookbooks. From the other end of the line, her mother made a clucking noise.

'Now, pet, I know you hated it. But it's unwise to quit a job unless you have another to go to.'

Anya wished people could stop saying things she didn't want to hear.

'Not to mention, what are you going to do for money?'

'I have some saved up,' Anya muttered. This was true. She had about a thousand pounds in an ISA, but she'd be paid again at the end of the month – although not much because she mainly worked on commission. Suddenly, things felt scary and sad. Even over the phone, her mother sensed the clouds descending.

'Now, it's just awful about Connor, love. I'm so sorry.'

Anya wished she wouldn't. Now she was definitely going to cry.

'Your father is furious,' she continued. 'Just a few weekends ago he was promising to drive out here to take a look at the lawnmower.'

'Well, isn't that the real tragedy.'

About four years ago, Irene and Stephen – now pushing the end of their mid-sixties – had relocated to Balfron, a genteel village about 45 minutes drive from Glasgow, where everyone knew everyone's business and talked about it in the queue at the Bank of Scotland on the high street. Her father was a doctor, who now worked part-time at the village practice, and her mother was a mostly retired music teacher, who still did the odd lesson. Anya blamed her for making her play the trumpet from the age of eight right up until the last day of sixth form, and therefore dooming her to be the object of unsophisticated jokes about sucking and blowing. To this day, Paddy still teased her about the assembly in which she'd played a solo in front of the whole school and turned purple, out of a combination of embarrassment and oxygen deprivation.

As they meandered through their last decade before full-time retirement, her parents were – as per the normal course of things – growing more interested in gardening and pottering, though her mother was also plugging the gaps of gainful full-time employment by inserting herself into the mechanics of the village's local politics, both formal and informal. A few months ago, her father had phoned and revealed, in a dark whisper, that he was concerned that 'your mother might be considering standing for the council'.

'Have you spoken to Connor at all?'

'No.' She wished her mother wouldn't say his name. 'He doesn't want to speak right now.'

'Right-o.' Irene swallowed. 'Well, Georgie says you're getting on very well at Claire's. Lovely house, isn't it?'

'Yes.' This came out as a hiss.

'Maybe you could come out and see us next weekend?'

'I'll probably be going out with Paddy next weekend,' she lied automatically and almost instantly felt guilty.

'Oh, lovely!' Her mother loved Paddy. Whenever he joined Anya in Balfron, they'd barely be through the door before Irene was bustling him into the best armchair – the one that reclined – and bringing him a massive drink and demanding 'all his news'. He called her 'Reeny', which Anya hated. He knew this, which was at least partly why he did it.

'Maybe I could come up next week though. I mean, I don't have anywhere else to be.'

'Oh, Anya—'

'Well, I don't. No job. No boyfriend. Paddy and Georgie and everyone else I know are all at work in the daytime.'

This was a mistake: Irene didn't believe in self-pity.

'Less of that, Anya – plenty of people would love what you have. Why don't you come down one day next week.'

'OK. I'll see.'

'Good.' Business-like again. 'And Anya, you make sure you're looking for another job, will you? Maybe you could hand your CV around, for a start. The West End has so many new places. It's so different even from when we lived there a few years ago.'

'Well, I've had an idea actually—'

'And,' her mother was on a roll now, and wasn't listening, 'I'll ask the ladies up here if they know of anything going. Something to tide you over, at least.'

Irene was gripped by many unshakeable misapprehensions about how the world worked (emails cost money; central heating actually made you colder). Obviously,

Anya would not find a hot tip for a new career off the back of one of Irene's conversations in the queue at the post office (why did their generation always have so many things to post?), but it would be pointless to attempt to explain this. Still, she was feeling self-destructive enough to try.

'That's not how the world works anymore, Mum.' She heard how snappy she sounded and felt mean. 'But thank you,' she added sulkily.

'You know Anya, you underestimate Balfron. It has a way of making things happen.' Irene had quite the mystic streak for a good Scottish protestant woman.

'I'm sure. And while you're at it, maybe you could also ask someone in Balfron if they've got a million pounds behind the sofa cushions.'

Anya knew it was a mark of quite how pitiful she had become that her mother did not rise to this.

'Anyway, pet,' Irene sounded brisk now. 'I must dash. I have errands to do. But look, your Dad and I will send you a bit of money to keep you going, all right? Just 'til you get back on your feet.'

Anya considered refusing this and then realized she couldn't afford to.

'Thanks, Mum.'

'Lots of love.'

'I love you too.'

5

Three hours. Three hours was all it had taken Anya's mother to find her a new job.

> Hi Anya. Have spoken to Fiona Morton who I bumped into at the post office and I have some good news. Her granddaughters Rosie and Rachel need a babysitter for a few hours after school, Monday to Friday. They're up in one of the grand houses near Park Circus! She's going to call you. They need someone ASAP. Looking forward to seeing you in Balfron next week. Love, Mum. X

As she read the message, Anya could feel something rising in her throat – fear? Fury? – and then realized it was the atom-deep humiliation of having her mother ask around to secure her an after-school babysitting job. She could vaguely remember the outline of Fiona Morton, a large-bosomed, though otherwise compact, woman who Anya was fairly certain was a member of her mother's gardening club.

Resuming the foetal position – Anya had been for a brisk walk around the park but was back in her bedroom now – she began tapping back a response (*Thanks Mum, not sure that's the*—) when her phone interrupted. It was an 01360 number, which would mean her parents, except she had their number saved. Oh, God. Already?

In a split second, Anya processed her options. She could ignore the call, but this was not really a solution.

Women like her mother were persistent and time-rich. Fiona Morton probably didn't have much else to do for the next few hours except make sure that Anya received this call – and possibly return to the post office – and if she did not pick up, Fiona Morton would not hesitate to deploy Anya's mother. A two-pronged attack was more than Anya could bear.

Sitting up, she leaned her back against the wall and pressed the green phone button.

'Hello?'

'Is this Anya Mackie?'

The voice on the other end of the phone was polite but commanding, and Anya sat up a little straighter.

'Speaking.'

'Lovely. I'm Fiona Morton – I'm a friend of your mother's. I live out in Balfron, just up the road from The Willows.'

The Willows was the name etched on to a small wooden plaque on one of the outside walls of her parents' house. Anya's mother had bought it at the garden centre near Drymen six months ago, hoping that it conferred a sense of authenticity. It appeared that this was catching on.

'Oh, hi. Yes, she mentioned you might call.'

'Did she now?' Fiona Morton sounded pleased; Anya could sense her impressive chest puffing out with pride. 'Now I'll get right to it – she says you need a job.'

Anya attempted to interrupt but was not heard.

'And I've got one for you. My granddaughters are looking for someone to mind them for a few hours after school.'

'Yes,' Anya managed.

'And your Mum said you'd be brilliant. It would be

every weekday, although you wouldn't have to pick them up from school. Their mum – my Aimee – she does that. But it would be a bit of homework, nothing too taxing. You can start on Monday. Can I give you Aimee's number and address? She's expecting you – needs you there about 4.30 p.m. Have you got a piece of paper to hand?'

Anya remained rooted in horror.

'Um, no, I—'

'What am I thinking! I can just send it to you in a text message!' A light laugh. 'What must you all think of us lot? Living in the dark ages! Pen and paper indeed! I'll send it over to you in a minute.'

Fiona Morton laughed again for a few beats too long, until she finally appeared to run out of steam. Anya felt a pitch of vertigo.

'Thank you,' she managed weakly, 'but I'm—'

'Oh, no need to thank me!' she purred. 'You're doing me the favour, honestly. Aimee's been so stressed with trying to find someone new after the last girl quit, so this is just really helping her out of a bind. I'll send the details now. Love to your mother!'

As quickly as the tornado had arrived, it departed, and Fiona Morton rang off. But there was another gust incoming. Just as Anya had begun to feel a cool, creeping sensation travel from the tips of her toes right up into her chest, her phone trilled again.

Mutely, Anya pressed the green phone button.

'Anya! It's Mum again. Just a quick one this time. I've spoken to Fiona and she's going to be in touch very soon.'

Her mother sounded pleased at her efficiency; Anya clenched her jaw.

61

'Yes, she's already called, actually.'

She assumed that her tone would convey her grim fury, but her mother seemed not to sense anything amiss.

'Has she! Well, that woman gets things done—'

'Mum, stop!' Irene stopped abruptly. 'Listen to me. I don't want to be a childminder!'

There was a brief, icy pause. Anya noted her breath was slightly ragged.

'I see.' Another pause; now Anya could hear the blood roaring in her ears. 'Well, I'm afraid beggars can't be choosers, Anya.'

'I only quit my job yesterday!' Was it really only yesterday? Time had stopped making sense. 'You haven't even given me time to find something on my own, Mum! I told you, I have a plan – I'm thinking of turning Anya Eats Too Much into a catering company—'

'Stop it.' Her mother's voice was sharp now. 'You will take this job. Fiona's made you a generous offer and you could do a lot worse.'

Anya could feel the childish tears threatening.

'But I told you, I have an idea, I was going to—'

'You don't have another job, Anya, and you don't have a plan,' Irene interrupted, flatly. Anya could hear the sound of a teaspoon hitting the inside of her mother's coffee mug. 'And pet' – it was clear that 'pet' was not being deployed here as a term of endearment – 'I know that what's happened with Connor is dreadful, and I'm truly sorry you're suffering. But the answer isn't to lie in bed all day at Claire's and wait for someone to come in and offer you a brand-new job and a brand-new flat and a brand-new life. You have to do something. You're going to be at Aimee's on Monday and that's final.'

The worst part was knowing she was right, although there was no way Anya was surrendering that easily.

'But—' she tried.

'Final, Anya.'

She rung off.

Anya closed her eyes and took three deep breaths.

When she was finished, she realized she still felt like strangling someone, so she pulled her laptop on to her lap, googled 'fancy utensils' and spent £23 on a pestle and a mortar shaped like a stone pig. Afterwards, she felt a little bit better.

Her hair was wet from the shower, and Anya brushed it roughly with her fingers. Somehow, she'd made it to almost midday of this shapeless, elastic day. She thought of the Berners Bilton offices, of her empty desk, computer dark. Everyone would know by now what Anya had done; those who hadn't witnessed her downfall would have been told in hushed tones by the printer, or in the tiny kitchen, by the sticky microwave.

She wondered whether the grapevine had yet delivered the news to Connor. She hoped not, because if he already knew, that meant he hadn't texted her to find out if she was OK. She hoped he was still to hear and that when he did, he'd send her a message.

She shook her head.

'Stop it.'

Lurching off the bed again, she navigated the chaos of spilled suitcases and tote bags stuffed with novels and boxed-up cookbooks and utensils, pulling on jeans and her 'cooking' shirt – a baggy, ancient navy blue one of her father's that she'd rescued from a bag destined for the charity shop one distant Easter weekend – and then plucked a cookbook from the pile on the floor. It was one of her favourite vegetarian chef's 'best hits'. Anya thumbed through it until she landed upon a recipe for a meat-free kheema, the beef substituted for lentils and chickpeas rolled in ginger and garam masala. She took a picture of the page and then set off to the Tesco Metro.

Back in the kitchen, she heated oil and onions, ginger, garlic and garam masala and chilli, adding tomato paste and peas, lentils and chickpeas, dutifully catching the flecks of spices with a wet cloth, as Claire had asked. The hob in Connor's flat was always in a state – blobs of tomato purée cemented to the tiling behind the stove, scattered rice and spices, barely time to clean it before Anya's next adventure – but at Claire's she felt her inter-loper status keenly. She still only hazarded cooking when she knew her cousin was out or busy watching something stern and joyless in the living room.

When she'd finished cooking the curry, she spooned a portion into a shallow bowl – all of Claire's crockery matched – and added a dollop of yoghurt. She sat at the kitchen table and ate her lunch, enjoying the feeling of ginger and garam masala fizzing on her tongue. She opened a Note on her phone and typed a title: @anyaeatstoomuch. Underneath, she added: 'Vegetarian kheema recipe – plus a naan'.

She spooned another dollop of yoghurt straight from the tub and then put the rest of the curry into a Tupperware in the fridge and sluiced the pans down. She ran a cloth over Claire's surfaces again, just in case, pausing to scratch at what looked like a fleck of garlic with the nail of her index finger.

Then she tiptoed back up the stairs to her bedroom. After the high of cooking, she felt a little low and pointless, the universe's spare part, so she emailed Tasha back. It was 2.30 p.m., which meant Tasha would be awake soon.

To: tasha.kelner@penandpencil.com
From: anyamackie@gmail.com
Re: S-O-fucking-S

It's almost morning where you are – in fact it's 6.30 a.m. – and that feels like the sort of time high-achieving people like you get up. In fact, you're probably reading this on your Peloton right now. I just made a curry for four and then ate half of it and am sitting on my single mattress in Claire's room in the middle of the working day. If someone put me on a Peloton I'd vomit lentils.

I haven't spoken to Connor once. I keep getting this thing where I see someone in Tesco Metro and am convinced it's him and my blood runs cold. And in the mornings, it still feels strange he's not here.

Claire's house is creepy. They have all this furniture made from hardwood so dark it's nearly black with all these sharp, unfriendly edges. And Richard is really obsessed with energy-saving lightbulbs, which I know is good for the environment but means it's really gloomy, so you don't see one of the sharp tables or sets of drawers until you've walked into it. Also, she has this weird antique doll from her grandma – her dad's side, not the one who's related to me – on a shelf that has a sort of Mona Lisa, always-watching-you, thing going on. I feel homesick but I'm not totally sure what for.

But there is some good news: I have a new job! The (enormous) downside is it's a babysitting gig that my mum got me. Imagine me looking after kids, Tasha. Also, they are twins. AM I IN A HORROR FILM!?

But you got to me with that food line, you sly dog. Do you really think I could do something like a catering company? I'd have to make a website and maybe get an accountant. Is that mad?

Vancouver sounds like f***ing paradise. Are you going to get really into ice hockey? I feel like you'd be good at ice hockey. You are naturally quite aggressive. Although maybe you're too tall. How's work? Can you WhatsApp me a picture of Loic please?

I promise I won't jump off a bridge today, though we'll see how I feel after my first day at my new job (imagine me silent screaming right now). Obviously, you and Paddy would have to do a joint speech at the funeral. Maybe Georgie could do a mournful dance.

Please can we FaceTime soon. I miss you a lot. I also have a lot of time on my hands.

Xxxxx

Feeling fidgety, Anya waited for ten minutes, just in case Tasha replied right away, but nothing came. She closed her laptop lid and drifted towards the window. The heavy curtains were still drawn, so she opened them on to the quiet street below. Hamilton Drive was a long terrace and the doors of the houses opposite like so many unblinking, unfriendly eyes. After a few moments of staring into the quiet mid-afternoon, she stepped away from the windowsill. Perhaps she was thirsty.

In the kitchen, she flinched: Richard was bending over the fridge, bottom bobbing. He straightened and she noticed he was eating her curry straight from the Tupperware with a huge spoon.

'Thanks for lunch,' he grinned, and she noticed he had a lentil stuck in his teeth.

6

It was drizzling and Anya's phone was getting wet. She wiped the screen with the corner of her trench coat and squinted into the map. It insisted this was the right street – its smart sandstone houses growing darker in the rain, like the colour of bad tea – but she couldn't work out which side number 36 would be on. Many of the houses had names, not numbers; a few sported golden plaques, with the titles of what Anya assumed were solicitors or high-end dentists.

She and Connor regularly used to wander around these roads, Anya dreaming of a shapeless, sunlit future. They'd definitely mooched this way in the summer, a meandering route on their way back from the cinema.

'Do you think someday we'll live somewhere like this?' She'd been marvelling at the tall, crenellated ceilings glimpsed through elegant, elongated windows. Connor hadn't answered, and Anya squeezed his arm. 'I can definitely see us in Park Circus.'

'I suppose we could always try winning the lottery.' He snorted.

Anya blinked fast, trying not to think of Connor, focusing her energy instead on dreading the afternoon ahead. A man in white jeans came out of one of the houses followed by a woman in heeled suede boots. Anya considered asking one of them which was number 36, but as she hesitated, they climbed into a 4x4 with blacked-out windows.

Eventually she found it. Number 36 was another long terraced house, behind a polished dark door with a big ornamental knocker. Through the big window to the left of the door she could see a huge living room with a grey sofa and a vast gilt mirror.

Anya had spent the whole weekend dreading this moment, muttering darkly as she tried to reorganize the chaos of her bedroom, chewing her lips as she stared at her phone willing Connor to text. Her dread had reached fever pitch now, but she didn't have time to fret because she was almost late. And so, with one long ragged breath, she pressed the cool metal button of the doorbell. Somewhere in the distance sung a low minor note, followed by a dog's yap.

The door was opened by a woman with expensive bottle-blonde hair that fell in loose, corkscrew curls. She wore spray-on jeans, thigh-high suede boots and a white, fairly transparent blouse. Her chest was similarly apportioned to her mother's, although rather perkier. She looked expensive and Anya felt dowdy in her Vans and ancient knitwear.

Aimee glanced Anya up and down, clearly coming to a similar conclusion.

'Are you Anya?'

'Yeah, hi.' Anya stepped forward and offered her hand. Aimee took it lightly and then dropped it.

'They're in the kitchen.'

With barely any time to be taken aback, Anya followed Aimee into a large hallway with a checkerboard flooring and more gilt mirrors everywhere. A large staircase with a plush silver carpet curled out of the hall on to a landing, but Aimee continued down the hallway. A warren of high-ceilinged rooms led off this main route – yet more mirrors, a few sprigs of twig in long clear glasses, Bose speakers on every surface – until they reached a kitchen, which glinted with chrome.

Two identical redheaded girls, with their hair in neat pigtails, perched at the kitchen island, jotters open in front of them. They presented a sort of mirror image: both with arms crossed, heads cocked, a smirk playing about their rosebud lips. They were spectrally pale, and had a smattering of freckles about their small, upturned noses. They wore identical school uniforms – complete with their scratchy wool blazers – which Anya recognized as belonging to the rival, and far better, school than the one she herself had attended.

'Rosie, Rachel, this is Anya.' Their mother waved a lazy hand in Anya's direction, and then started tapping at her phone with long, frosted fake nails. She wandered back towards the hallway before she remembered. 'She's your new babysitter.'

The girls said nothing, although an identical smile stretched across both faces. It was not a warm one.

Aimee had paused in the doorway, still tapping away at her phone. 'Maybe you could do their homework with them.' She looked up. 'Girls, do you have homework?'

'Yeah,' said one of them. 'English.'

'Great,' Aimee was walking away again now and her voice sounded faraway, 'why don't you do that then. I've got a call now.'

For a few moments there was silence, apart from the

disappearing sound of Aimee's heels clicking on the smart floor in the hall. When this had stopped, Anya waved and instantly regretted the awkward, self-conscious gesture.

'Hi, then. I'm Anya.'

In response, one of the children snorted.

'I'm your new babysitter.'

'Duh,' said the other one.

Anya smiled tightly and observed they both appeared to be blinking almost in unison. She pointed at their blazers.

'I went to Kelvinbridge Academy.'

'Unlucky,' said one of them.

Anya was trying to think of a response to this while in tandem, both reached for their schoolbags and extracted a jotter and textbook each. At least their pencil cases had their names on them, so she could tell them apart, albeit briefly.

'What kind of homework do you have?' She moved tentatively closer to them.

Both scowled.

'English,' Rosie said very slowly, as though speaking to someone very stupid.

'Sorry, yes,' Anya slithered into the third stool at the kitchen island. She was also still wearing her coat, and awkwardly shrugged out of it and left it resting in her lap, damp on her knees. 'I just mean what type of thing. Like, spelling, or the alphabet?'

The girls exchanged a glance.

'We're eleven,' Rosie said pityingly. 'We know the alphabet.'

'Of course.' She was starting to feel a little desperate. 'Well, why don't you show me?'

They both ignored her and instead started wordlessly scribbling, hands cupped protectively around the pages, their heads down and close to one another.

For twenty minutes, Anya barely dared to breathe as the twins scribbled. She watched the wall clock above the kitchen door and tried not to picture her empty desk at Berners Bilton and the salary that was no longer being deposited into her bank account on the fifteenth of every month. The house was silent – she had no idea where Aimee had gone – and smelled of something sweet that made Anya's nose tickle. The cool from her damp trench coat continued to seep into her jeans.

Eventually – and again, almost in complete unison – the twins appeared to finish. Rosie whispered something inaudible to Rachel.

'We're going to get changed now.'

'OK.'

'And then we're going to play football in the garden.'

'Great.'

'You have to go in goal.'

Was she mistaken, or was that a synchronized, malevolent grin?

'OK.' At least she'd worn trainers. 'I'm not very good—'

The girls had already left. While they changed, Anya cased the kitchen, keeping an ear cocked for Aimee's heels or the twins rattling across the floors.

From the contents of her cupboards, Aimee did not look like someone who cooked a lot. One was entirely empty except for a multipack of lunchbox-sized raisins. Another cupboard had a carton of Special K, a bottle of extra virgin olive oil and a (sealed) packet of sushi rice. The fridge was similarly dispiriting: oat milk, several containers of pre-prepped salad from a company called Detox Queen; nothing that looked like food that children would like.

Still, the kitchen was flash. Although it seemed likely they were virtually unused, Aimee seemed to have all of the mod-cons: state-of-the-art espresso machine; a shiny Nutribullet; pestle and mortar, vegetable steamer and shiny, stainless-steel pans suspended above the pristine hob, like a pre-fab, ultra-kitchen. She stroked one of the saucepans longingly.

Footsteps: she slid back into her chair just in time for the twins to appear in the doorway, wearing green-and-white hooped Celtic kits and football boots.

Anya tried a game smile. 'I'm a Partick Thistle supporter, I'm afraid.'

The girls gave her a look of matching derision.

'They're rubbish,' one of them said authoritatively, and Anya wished she could disagree.

The other girl opened the back door – without the pencil cases she was no longer sure which was which – and Anya followed them into a long garden, complete with a trampoline, a small ball and a set of goals and – at the other end of the garden, far from the goal and near a tall wooden fence – a large, high-end shed. One of the walls had been replaced with glass, inside which Anya could see what looked like a yoga studio. She was about to ask the girls what their mother did when a ball hit her in the side of the head.

'Ow!'

73

The girls were clutching one another, bent double with glee.

'Oops,' one said when they'd finally stopped. 'Sorry.'

Anya soon suspected that the girls had no intention of attempting to score goals. Instead, the name of the game was to hit Anya – ideally full pelt in the face, which meant a high five exchanged, but anywhere on the body would do (earning a low five).

'Wait,' she huffed as she straightened up after a missile to the stomach, 'I'm getting really muddy.' This was an understatement: she was filthy, her knees damp, her trench splattered with mud. In response, one of them started taking a run-up. Before she could think about it, Anya had leapt out of goal.

'Hey, you said you'd go in goal!'

Anya bit her tongue and moved back. The twin collecting the ball stood on her toe.

Whenever Anya met a toddler, she marveled at the small creature's patience for repetitive games; the twins', it turned out, was superhuman. For what seemed like hours, she took countless more body blows while the twins cackled; she was practically breathless with relief when Aimee's silhouette appeared in the doorway, although she might have just been winded.

'Girls,' she snapped. 'Dinner in twenty minutes. I'm heating you one of my meals up. Go get changed.'

Wordlessly, both moved towards the door, a bedraggled Anya in slow pursuit. Aimee glanced her up and down and smirked.

'What happened to *you*?'

'They kept kicking a ball at me.'

Aimee just rolled her eyes and turned on her heel. Anya followed her back into the kitchen and she spun around.

'Shoes off.' Aimee pointed to the twins' football boots, arranged in their pairs by the door. Obediently, Anya removed her own trainers.

The wall clock in the kitchen read 6.30 p.m. now, which at least meant it was home time. She could hear the sound of the twins' feet ascending the stairs above. In the kitchen, leaning against one of the marble counters, Aimee was texting again, talons flying across the screen. Anya padded across the floor towards Aimee, carrying her trainers meekly.

'So – is it OK – if I go?'

Aimee continued to text. When she was finally finished, she placed her phone on the kitchen island and appraised Anya again, an eyebrow cocked disdainfully.

'Yes, I'll do their dinner.'

'I'll see you tomorrow then?'

Aimee looked at her as though this was a rhetorical question, and then picked up her phone again.

'Money's on the table in the hall.'

Anya felt the rush of relief: she'd been terrified to ask.

'Thank you.' She stepped towards the doorway. 'Have a good evening.'

Aimee didn't look up.

The first two weeks at Park Circus passed in a blur of indignity.

On Thursday – her fourth day on the job and a week since she'd quit Berners Bilton – the twins had locked Anya in the downstairs utility room with all the lights off (the switch was on the outside of the door) for a disquieting and increasingly desperate forty-five minutes. For a while she had drummed both fists on the door and tried to sound convincing as she urged the girls to 'let me out – now!' but this had inspired only giggles and eventually Anya had given up and slumped against the door, a defeat that reminded her of the moments after Connor had left, which only made things worse.

Just as she'd started to dig her fingernails into her palm to quell the panic, with no warning they'd unlocked the door and Anya had fallen backwards on to the kitchen floor. She stood, blinking and brushing herself off, her eyes still adjusting to the bright light, and noticed that they had produced a shaggy, rather senile white dog.

'This is Corrie,' said whichever one of them was wearing a ponytail.

'Right.' She felt like she was in a strange dream.

'She needs to go outside,' said the other one snappily.

On cue, Corrie started scratching at Anya's jeans.

'OK.' Anya moved towards the back door but a twin snapped.

'No! Mum doesn't let her go in the garden.'

'Oh. Well, shall we go for a walk, then?' The art of authority was still eluding Anya; she phrased everything as a sort of desperate question.

The girls had their heads together as Anya closed the front door behind them, Corrie now on a long red lead. She was grasping several small dog poo bags and trying not to think about what she'd have to do with them, although they certainly felt like a cosmic metaphor for something.

'Shall we head around the block a few times? Or we could go to the park?' Again, the questions. But before she could attempt assertiveness, the girls had exchanged a glance and legged it in opposite directions.

'Wait!'

Anya tugged at Corrie, but the dog was already squatting in the middle of Aimee's front path. Immobilized, Anya waited to collect the spoils, clenching and unclenching her fist and trying to ignore visions of the twins being kidnapped, or struck by a 4x4, or falling down an open manhole.

Once Anya had a bag of shit for her troubles, she set off at pace, dragging the old dog behind her, but after forty-five minutes of increasingly frantic searching, she was back at number 36, with neither twin (and still holding the dog bag). On the doorstep were the girls. Both were playing on their Nintendo Switches; neither acknowledged Anya.

There had also been an incident with her phone – after a seemingly endless search, her cheeks growing redder and redder in frustration, she had found it in the washing machine – and the Wednesday evening when she had been unable to leave because her left shoe had gone walkabout. This, she eventually located in Corrie's smelly basket.

'I know it wasn't you,' Anya said, tickling the dog's ears, though she remained unmoved.

Anya had also put paid to any fantastical notions about she and Aimee forming an unlikely friendship. Indeed, the twins were only half the problem; Aimee's disdain for Anya occasionally curdled into pure spite (she had sniggered when Anya had stiffly explained about the door locking incident) and made her feel a little bit like she was trying to win the approval of a school Queen Bee.

Indeed, it was abundantly clear that Anya was simply one of a legion of people whom Aimee employed to serve her. For Aimee was a star – or at least a beauty influencer with 178k highly engaged followers. A recent image of her wearing electric blue eyeliner and a pink bodycon dress while walking Corrie (who had definitely been 'done' for the cameras – she was never usually that clean or fluffy) had inspired strings of heart eyes and lipstick emojis from legions of women just a little older than Anya.

And so, when Aimee was not collecting likes for Instagram posts marked #ad, she was WhatsApping her demands.

Aimee Twins

I need you to pick the girls up today

3.50 pm

Don't be late

Anya

OK no worries!

Aimee Twins

Please don't let the girls have Diet Coke

They told me you'd let them have one each

Anya

I'm so sorry!

They said they were allowed

Aimee Twins

I'm sure they didn't.

They know they aren't.

Anya

So sorry!

Won't happen again

Aimee Twins

Need you to stay late tonight

Have a shoot

Anya

Ah, I'm actually going to my sister's for dinner!

What time?

Aimee Twins

Don't know

Probably be home by 8pm

See you later

Actually make it 9pm

9.30 pm

Aimee Twins

Hi Anya the girls told me you let them watch *The Hunger Games*.

They're not allowed to watch that.

Please consider what's acceptable for two eleven-year-olds Anya.

Anya

Oh I'm so sorry!

I thought it was a good film for them

Aimee Twins

Rosie had nightmares.

I didn't get any sleep.

Don't let it happen again.

Anya

Of course. So sorry again.

Aimee Twins

Please can you do the pile of laundry that's in Rosie's room

DO NOT put it on the wrong temperature

Anya

Of course!

What type of wash should it go on?

Aimee Twins

I don't know check the labels

Anya had gleaned from Aimee's one-sided phone conversations that she was separated from the girls' father, who lived in Dubai and appeared to have little to no emotional interest in either girl. This, Anya suspected, explained at least some of their behaviour, and possibly some of Aimee's. It didn't make it any easier to bear, though.

By the Friday evening of Anya's second week in charge – loose term – she was exhausted, watching the clock out of the corner of her eye as she prepared a snack for the girls: homemade red pepper hummus, which she'd blended in Aimee's Nutribullet, with wholemeal breadsticks. It was the first thing she'd dared to prepare in Aimee's kingdom, and was a sort of last resort – an attempt to feel in control of something. Still, she had a fanciful notion that the girls might enjoy something home-cooked, rather than heated up by their disengaged mother. She dabbed a finger into the mixture, tasted it and then added a sprinkling of the salt (she'd brought it with her – from the sight of her cupboards, Aimee didn't seem to believe in flavour). She took deep, meditative breaths and plated up two portions, trying not to listen to the twins, who were sitting at the kitchen island, legs swinging, speaking in tongues, which was something they did a lot.

'Blip blip jaaar, belb belb belb,' came one voice.

She ignored them.

'Reen ka ka ka. Naaaar.'

They both giggled again. Summoning on reserves of strength, Anya turned, smiling without her eyes, and placed two bowls in front of them. Each had a dollop of hummus and five breadsticks.

'What's this?'

They were both eyeing the bowl suspiciously.

'Red pepper hummus and breadsticks.'

They narrowed their eyes further.

'Did Mum make it?'

'No, I made it. Just now.'

Their brows knitted.

'Try it,' Anya said.

They exchanged a dark glance and then simultaneously picked up a breadstick and bit off an end.

'You're meant to have it with the hummus,' Anya said patiently.

They both stared at her, although at the sight of food, they looked more curious than hostile, which was at least something. Anya turned back to the sink and started rinsing the Nutribullet in soapy water. While she dried it, she heard both twins sidle out of the kitchen without a word. Their bowls were empty.

Trying not to feel too pleased with this smallest of victories, Anya collected them from the kitchen island and washed them too. As she was drying the crockery, she heard the click of stilettos on the floor. Aimee appeared.

She was in her uniform of spray-on jeans and a blouse and carrying a vast patent handbag with a very loud logo.

'I take it they behaved.' This was not a question, and Aimee did not look at Anya, but started rootling through her handbag, which she was resting on the counter. She was examining a nail extension but seemed to feel Anya's eyes on her. She looked up and blinked spidery lashes. 'You can go now.'

It was only 5.55 p.m. – early release.

'Wow. Thanks.'

'I'll see you on Monday.'

Aimee was back in her handbag and said nothing, so Anya headed for the front door. The geriatric Corrie was curled in her basket in the hallway. Anya gave her a pat on the head, and Corrie flicked her fluffy tail lazily. Anya put the envelope of cash into the inside zip pocket of her coat and opened the front door.

She felt her shoulders fall as she closed the heavy door behind her. She'd managed two weeks – and if they hadn't gone well, at least they were over. And it was only part-time: during the daytime, before she was expected at Park Circus, she had been cooking a lot – thick autumnal stews, spicy daals, roasted vegetables glazed with miso. She was particularly happy with her pea, mint and feta filo tart: buttery and flaky and salty and moreish.

Anya had developed a new plan of action, of sorts. During an interminable night towards the end of last week, she'd been under the covers, eyes itching from insomnia, re-reading the introduction to a cookbook she'd pored over many times. The book was by her favourite chef, a buzzy Instagram type with a messy bob who produced meals that were designed to look like you'd barely tried and that you'd cooked everything with a sloshy Martini in hand. Anya had read her fairytale before: about how this woman got a job front of house at a restaurant in Soho and how listening to the chef's patter had inspired her to start a supper club, which led to catering gigs and then a book deal. Anya found herself drinking in these details while quietly seething with jealousy – the gall of the woman, to make it seem this easy! – but on this occasion, with the lightly manic zeal of someone awake at 4 a.m., she had started to wonder whether perhaps it was. Well, almost.

She didn't fancy supper clubs and she'd have to do them at Claire's – Richard attending in his Crocs – and writing a cookbook as a relative nobody would be nothing but a vanity project. But this woman's fairytale had strengthened her resolve: Anya Eats Too Much could be a catering company! The adrenaline had surged as she imagined developing a menu in precise typographic letters, starting a website, writing her own story. She could use her Instagram to drum up a little business and then take it from there. She'd have to work for the twins at the same time, unfortunately, until the business started to make any money (a big if). But even if it was just the insomnia talking, she liked the idea. Very much.

So, she now spent her mornings before she went to the twins working on a proto-menu, trying to work out which meals could be done at scale and at speed, and which would prove too fiddly, complicated or expensive. The industry was like a balm for her soul: when she was cooking, the rest of the world seemed to fall away, if only (very) temporarily.

Anya pulled her coat around her: the city was dark and the wind had bite. Tonight, she didn't want to cook for research – she just wanted nourishment, to go home and make a fish finger curry from this food blog she followed and watch Connor appear online and offline on Whats-App. But her cavalry – Paddy and Georgie – had mobilized and were insisting they all went out that evening.

'We haven't been out in ages.' Paddy had called last night when she was reading her newest cookbook, a fizzy Japanese tome with very stylish photography (the recipes were a little too cheerful for Anya's current state of mind). 'And it's the end of the second week of your new job. We really should have marked it by now.'

'I don't think my new job is any cause for celebration.'

'Fine. We can celebrate you leaving your old one. I've checked and Georgie's free too. We'll go to Ashton Lane. No arguments.'

It appeared Paddy had, as ever, been deadly serious: her phone was twitching.

Paddy

Right

Plan for tonight

I did all my weekend marking last night so

that we could have fun this eve

Georgie

Yay!

I'm excited

What time shall we meet?

I'm just about to get on the Subway home from work

Paddy
7?
Maybe we can even go out after
. . .

Georgie
Let's not go overboard

Paddy
Anya?

Georgie
We can see you're reading these

Anya
Hi

Paddy
Tonight
Ashton Lane
7 pm work for you?

Anya
I'm quite poor
And I had plans to make a curry

Paddy
I'm not having this
You can eat a curry when you're dead
Or when you get home, drunk, from Ashton Lane
after a night with your BEST FRIEND

Georgie
Um and your sister

Paddy

Yes, see even G is coming

Georgie

Hey

ANYA WE CAN LITERALLY SEE YOU READING THESE

Paddy

Pay attention to us

Anya

I'm not really in the mood

Paddy

We know

That's why you should come

We have arranged this in your honour

Georgie

Yes you can't sit at home moping all evening!

Paddy

Don't give her ideas

Anya?

Georgie

ANYA

Anya

OK FINE

Georgie

Hooray

Did we agree 7

?

Paddy

Yes

I'm home now but need to shower and get ready etc

Anya that gives you time to make your curry now

if you're so desperate

Anya

Oh shut up

Plus it really doesn't

You can't rush art

See you bastards at 7

Still, perhaps Connor would be out on Ashton Lane later. It was only a ten-minute walk from his flat, plus it was a Friday, and payday (that morning she'd received her last lump sum from Berners Bilton. Another email from HR Pam, with a P45, had arrived that morning). Perhaps – a shiver – he'd end up in the same bar as her, in a corner with Duncan and Chris and a few of the insipid girlfriends. She quickened her pace, feet slapping the pavements so that she'd have time to put on make-up.

But life, Anya reflected a few hours later, installed in a booth with a rather weak gin and tonic, was just one long, cosmic disappointment. The flicked eyeliner and heeled boots – a Boxing Day purchase last year, which Connor had once told her made her look like 'someone else, in a good way' – so far appeared to have been for nothing. He was nowhere to be seen. Her head turned every time a group of men swaggered in, every time she heard a chorus of cheers or laughs or grunts, but he wasn't there, of course he wasn't there, and she felt bruised and let down and silly.

She tried to concentrate on Georgie, who was saying something, her eyes characteristically deep and concerned.

'And anyway, it's just a temporary solution.' Georgie sounded encouraging, although her brow was furrowed. 'You're not going to have to look after them forever. And at least you're getting paid again.'

'I *know* that, Georgie.' Her sister opened her mouth, but Anya beat her to the punch. 'And obviously, I need the money. But knowing that doesn't really help when the little witches are kicking a ball at my face or locking me in the laundry room, in the dark.'

Paddy snorted.

'Sorry. It's not funny.'

Anya glared at him and put her chin on the sticky table.

They'd ended up at Vodka Wodka, which was at that risky, transitional stage of a Friday night – the 'just a few drinks' crowd reaching the end of their stint, the 'big one' crowd increasingly revved up for theirs. There was a crackle in the air. Beside them was a hen do armed to the teeth with willy straws and sashes, although they'd so far been very well-behaved: sipping not slugging Prosecco; all of them still seated, rather than standing on their chairs scouting for willing accomplices. But Anya had been on a hen do, and knew it was only a matter of time.

Paddy nodded in their direction.

'When do you think they'll start having fun?'

'Sssssh.' Georgie stole a sideways look at the hen party. 'They'll hear you.'

Paddy rolled his eyes.

'I wonder what Claire's hen will be like.' Georgie was examining her split ends now, which felt like a rather unfortunate reflection on the evening.

'What hen do?'

'Oh.' Georgie contorted her mouth, like she was trying to swallow something she'd already said. 'Did she . . . did she not invite you in the end?'

'No,' Anya snapped. 'She didn't.'

There was a squirmy silence, during which time Paddy stuck his head under the table to take a drag on his e-cigarette.

'That's not very subtle.' Anya took another sip of her watery gin and tonic.

'Sorry, Anya – I really did tell her she should invite you.' Georgie was knotting her hands, and Anya suddenly felt very tired.

'Georgie, don't be silly. It's *Claire's* hen do. She can invite whoever she wants.' But she jutted her chin, just a little bit. 'I don't want to go anyway.'

Georgie stopped knotting her hands and nodded. After a beat, she added: 'I think it'll be pretty quiet. We're doing a scented candle workshop. Magdalena's idea.'

Magdalena was Claire's best friend. She was so haughty that Anya often found herself getting the giggles in her company – which she tended to avoid, apart from when it was thrust on her at family gatherings – out of sheer panic. Frankly, she was surprised that Magdalena had lent her endorsement to something as frivolous as a scented candle.

'In that case, I am thrilled not to have been invited.'

Paddy, who had gone for another drag, re-emerged.

'What are you talking about?'

'Scented candles,' Anya said.

'Right.' He took a sip of his pint. 'So, I applied for that job in the end. I wasn't going to go for it at first, but then I realized that it'd look bad if I didn't. And Mrs Dean said I should apply, so . . .' He put his drink down on the table and Anya saw the delight in his face. Mrs Dean was the head, a stern but brilliant woman whom Paddy was slightly awed by.

'This is the head of English job, yes?' Georgie was definitely pleased that the conversation had moved off Claire, hen dos and cedarwood candles.

'Yes.'

Paddy had mentioned it to Anya at the pub on the afternoon she was packing up at Connor's; she felt a twist of guilt that she hadn't asked him about it since. Self-indulgence was time consuming.

'So, what happens now? Do you have an interview?' She tried an intent, interested frown, which earned only a tight smile from Paddy. She hadn't quite got away with it, then.

'I have to present my ideas to a board including Mrs Dean.' He picked up his pint again. 'I won't get it. But still. Good to look like you want these things.'

'Definitely.' Anya tried to clink her glass against Paddy's but instead knocked his pint, which swilled over the rim. He gave her a hard stare but couldn't keep it up, and she was relieved when it became a forgiving smile.

'Anyway.' He extracted a packet of cigarettes from his top pocket. 'Anyone?'

Georgie rolled her eyes; Anya nodded. She was mainly a social smoker now – a vulture, Tasha called them, as she sucked on a Marlboro Light – but in her current mood, it didn't seem like the time to be depriving herself of anything that offered a hit. She followed Paddy, who had almost collided with a member of the subdued hen do, returning with a single bottle of Prosecco for the table. She was glassy-eyed and didn't seem to notice.

'Only a matter of time,' she muttered but Paddy was ahead of her, elbowing his way through the throng towards the smoking area outside.

Despite the temperature, it was heaving and Paddy and Anya positioned themselves on the fringes of the crowd. In sync, they lit up and took a hungry, grateful drag, Anya relishing the new, chemical lightness in her head and legs.

'The job is exciting—' she started, but Paddy was already talking.

'OK, so' – he took a deep breath – 'I wasn't going to tell you this, but I saw Connor the other day.'

Anya's blood ran cold. There she had been, willing Connor to materialize, but the prospect that Paddy had seen him made her feel terrified and unprepared, like those anxiety dreams about exams she hadn't revised for. She managed to fix her face into something approximating calm.

'Where were you?'

'In that running shoes shop near the school.' Anya looked blank, so Paddy added, 'Sort of between school and his flat.'

She contemplated this.

'But Connor doesn't run.'

'Maybe he's started.' Paddy was matter-of-fact. 'He didn't see me though. And I'd just realized spending £90 on new trainers was ridiculous, so I left pretty quickly.'

'Was he alone?'

'Yes. He had headphones in.'

Anya was weirdly grateful for this detail.

'How did he look?'

'The same. He was wearing work clothes.'

'Are you sure he didn't see you?'

Paddy exhaled again before he answered.

'Well, I obviously can't be sure, but it didn't look like he had.' Anya nodded, and he added: 'Georgie told me not to tell you.'

Anya felt a little hot rush of shame – and a little satisfaction – that they'd been talking about her.

'I'm not going to fall apart because Connor's doing *Couch to 5k*.'

She wasn't quite sure if that was true, but it sounded good; Paddy smiled a measured smile.

'That's what I said.'

Anya chewed her lip.

'I hope he isn't going to undergo some sort of transformation. You know, like I was the only thing keeping him from this athletic, healthy, better life.'

'It's just a pair of trainers, Anya.'

Paddy and Connor's relationship had always been cordial. They embraced each other warmly at pubs and birthday parties, although it had not escaped her attention that over those evenings and afternoons, they'd rarely said much to each other except hello and goodbye.

Admittedly, their characters were not a natural fit – Paddy was dry and wry, Connor rather more sweetly earnest – and their idea of what constituted a good time was very different. Anya definitely laughed more with Paddy: he was far sillier.

One rare afternoon, when the three of them had gone to the cinema, Anya and Paddy had amused themselves on the way home by doing an impression of the villain in the film they'd just seen. All it took was a look from Paddy to set Anya off again, and on the Subway they were hysterical.

After Paddy had gone his separate way, Connor had been quiet. They'd been walking back up to the flat from Byres Road.

'Are you OK?' Anya squeezed his arm.

'I'm fine.' He unlinked his arm. 'Just don't really enjoy feeling like a parent taking his two kids out, that's all.'

'What?'

'You and Paddy. Your stupid act on the Subway. It was quite embarrassing.'

'We were just messing about. Don't be such a killjoy.'

They hadn't hung out much as a three after that.

Paddy jabbed her on the shoulder now. 'Stop staring at your shoes.' Anya tried a weak smile. 'And don't give me that martyred smile.' He prodded her again.

She felt another twist of guilt. She hated this version of herself – martyred, mopey, self-indulgent. It was so boring, and if she was boring herself, she could only imagine how Paddy and Georgie felt. She made her umpteenth resolution to pull herself together. For some reason, it helped if she imagined herself doing this in her mother's voice.

'Sorry, Paddy. I'm being such a drag, I—'

He waved the hand with the cigarette dismissively.

'You got dumped; you live with Claire. I'd be the same.'

'Yes—'

'But saying that,' he interrupted firmly, 'even I have limits. And I'm not tolerating a meltdown because your ex-boyfriend is considering buying a pair of Asics.'

She grinned automatically and was pleased.

'Point taken.'

'Sorry for the tough love.'

Paddy stubbed his cigarette out on the metal bin, which was scarred with ash and overflowing with butts.

'It's what I need.' Anya copied him.

'Yes, it is.' He did an exaggerated shiver, gripping his shoulders. 'Right, come on. It's fucking Baltic out here, and I want another drink.'

They'd stayed for two more. The hen do started, finally, to rev up: the maid-of-honour was leading her coven in a game of truth or dare that included challenges to 'steal a bottle from behind the bar' – the bridesmaid in question chickened out and had to drink – and to 'proposition an eligible bachelor'. To his delight, Paddy was selected.

'Will you buy me a drink?' The girl was going for coquettish, although was slurring her words, and one fake eyelash was drooping from her eyelashes. Paddy grinned beatifically at her.

'Since you asked so nicely, I will. But you have to make them do a dare.' He pointed at Anya and Georgie.

'Deal.' This was the maid-of-honour who was, clearly, running proceedings.

When Paddy returned with a tray of shots, the bride

had insisted that the three of them join the hen table. Determined to make amends for her sour mood, Anya concentrated hard on playing along, accepting her own dare – to lead a conga line through the bar – with enthusiasm, while praying harder than she ever had that Connor would not suddenly emerge from the men's in time to catch her. When she returned, red-faced and a little breathless, she was rewarded with a hug from the mother-of-the-bride, which she returned clumsily. Paddy smiled at her.

After Georgie had been frogmarched by the bride to the bar to ask out the barman, the hens shrieking with delight, they'd decided to call it a night, much to the dismay of the bridal party, although not before the barman had returned to talk to Georgie. He was wearing the customary uniform of a very tight black T-shirt, which was stretched across a quite magnificent set of pecs and biceps.

'Who's your friend, Georgie?' Paddy asked, as the man retreated, though not without a rather sultry smile in Georgie's direction.

'His name's Alex,' she said, casually, pulling her coat around her shoulders. 'I gave him my number.' Paddy and Anya's jaws dropped, and Georgie looked pleased.

They walked back up Ashton Lane, Paddy in the middle. Warm light from bar after bar pooled on the higgledy-piggledy cobblestones, and the din of revellers was enough to make Paddy gaze wistfully into each establishment. When they reached the end of the road, he crossed his own.

'So, what's the plan then?'

Georgie shrugged. Anya knew she was the deciding vote. If she wanted them all to continue on at Georgie's, they would. Surprising herself, she felt a powerful urge to be alone.

'I'll . . . I'm going to go back to Claire's.'

'Are you sure?' Georgie narrowed her eyes. 'You're welcome at mine, honestly. I can take the sofa again, I don't mind.'

This made Anya feel more sad.

'No, it's fine.' She had to stop this. 'I want to sleep in my own bed, honestly. Well. Mattress.'

Paddy and Georgie moved in to envelop her, and Anya was cocooned. She could smell Paddy's cigarettes and Georgie's detergent.

'Will you be OK getting back?' Georgie looked anxious. Anya nodded. 'Text us when you get home.' Georgie squeezed her shoulder.

'Do you want a ciggie for the road?' Paddy offered.

'Go on then.'

It was a fifteen-minute walk home, and Anya gripped her keys the whole way back, though on this Friday night the city felt warm and friendly, rather than frightening. Still, it was very cold, and she was relieved when she reached the doorstep, even if Claire had locked the huge, double storm doors and it took Anya a while to grapple with the unfamiliar keys. She wasn't sure if Claire had locked them because she thought Anya was at home and in bed, staying at Georgie's or whether there were more sinister overtones.

In the hallway, she was grateful for the heat and observed she was drunker than she'd realized. So drunk that she took a few beats to notice Richard. He was standing at the end of the dim hallway, beside a heavy oak desk, reflected in the mirror that hung at the end of it. He wore striped pyjamas that made him look like a Victorian child, his face illuminated by the ghoulish light of his iPhone.

'Richard!'

At the sound of Anya's voice, he dropped the phone into the pocket of his nightshirt.

'Anya.'

'You gave me a fright.' She stepped forward a few paces and shrugged out of her coat, which proved tricky. 'What are you doing?'

It was hard to tell in the dark, but he seemed a little twitchy.

'Nothing.' He patted his top pocket. 'Just looking for my phone. Which I have found.'

'OK.'

'So, now I'll go to bed.'

'Right.'

She started climbing unsteadily out of her boots, aware that Richard was still at the end of the hallway, fumbling around in the desk drawer. He straightened suddenly.

'Good night, then.'

'Night Richard.'

He moved up the stairs like a spectre. Once he'd disappeared, Anya tiptoed towards the desk and pulled open the drawer, which was empty except for an iPhone, an old model. Anya jabbed at the screen but it appeared to be off. She closed the drawer again.

Her legs were leaden and she was grateful to reach the top of the stairs. Closing her bedroom door as silently as she could, she tiptoed across her bedroom to switch on the tiny lamp that sat on the floor beside her mattress. The curtains were already drawn.

In the gloom from the lamp, her life felt even more makeshift: the spilled suitcases, the boxes of utensils and cookbooks and silly Anya miscellany that her parents had offloaded on to her when they'd moved to Balfron and which she'd been carting around for years.

She sat down on her mattress and, to her surprise, found that she was crying – silly, drunk, heartbroken tears that came from nowhere. She wished Paddy hadn't seen Connor; she realized how much she had hoped she would see him that evening though, how many times she had peered over Paddy and Georgie's shoulders across the bar, watchful and distracted.

Just as abruptly as she'd started crying, she stopped and wiped the rivulets of eyeliner from her cheeks. There was a box on the floor near her and she nudged it towards her with her toe. She parted its cardboard flaps. It was the stuff from her parents: a sports day ribbon; her S6 report card (she didn't open that); a flyer from their S5 production of *Animal Farm* (Anya had played Cow #2); an employee handbook from the McDonald's in Partick, where she'd worked for about four months when she was sixteen, before she got the silver-service waitressing gig. Her mother had been furious when she'd quit that job ('We've spoiled you,' she'd said bitterly. 'That's not it, Mum!' Anya had protested. 'I'm just sick of smelling like a Big Mac!').

She sniffed thickly and then went deeper. There were bank statements from her first 'Junior Saver' account with Bank of Scotland (she remembered visiting the branch on Byres Road with her dad and going home and boasting to Georgie about the little blue book where the transactions would be recorded); and birthday cards from both sets of grandparents, long dead now – written in her Granny Mackie's neat hand, and her Granny Williamson's loopy one.

At the bottom of the box was her yearbook: royal blue, like the uniforms, imprinted with the school's crest on the front and 'Class of 2007' in gold embossed letters. Nostalgia got the better of her, and she opened its hardcover warily. The fonts and graphic design were comically outdated, and the opening sections focused entirely on the performances of their hockey and rugby teams, with reports by the captains and the coaches. Anya flipped past to the middle of the book, where there were ten or so pages of pictures through the ages, snaps taken from school trips and sports matches and school dances and charity events. She pulled it closer in order to better scrutinize the photos in the low light from the small lamp and, as she did so, something slipped from the book's pages and fluttered to the floor.

It was a scrap of lined paper, roughly torn. It appeared to be blank, apart from a scribble of blue in the corner. Still, Anya picked it up and turned it over and discovered that it was not blank.

I, Euan Carrick and I, Anya Mackie, declare that if we are still single at the age of 30 years old, we will find each other. This is a **LEGALLY BINDING CONTRACT!**
Signed by Euan and Anya, on the evening of 26 June 2007

7

From the top of the hill in Kelvingrove Park, Glasgow looked infinite, a repeating pattern of gables and spires and Victorian terraces, as far as the eye could see. Although it might just have been because Anya was seeing double.

She was blinking to try and right her sight when Euan passed her the lemonade bottle, which was filled with an inexpertly mixed cocktail of apple juice and Famous Grouse (about three parts Grouse to one part apple juice). Anya accepted it and stifled a burp, which burned the back of her throat. Stricken, she took another glug and hoped that Euan hadn't heard it.

He didn't seem to have done: he was too busy trying to light a cigarette. The lighter was cheap and temperamental; the wind – even on a June evening – nippy and forceful. Eventually, he succeeded and took a deep inhale, releasing the smoke in a flourishing billow that made Anya's head spin even more.

'I can't believe it's over,' Euan said, for what might have been the fourteenth time that hour. They'd reached the solemn, reflective period of their evening already.

'I know,' Anya replied gravely.

But it was momentous: school was over forever, as of 3.50 p.m. that afternoon. They were done with it all for good – no more school ties or clock-watching in a double period at the end of the day, willing the bell to ring. No more schoolbags or abrasive wool blazers or acid enquiries from form teachers ('Oh, I'm sorry, Miss Mackie, am I *interrupting*?'). No more after-school detentions or playground duty or pretending to your parents that there actually wasn't a parents' evening this term and, yes, it was a bit weird.

Instead, there was freedom, stretching out ahead of them, a sense of possibility and opportunity and change that gave Anya vertigo if she thought about it for too long. Though it might have just been the whisky and apple juice. Euan stretched out his hand and Anya passed him back the sticky bottle, and he threw his head back, took a gulp and spluttered, spitting the drink everywhere, and she giggled.

They were alone now, at last, for the first time in hours: Ciara, Kaye, Arpita and Billy had sloped off home to get ready for the party at Gordon's house later on.

'Aren't you coming?' Ciara had stood over Anya, one hand on her hip, the other arm slung through Arpita's.

Anya shrugged. 'I think I might stay here a bit longer.' She'd tried not to look at Euan as she said this.

'OK.' Ciara stumbled, a little unevenly. She'd brought a big Smirnoff Ice bottle with her and had finished most of it, and Anya wondered if her parents were home. Ciara's parents were very strict. 'Text us when you're coming.'

Billy and Kaye were already halfway down the hill, she piggybacking on his shoulders, shrieking as he accelerated down the grass. With a final wave, Arpita and Ciara followed them, a cigarette dangling from Arpita's spare hand.

Euan had been outstretched on the grass opposite, but as soon as the rest of them had disappeared, he moved next to Anya. She smelled whisky and cigarettes and sweat, and her stomach flipped over, and then he kissed her, a little sloppily. When he pulled away, he was grinning, and she laughed.

'I was waiting for them to leave.' He slung an arm around her shoulders.

'Me too.'

Euan and Anya had been kissing on the top of the hill in Kelvingrove Park on Friday nights for months now. It had become a routine: Anya and Ciara and Kaye and Arpita and Billy and Euan, often joined by Jamie and Gordon, would come to the top of the hill and drink tinnies and mess around and then eventually, one-by-one, everyone else would peel off and Anya and Euan would remain. She knew the others knew – she'd told the girls about it, a little giggly, besides it was obvious – but hers and Euan's 'thing' was unofficial and they were still a little shy around the others. They preferred it when it was just them.

Still, Anya was grateful for the wider group. Paddy had left at the end of the previous year to go to college in Paisley, and all last summer her stomach had been in knots. He had been her best friend since they were both twelve, when he'd sat down next to her in French and pointed out that the kids on the front of the textbook looked like members of a 'really sad cult'. She'd been desperately worried she was going to be an outcast without him.

But within a few weeks of the start of term, she'd been adopted by Ciara, Kaye and Arpita, and integrated into their gang. She'd always been friendly enough with the three of them – she liked Ciara especially, with her dark ringed eye-liner and her shocking pink headphones, which she wore in class, even when instructed not to – and now she was one of them. Billy was Kaye's boyfriend, and Gordon was his best mate, and Euan and Jamie came as a sort of package.

They'd linked up after class that first Friday, sidling through the gates with swagger, big fish in the small school pond, shooting a cool glance at a gaggle of S4s that included Georgie. Anya had waved at her sister – whose eyes were wide and surprised at the sight of Anya's new gang – when she was sure Ciara and everyone else weren't looking.

The boys were at the top of the hill already. Anya knew Jamie and Gordon, but she'd never spoken much to Euan. He had been new last year, and their paths only crossed in History class. He always arrived late, shirt untucked, hair sticking up.

'Hey,' he nodded as she sat down.

'Hey.'

They hadn't spoken much on the first Friday night – she'd mainly sat with Ciara and the girls – but the following Monday he'd sat down next to her in History, and she hoped he hadn't seen her smile.

He started sitting next to her every lesson, and the two of them had quickly fallen into a fluent banter that involved plenty of eye contact and gently disruptive behaviour designed entirely to amuse the other; one Friday after-noon, thanks to Euan, they were finally both reprimanded by their teacher for laughing at a picture of an Iron Age fork, which Euan had jabbed at in the textbook, and Anya had giggled without really knowing why. She had started thinking about him, reordering her route around the school in order to try and choreograph an accidental collision. And every time she pulled it off, she was rewarded; that grin when he spotted her, the occasional raffish wink that she should have found ridiculous but didn't.

Still, the first night they kissed took her by surprise. It had been a small group that evening – no Arpita or Jamie or Billy – and the others had tired, hijinks no match for the siren call of parents' living rooms and central heating. But Euan had given her a look and she'd felt something and known that the right answer was to linger behind, on the pretence of finishing their lukewarm beers.

And just as she'd hoped, Euan had drawn Anya close to him and left his arm around her. There'd been a moment of hesitation when their faces were close to one another, and then they'd kissed.

After that, things changed. At school, there were more glances that lingered and smiles that seemed like they might contain a subtext. Two or three times, they'd bunked off just the two of them, afternoons Anya liked to think of as dates. The first time, he'd surprised her, grabbing her school bag from behind.

'Guess who?'

She'd turned, secretly delighted, but rolling her eyes to pretend she wasn't.

'Hi.'

'Let's go.' He glanced left and right. 'Hurry.'

'What? Where?'

'Out of here!'

Before she'd had time to argue, he'd guided her down the stairs that led to the back exit and then on past the gates. Anya's heart was thudding, convinced that every teacher and pupil in the school had their nose pressed to the window right now, watching them leave, certain that someone was already calling her parents. But Euan had an arm slung casually around her shoulders, so she didn't say anything.

He'd led her to the walkway that stretched down beside the River Kelvin, about ten minutes' walk from school, and they'd strolled along beside the water, blazers stuffed roughly into their schoolbags, Euan's tie hanging out of his trouser pocket. It was quiet on this mid-week, mid-afternoon, and they relaxed slightly.

'Dressed like this, they won't know what school we're from anyway,' Euan said authoritatively. 'Or we could be on a break from work.'

Anya snorted.

'Who goes to work like this?' She grabbed a handful of her scratchy tartan skirt. 'And your shoes are definitely from Clarks.'

Euan shrugged.

'Fine. Let's just keep our eyes open for people.'

But luckily, no one walked past and so they carried on moseying around for another hour or so, chatting and bickering and flirting, Euan occasionally pausing to mount a half-collapsed stone wall or play keepie-uppies with a discarded plastic bottle.

Eventually, Anya called time.

'I think we should go back now. I've got Art at two fifty.'

'It's just Art though. You won't miss much.' Euan was swiping the air with a thick stick of wood.

'Yeah, but I think we're getting some work back. So, it'll be obvious if I'm not there.'

'Fine.' He was play-fencing now, showing off. 'But I'm going to stay hanging out.'

Anya immediately wished she hadn't suggested it and was about to say she'd changed her mind when he gave her a kiss on the cheek.

'Off you go, nerd.'

She smiled reluctantly and turned back in the direction of the school playground, hoping he was watching her walk away but afraid to turn around and check.

And this was how it went. Sometimes, he'd miss a History class – the only class he and Anya had together – and she'd feel uneasy, worried he was with someone else. And then she'd see him in the park and her anxiety would recede.

They'd started meeting at the gates, holding hands as soon as they passed through into the park. There had never been a conversation – no words like 'official' or 'boyfriend' or 'girlfriend' – but Anya didn't really mind. She was happy with what they had, and he seemed to be too, and she didn't want to break the spell. On Sunday nights, school looming in the morning, she'd find herself replaying the moments on the hill, not always trusting the whisky-soaked memories, excited at the thought of seeing him the following day.

She was startled: Euan was spluttering on his drink. She shot him a teasing glance through her eyelashes, and he passed her back the bottle, which she swigged with bravado, her head lightly swimming now.

'I can't believe it's over.' He shook his head, and she laughed.

'Euan, you've said that like four times.'

Anya was going to Glasgow University when the summer was over, Euan to Aberdeen. She knew she wasn't intrepid enough, going to university in her hometown – in streets so familiar to her that she drew them in her head when she couldn't sleep – but when she imagined university, it looked like the cloistered courts of Glasgow University and she didn't know how to make it look any different. She wasn't sure what Aberdeen looked like. Euan would know soon, though.

She took another sip of the whisky to distract herself and felt it burn the back of her throat. As close as she felt to him, as much fun as she had with him, their connection also seemed fragile. She didn't really know much about him; their conversations were always very of the moment. She'd told him about Paddy and her family, how she sometimes felt jealous of Georgie because she worried their parents liked her better and she was more academic, more conscientious. Euan was a good listener, quiet and encouraging in the right places, but he never really spoke about his own family. He'd mentioned – once – that his mother had died when he was very small, but she hadn't really known what to say. A parent's death was a huge, gaping, real thing, and she'd felt terrified in the face of it. In the end, she'd muttered an anguished, 'I'm so sorry,' but Euan seemed not to have heard her and he'd never mentioned it – or anything personal, really – since. This added to this sense she only half-knew him, that he was only real on this hill, in the park, sipping whisky and lemonade from a plastic bottle. It was quite easy to imagine him disappearing; in fact, sometimes, when she wasn't with him, she wondered if she'd made him up.

Or maybe she was just drunk. Euan was chugging from the bottle again and Anya stretched out a hand.

'Give it here.' If she was going to say anything, she needed a few more slugs of Dutch courage.

Euan passed it to her and she took a bold swig, sweet liquid dribbling down her throat and chin. He laughed at her and then kissed her casually on the cheek.

'What time is it?' He pulled away. 'We should go to Gordon's soon.'

Panic countered the alcohol and chilled her veins. She wanted more time, just the two of them.

'Shouldn't we finish the whisky first?' she asked, hoping she sounded casual.

'OK.' Euan had sussed her out, and gave her a half-cocked smile, eyes like black mirrors. 'I guess he lives quite near here.'

Nearby, there was another crowd of boys and girls, who also looked like new school leavers, rolling on the grass and whooping at one other. In the advancing dim, she couldn't tell if they were from Kelvinbridge too. She was about to ask whether he recognized them when he kissed her again, quicker and more urgently this time. When they pulled apart, he was grinning again.

'It's the first night of the rest of our lives!' He whooped and she rolled her eyes, wrapped up in him but feeling self-conscious. He was on a roll now, Euan the mischievous showman. He grabbed the bottle back and took another hungry gulp.

She calculated there was still about a third left. Emboldened by the jet fuel in her veins, she shifted a little so that she was facing him, awkward, shoulders sloping.

He found her eyes and his sparkled. 'What?'

'Do you think we'll still, like, see each other?' she said, quickly. 'Next year I mean.'

He dropped his gaze and started fiddling with the lighter again, sparking the flame, not looking at her, and she felt suddenly, quietly devastated.

'I'll be in Aberdeen,' he said, eventually.

'Yeah, I know.' She was winded. 'And I'll be here. That's what I mean. But in the holidays and stuff.'

He dropped the lighter and found her eyes again.

'Um.' She could feel the goosebumps on her arms. 'Well. We're moving actually. Back up to Perth. To be near family.'

'Oh.'

'So, I won't be here in the holidays so much.'

He hadn't told her this, and it felt like another body blow. There was a sad pause, long and loaded with unsayables, and then he brightened slightly. 'But we'll still see each other. Definitely. I'll come into Glasgow to see you. And Jamie. And everyone.'

'Right,' she said brightly, trying to smooth the edge from her voice.

The sun was setting now and their figures cast long shadows on the grass. She couldn't tell whether that was her chance, over, when he started speaking again.

'If I wasn't moving away, it would be different.'

She felt the hope and panic rushing all at once.

'What would?' she asked eventually.

'Us.'

He gave her a sad smile.

'Oh,' she managed, her breath ragged. 'Of course, I mean—'

He started kissing her again, his mouth hot and metallic and tasting of whisky and Mayfairs. She closed her eyes, even though it made her head spin a little. It can't have lasted more than a few seconds but in the moment, felt infinite.

He leaned back and grinned again, and she grinned too.

'I'll miss doing that.'

'Me too.'

For a horrible second, her stomach roared hot and cold and she worried she was about to cry, but luckily he reached out his hand and interlaced his fingers through hers. So they sat like that for several minutes, not saying anything, but occasionally squeezing their palms together. Anya watched the spires of her city disappear against the darkening sky and tried to remember to breathe. This was all happening very fast.

Eventually he took his hand from hers and brushed both palms on his school trousers. He looked contemplative.

'I'm sorry,' he mumbled. 'I just – I dunno – I don't think we want to do that long-distance thing. You coming up to Aberdeen and me coming down here every weekend.'

All term, the couples in their year had been debating this question. Those who had decided to try it uttered sacred vows about £1 Megabuses, regular phone calls and long holidays and how a semester wasn't even that long, anyway. Those who had decided not to, had tried to carry on all term as normal, the expiry date of fresher's week looming like disaster on the horizon.

And so, despite her yearning, Anya did sort of agree. Well, on paper anyway. She didn't want to have to get on a Megabus – the smell of egg sandwiches lurking in the air – and go all the way to Aberdeen at weekends. When she imagined university, she didn't imagine it involving her shuttling halfway across Scotland regularly, saying goodbye at grey bus stops, a relationship via screens, stomach tightening over every dashed-off text ('Can't talk now! Maybe later?').

He took her hand again and squeezed it lightly.

'This isn't the end.'

'It sort of feels like it.'

They kissed again. When they broke apart, she felt a little teary again and screwed her eyes up in case he noticed, but he was shuffling a little now, more alert.

'No, it isn't the end. Because I've got an idea.'

In the half-light she could see the bright mischief in his eyes again.

'What do you mean?'

He reached for his school bag and started scrabbling around for something. After a few moments, he removed a pad of lined paper and tore a sheet from it.

'You got a pen?'

'Um—' Anya reached for her own school bag, unzipped it and hunted for a Biro.

'Here. Dunno if it works though.' She passed it to him.

Using the pad of lined paper as a surface, he scribbled in one corner. It worked.

'Bingo.'

'What are you doing?'

'Well.' Euan flipped the paper over. 'Why don't we make a promise? A vow. Not to forget about each other.'

'What, to like, text each other?'

'No.' He shoved her lightly. 'More than that. To – well – find each other again. A contract!' She couldn't work out if he was teasing her but he was growing more animated, sitting up straighter, fidgety and thrilled. 'When's your birthday?'

'July seventeenth.'

'Mine's September fourth' – he nodded, almost to himself – 'so that works perfectly. If we're not with other people by the time we're' – he broke off to think for a second – 'thirty. Then we'll find each other again.'

Anya couldn't help it: she burst out laughing, and he put the pen down and laughed back.

'Fine, then.' He grinned.

'Sorry, sorry.' She nudged him. 'No, it's a good idea! Sorry. Thirty just sounds a really long time away.' She wrinkled her nose and kissed him on the cheek. In return, he shoved her lightly, though she could tell he was pleased.

'But wait,' she felt suddenly panicked, 'do you mean that we won't see each other until we're like, thirty?'

He shoved her again.

'No! God, you're taking this the wrong way. It's a thing. To bring us back together again. Once we've lived some of our lives. I'm your back up man.' They shared a shy smile. His became a sloppy grin. 'Not that it'll matter because there's no way I'll be single at thirty. Unlike you.'

'Hey.'

Their faces were close again, so close she could feel his breath on her face. After a moment, he started writing.

I, Euan Carrick (17) and I, _____, (also 17) declare that if we are still single at the age of 30 years old, we will find each other. This is a LEGALLY BINDING CONTRACT!

'OK, you write your name there.'

He extended the pen, the lined paper and the sheet to her. The pen was slightly greasy. Anya wrote her name in careful cursive – he hadn't quite left enough space for it, so the 'Mackie' was a lot smaller than the 'Anya' – and passed the lot back to him. He started writing again.

'What's the date?'

'Twenty-sixth.'

'What month?'

'June. Duh.'

'Shut up.'

He extended the pen to her again.

Signed by Euan and _____, on the evening of 26 June 2007

She leaned close to the paper to fill in the blank again. She could feel him watching her, and solemnly she passed the paper back to him. He grinned.

'Right, now we have to do the ceremonial shot to make it official.' He passed her the bottle. 'Ladies first.'

She made a face and gulped the whisky down, tears springing to her eyes as she felt the fire in her throat once more. She passed it back to him and smiled.

He stood up unsteadily, and brushed his trousers, then extended an arm to pull her up. She stumbled, feeling much dizzier now she was standing up. They kissed again, hot and clumsy and urgent. When they pulled apart, he was watching her, grinning a dopey, silly smile.

'See you in twelve years, then.'

8

Suddenly, horribly awake, Anya lurched forward and took a gulp of air. Panic rising, she reached for her phone, but fortunately she had neither WhatsApped Connor, nor posted something performative on social media.

The relief was anaesthetizing and, for a few moments, she lay staring at the ceiling. Her small bedroom lamp was still on, and she closed one eye against the dull glow. With the other, she observed that her clothes formed an outline on the floor where she'd stepped out of them last night. And then, like dragging something from the bottom of the sea, the memory surfaced. In the cold light of sobriety, the contract, which she appeared to have placed by her mattress before she fell asleep – the end of the night had slipped and blurred and she didn't remember going to sleep at all – looked even grubbier and more ragged than she remembered it feeling in her hands last night.

Rolling on to her stomach, she examined it again, noting the way the 'Y' in 'Anya' looped, long and ludicrous. She must have put the paper in the yearbook for safekeeping that evening.

She no longer kept in touch with Ciara, Arpita and Kaye; their bond had been too new to be solid and at university she'd been reunited with Paddy and found Tasha and a wider group of boisterous kindred spirits. She had crossed paths with the school lot a few times in the years after they'd left school: at the pub on Christmas Eve, where ghosts of schooldays past were guaranteed; at a New Year's Eve party, crammed into a kitchen, where the walls wept condensation. But mostly, their lives had sidled off in separate directions; she didn't even remember where they'd gone to university. Every so often, Anya would see one of them pop up on Facebook and they would feel like a stranger, which she supposed at this stage, they were.

But Euan: when did they even say goodbye? The evening in the Kelvingrove Park wasn't their last: there had been a few more nights with the others that summer, sharing shy, wistful kisses despite knowing they were doomed, that they had decided to be one of the couples with an expiry date. She remembered a cinema trip, riding up the escalators to the screen at the very top, him pinching pick 'n' mix from the big barrels, showing off for Anya.

They had tried to keep in contact at university, especially at first. She could just about remember sitting on the scratchy carpet of her tiny room in halls, talking to him on the phone, both of them swapping slightly competitive stories of wild capers and crawling into bed at dawn. She'd often wondered if there was ever a girl there too. Until one morning, she woke up and there was a boy there with her. She and Kris never really turned into anything, but they'd done something she'd never done with Euan, and that had mattered a lot at the time. After that, she'd felt a little guilty, while also knowing that she needn't. They'd agreed: they weren't together.

They had texted on and off, although she couldn't remember any specifics, and was sure the phone calls had tailed off by Christmas. And at the same time, there was the joy of having Paddy back by her side, and the mischievous thrill of seeing her hometown transform into a playground: pubs; clubs; parties. And then Anya had spent the summer after her first year of university working all hours and then Interrailing with Tasha; by which point it would have been a year since she and Euan had even seen each other.

It didn't help that Paddy had always been so determined to move forwards not backwards and had been rather cut-throat about avoiding people whom he'd once shared a French listening class with, and that Anya had always played his willing accomplice – especially at that age. And really, they'd had such fun gathering their new group: Tasha and Tom and Sara and Andy and Kelsey; living in halls; making milestone mistakes (lost keys; lost virginities; lost dignity). She and Euan had made the right call not to let them tether themselves to one another at university and beyond.

And beyond it was: she was thirty now, as of July. Which would mean – according to the ragged, grubby slip of paper she held in her hand – that Euan was too. In fact, he'd turned thirty-one a few weeks ago.

She unlocked her phone, opened Facebook and typed Euan Carrick into the search bar. Two accounts appeared, and she felt something in her stomach, but neither was the right person. One was based in Springfield, Missouri, and looked to be about sixty-odd, the other was a teen-ager, his hair greased into hedgehog spikes, wearing a vast, mirrored pair of sunglasses.

She tried Instagram but the closest she could find there was a Euan Carr, whose last post, three years previously, showed an older gentleman in a generic beach bar, grip-ping a sloshy pint, and whose flat and ruddy face suggested that he was a man who used the term 'the missus'. She hoped this wasn't Euan.

There was noise on the landing.

'We've – I've – paid the deposit.' Claire's voice was echoed slightly as though she were already off down the stairs. 'We still have to pay off the rest of the balance.'

Anya waited for Richard's response but heard nothing except the sound of the bathroom door close and then lock. She pulled the duvet to her chin with one hand and with the other picked up the yearbook.

She flipped through it quickly, past entries about rugby and Computer Club and Gold Duke of Edinburgh expeditions and school plays, until she found the profile pages. Euan's was on one of the first pages, the picture grainy, probably taken on a camera phone in 2007. She could just about make out his gelled-back hair but it wasn't a lot to go on in order to reconstruct a version of what he might look like now.

Name: Euan Carrick
Year joined: 2005
Nicknames: Farmer boy, Wee man, Carro
Most memorable moments: Throwing a water
    balloon at those S3s, Poolgate, THAT charity auction
    dance routine
Mortal enemy: Mr Wood
Most often seen: Mucking about with Jamie Kildare;
    trying to impress Anya Mackie
In five years: In jail

She read it a couple of times, surprised and embarrassed

by how gratified she was, all these years later, to see her name on his page.

She made a fly-by to her own profile ('**In five years:** Still taking stick for that trumpet solo' – she hastily flipped past it), then turned to the photo collages in the middle of the yearbook: albums of school trips and sports days and dances. He'd only been there two years, but Euan made it into a surprising number of the pictures (unlike Anya, who'd gone to the school her whole life and only made it into a few of them). There he was on the sixth form residential trip during September half term – hanging off Jamie's shoulders – and sitting on the benches in the PE hall during the twenty-four-hour sports challenge, laughing at something or someone out of shot; and on stage at the aforementioned auction (although before the half-naked dance that was referenced in the yearbook and, Anya remembered still, earned him a detention).

And there they were together, although only incidentally, a class picture of their Advanced Higher History Class examining some old coins (she felt bored just looking at it – she wondered who had thought to take a picture to mark such a tedious occasion). They both looked rather solemn. She wished there were some photographs of those nights in the park.

Her phone, on the mattress, glowed: Paddy was Face-Timing. She considered ignoring it then felt mean, so pressed the accept call button, smiling as the close-up of his face came into focus. His eyes were small behind his glasses, pink and blinking.

'Morning sunshine.' Paddy moved the phone and the

scene blurred for a moment, and Anya felt hungover. 'How are you feeling?'

'Could be worse. You?'

'Bad. Ordered a Domino's when I got in.' He grimaced. 'Including potato wedges. So, when I woke up there were all these chunks of potato congealing in the BBQ sauce.'

Anya made a sympathetic noise, and Paddy scrunched up his nose.

'It's very dark in your room.'

'Sorry. One second.'

She placed the phone face down on the mattress and moved to the window. She pulled the curtains open and then returned.

'That's better,' Paddy said. 'Your face looked really weird in the dark.'

'Thanks.'

'What are you doing today? Do you want to go for a walk?'

Strictly, Anya had earmarked this weekend for @anyaeatstoomuch admin. While she had been cooking like a woman possessed, she knew that she needed to do the practical (read: boring) parts too. This weekend, she'd vowed to look into a Squarespace website properly, and possibly ask her dad about borrowing his fancy camera for taking proper pictures of the food.

'Where were you thinking?' she asked. 'I have things to do today.'

There was also the question of Euan, who was surely worth another hour at least of internet-stalking.

'Me too!' He sounded lightly indignant. 'I have to prep

for this head of department job. We wouldn't be out for long.'

'When's the presentation?'

'In two weeks.' He made a face. 'So, I have a lot to do. I thought we could go to the Necropolis, and then we could go our separate ways and have our separate boring work weekends.'

Anya knew Paddy was checking up on her, in his own way; she smiled.

'OK. That sounds good.'

He looked pleased.

'Shall we meet there at eleven thirty? I'll text Georgie too.'

'Let's do it.'

'Right. I'm going to go shower.'

Paddy always waved before he ended a FaceTime call. It reminded Anya of her mother. She waved back.

'See you in a bit.'

She closed the FaceTime screen and spotted a red bubble on her Gmail app: Tasha. In her hungover stupor, she hadn't noticed a reply.

To: anyamackie@gmail.com
From: tasha.kelner@penandpencil.com
Re: S-O-f***ing-S

I changed the subject line so it doesn't have a swear word in it. We're better than that. Also, Anya I'm offended you think I'd ride a Peloton at 6.30 am.

I have been really busy at work though – sorry, that's why it's taken me so long to reply, and why I'm sending this on a very rare Friday night in. Not usually my style as you know but they've had us in the office until 11 pm most nights this week and I feel like a total zombie. Ted (other more senior account exec, who's so demonically positive it's an insult to my cold Britishness) has been making us play show tunes from musicals to 'keep our spirit going' while we sit at our screens at 9 pm hating the company. So, I'm having a wine on the sofa and emailing you and waiting for Loic to come round. (I'm not that tired, etc etc.)

OK, what do you mean you're working with kids???? I would never laugh at you about anything (that's a lie) but also haven't you heard that old thing about never working with kids or animals????? Seriously, can you tell your mum where to go? (No offence, that's just the sort of thing I say to my mum all the time but, as you know, she is a bitter old battleaxe.) But what about food! I would literally love to plan that dream with you. I will be your *Dragons' Den* dragon any time!!

How are you feeling about Connor? Any emotional progress? Done the rite-of-passage, got drunk and called him yet? Obviously really hope not but I would not judge you if you did (Paddy would, but you can tell me). And also, it's going to happen and sometimes it's best to accept something and lean into it. People at work are always leaning into things so it's one of My New Sayings. Keep me posted on any developments in your life please.

Xxxxxxxxxxx

*

Anya's parents used to take them on walks to the Necropolis – a sprawling gothic graveyard near Glasgow Cathedral – when they were children. Her mother had grown up in the area, in a small tenement house at the foot of the low hill on which the cemetery sprouted into the sky, surrounded on three sides by roads. As adults Anya, Georgie and Paddy made regular pilgrimages there a tradition of their own. Anya remembered the first time they'd brought Connor here, on a sunny spring day, and he'd teased Georgie and Anya about liking it so much. She'd been so keen to impress at the time that she'd agreed it was silly, and then later felt guilty.

On this crisp Saturday morning in early October, the city looked dark and dramatic against the low-hanging white clouds, a little unreal, like a stage set. As the three of them walked through the ornate gate, towards the first block of higgledy-piggledy headstones, Anya was already grateful for the cold air blowing her cobwebs free. Making her way here, standing on the platform with the Saturday shoppers who were piling into town, her head had been full of too many things: menus, Connor, and trying to pinpoint exactly the moment when she had seen Euan for the last time. Her mind felt muddled, and a hangover had settled in her temples; the rush of the cool air felt vaguely medicinal.

They had set off on their usual circuit, hands stuffed in pockets, paces purposeful. They soon passed their first set of graves, some crumbling and grand, others pauper-like by comparison.

'When I die, I want a massive headstone,' Anya pointed at a tomb to their right. 'With a cherub. And a big cross.'

'Noted.' Georgie nodded briskly. 'But please don't die. Ever.'

Anya looped her arm through her sister's.

'OK. I promise.'

'When I die, I will haunt you.' Paddy was already striding

ahead, leading the way up the low hill ahead of Anya and Georgie.

For a little while, they loped on in comfortable silence, air forming hot clouds in the chill, Georgie's nose growing pinker and pinker. Anya knew the Necropolis was in the middle of a city, but it felt miles away from clogged bus lanes and heaving Subway trains with low roofs that smelled of armpits. Still, her thoughts remained noisy and cluttered with ingredients and yearbook photographs and kisses on top of hills, and the fuzzy image of a boy she hadn't seen in a decade.

As they rounded another cluster of headstones, Anya tried what she hoped was a nonchalant tone.

'So, after I got home last night, I ended up going through all these boxes of all my old stuff.'

Georgie, to whom Anya was still looped, looked politely interested; Paddy remained ahead but his head popped over his shoulder to show he was listening, and so she continued.

'Do you remember Euan Carrick? We were at school with him.'

Paddy half-turned again.

'Who?' he called out.

'Euan Carrick. I don't think you really knew him. I hung out with him a lot after you left.'

Georgie, who was making a face like she was trying to remember the answer to a pub quiz question, suddenly clapped delightedly, jerking Anya's arm as she did so.

'Yes! I remember him. The one you really fancied,' she added, matter-of-factly.

Paddy had stopped to let the two of them catch up and they walked on as a three.

'I don't remember him,' he said.

'He was part of this big group I used to see in the park on Fridays after you left – we had a bit of a thing in sixth form.' Georgie nodded authoritatively, pleased she'd been correct. 'But then he went to university in Aberdeen and I stayed here and we never really saw each other again after that.'

They sidestepped a beheaded headstone, no more than overgrown rubble poking from the ground, and Anya felt a little sad for its forgotten owner. Both Paddy and Georgie were looking politely blank now.

'What about him?' Georgie prompted eventually.

'Well' – Anya felt a bit dizzy – 'I found this note. Last night. A sort of *contract.*' It sounded even sillier said out loud, but she carried on. 'We wrote it on the last day of school. We'd spent the evening together in the park drinking and snogging.' She knew she wasn't explaining this very well. 'It was silly. This stupid thing about how if we were both single at thirty then we'd find each other—'

She broke off and stopped walking, breaking Georgie's grip. She and Paddy both looked a little nonplussed.

'Not a real one, it's not *legally binding.*' The joke fell flat, so she took another few paces towards a low wall and the other two followed. 'It just made me think. About how we totally lost touch after that. I haven't spoken to him since that summer, but we were so close.' The wall was just ahead of a small set of stone stairs blanketed with damp russet leaves. Georgie and Paddy stood in a cluster of two and Anya felt lonely; more so when she saw them exchange a quick look.

'Well, anyway. It all just made me think how sad it is,' she finished lamely. 'That's all. Drifting apart from someone you were so close to. Not knowing what happened to him. Maybe we should have got back in touch.'

There was a pause.

'I feel like we're missing something here,' Paddy said eventually.

She was going to have to say it.

'Well, fine, what I really mean is – do you think it would be weird if I looked him up? On Facebook or something.' She said this rather fast. They exchanged another glance, and so she added quickly: 'Not to call in the stupid contract – it's not about the contract. Just as friends. Maybe it would be nice to see him again.'

But she'd run out of steam and found she couldn't look at either of them, though she felt their eyes on her. She rubbed the toe of her boot on the step, virtually feeling the charge of their telepathic communication.

'I'd be careful.' Georgie, of course, gentle but firm.

Anya dared a glance at her now, and her sister continued.

'You're in a . . . a bit of a state at the moment. So, I'd be wary about hunting down anyone who might . . . upset you . . .'

'Oh, shut up Georgie,' Paddy interrupted crisply. He turned to her. 'Anya, that is one of the saddest ideas you've ever had.'

There was a long, stung silence.

'Thanks, guys,' Anya finally managed. If she pretended to sulk, perhaps they wouldn't realize she was hurt.

'Sorry!' Georgie looked upset, but Paddy shook his head and fixed Anya with a beady eye.

'Anya – don't text your high-school crush from a decade ago. Download Hinge like a normal person.'

Anya hadn't yet made the inevitable journey on to the apps, because every time she thought about doing so, she felt hot and a little panicky, and the world too bright and real. She hadn't used the apps before she started dating Connor, and she was terrified that she was way too late to start now, that she'd aged out of modern love and would never get a grip on its rituals and customs. Not to mention that her impressions from Tasha and Mhairi and her other former colleagues was of a human safari, and Anya was certain she'd rank as a lower-tier animal, something parasitical and undesirable. A rat, say.

She shook her head.

'I'm not ready.'

'Oh, that's a good idea.' Georgie ignored her, her wide eyes aimed on Paddy instead, and Anya felt ganged up on again. 'It'll show you what else is out there.'

'Exactly.' Paddy nodded sagely. 'Plus, it's always a bit of an ego boost.'

'I highly doubt that.' But already Anya had the panicked feeling of a situation slipping from her control.

'You'll clean up.' Paddy nodded firmly, the matter settled. 'We'll make your profile now.'

'No!' She pointed up the low hill. 'I want to keep walking. It's cold. Look at Georgie's nose.'

Georgie touched it.

'Is it really red?'

'Yes,' Anya replied. Maybe this would work.

Paddy had started walking again.

'Fine. We can make your profile while we walk.' He called over one shoulder. 'Come on.'

Anya considered turning around and flouncing off but

couldn't be bothered. Georgie was already following Paddy; with a theatrical sigh, Anya brought up the rear.

'Stop sighing.' Paddy turned and started walking backwards in order to watch Anya's face. 'This will be good for you. Now, first, we'll need to find some good photos to use.'

'There aren't any.'

'Then we'll take some.'

He really wasn't letting up.

'Please.' Perhaps begging would work. 'I'm too hungover for this.' The cold air was stinging her lungs, and she regretted smoking last night.

'That's exactly why you need us to help you.' Georgie had slowed down in order to elbow her in the ribs.

'Exactly.' Why did Paddy have so much energy? He'd drunk as much as she had, and he'd fallen asleep with some potato wedges. 'Give us your phone.' He stretched out a hand, and Georgie elbowed her again.

'I haven't even downloaded any apps yet.' But her voice had a whine of surrender.

Strictly this wasn't actually true: Anya had downloaded Hinge and Bumble one evening, after enduring a stilted, tedious dinner with Claire and Richard, and reasoning that dating couldn't be a worse way to spend an evening. But she hadn't dared open either; they sat, pointed but pointlessly, on her home screen, making her feel worse about everything.

'Start with Hinge.' Paddy turned around in order to skip nimbly up another set of stone steps, waiting at the top for Anya and Georgie, and Anya considered running again.

'You should definitely start with Hinge,' Georgie nodded, taking the stairs more carefully, wary of the slippery autumn leaves. 'The men are way better looking and have way better grammar.'

'Do *you* have a dating profile?' Paddy sounded amused.

'Of course! Everyone does!'

'Download it, Anya, and then we'll start with pictures. It's really all about the pictures.' Paddy smiled wolfishly.

'Wow, what an insight.'

'They can't have Connor in them,' Georgie said, apologetically.

'Give me your phone,' Paddy demanded. She hesitated, but he gave her a look and she surrendered it. 'What's your passcode?'

'170594.'

'My birthday!' Georgie sounded pleased.

Paddy had opened Facebook and was scrolling through her tagged photos. After a few moments, he turned the screen around for Anya and Georgie to examine.

'This one's OK.'

'I'm about twenty-three in that,' Anya pointed out. It was from a Mackie family holiday to Crete, where she was sitting on a stone wall, silhouetted against the sunset. 'Also, you can't see my face.'

'Neither of these are major problems.' Paddy was scrolling again.

'What about that one.' Georgie had jabbed her finger at the screen and Anya felt hemmed in again. It was a picture of her sitting in the back of someone's car, on the way back from a festival, gripping a can of Irn-Bru. 'When was this?'

Paddy withdrew the phone from Georgie's reach.

'Georgie, she should have detagged that photo years ago. Her face looks like brie.'

'OK, we're not doing this.' Anya snatched the phone back clumsily.

They both blinked at her.

'I'll do my own profile.' She drew a haughty breath. 'This is something I need to do myself.'

Paddy shrugged.

'OK. But I'm not making a pact to marry you when you're still unwed at forty.'

9

When she returned from the Necropolis to an empty Hamilton Drive, Anya remembered — with a thrill — that she had the run of the house. This was exceptional: although Claire was often out — at work, at yoga, having coffee with Magdalena — Richard was always in his study, jabbing at his keyboard and shelling the pistachios he snacked on from morning until evening. But this weekend, he and Claire were doing a recce at their wedding venue, back on Sunday evening, which meant Anya would be home alone for almost thirty-six hours. Despite the hangover, she grinned.

The energy of the house already felt different: friendlier and more sympathetic. After shrugging off her coat, Anya was unable to resist a rare opportunity to trespass in Richard's study, the first door off the front hall. The door creaked as she opened it; inside, it smelled of stale deodorant and hot computer. Stepping a little closer to the desk, she noticed his orthopaedic chair had a distinctive bum groove. She made a face, then retreated, closed the door and walked, rather than tiptoed, down the stairs. She'd gone via the tiny Tesco on the way home and, in the kitchen, she hooked her phone up to the Sonos to play a podcast while she prepared a rich, buttery cacio e pepe: her signature hangover meal. She ate a steaming bowl of it in the living room, on a tray, watching the big television.

The last time she'd felt this relaxed was the night before Connor had turned the world on its axis, although realizing this made her think of Connor, so she had a second serving of pasta instead. She passed the day in a stupor of television, occasionally waking up to discover she'd fallen asleep in the big chair.

Later, once she'd hauled herself to bed, and was full and sleepy and almost content, she had allowed herself another look at the yearbook. The Anya in the pictures felt like looking at another person and, vainly, she tried to remember being that person – the one who'd kissed Euan on the top of hills and had thought about him on Sunday nights before school, excited about the prospect of colliding with him in the corridors. Paddy and Georgie hadn't put her off, exactly, but she wasn't sure what she wanted yet, and nostalgia was tiring. She placed the yearbook beside her bed and was asleep moments later.

On Sunday morning, she'd woken without a hangover and therefore with a new lease of life and determined to focus on Anya Eats Too Much. Feeling something like excitement, she padded to the kitchen in her pyjamas and slippers and, after she'd made a coffee in Claire's Nespresso machine – and then another one – she opened her ancient, wheezy laptop and got started.

The first move was to make a proper website. Every podcast she ever listened to recommended Squarespace, and so she visited the site, noting with pleasure that no one else had purchased the domain anyaeatstoomuch. com. This, she decided – plugging in her card details – was kismet, just the kind of sign she hadn't realized she'd needed the world to offer up. Fifteen pounds a month felt like a bargain for that sort of cosmic satisfaction.

Anya wished she'd paid slightly more attention in her Standard Grade IT classes, though: it took a morning of slightly laboured fiddling – and plenty of googling 'how to make a food website' and 'good website layout' – before she had a proper 'About Me' section, rendered in white over a smart blue background. But eventually, she had one up there, along with a sample menu that included the pea, mint and feta filo tart that she was so proud of. She liked her font, and she liked her blurb, although she definitely needed a proper logo. Perhaps Tasha could help with that.

For the umpteenth time that morning, Anya read the blurb aloud.

Anya Eats Too Much

Hello! I'm Anya. I like cumin and lunches that last until dinnertime. I don't like coriander or the concept of breakfast 'to go'. I'm a chef and enthusiastic eater from Glasgow, which is where I live. No, I have never had a deep-fried Mars Bar, but yes, I do like haggis and think it's criminal that we only eat it one evening a year.

If you've found yourself here, you must be hungry. Good news! I currently cater small-scale events of up to 30 people. I have a sample menu, but I'm also very happy to discuss personalized menus and can cater to any dietary requirements, too. If you'd like to see more of my food, visit my Instagram @anyaeatstoomuch.

I don't do Twitter because it seems like sitting in a room where everyone won't stop arguing and being unable to find the door.

If you'd like to chat menus or the merits of coriander (good luck), you can email me on anya@anyaeatstoomuch.com.

Anya x

She hit save again, and rubbed her eyes, which were stinging slightly. It was 1.35 p.m., which meant she'd been at her screen for several hours, and she could do with a shower, not to mention she still needed to hose down the hob, which was still covered in pools of melted butter and grated Parmesan, to ensure it met Claire's exacting standards.

She was just summoning the energy to consider doing this when she heard the grind of a key in the lock upstairs and the sound of voices. Bickering voices; Anya froze.

'I don't know what you want me to do. We've already sent out the invitations, Richard!'

She heard the buzz of Richard's voice, but not what he said. Whatever it was, though, Claire didn't seem to like it.

'It's not how you imagined it? We've visited it before! We decided to have it there together! You can't just decide you don't like it now!'

Anya squirmed – she definitely shouldn't be hearing this. They'd been having a few arguments about the wedding recently; although from Anya's extensive experience as a bridesmaid, these seemed fairly par for the course. Still, Claire's tone scared her. Slamming the laptop lid closed, she washed her mug in the sink and then used the damp sponge from beside the sink to scrub at the hob, trying to ignore the raised voices, then tiptoed up the stairs, laptop under one arm. Claire and Richard were standing in the hallway now, several metres apart, both furiously tapping on their phones. Neither of them had seemed to notice she'd appeared.

'Hello!' Anya tried brightly, affecting the look of someone who had not been – however inadvertently – eavesdropping on an uncomfortable row. 'Did you have a good trip?'

Claire looked up sharply at the sound of Anya's voice. 'Hi, Anya.'

Richard didn't say anything.

Anya gestured to her laptop. 'I was just doing some work in the kitchen.'

But Claire was back tapping on her phone again, so Anya just continued up the house. When she was halfway up the curving staircase, she noticed Claire flounce off down the hall without a word to Richard, her long cardigan swooping in her wake.

After Anya closed the door of her bedroom, she reflected that sometimes it wasn't so bad being single.

The twins had suggested 'playing' football again, but this time, Anya had come prepared.

'What is it?'

The girls nearly knocked their heads together in their eagerness to examine the Tupperware box of courgette and Parmesan fries.

'They're crisps. Made of cheesy vegetables.'

They exchanged a telepathic look.

'OK,' said whichever one had pigtails that day. In a synchronized movement, they sat at the kitchen island and gave Anya the sort of look a queen might give a subject.

She plated the chips up with a homemade chilli dip and sat at the table, pretending not to watch while the twins feasted. But there was clearly an opportunity here. As she'd clocked the first time she tried it, the girls were tranquillized by food. Anya reckoned that were she to try proper cooking with them, she could keep them entertained, avoid being brained by a football, and use afternoons at Park Circus to trial easily scalable recipes for Anya Eats Too Much. She was happy with her menu in principle but suspected some of the dishes would be easier to make at speed and in large quantities than others. Plus, it would probably be good to attempt cooking in a hostile environment.

'You can make those again,' said one of the girls, while the other licked her fingers, one-by-one. Anya took the plates to the sink so they wouldn't see her smiling.

Later, as she shrugged into her coat near the front door, she spotted Aimee, who was staring rather vacantly into a vast mirror, curling a blonde wave around her index finger.

'Aimee?'

The woman gave no indication that she'd heard her.

'I wondered if it would be OK if I started cooking with the girls?'

There was a pause so long that Anya wondered again if she'd heard her, but eventually Aimee drew her eyes away from the gilt-rimmed glass.

'I don't understand the question.'

'Well' – Anya stepped cautiously closer – 'like, make them snacks. And meals. And things like that. They could join in, learn how to cook a few things.'

Aimee gave her a look as if she smelled bad.

'Why?' she asked eventually.

'Well – um – I just thought they might . . . like it.' And it meant that they wouldn't brain her with a football.

Aimee narrowed her eyes and, for a moment, Anya thought she was going to say no, but instead she shrugged.

'Knock yourself out. Just as long as you clean up afterwards.'

The next day, she'd *almost* looked forward to 3.30 p.m.; she planned to make a green risotto with hazelnuts, for which she'd bought the ingredients on the way over. As she placed the shopping bag on the counter, she could sense the girls were intrigued.

They both watched her, open-mouthed, as she set to work, time vanishing as she melted the butter and stirred in the rice and seasoning (she was skipping the wine that her recipe usually demanded, for obvious reasons).

Another telepathic look, and then one spoke.

'What are you doing?'

'I'm making a green risotto.' A studied pause. 'Do you want to help?'

Cautiously, they both stepped forward.

'What, like cook?' They were both blinking fast.

'Yes. You could help.'

Another look, and then they both nodded slowly.

'OK. I need you to mix this goat's cheese and cream and oil in a bowl. You can take it in turns to stir the mixture.'

'Me first!'

'Rosie always gets to go first.' Rachel had the mournful tone of someone who had accepted their lot as second best. Both had pigtails today, but Anya noted Rosie had two blue hair ties, and Rachel one blue and one green.

'I'm older.' Rosie turned to Anya, smirking, and Anya

decided she liked the younger twin better. 'By seventeen whole minutes.'

'OK, you can go first.' Anya handed her the spoon. 'But you have to share, or you can't help again.'

Rosie nodded.

Anya held her breath but the girls played nice, and whipped the goat's cheese, cream and oil into a relatively smooth paste. She kept one eye on them, while she stirred her risotto rice. When it was ready, she brought the cooked rice to the kitchen island. Both of them watched her with big eyes.

'OK, now we mix it all together.' She had cheated and brought pre-prepped pesto, which she tipped on to the rice. 'Now add some dollops of your mixture.'

Rosie went ahead, adding her dollop with gusto, though Rachel waited for Anya's nod of permission.

'OK, that looks good. Do you want to try some?'

They both nodded slowly, and Anya doled two small portions into two bowls. The girls took a few careful, suspicious mouthfuls – it was, Anya supposed, very green – and then quickened their pace, spoons flying into their mouths. Anya took a few mouthfuls straight from the pan and pretended not to watch them.

She had continued to test recipes on them for the rest of the week, both of them playing small, slightly haughty sous-chefs. Neither had been that keen on the beetroot dip with feta and quinoa, but they'd finished the spicy ginger and edamame, and the bulgur pilaf with spicy tomatoes.

Before she presented each dish, Anya took a careful picture of it, hoping someone would mistake Aimee's pristine kitchen tiles for her own showroom. Later, she'd post a picture on @anyaeatstoomuch ('Arancini balls! Working on my menu – watch this space #balls'. That one got 1,367 likes). She'd posted a story saying 'something exciting – coming soon', which had received thirty-odd messages – heart eyes and question marks – from followers. It was early days, but it felt like something was happening.

'You can take my plate now.' Rosie pushed away a bowl that had once featured teriyaki tofu but was now almost licked clean.

'Of course.'

The rest of the time, of course, they were still beastly: sneering; rude; on occasion unkind. It was all childish – they were, after all, eleven – but exhausting. They laughed at her clothes, her expressions. When she wore her hair in a bun one day, they told her she looked like a bug. They'd planted a stolen candlestick in Anya's bag and Aimee had narrowed her eyes at Anya's panicked protestations. Shortly after licking their risotto bowls clean, they had commandeered the vast Bose sound system in order to play a single pop song on repeat, watching Anya for a reaction (later, as she struggled to sleep, the song ricocheted around her head like a bubblegum grenade). On Thursday evening, when she took the bins out, they locked her out without her coat for almost forty minutes. But at least when she cooked, she got some brief peace, she felt in control. It had always been that way.

Still, by the end of the week she was run ragged, too tired to make anything for herself other than an omelette (she did at least have some truffle oil left over). Claire and Richard were watching a 'challenging' BBC4 drama – mercifully,

Anya hadn't been invited to join – and so she holed up in her room, eyes burning with tiredness.

Missing Connor and her old life no longer felt raw; it was more like something that had taken residence in her chest and her shoulders. She missed her lightness. Still, the more time passed, the harder she found it to remember what it had been like: she and Connor seemed like other people, characters in a book or show she'd loved but whose plot lines she only remembered as a vague tangle.

At the same time, the memories of Euan had started to drift around her consciousness. She hadn't been thinking about him non-stop, but snapshots appeared periodically, almost out of nowhere: in the daytimes before she went to the twins, or in the supermarket as she bought stock cubes and spices, gauzy images that made her wistful. An afternoon bunking off by the river passing a cigarette back and forth. In the sixth form common room, his face lighting up when she appeared. Squeezed on to a couch at another of those hopeless house parties, ignoring the hubbub of mayhem around them.

She suspected her mind of doing something strange, of displacing the recent pain of Connor's departure with soft-focus memories into which she could retreat more happily. She had no doubt it was normal to find yourself wondering about old relationships when a new one ended. Indeed, she could see that there might be a strange sanctuary in doing so (and certainly, it was more appealing than using the Hinge profile that she hadn't touched since Paddy and Georgie strong-armed her into making it).

At first, she wasn't sure if she'd actually do anything about any of it, whether she'd send one of the messages she occasionally composed in her head before she drifted off ('LONG time no speak – fancy a drink?').

Or if she'd even be able to: she couldn't find him anywhere. There was nothing on Facebook, Twitter or Instagram, nor on Billy, Ciara, Arpita or Kaye's profiles. There was no evidence he'd ever been educated or employed anywhere. He appeared to have no digital footprint; perhaps he'd died she'd thought, queasily, one evening as she brushed her teeth.

But after a week, more out of frustrated curiosity than anything else, she stumbled on an idea: contacting Gordon Wilson, who she'd known at both school and university and who'd been a good friend of Euan's at Kelvinbridge Academy. To her surprise, their Facebook Messenger history confirmed she'd even gone to his birthday drinks seven years ago ('see you soon!' – she blinked at the words of yet another unfamiliar Anya), an evening she didn't remember at all. He might think it a bit odd she was trying to track Euan down, but frankly she wasn't that fussed about what Gordon thought of her. His profile picture was an image of a street sign reading, 'Balls Close'.

> Hi Gordon – long time no speak!
> Hope all's well
> Weird one
> You wouldn't happen to be in touch with Euan Carrick would you?!

She'd sent it yesterday, but there was still no response.

To distract herself this evening, she tortured herself by going via Connor's page. His profile picture was no longer the photo of the two of them, squished into frame, at the top of Table Mountain (their most intrepid holiday, eighteen months into their relationship). He had changed it to a picture of himself that she didn't recognize, sitting at a pub table, grinning self-consciously. She suspected that this was a picture he'd taken to use on Hinge. Anya blinked hard.

Mercifully, her phone lit up: Tasha. She had today, Friday, off, and they'd agreed to FaceTime at some point.

Anya angled it above her face, the most flattering angle, and then pressed accept. She could see a pile of honeyed, freshly highlighted hair, and then Tasha's face loomed into view: big eyes, big mouth, skin clear from skating on frozen lakes, or whatever else she did in Vancouver.

'Aaaaaaaaaah!' Tasha was sitting cross-legged on a slate grey couch in a bright, airy apartment. 'It's really you!'

Anya felt a bubble of affection rise in her chest.

'God, you look annoyingly healthy.'

Tasha flicked her hair.

'Sorry, I know. I had twelve hours sleep last night and I've just got back from yoga.'

'I hate you.'

'No, you don't.' Tasha loomed towards her again. 'Let me get a look at you.'

Anya covered her face with one hand.

'Don't. I have just eaten an omelette doused in truffle oil and I feel like a slug.'

'Oh, you look fine.' Tasha beamed. 'Tell me things!'

'You know all the things. Life. Disaster. Etcetera.'

'And to cap it all off, you're home on a Friday night.'

'Hey. Don't kick me when I'm down.'

'Sorry.' She grinned.

'How's Vancouver, besides perfect?'

'Very glad to have a day off. This evening I'm going into

town to meet some people for tacos and tequila.' Tasha wriggled on the couch. She was a fidgeter. 'I'm bringing Loic, which is an experiment. Partly because I don't think he's going to understand anything they're saying.'

'That's exciting.'

'We'll see.' Tanya shrugged. 'Tell me about Connor.'

Anya sighed.

'Well, I just went on his Facebook page and he's changed his picture from a picture of us to one that's just him. So that hurts.'

'Oh, Anya.' Tasha tucked her hair behind her ears. 'Still, it had to happen at some point.'

'Yes. Well. Paddy and Georgie tried to set me up on Hinge last weekend until I put a stop to it.'

'I met Loic on Hinge. It might be just what you need.'

'I can guarantee I won't meet a Loic.'

'Don't be so defeatist, Anya!'

She could sense Tasha revving up for a motivational address and so blurted out, 'I've actually been trying to track down my ex-boyfriend from school.'

'What!' Tasha leaned forwards again, long hair swinging around her face. She looked thrilled. 'Who is he?'

'His name was Euan.' Saying it felt strange in her mouth. 'It's all silly. I found this note we wrote each other years and years ago and had the idea of looking him up. Although all I've managed is a message to an old friend . . .' Tasha was still grinning. 'Do you think I'm really tragic? Paddy and Georgie practically had me sedated when I told them.'

Tasha shrugged.

'People do it all the time. Sometimes it works out. No harm in trying.'

'That's what I thought. They didn't agree.' She chewed her lip. 'I mean I haven't got anywhere yet. And I don't even know what I'd say. I don't know . . .' Tasha was smiling her encouraging sunshine smile from 4,000-odd miles away. 'The idea of having to find someone totally new feels too . . . terrifying.'

Tasha nodded.

'I get it.' She tossed her blonde hair with the hand that wasn't holding the phone and smiled. 'I think it's OK to cautiously see what happens. Just as long as you promise you won't message Glenn.'

Glenn was a lean, cocksure musician in a very unsuccessful band, with whom Anya had been infatuated in their early twenties. He was a cliché of a fuckboy: handsome; sneering; kind for about fourteen minutes a week; always shagging someone else; never texted unless it was a 2 a.m. 'u up?' text. Anya had slept with her phone on loud for six months until Paddy and Tasha had staged an intervention.

'I don't think we could class that as a relationship. More a mistake I kept making.'

'God, I miss our youth.' Tasha grinned. 'Kidding. Anyway, see what happens. And I want updates.'

Anya smiled. Tasha always understood.

'How's the babysitting?'

The smile vanished.

'Horrible. The only thing they don't hate about me is my cooking. I'm using them as my guinea pigs.'

'Tell me about the cooking!' Tasha had been enthusiastically liking everything that Anya posted on @anyaeatstoomuch. 'The beetroot thing looked amazing.'

'That didn't go down too well. But they are eleven. I don't think I liked beetroot when I was eleven.' Anya switched the phone into her other hand and continued: 'Anyway, I'm trying to perfect a repertoire. And I've done my website. In fact – I meant to ask you – do you think you could help me get a logo done?'

'Definitely!' Tasha was nodding violently and Anya felt a hot rush of excitement. 'This is so exciting! You might have to pay them but I can get it for mate's rates, I'm sure. Or screw them on the exchange rate.' She grinned. 'Kidding. Leave it with me though.'

'That would be amazing. I had been thinking of asking Paddy's ex, Johnny.'

Tasha frowned.

'Was he a graphic designer?'

'Yeah. I think so? Or maybe he just wore a lot of Japanese T-shirts.'

Tasha snorted.

'I'll ask our lot on Monday.'

'Thank you so much.'

Tasha was gripping both feet now, in a yogic pose. 'OK, so work, men' – she reeled off – 'how is the house of horrors?'

Anya shrugged.

'No worse than usual. They're downstairs watching some sinister BBC4 show. The other day Claire asked me to wash my hands before touching a light switch, and this evening I found Richard using my electric whisk to kill a spider. The expensive one.'

'How rude.'

'He does this thing where he always licks his lips when

he's talking to you, and it makes my skin crawl. And they keep leaving the Hoover outside my door.'

'Can you move out?'

'Not until my income is more stable. Or Paddy evicts Ivy and takes me in.'

Tasha made a face.

'How is Paddy? He hasn't replied to my last two emails.'

'He's busy. Prepping for this head of department job he's going in for.'

'Tell him to send me his news.'

'I will pass on your kind regards.'

Anya rubbed her eyes with the heel of her hand.

'You're tired.'

'I am. It was a long week. And I'm going to my parents' tomorrow.'

She had submitted to an afternoon in Balfron, on the condition that Georgie also came along.

'Go to bed.' Tasha tossed her hair. 'I've got to go shower anyway.'

'OK.' Anya felt relieved. 'But do not take this as a sign I wasn't thrilled to speak to you.'

'Oh, I know you were.' She grinned. 'I'm all about the hyper-efficient catch-up these days anyway.'

'Of course you are.'

Tasha grinned even wider. 'Let's do it again soon. And keep me posted on the cooking. *And* on your long-lost lover.'

'Shut up.'

'Love you.'

'Love you too.'

10

Anya made the X10 bus that would take her to her parents' house with two minutes to spare, sliding into the seat beside Georgie. Her sister had her earphones in and was staring out of the window, but sensing Anya's presence, she turned and beamed, picking the earbuds out of her ears.

'I was worried you'd miss the bus.'

Anya put her tote bag between her feet. 'Thanks Georgie. Your faith in me is touching.'

Her sister rolled her eyes.

'Sorry. I'm just nervous about seeing Mum.'

'She's excited to see you.'

This made Anya feel more nervous.

Both of them watched the last few stragglers climb on to the bus, eyes lighting up at the sight of the plentiful empty seats. The route out to what their mother fondly called 'the sticks' was clearly not in favour on a Saturday morning: the crowd was sparse and eclectic. One man – definitely a student – was gripping a Burger King paper bag in one hand. He slid into an empty double seat a few rows ahead of them. Anya watched rather enviously as he produced a cheeseburger out of the bag.

'Can we go to Burger King when we get back?'

Georgie ignored her, and instead wrapped up her scarf and rested it on her knees.

The bus was pulling out on to Sauchiehall Street, lumbering down the road, the driver honking the horn at regular intervals to scare lazy or unwitting pedestrians out of its path.

'How was your week?' Georgie put her head on the window and winced: it was damp with condensation.

'Fine,' Anya replied, trying not to smile as her sister smoothed her hair with her scarf. 'I've been sedating the twins with my cooking.'

Georgie gave her a strange look.

'Kidding. I've just been trying out a few recipes on them. It's the only thing that stops them from throwing a ball at my face, plus, it's good content for Instagram.'

'I've been liking all the posts.'

'Your enthusiastic pasta emojis have been noted. How was your week?'

'Long. And my boss is still being . . .' she made a face.

Georgie's boss – a woman called Sheila Dawes – was the only person about whom Georgie could not find a single good thing to say. She was critical to the point of pathology, nitpicking and pedantic and irritable, a stranger to words like 'please' and 'thank you' and 'well done'. To someone like Georgie, for whom validation and acceptance were a lifeblood, this was very difficult, and the relentlessness of it got her down.

Anya squeezed Georgie's hand.

'Sheila is a cow.'

'Thanks.' Georgie sighed. 'I'm glad it's Saturday.'

'And we're on our way to spend the day with our parents.' But Anya smiled too. 'I'm just joking. I'm looking forward to it. Probably. Deep down.'

The bus edged out of central Glasgow and started to pick up pace, the two of them sitting in companionable silence as the familiar route flashed past. As the bus approached Milngavie's manicured lawns, electronic gates and blacked-out Subarus, Georgie extended one of her earphones to Anya. She was listening to a true crime podcast. Anya had accidentally read a spoiler about whodunnit, so she felt strangely qualified to start listening midway through the third episode.

Still, as the bus got closer and closer to Balfron, Anya's fidgeting clearly became impossible to ignore, and Georgie pressed pause on the podcast and removed her own earbud.

'Are you OK?'

Anya gave her a look.

'They will ask you about work and your longer-term plan because they're parents,' Georgie said matter-of-factly. 'The best approach is to be easy breezy about the catering plan, which is very good and very exciting. They'll think it's risky, but just try not to let them get to you.' She held a palm out and Anya dropped the other earbud into it. 'If they ask you about Connor, I think it's within your right to politely decline the questions. Just act casual.'

'Act casual. Listen to you.'

Georgie widened her eyes but said nothing.

The bus continued on down the narrow road, slowing a little as it entered Balfron. The bus stop was near the post office, and Irene and Stephen were there to meet them, their mother wearing new glasses whose lenses flashed in the weak sunlight.

The family sedan was parked just beside the stop: it was another ten minutes up the road by car to their parents' house. Georgie gave Anya a last fleeting, cautionary look, which Anya knew meant 'be nice'.

'There you are!' Irene was already bustling towards them both industriously. 'I was starting to worry the bus had broken down.'

Stephen, the more reserved of the two, raised a palm in greeting.

Anya could be prickly with her parents, mainly because she worried endlessly about them. Now in her thirties – and always of a fairly morbid bent – she had braced herself for their steep decline. She knew it happened. Paddy's father had died a couple of years ago, a cancer that had taken under a year to claim him, and many other university friends spent weekends shuttling to small, retirement suburbs to check in on ailing parents. And so every time she saw hers, she checked them anxiously for signs of frailness or general doddery, listening out for words forgotten, counting how many times they walked into a room and forgot why they'd ventured there.

Fortunately, she thought, as her mother bustled towards her at pace, her father with an arm slung over the roof of the sedan, they both appeared as fit as fiddles. Stephen was tall and lean and, unlike so many of his unluckier friends, still sported a full head of hair, albeit tufty and greying. Irene, meanwhile, was smaller and softer: her own hair kept shortish and neat, and close enough to her natural dark by regular visits to Adrian on Balfron High Street.

It was a relief, too, that they had been married for

thirty-three years and remained visibly, endearingly delighted by the other. In all their years alive, Anya and Georgie had never witnessed anything worse than a bit of clucking between them, perhaps the odd rolled eyebrow. He teased her mercilessly, but always with a sparkle in his eye, and she was far too assured to be anything but amused by it.

'Well, isn't this a treat!' Their mother looked so pleased that Anya couldn't help but smile back. Stephen had ducked into the car and through the windshield Anya could see him methodically checking his mirrors before he started the engine, and smiled again.

'Sorry we kept you waiting,' Georgie said, giving her mother a peck on the cheek.

'Not to worry, you're here now. Anya!'

Her mother widened her arms and Anya walked into them.

'Hi Mum,' she said, from over her mother's shoulder. Irene was about a head shorter than her, and Anya was never sure what to do with her arms when they embraced. But it was still nice. 'I like your glasses.'

Her mother rolled her eyes, always on high alert for teasing.

'Thanks. Now get in you two. I've got a shepherd's pie in the oven.'

Georgie and Anya feigned enthusiasm as they climbed into the back seats of the sedan. Their mother's stodgy staples regularly made the whole family lethargic for hours afterwards.

'Nice to see you too, Dad,' Anya quipped as their father careered around a hedgerowed corner. Stephen had accelerated as soon as Georgie closed the car door.

'Yes, yes, there'll be time for all that but you had me parked on a double yellow.'

Still, Anya saw her father's eyes sparkle in the rearview mirror.

'So, how's Paddy?' Her mother swung around in her seat. Even when Connor was in the picture, Paddy was always enquired after first.

'Same old. Still teaching – he's applying for the head of English job. I'm fine, by the way.'

Under a minute before Anya's first grizzle, although her mother politely ignored her.

'Has he got a boyfriend at the moment?'

Paddy's last relationship had fizzled out about four months ago. He'd been a teacher too, at another school. ('Chemistry, though, which should have been a giveaway.')

'Not right now, no.'

Irene sighed.

'When am I going to get to go to a wedding, eh?'

'There's Claire and Richard's coming up,' Georgie said dutifully.

'And that'll be a right laugh,' Stephen said, wryly.

They had pulled into the driveway now and he parked up.

Their parents' house was a detached, two-storey stone house, with rose bushes in the front garden and a vast, verdant lawn stretching out the back. There was a terrace and a greenhouse, where Stephen was trying to grow tomatoes, but the Stirlingshire weather gods were winning.

Anya and Georgie had been heartbroken when their parents had told them they were selling the West End house, although the relative idyll of the new Balfron one had rather sweetened the pill. Sunk into an armchair, wiggling her toes in the plush carpet while Georgie stretched out on the sofa opposite, Anya was surprised to realize that she felt more relaxed than she had in weeks.

Or at least she did until Irene bustled in, wearing an apron.

'What are the pair of you doing?'

'Sitting down.' Anya gestured to the armchair.

Irene crossed her arms.

'I can see that, Anya. Instead, can you stand up and come and help me in the kitchen? We need a dressing made, and the table laid. I thought we'd eat on the terrace.'

'I thought we were having shepherd's pie,' Anya said. 'Why do we need a dressing? Also, it's October.'

Her mother's face hardened.

'For the side salad, Anya. And you can put a coat on.'

Anya was gratified to see Georgie roll her eyes, but both knew better than to ignore an instruction. In the kitchen, which was fridge-like due to the doors being flung open on to the terrace and lawn beyond, their father was chopping cucumbers.

'Got you too, did she?' Anya said.

Her father winked.

Automatically, Georgie started laying the table and Anya started making the dressing. The Mackies were a well-oiled machine, and lunch was on the terrace in five minutes flat, with Irene's good mood reinstated. Their father was now wearing a bobble hat.

'That's better,' their mother said, as soon as they were all seated, a steaming serving of shepherd's pie in front of them. Anya tipped the vinaigrette on to the salad. The shepherd's pie was too thick, and Anya tried to scrape some of the potato off the top and into her napkin without her mother noticing. When her father spotted her, she gave him a guilty grin.

'Right, so – Anya. Paddy's well. What about work?' Her mother had paused, the salad tongs suspended over her plate, a tomato balancing perilously.

Anya took a mouthful of pie and chewed it slowly and deliberately. Eventually, when the pie was nothing but mulch in her teeth, she started.

'It's OK. Working with the girls is very ' – she searched for the choice word – 'enlightening.'

Georgie was concentrating very hard on eating her own pie.

'Fiona Morton said they were good girls.'

'They're certainly girls.'

Her mother frowned, not getting the joke, but her father was grinning.

'And when you stop being a babysitter,' he grinned even wider, 'what next?'

The whole family was watching her now. She speared a salad leaf with her fork.

'I'm thinking about starting my own catering business, actually.'

'It's very exciting.' Georgie's interjection was a little too quick. Stephen raised his eyebrows, and her mother looked confused.

'A catering business?' she asked. 'What do you mean?'

'Well, I've started a,' – she considered trying to explain Instagram to her parents and then decided it wasn't worth the bother – 'a website. And I've got a menu of dishes.

And Tasha's getting someone she works with to design the logo. So, I've just sort of . . . launched it.' She skewered a cherry tomato with her fork and shivered, which was probably the cold but might have been the alarmed look on her mother's face.

Her father was more diplomatic. 'Sounds very modern.' He cleared his throat. 'And entrepreneurial.'

'Thanks, Dad.' But Anya was watching her mother.

'I'm sorry, I don't really understand.' Her tone was slow and measured, although Anya was sure she could detect a crackle of displeasure. 'How does that make money?'

'Well, it doesn't yet.' A steadying sip of wine. 'But once I start catering for people, then hopefully it will.'

'But who will you cater for?'

'Weddings or parties or corporate . . . things. All sorts. Wherever people need food. I've launched the website, and I'm registering for self-assessment' – a triumphant flourish – '*tax*. And I've done a budget on the menu and the costs and things.' She speared another tomato. 'I'm actually thinking of making it all vegetarian. There are so many vegetarian restaurants in Glasgow now.'

Anya had sent Tasha a brief for the logo on Friday ('funny, a bit quirky, I like red and HATE yellow. Maybe something with a vegetable or a spoon. But you're the expert') and then knocked up the budget, all while she was hiding from Claire and Richard and their loud, vicious stage whispers. It needed a bit of work: she'd done a little more guesstimating than she suspected was wise in an industry that pivoted on fine margins, and a little too much consulting of the prices on the website of Garden of Eden, run by a couple who were also based in Glasgow and made four different types of dhal, and whom she had already cast as her bitter rivals. She'd decided the sweet potato dhal with coconut crust looked too oily and hoped that soon they'd know she existed.

Irene had opened her mouth but Stephen gave her a politely cautionary look, and Anya felt her heart rate level out.

'Well. I hope this means you'll be cooking the Christmas dinner this year.' He pushed his glasses further up his nose. 'Although . . .' his eyes sparkled behind the lenses, 'I don't much fancy a nut roast.'

'Deal.' Anya smiled.

With great effort, her mother managed: 'It all sounds very smart. Will you keep babysitting the girls alongside while you . . . work it all out?'

'I will.' Anya sounded as conciliatory as she could muster. 'Until I sort everything else out.'

'Good,' Irene gave a satisfied nod. 'It would be good not to make an enemy of Fiona.'

Anya resisted very hard the urge to tell her mother that Fiona Morton was not a hard gangland moll, and that Irene could probably survive the odd cool look in the post office, but instead took a large gulp of the wine her father had refilled for her.

'And are you enjoying living with Claire?'

'That has also been enlightening.'

Her father snorted. He had never been very keen on Claire. 'Not much fun, is she?' he'd say, whenever Claire had refused to play in the garden with Anya and Georgie or help him repair their bikes in case she got oil on her school pinafore.

'And what about Connor, then?' Irene ignored them both.

'What about him?' Anya concentrated hard on moving her shepherd's pie around the plate so it looked like she'd eaten more of it than she actually had.

'Any word from him?'

'No. Not in weeks.'

'Coward.' Her father was gruff. 'Never thought much of him.'

This remark lingered for a moment, until Anya managed a strangled, 'Thanks, Dad,' then worked on excavating another cherry tomato from the mush of shepherd's pie that remained stubbornly on her plate. Irene opened her mouth again, but Georgie got there first.

'No one's asked me a thing about me today!' she said crossly.

'Sorry, pet.' Irene smiled. 'How are you?'

Across the table, Anya mouthed 'thank you' at her sister.

After dessert – a trifle, of course – they went into the living room, where Anya was grateful for the central heating. They started a game of Scrabble, but after a few rounds, even Georgie and Stephen were losing interest, although both swore it had nothing to do with the fact that their mother had tried to play the word 'fromulent'. Once the game was finally over, Anya gave Georgie a pointed look.

'I think we might get going, Mum,' her sister said, knowing her line.

'Already!' She sounded disappointed and Anya felt a flicker of guilt. Whenever it was time to leave, she suddenly felt a rush of regret at all the things she hadn't said to her parents, although she wasn't ever sure what they were. She loved them both, but wished she knew how to relax around them, to stop feeling like a hunted teenager.

'We'll come back soon.' Anya gripped her mother hard, hoping perhaps this would communicate something. When they separated, her mother was smiling and she felt both better and worse. 'I'll even bring Paddy next time.'

Her mother smiled more broadly. 'All right then. If you promise.'

While Georgie and Anya collected coats and wallets and phones, their mother disappeared into the kitchen and then re-emerged with a Tupperware.

'Now, take this,' Irene said, pressing it into Anya's hands. It appeared to contain a second shepherd's pie. 'And send my love to Claire.' She remembered. 'And Richard.'

'As soon as either of them become capable of love, I'm sure they'll return it,' Anya said, giving her mum a peck on the cheek and earning an eye roll.

Their father was already waiting in the car, the engine running. Anya squeezed into the back seat next to Georgie.

'Well done,' she muttered.

Their mother tapped on the window and Anya rolled it down.

'Keep us posted on everything, will you, Anya?'

'Yes, Mum.'

'Love to Paddy.'

'He'll be delighted.'

Their father turned from the front seat.

'Let's get rid of you then.'

He shot out of the drive, their mother waving animatedly

from the doorstep. Anya knew she'd stay standing there after they'd disappeared from view. Once deposited at the bus stop, their father rolled down his window.

'Mind yourselves, the pair of you,' he said solemnly. It was his customary salutation.

'Yes, Dad,' Georgie said.

'And let me know when I can book you to cater my next party.' He winked at Anya, then wound the window up and accelerated back up the hedgerow-lined country road.

Anya took the window seat this time, resting her head against the cool glass while the bus made its reverse journey. Dark had long since fallen and every so often a car loomed into the distance, headlamps like wide eyes in the gloom. The bus lighting had a slightly nauseous feel, and Anya grimaced, although perhaps it was just the stodgy shepherd's pie.

Despite the inevitable bittersweet ending, she'd had a good afternoon, much better than she'd imagined. She closed her eyes and replayed her father's comment about Connor. 'Never thought much of him.' She supposed it had not escaped her notice that her father and Connor had never seemed entirely comfortable in each other's company, her dad a little gruff, Connor tending to pontificate a little on topics only he cared for. She could remember, on occasion, catching her father looking visibly bored.

Still, you couldn't please everyone; she supposed Connor's mother had probably said something similar about her. And it didn't really matter, anyway. It was over now and her father and Connor would never have to share a shepherd's pie again.

She WhatsApped Paddy.

How's work going, she typed.

He was online immediately.

Stressful
I know two other teachers are def going for it
Including Mrs Cricklewood
Which has obv made me want it much more

Mrs Cricklewood was Paddy's professional arch-nemesis. From what Anya had gathered, her teaching style was cold and sterile and her discipline rigid. Paddy was convinced she thought he was a soft touch and a useless teacher.

'Even though my Standard Grade class did better than hers overall!' he'd explained, as they'd walked home from the cinema on Wednesday evening, Anya nodding seriously. 'And I took my S2s to the Tron Theatre twice last year, which was more than she managed! She just sits and makes the poor little bastards read the plays quietly – doesn't even get them doing voices or anything. I mean, no one who ever *read* Macbeth liked it.'

'No,' Anya said. 'Definitely not.'

Anya
Hang in there
And think of the look on Mrs Cricklewood's face when you get it

Paddy
That's what's keeping me going
How was Balfron

Anya

Fine, actually

Told them about my catering biz plans and my
mum didn't self-combust

Barely talked about Connor

So, all round a success

Paddy

Well done

What are you doing for the rest of the weekend?

Anya

Counting down the hours until it's
acceptable to go to sleep

Paddy

It's always acceptable to go to sleep

Anya

Ha

True

Probably just going to go home

There's this recipe for freekeh pilaf I want to try

Paddy

You are such a nerd

Anya

Good luck with work

YOU GOT THIS XXXXX

Paddy sent back the arm-flexing emoji and a last reply:

Well duh

By the time they reached the outskirts of the city centre, it had just turned 6 p.m., although Saturday night had begun in earnest, its safari of Glasgow city tribes already stalking the concrete jungle. There were the Rangers fans, wrapped in flags and scarves, spilling out of pubs with pints and polystyrene boxes of fat, limp chips; and the crowds of blow-dried girls in minis and heels so high they looked like they were walking on stilts, on their way to the cocktail bars of the Merchant City.

'What are you up to this evening?' Georgie asked.

'Going home. I'm hoping by some miracle that Claire and Richard are going out.'

Georgie smiled.

'I'm seeing Claire on Wednesday for lunch.'

'Lucky you.'

The bus lurched into its resting stop and the engine stopped.

'Shall I leave it here?' Anya indicated towards the shepherd's pie.

'No! Mum will want the Tupperware back.'

She rolled her eyes.

'Fine.'

When they were off the bus, Georgie zipped up her padded turquoise cagoule.

'You look like a scout leader.'

'Shut up.' Georgie zipped it up further. 'I knew she'd make us eat on the terrace.' It was even colder now, the evening settling. 'How are you getting back?'

'Subway?' They were still standing in the middle of the pavement, crowds of Glaswegians moving around them. Georgie nodded.

The Subway was busy, though Georgie slipped easily through the shoals of travellers in the entrance hall and barrelled towards the barriers, gripping her monthly travelcard.

'Wait. I need a ticket,' Anya blurted stupidly. She hadn't needed a travelcard since she left Berners Bilton.

'Oh,' Georgie hadn't considered this. 'Of course. I'll wait here then.'

Georgie shuffled towards the wall to wait, while Anya got into the queue for the middle machine, which turned out to be a mistake. The woman at the front couldn't grasp the mechanics of the ticket machine and kept having to start her search from the beginning.

Anya had turned around to motion something to this effect to Georgie when she saw him, a couple of people behind her, headphones around his neck, a new jacket; unmistakably him.

'Connor!'

He couldn't disguise it: his face fell.

'Ah. Hi Anya.'

11

He looked deeply uncomfortable already, the definition of a man praying for a spontaneous sinkhole to appear and drag him into hell, where things would surely seem better by comparison, but Anya felt a rush of excitement, in spite of it all, to see him.

'How have you been?' he had tried hoarsely from across the queue, when a woman who was between them in the line – a gruff, leathery broad, whom Anya estimated to be in her seventies – saw her chance.

'Oi, hen, ye wanna swap wi' me?'

The woman stepped out of the queue, pointing with a red lacquered fingernail at Anya's spot. Helplessly, Anya stepped aside and took the woman's place in front of Connor. She dared a look at his face, although it felt a little like staring into the sun. He looked older, the horizontal lines on his forehead more furrowed than she remembered, although perhaps he'd looked like that for years and Anya just hadn't noticed. She did notice he was holding a bottle of red wine, with a label that looked expensive, and Anya stared at it for a beat, feeling unsettled by it.

'Right.'

'Can we?' Anya motioned to the escalators.

Connor looked like he wanted to do anything but leave the station with her, but nodded, and they stepped out of the queue. Anya felt more eyes on her now and had an urge to explain the context of the situation to the assembled strangers. ('He dumped me!' she imagined shrieking. 'This is his worst nightmare!')

Georgie was still near the wall, although there appeared to have been a development: shepherd's pie was splattered across the floor of the station, and her sister was trying to scoop it into the container with her bare hands. Anya decided now was not the time. As they passed, Connor gave Georgie a nod.

'Hi Georgie,' he said, solemnly.

'Hiya!' She looked up, smiling what Anya and Paddy called her 'lobotomy smile', all teeth, no eyes.

Anya and Connor boarded the escalators in silence, leaving Georgie behind. He was standing in front of her, facing straight ahead, so she stared at the back of his jacket and tried to work out what she was going to say. They got to the top of the escalator and he drew her to a silver bollard beside the Subway entrance. It was dark now, and bitter and mizzling, and everyone around them looked miserable: coat lapels pulled around their necks, noses fixed to the ground, lips pinched.

'So, um, how are you?' His voice was thick, a little throaty, like he had a cold.

'I'm OK. Just coming back from my parents' house.'

'How are they?'

'They're fine.'

'How's the garden looking?'

This was a man to whom she'd confessed her deepest, darkest inadequacies, and now he was pretending to care about her father's flower beds.

'Green. Where are you going with such a nice bottle of

wine?' She was trying to sound casual and funny and unbothered but for some reason the wine was really bothering her.

He looked even more uncomfortable.

'What's the matter?' Her voice was still jokey, but an edge she couldn't control had crept into it now. 'Are you going to meet someone?'

Something unmistakable crossed his face now and her heart did a violent twist.

'Are you?' A stranger brushed past Anya, their shopping bags knocking the backs of her knees and she flinched but didn't stop watching his face.

'I'm just going for dinner—' He stopped.

Anya's ears were roaring so hard, and she barely heard herself say dully: 'That was fast.'

'Wait, Anya, it's not—' but his heart wasn't in the denial, and he halted, worrying at his stubble. She had an urge to grasp his hand so he'd stop.

'It's not what?'

'I'm sorry, Anya.'

'How long has it been going on for?' She'd made it so easy for him: agreeing to his 'rule' not to text one another, silently moving out. She was angry at herself for being so passive, but angrier with him.

He looked miserable now.

'Not long. Really.'

She weighed this.

'Yes, but how long? In this case, you see, timing is quite important.'

The truth was etched into his face, but she wanted him to tell her anyway, to make it real. It struck her that there had been a part of her that expected Connor to still love her.

'It's been a few months.'

He was really going to make her do the sums.

'We only broke up six weeks ago, Connor.'

Her hands were starting to burn with the cold, and she put them both in her pockets. She both wanted this horrible moment to end, and wanted to drag it out indefinitely, because as soon as it ended, they were really over for good. But he knew he was caught.

'Nothing really happened.' He changed tack. 'It was only at the very end.'

The inadequacy of this excuse hung in the air for a few moments and she was proud of herself for not breaking his gaze. Eventually he managed:

'I'm sorry. I should have told you.'

'Yes. You should. Is it someone you work with?'

'Anya.'

'Sorry.'

'No, don't apologize' – he sounded irritated but caught himself – 'you don't have to apologize. I should be the one to apologize.'

Tears were threatening now, so she screwed up her nose to try and stop them.

'Goodbye.'

'Wait—'

But she was walking off. He might have called her name, but she wasn't sure: they existed in different worlds now. Suddenly, she was standing on the escalator, which was making its slow descent into the bowels of the Subway station. She was pleased – at least – that she hadn't looked back. Her heart was ricocheting off the inside of her chest, her stomach roaring hot and cold, her legs like helium, but she hadn't looked back. When she got to the ticket hall at the bottom, Georgie was walking towards her at pace.

'What happened?' She steered Anya away from the escalators towards an unmanned information desk, with an anxious backwards glance to confirm Connor wasn't descending towards them.

'It was bad.' Anya's voice was tight. 'Can we go? Now?'

Wordlessly, her sister produced a ticket from her cagoule.

'Thank you.'

On the platform, boisterous but harmless football fans were chanting something. One lurched towards Anya and Georgie, but Georgie steered them both out of the way with a polite smile towards the very end of the platform. There were four minutes until their train.

'Are you OK?' Georgie's eyes were huge.

'Sort of. No. I'm not sure.'

Georgie nodded as though this were a reasonable answer.

'Do you want to go for a drink?'

'Yes.' Anya chewed her lip and tried not to think about Connor's face. Georgie was frantically texting.

'Paddy says he's knee-deep in work, but we're welcome to pop over for one.'

'OK.'

They watched the clock count down and then Anya remembered the shepherd's pie.

'What did you do with the pie?'

'One of the Subway staff said they'd chuck it away for me.' Georgie looked guilty. 'Please don't tell Mum. I'll buy her a new Tupperware, obviously.'

Anya nodded, not really caring.

'Do you think I should move to South America and start a new life running a beach bar?'

'No.' Her sister had not hesitated. 'You can't even speak Spanish.'

'I'd learn,' Anya tried defensively, but her heart wasn't really in it.

'You're going to stay in Glasgow,' Georgie continued. 'Start your catering company, and then . . .'

It boded poorly for Anya's new life plan that Georgie couldn't conjure what came next. When the train arrived it was busy and Anya was glad of the people. Packed in like a sardine, she felt more real.

At their stop, Hillhead, Georgie led the way, following the swelling crowd out of the station. On a bustling Byres Road, warm lights of pubs pooled their glow on to the dark, wet streets, and Anya felt a little better.

Close to the top of Ashton Lane, they spotted Paddy on the corner. He was holding an umbrella in one hand and an M&S bag in the other. When he saw them approaching, he opened his arms and Anya walked right into them. She felt him give her a kiss on the head.

'I thought I'd pop out and get us some supplies.'

'Thank you.' Her voice sounded small and a little rusty.

Paddy nodded at Georgie.

'Nice cagoule.'

'Shut up.'

Paddy and Georgie flanked Anya and the three of them

set off up the hill, away from the twinkling lights of Ashton Lane, towards Paddy's flat. He held the umbrella over her so she wouldn't get wet. Georgie had put her waterproof hood up.

'I'm afraid Ivy's in,' Paddy apologized, as he let them into the building. The three of them trudged up the three floors to Paddy's flat. Every few steps, he shook the rain out of the umbrella.

'You're getting me wet!' Georgie protested.

'You're wearing a cagoule.'

She sighed loudly.

When they reached Paddy's floor, they could hear Katy Perry trilling through the door, and the three of them exchanged a glance.

'It seems the evening has evolved.' Paddy slotted his key into the door. 'But they're harmless.'

Inside, in the big hallway, it smelled strongly of hairspray. Ivy – tall, blonde, lithe – was slugging something dark from a tumbler; while a friend of hers – tall, blonde, lithe – was frowning into the mirror, trying to rearrange her top so her bra strap wasn't visible. A third girl – tall, blonde, lithe – was squinting into her phone.

'Paddy!! You're back!' Ivy bounded towards him, dark liquid sloshing perilously around the glass. She wrapped herself around him and then extracted herself, smiling.

'Ives, I was only gone about fifteen minutes.'

'Was it?' Ivy grinned drunkly. 'And Anya! There you are!'

Anya assembled what she hoped was a smile.

'Here I am!'

Ivy moved towards her. When they hugged, Ivy's

perfume – sickly and sweet – tickled Anya's nose, although with her face buried in Ivy's hair, she was able to let her grin go, which felt good.

'And who's this?'

'Georgie.' Georgie gave a little half-wave.

'Amazing!' She pointed at her two friends, still distracted. 'This is Calgary and that's Lucy.'

Paddy was kicking his trainers off. 'Where are you guys going out?'

'Sub Club. But we're going for drinks in town first.'

'Fun.' Paddy picked up the M&S bag. 'Can we have the kitchen?'

Ivy made a pouty face.

'You guys should have a drink with us!'

'Nah,' Paddy said lightly. 'We're just going to sit and have some snacks. I've got work to do tomorrow.'

Anya was so grateful.

Ivy elbowed him. 'OK, fine. Killjoy. Have fun!'

Anya, Georgie and Paddy shuffled towards the kitchen as Ivy shimmied towards either Calgary or Lucy – Anya had not been paying attention – at the mirror. With the kitchen door closed, the sound of Katy Perry dimmed. Paddy gave them both a warning glance.

'She's really sweet.'

'I know,' Georgie sounded forlorn. 'But she does forget she's met me every single time I see her.'

'Maybe it's the cagoule,' Paddy smirked. He had moved to the counter and was unpacking his M&S bounty.

Paddy's kitchen was small and chaotic. Its centrepiece was a huge wooden table, half of which was consumed by a vast ecosystem of takeaway leaflets, old water bills, free newspapers and Subway tickets. Taped to the fridge was a piece of curling paper, 'Paddy and Ivy's chores chart'. On the windowsill were a trio of bedraggled pot plants, suffering from neglect (the windowsill was Paddy and Ivy's smoking spot, and most of the plant pots doubled as ashtrays). All the pots and pans stacked on the shelves were mismatched and, this evening, it appeared that all the lights except one were out. Anya was enormously glad to be here.

Across the table, Georgie flashed her a hopeful smile, while Paddy placed a big bag of ridged salt-and-vinegar crisps in front of them, packet torn wide open, and then a bottle of wine and three glasses in the middle of the table.

'OK. Go.'

Haltingly, eyes fixed on a patch of hardened candle wax in the centre of the table, Anya told them both the sorry tale, feeling winded again by the humiliation of it all.

'I feel so stupid.'

'You're not stupid,' Georgie said automatically.

'You're not,' Paddy agreed.

Anya shrugged them both off.

'It's not like I actually thought we were going to get back together.' Was this true? 'But' – her voice was breaking a little now – 'but I thought maybe he at least might miss me. Maybe. That he was biding his time and then . . . I don't know. That he'd get in touch and we'd somehow sort things out.'

Neither Paddy nor Georgie said anything for a while.

'At least, this way you're kind of allowed to hate him,' Paddy offered, finally. 'Moving on that fast is definitely a black mark against his name.'

'I didn't really want to hate him.'

Neither of the two of them had an answer to this.

In the silence of the kitchen, the sound of Ivy and her friends was newly amplified. There was a squawk now – 'Who's calling the Uber?' – and they all exchanged a glance.

Paddy stood up.

'Cigarette?'

Anya nodded. The two of them moved to the window and Paddy pulled it open. It admitted a cold, pure draught that Anya found strangely exhilarating. Georgie set up a chair nearby.

Anya lit her cigarette and nodded at Paddy. 'How's your work going?'

'It's OK.' He followed suit. 'It's quite hard to know exactly what they're looking for.'

'I think you'd be a brilliant head of department,' Georgie said loyally. 'Way better than any of the ones we ever had.'

Paddy smirked at her.

'You have to say that.'

'Well. Yes. But you would.'

'Thanks.' He elbowed Anya. 'Sorry you had such a shit day.'

She smiled tightly.

'I want it on record that I never liked him that much,' Paddy said.

'I've heard a lot of that today.' He gave her a quizzical look, so she added, 'My dad apparently felt the same.'

He put his arm around her.

'You're ashing on me.'

'Sorry.'

When they'd stubbed their cigarette butts out in a particularly sad-looking prayer plant, they turned back to the table. While Paddy filled a glass with water and gulped it at the sink, Anya prodded disconsolately at her phone. She had a text, from a number she didn't recognize, and felt a trickle of irrational panic. Could it be Connor's new girlfriend? Warning her off? Feeling skittish, she opened it.

Hi Anya. Hear you're looking for Euan Carrick. Me too. I suggest we join forces.

12

She blinked very fast, and the screen blurred and swam.

'Anya?' Georgie must have asked her something.

'What?'

'Are you texting Connor?'

Paddy had started washing some of the dishes stacked in the sink but whipped around when Georgie asked this.

'No!' Anya said indignantly.

Feeling the glare of her sister's suspicious eyes, Anya angled the phone under the table.

Who is this?

One eye still trained on the phone, she watched for a response, but none came immediately. Paddy clattered a saucepan in the sink and she winced.

'Sorry.'

Anya suddenly wanted to be alone. Pressing her phone into her jeans pocket with urgent, clumsy fingers, she stood up and Georgie tensed like a guard dog.

'Where are you going?'

Anya fixed her most pleasant smile.

'To the bathroom, Georgie. Would you like to come?'

This earned a glower, and Anya continued to the loo down the hall. Sitting on the edge of the bath, Anya typed the number into Google and hit search, but got nothing. Facebook? She copied and pasted it in and hit search but this also produced nothing. The bathroom smelled of strawberry shower gel.

What else could she try? Emails? She tested the number in the search bar on her Gmail account. Also, nothing.

Her phone vibrated again and she eagerly tapped the notification at the top of the screen.

It's Jamie Kildare. Wednesday evening?

Jamie! Euan's schooldays sidekick. She hadn't thought of him in years, let alone spoken to him. Gordon Wilson must have told him about her message, although he'd never replied to her . . . So, Jamie was looking for Euan! She wondered why; perhaps he really had fallen off the face of the earth.

She drummed the edge of the bath with her fingernails. This evening was getting stranger and stranger. There was no way she wanted to tell Jamie precisely why she'd been curious about Euan. She gnawed on her thumbnail and with the other hand, she typed her response, quickly, before she could change her mind.

Long time no see. Yes, Wednesday works.

She watched him typing.

Excellent – looking forward to it.

Anya started typing 'Me too!', and then decided this was overkill. Instead, she stood and pointlessly flushed the loo and washed her hands, gurning into the mirror. She hadn't looked at her reflection since her parents' house: her hair was flat and mascara had crumbled a little, sitting like soot in the creases under her eyes. She hoped she had looked a little better when she had seen Connor.

In the kitchen, Paddy and Georgie were wolfing down portions of rubbery tomato pasta.

'That looks . . . old.'

Paddy grimaced, tired tomato clinging to his teeth.

'We're not all master chefs.' He swallowed. 'There's plenty for you.'

'No thanks.' She paused. 'I think I might go back to Claire's actually.'

'Are you OK?' Georgie looked anxious, and a little suspicious.

'Yeah, I'm fine. I'm just tired. It's been a long, very weird day.'

Georgie stood up and Anya stepped dutifully into her embrace. Afterwards, Georgie tucked Anya's hair behind her ear.

'Will you text us when you get home? Or if you need us?'

'Of course.' She pulled her jacket on, pleased to be leaving. 'Paddy . . .' he was still shovelling food into his mouth, but she reached over his shoulders for a sort of vice grip of an embrace, and a kiss on the cheek. 'Good luck with your interview on Monday. You'll be brilliant.'

'Thanks.' He wiped his mouth with the back of his hand, and half turned to find her eyes. 'Are you sure you're OK?'

'Yes. Promise. I'll see you both very soon.'

The quiet route home was quicker, but it would take her within a parallel road of Connor's flat, and she was worried that he'd be there now with the new girl and they'd both see her out of the window. So Anya flung herself back into the Byres Road throng, sidestepping girls in stilettos and boys swilling from tins, heads thrown back in laughter.

She was pleased when she got back to Claire's, even though the house was dark and uninviting, flanked on either side by houses whose illuminated windows showed couples curled in front of flickering televisions. It was only 9 p.m., but the door was already bolted. Anya unbolted it. Richard was standing at the end of the corridor, next to the dark wooden drawer again, but as Anya stepped through the door he melted into the shadows.

'Hi Richard,' she called out, removing her boots and jacket, but he didn't respond. Anya double-checked the door, then climbed the stairs to her cell.

Cocooned inside her duvet – the radiator in her room certainly wasn't firing on all cylinders – Anya palmed through the yearbook until she found Jamie's page.

Name: Jamie Kildare
Year joined: 1996
Nicknames: J, Jambo, Killy
Most memorable moments: Breaking his foot on the
  ski trip
Mortal enemy: ?
Most often seen: With Euan Carrick
In five years: Busting Euan Carrick out of prison

She flipped through the hardbound book until she found the photo pages. There he was in the back row of the football team picture, and standing on a podium at sports day, hair slick, triumphant with his silver medal.

She remembered Jamie from the park, him and Euan

advancing up the hill, their ties hanging out of their pockets. He had always seemed quiet, a brooding foil to Euan's sunshine energy. Apart from that, they had rarely overlapped outside the classroom, or inside it. Before Euan arrived, she was sure he was involved with the large indistinct cluster of 'sporty' boys, although again more as a sidekick than a protagonist. His name had never been first on girls' lists during giggly conversations in the changing rooms after PE, although he'd invariably get mentioned eventually (pickings were fairly slim at Kelvinbridge Academy). Had there once been something with Arpita, one of those awkward, teenage half-things that fizzled quick?

And now he was looking for Euan too. Unlike Euan, though, Jamie was easy to find on Facebook, and he and Anya had plenty of mutual friends, though his profile was private – all she could see was a picture of him in running kit, a medal proud around his neck – and the information that he had attended Kelvinbridge Academy and Edinburgh University.

She clicked 'add friend' and then closed the shell of her laptop.

13

To: anyamackie@gmail.com
From: tasha.kelner@penandpencil.com
Re: Logo!

OK, see what you think of the attached. It's a first draft but I
told one of the guys here about you doing veggie stuff (is that
still right?) and so I think that's why the broccoli is so front and
centre, but he's very happy to take any notes at this stage. It's
very much a work-in-progress. He also says he's happy to look at
the website – so let me know if you want me to get him working
on that? Think of me as your project manager.

Xxxxx

Anya clicked on the attachment. The graphic was a smart,
sleek red A, wearing a chef's hat. It appeared to be sort of
high fiving a wooden spoon, which was wearing an apron.
She wasn't sure whether it was too silly or totally brilliant,
which rather summed up how she felt in the face of all art.

'Where's Corrie?' Rachel – today they were wearing
name headbands, although for all Anya knew they'd
swapped them – had appeared from the garden. Anya had
been dodging another game of football.

'I don't know.' She placed her phone on the counter.
'Have you looked for her?'

Rachel gave her a withering look.

'Right, no, I'll look.'

As Rachel flounced back into the garden, leaving muddy footprints across Aimee's pristine floor, Anya walked into the grand hallway. She couldn't smell Corrie, which meant the dog had to be a fair distance away.

'Corrie!'

Every room in this house seemed to be a living room with the charmless international interiors of a high-end hotel. Corrie wasn't supposed to go in any of them, although Anya had definitely discovered her sitting on the sofa between the girls before.

'Corrie?' she repeated.

She'd only been upstairs once to try and help Rosie find her recorder, which had later turned up inside the fridge. (It was of some solace to Anya that the girls bullied each other as much as they bullied her). She ascended the house slowly and cautiously, listening for the shake of a collar, peering behind every door as she did so. The dog was not in the first-floor bathroom, the first-floor living room or either of the girls' bedrooms, so Anya proceeded up another level to Aimee's floor. Victory, of sorts: she could smell Corrie up here – and something else that made her nose wrinkle.

'Oh Corrie!'

The dog was sitting in the middle of Aimee's home office, its paws resting triumphantly in a pile of vomit.

By the time Anya had cleaned the thick pile carpet, praying that she hadn't eaten any of the lipsticks that were earmarked for some influencer project of Aimee's, it was almost time for her to leave. It was Wednesday, and she and Jamie had agreed to meet at 7 p.m. at a bar called

Metropolitan in the Merchant City, a flashy place with twinkling lightbulbs over a terrace and usually packed to the exposed rafters with suited and booted twenty- and thirty-somethings who huddled around wine coolers. It was the sort of place that assumed it could purchase charm with expensive glassware; Anya could barely afford a drink there when she had a proper job. She'd dressed in dark jeans and a half-sheer top and knee-high flat boots for the occasion, which she'd rather regretted when she'd been down on her knees scrubbing Corrie's chunky vomit from the carpet.

Mercifully, Aimee had returned on time: five minutes after Anya had tossed the rubber gloves back into the utility cupboard, and just as she'd finished serving the twins two steaming bowls of ramen, tofu bobbing in the salty broth (she'd made a vat at Claire's last night and brought it over). Neither twin said anything when she placed the food in front of them, but she heard slurping as soon as she'd turned her back.

At the sound of Aimee's key in the lock, Anya smoothed her hair and assumed an innocent expression. She hadn't told the twins about Corrie's mishap. There were heels on the marble floor and, moments later, Aimee appeared, nails tapping on her phone screen, as always.

'What's this?' With a frosted talon, she pointed at the ramen.

Anya stepped forward.

'Oh, just tofu ramen. Don't worry, it's very healthy.'

'Where did you get it from?'

'Well, I made it.'

Aimee looked affronted.

'What do you mean *you* made it?' The emphasis on the

'you' was accompanied by a sneer. She glanced around the kitchen. 'How did you make it?'

'It's quite an easy recipe actually. I made a vat last night and then brought some over for the girls.' When Aimee blinked, her fake eyelashes looked too heavy for her eyes. 'Although I've also been doing some cooking with them. Remember, I mentioned . . .'

Something like recognition flashed behind Aimee's eyes.

'Mmm. Yes, I think they did say something about cooking.'

Aimee's face was inscrutable; inspired, Anya decided to try a different tack.

'I'm actually . . . well, I'm starting a catering company. This is on my menu.'

'A catering company?' Was she mistaken, or was that a note of interest?

'Yeah, it's early days. I just got the logo and have launched the website.'

'So will you do events?'

'Hopefully. That's the plan.'

Aimee narrowed her eyes now.

'I do events.'

'Oh—'

'I wouldn't want' – pointed talon out again – '*that*. But if you do other things.'

'Um, yes, it's all veggie and—'

'Just you send me your thingy – website or handle or whatever? I can have a look.' Aimee was bored now and had returned to her phone. Corrie, meanwhile, had trotted into the kitchen and was sitting in a corner, watching the scene unfold.

'Yes, I will. Thanks.'

But Aimee was gliding off into the hallway again, almost tripping over Corrie.

'Corrie, move! Girls, will one of you take her out, please?'

Both girls were hunched over their bowls, slurping noodles, and didn't reply.

'Bye, girls.' Anya felt a little lighter. 'I'll see you tomorrow.'

Neither said anything, but Anya got a small, slightly grateful wave from Rachel.

At five to seven, Anya stepped off the pavement on Wilson Street and straight into a deceptively deep puddle, sending a spray of dark water up the flapping front of her trench coat.

'Fuck.'

Unthinkingly, she stopped in the middle of the road and a taxi swerved, honking its horn and Anya flinched. A red-faced driver stuck his head out the window.

'HEY! WATCH WHERE YOU'RE GOIN'!'

'Sorry!' she called as the taxi disappeared into the dark, its rear lamps like unblinking eyes.

When she pulled up a few paces from the half-full terrace, she scanned the outdoor tables for dark-haired men. Jamie had accepted her friend request and so that afternoon, on the way to Park Circus, she'd examined the sparse page, in the hope she'd recognize him immediately. There were several boisterous groups huddled around wine coolers, faces aglow in the light of the outdoor heaters, but no one who looked like he could be Jamie. She felt nervous.

'Can I help you?'

Anya gawped at the sleek brunette in a black jumpsuit who was now addressing her.

'Do you have a table?'

'Sorry' – she could feel herself reddening – 'no, I'm here to meet someone.'

The girl blinked languidly at her, and Anya noted enviously that her eyeshadow managed to be both dewy and sparkly.

'I think they must be inside,' she spluttered, pointing towards the entrance.

'No worries.' The girl sashayed off towards a table of baying, braying men, who all looked a little like Marc di Marco.

Inside, the place was all stone walls, wooden floors and heavy cutlery. Anya moved towards a vast backlit bar, still scanning the tables. There was still no sign of him and nerves trickled down her spine, leaving her feeling immediately certain that her make-up had run all down her face and was now pooling under her cheeks.

7.05 p.m. She could surely make it to the bathrooms quickly to check it before she came back for a proper recce. Luck: they appeared to be straight ahead, just across the bar. With a furtive glance left and right, she started walking, her pace quickening as she passed the tables on the left-hand side of the room.

'Anya Mackie?'

She whipped around and knocked a set of the heavy cutlery off the table with the edge of her bag.

She'd have picked it up, except Jamie was holding his hand out. He was wearing dark trousers and a blue shirt, sleeves rolled to his elbows. His shirt was unbuttoned a few times – exposing a light thatch of dark chest hair – and he had dark curls, three-day-old stubble and an open smile.

'Jamie!'

He raised both palms in surrender, slightly amused.

'You gave me a surprise.' She instantly regretted how stupid this sounded.

'Sorry,' he said cheerfully. 'I've grabbed us this table.'

'Great.'

It was situated inside a cushiony leather booth on which stood a half-drunk pint, condensation rolling down the outside of the glass. Slowly, Anya shrugged out of her trench coat and placed it on the banquette, then lowered herself into the booth.

Automatically, another sleek waiter popped up like an otter.

'Good evening,' he said in a lilting voice. 'And how are we this evening?'

'Good.' His attentive grin was a little unnerving. 'Can I just have a glass of wine, please?'

'Absolutely,' the waiter responded superciliously. 'And have you consulted our wine list this evening?'

Anya stared at the menu in front of her, the words a mass of curly italics and pound signs.

'Dry. White. Please.' Jamie was watching this exchange with a pleasant smile on his face, and for some reason she felt self-conscious.

'Of course,' simpered the waiter, collecting the menu from in front of her. 'Good choice.'

For a few beats too many, they watched him sashay back towards the bar. Then, feeling herself flushing, Anya crossed her arms on the table. Jamie had an eyebrow raised in light amusement, which made her feel even more flustered.

'So,' she managed, 'hi.'

'Hello.' He nodded, more at ease than she was. 'It's been a while.'

Anya noted that he seemed to have grown into the cheekbones that had made him look a little pointy at school.

She hadn't managed to say anything else; Jamie grinned. 'This is a bit weird, isn't it?'

'A little.'

'Sorry, it's my fault. My slightly cloak-and-dagger text—'

The waiter reappeared at her shoulder, holding a chilled bottle swaddled in a napkin.

'I've brought the Chenin Blanc for you to try.'

'Great.' Anya nodded vigorously. 'Looks great.'

He bowed his head, flipped her glass and poured a thimbleful into the glass and Anya knocked it back in one gulp. She'd brushed her teeth at Aimee's furtively before she came out; whatever she'd ordered, it would have tasted horrible.

'It's lovely.'

The waiter nodded and topped up her glass then stepped silently back into the scenery.

Still smiling, Jamie raised his glass and Anya knocked it a little clumsily.

'It's very nice to see you.' He put his glass down.

'You too.' She paused, 'I can't remember if we've seen each other since school.' When he laughed, she added: 'Sorry!'

'No, don't be, I'm just teasing. I don't think so. Or if we have, I don't remember either.' He laughed again.

'I don't really see that many people from school,' she added by way of apology.

'Me neither. In fact' – he gave her a meaningful glance here – 'Gordon is one of the few people I am still in touch with. Just from time to time.'

'I assumed that was it.' She blinked fast. 'He didn't message me back.'

Jamie took another polite sip of beer, then asked: 'So, what do you do now?'

Anya giggled. It was the nerves.

'Sorry. It just feels a bit like: so, *tell me about the last thirteen years of your life.*'

She wasn't sure where that deep, solemn voice had come from, but he laughed again.

'OK, good point. Just give me the highlights reel.'

His charisma took her aback; in her mind's eye, he was still taciturn and mumbly.

'Um, well, I still live in the West End,' she began. 'I went to university here too. And' – she decided to cut Connor out of this potted biography – 'I'm sort of trying to work a few things out right now, but I'm starting a catering company.' Saying it aloud sounded funny.

'Wow.' He nodded encouragingly, so she shook her head.

'It's early days. But, yeah.' She took another sip; this wasn't so hard, whatever it was. 'How about you?'

'Well, I went to Edinburgh. For university. And now I'm an engineer.' Anya nodded politely this time, but he added: 'Don't. It's definitely quite boring.'

'Really?'

'Well. No, I like it. But it's not as cool as being a chef.'

'Chef is definitely a stretch.' But she smiled. 'So, um, are you married?' She felt instantly mortified by the question in case he thought it was a clumsy come-on, so added,

'Everyone seems to be married. And have children and live in Milngavie.'

'No.' He had a kind smile. 'No wives or dependents.'

'Four by four?'

'Just a Nissan Micra. The windows don't roll down.'

'Excellent.'

After this successful exchange, there was a slightly self-conscious pause. They both smiled at each other over the rims of their drinks; she was grateful when he took the lead.

'So, now that we've both been suitably self-deprecating' – his eyes were twinkling again – 'shall we talk about Euan Carrick?'

It felt weird to hear the name aloud; weirder than her telling Jamie she ran a catering company.

'How come you're looking for him?' Jamie asked. His tone was light and interested, but she still felt a flicker of panic. She had been thinking about how to answer this question all week.

'What are *you* doing looking for him?'

'Hey, I asked you first.' He laughed again.

'True. I . . .' Her mind felt blank and Jamie was starting to look amused now. 'I . . . I remember his uncle owned a chain of restaurants.' She did dimly remember this. 'And with my new catering gig, I wanted to ask for some advice.' Jamie was frowning now, so she added, with more conviction: 'And I thought it would be a nice excuse to get in touch.'

He didn't say anything for a moment or two and Anya worried that he'd seen through her, but then he nodded lightly.

'Fair enough.'

As improvised lies went, she'd impressed herself.

'What about you?' she asked before he could press her any further.

'My dad just died.'

Anya winced.

'Sorry, that's—'

'Yes,' he interrupted firmly, 'I know. Anyway, as a result of this I ended up in possession of a box of old things – yearbook and rugby tops and sports day medals, all that guff. He'd had it in the garage for years.' Anya felt her cheeks start to burn, but mercifully, he started speaking again. 'And, going through it all, all the old stuff, it made me think of the olden days. Of school, Euan ... Well, I weirdly found it was him I wanted to speak to most, after all those years.' He found her eyes. 'I haven't heard from him in a while. Not since a few years after we left university.'

So, his story was almost exactly like hers then; she almost regretted the lie.

'That's more recently than me. I don't think I've spoken to him since our first year of university.' She added, in a softer voice, 'I'm really sorry about your dad.'

'Thanks.'

There was another awkward silence, which Anya filled by tipping her already nearly empty glass into her mouth. She should have ordered a large. Jamie rolled his pint glass in his hand.

'Anyway, it happens. We went to different universities, and he never was very good at staying in touch, in fact, he was always pretty hard to track down, even at school. I'm sure you probably remember.'

'He was always losing his phone.'

'And it never had any credit.'

They shared a self-conscious, wistful smile.

'It is a bit weird, isn't it,' Anya leaned forward, 'that neither of us has been able to find him. I feel like I've tried everything. Facebook, LinkedIn . . .'

She trailed off. Jamie appeared to consider this carefully.

'It is weird,' he started slowly. 'But on the other hand, Euan feels like someone who wouldn't really use any of that stuff. Social media, and the rest.' He added, a little wryly: 'He feels like someone who might just disappear, and not really think about the consequences.'

Anya considered this.

'Yeah. I suppose I'd be far more surprised to find out Euan had a, a . . .' she was gesticulating and caught Jamie eyeing her hand, 'a YouTube channel' – where had that come from? – 'than to hear that he lived entirely off-grid in a hut somewhere in the Highlands.'

'Exactly. Plus, there's more to life than Facebook.' He smiled. 'Anyway, what do you think? Should we join forces? Try and find him?'

After a surprised beat or two, she laughed.

'What, like amateur detectives?'

'I hope it will be exactly like that.'

She laughed again; he couldn't keep the deadpan up, and his face softened also into a smile.

'Um . . . I mean, it depends. What exactly would it involve?'

'Well, for a start you'd have to quit your job so we could go on the road full time.' She was slow and he shook his head in delight. 'Anya, this is too easy. We're not going to spend all of our waking hours on the trail. I just meant, share whatever we learn. A sort of team effort.'

She tucked her hair behind her ear while she considered this.

'And then what would happen?'

'I'm not exactly sure. Hopefully a nice reunion drink. Dinner if we get hungry. That sort of thing.' He seemed very different to how she remembered him.

'I guess that sounds fun.' It did, if also completely fantastical. 'Although I'm not sure I'd be much help. I lost touch with him long before you did.'

'Well, maybe not.' Jamie shrugged evenly. 'But you never know. Plus' – he picked up his pint glass again to drain the last of it – 'it would be nice to have the company.' She blinked in surprise, although he didn't seem to notice. 'And two heads are better than one. You might prove to have some clue that you don't yet realize you have.'

'Clue?' She raised a teasing eyebrow.

'Yes. Clue.'

'OK.' She folded her arms across the table. 'So, if I were to agree to this in principle, what would we do first?'

'I was hoping you'd ask that.' He leaned forward now too, hands clasped. 'Well, as we've obviously both done extensive online searches' – Anya nodded in confirmation – 'then I thought we'd begin with a few trips. To Euan's old haunts, that sort of thing.'

'Wow. You really mean it.'

'I do. So?' He looked a little bashful now. 'What do you think?'

Anya considered it. Certainly, this was an unorthodox proposition. Jamie was virtually a stranger – if a handsome one whom she'd sort of known more than a decade ago – and she really wasn't certain if any good could come of hunting for Euan. Plus, she really ought to be spending any spare time she had working on Anya Eats Too Much.

On the other hand, the wine had hit her empty stomach, Jamie didn't seem like a total psychopath and maybe – maybe – something good might come out of hunting for Euan. Plus, Tasha, if no one else, would probably approve. And she was feeling newly reckless.

'OK.' What the hell. 'Let's do it.'

'Excellent.' She was rewarded with a grin. 'Are you free on Saturday?'

His enthusiasm was sweet; she laughed.

'I think so?'

'Great. I was thinking we could go to Aberdeen. I've got the address of his old flat there. I've tried writing and calling, but no luck.' He paused. 'So, I thought we could head up and ask a neighbour if they know anything. I know it's a long way, but it just seemed like a good place to start. You're always meant to look for lost things in the last place you saw them.'

'When did he live there?' She was surprised to feel a shiver of excitement.

'Until quite recently, I think. So, I was thinking we could take a recce. I've got a car. We can drive.'

'Can you promise a stake-out?'

'I'll do my best.'

'In that case, I'm in.'

'Great.'

He held her gaze for a moment or two, and then tapped a palm to the table.

'I have to go in a minute, I'm afraid, I've got to meet someone.' He looked genuinely sorry and she found herself wanting to apologize too. 'But it was really nice to see you again. And I'll text you,' he'd swung out of the booth now and was putting his coat on, 'about Saturday?'

'Yes.' She wondered who he was going to meet. She could imagine Jamie having a quiet girlfriend, someone petite and self-contained and not very expressive, with a short pixie haircut, possibly from the Borders or one of the Islands. 'I'll see you then.'

'Great.' He gave her a half-wave. 'See you soon.'

She watched him lope off, feeling slightly dazed. He stopped by the door to pay for his half of the bill and when she left a few minutes later – giving him time so they wouldn't end up on the same Subway platform – she discovered he'd paid hers too.

Anya unlocked the front door and jumped. Claire was standing so close to her she could see the pores on her nose in the light of the energy-saving bulb in the doorway. Her cousin looked very small in her thick pile dressing gown.

'I thought you were Richard.'

'Afraid not.'

'He's not home yet.' Claire sounded agitated, which was normal, but also a little anxious, which wasn't.

'Oh, where is he?'

'I don't know. Obviously.'

Anya was about to say something, but Claire had already disappeared into the darkness.

'There's spare pasta in the fridge if you're hungry.' Her

cousin's disembodied voice came from down the hall. 'Aubergine and pesto.'

'Thanks,' Anya called weakly after her. Claire was a better cook than Georgie, and Anya was grateful for the evenings when she benefitted from her leftovers – even if she'd never have admitted it to her cousin.

Eventually, Anya groped the right part of the wall and the kitchen was brought to life. She fetched a fork from a top drawer. The whole place was as clean and solemn as a laboratory; on the counter nearest the fridge, there sat two bowls containing two pieces of Weetabix each, and two mugs, each containing a teabag. Claire and Richard optimized their mornings down to the last second.

On the top shelf of the fridge sat a container of pasta. She opened it and stood in the fridge door, shovelling hungry mouthfuls, barely pausing for breath. After she'd wolfed down half of the contents of the box, she noticed the lid read 'RICHARD LUNCH', and spotted another, smaller box on the top shelf, without a label.

'Oh, shit.'

Anya reached for the Tupperware and tipped it into Richard's lunch box.

After filling a glass with water, she went to sit at the kitchen table.

She had already decided she wouldn't tell Paddy and Georgie about any of this yet. They'd exchange one of those customary alarmed looks, and then tell her it was all a bad idea, and ask if she'd considered seeing a counsellor (Georgie) or getting a fucking grip (Paddy). She was curious, that's all, she thought a little defensively. Jamie was right – it was an extraordinary coincidence that they'd both been thinking of Euan at the same time, even if she'd lied poorly about the real reason why. She squirmed, feeling a little guilty now. Jamie was nothing like the surly presence on the outskirts of her memories.

The wall clock chimed once: 10.30 p.m. She had work to do on Anya Eats Too Much tomorrow – to send her notes back to Tasha about the logo and to 'announce' the website on her Instagram – then Park Circus after school. She gulped the last of her water down and put both glass and fork in the dishwasher, and then tiptoed up the dark stairs towards her bedroom.

Jamie texted as she was climbing into bed.

Nice to see you this evening. I think this is going to be fun. X

14

To: tasha.kelner@penandpencil.com
From: anyamackie@gmail.com
Re: Logo!

Tasha!!!! Thank you SO MUCH. Four immediate thoughts:

1. Does the aubergine in the background look a bit 'sexy'?
   A bit like a shit dating app innuendo (to be fair, I wouldn't
   really know . . .)
2. Maybe the chef's hat is a BIT big?
3. Obsessed with the A though! Red is exactly the right
   colour. POWERFUL.
4. On which note, this is basically exactly the motif I want for
   the website – red, big typographic vibes, a few vegetables.
   Do you think he could make it so that the cursor, when you
   hover over things, is a carrot? Or would that cost loads of
   money?

In other news, it's 9 am here and I'm already sitting in a café
with an oat flat white (less nice than real milk). I feel like Mark
Zuckerberg!

Plan is to post on my Instagram with my menu and telling people I
am open for business! Also, did I tell you that Aimee – the mother

whose spawn I look after – said maybe I could do some catering for her?? She probably didn't mean it but she is a make-up influencer (I know) with lots of followers so it could be quite useful. ANYWAY, I just wanted to boast about how I am up and alive and doing things. Thank you again for the logo, I owe you xxxx

PS Is this an email only about professional things? Because I have a number of serious life updates, including how I found out Connor has a new girlfriend (I sort of don't want to talk about this) and also how I have now joined forces with a man from my past to find the long-lost teenage ex-boyfriend.

PPS I believe that is what they call a cliff-hanger.

Anya's first official day in business had been low-key. This was only the soft launch: while Tasha's colleague worked on rejigging bits of the website and fine-tuning the logo, Anya wanted to see what impact an Instagram post could have.

'Don't worry too much about how much the website will cost,' Tasha had said in a voicenote earlier this week. 'He's our best designer but owes me big time for not telling his boss about the time he missed a Saturday shoot because he was hungover.'

Anya had priced up her menu properly this time and asked her father to review the sums.

'I can add and subtract all right,' he'd told her. 'But I don't know much about food. However, as long as you're making more than you spend, I'd say you're doing well.'

She'd dropped her menus on to Instagram with a link to the website, and then spent an obsessive hour refreshing the notifications and clocking the likes (789 after an hour, although not a single enquiry) until she forced herself to put her phone away and go to the super-market. She was expected at Aimee's in an hour.

It was in Tesco Metro that she received her first DM and almost dropped the box of eggs she'd been clutching. Someone had enquired about a dog's birthday party (they wanted Anya to do the humans' food, not the dogs'). Heart thudding, she had replied saying she'd love to – when, where and which dishes were they keen on? Waiting for the customer to reply felt like waiting for a date to text back (she imagined), and she left the supermarket with her heart still pounding, gripping the eggs. This evening, she was going to teach the girls to make an omelette.

That was, if she could get them to stand still for the five minutes it would take to make one. It was chaos at Park Circus when Aimee let Anya in: Rosie and Rachel were bickering loudly, which for some reason kept triggering the Amazon Alexa, and Corrie was running around yelp-ing, which was her version of joining in.

Aimee opened the door and virtually dragged Anya through it.

'*Finally.*' She wasn't late. 'They're all driving me mad and I've got a call in fifteen minutes. Can you just keep them quiet . . . take them out or . . . Corrie!' The dog abruptly stopped chewing a flip flop. 'Stop that!'

Aimee was already halfway up the stairs before Anya had taken her coat off. She paused to give Corrie a pat on the head, removed the flip flop from her clutches and then walked into the kitchen, where the twins were squab-bling over a pink Polaroid camera.

'It's MY turn.' She was getting better at spot-the-difference, but in the blur of limbs and red hair, Anya had no chance of telling who was who.

'Hi.' They didn't look up. 'Hey, Rosie, Rachel?'

They continued to wrestle, so Anya stepped towards them and they broke off, panting.

'Give it to me.' She wasn't sure where this tone had come from, but it seemed to work. Rachel – she could see now it was Rachel – handed her the camera. They both struck an identical pose: arms crossed, lips stuck out. Before either of them could catch up, Anya pointed towards the eggs on the counter. 'Today, we're going to make an omelette.'

They exchanged a glance.

'What's an omelette?' Rosie tugged at her woollen school skirt, which was on backwards after her fight with her sister.

'It's made with eggs. Easy, tasty. I'm going to teach you.'

They didn't say anything but both sidled up to the kitchen island.

As ever, Rosie and Rachel were slightly sullen students – Anya felt sorry for their teachers, although she suspected they were rather better paid than her – but at least they'd stopped fighting. She set them to work chopping mushrooms with a table knife – she wasn't risking anything that might work as a real weapon – while she commentated on her every move.

When Anya opened the egg box, Rachel perked up.

'Does it have a chicken in it?' She pointed at an egg.

'No. These are eggs we eat.'

The girls looked disappointed.

They didn't look particularly enthused by the finished

product either, although Anya had clocked a certain zen-like contentment on their faces as they'd whisked the eggs and she'd tried not to smile. It was exactly how she felt when she was in the kitchen.

'Whose is better?' Rosie demanded when they'd both finished frying.

'They're both good.'

This was the wrong thing to say; the twins exchanged a scowl.

A couple of hours later, when Anya was leaving (she'd left the eggs in the cupboard so she could repeat her trick another time), Aimee reappeared on the stairs in a pair of pink, slightly saggy Ugg boots. Anya had never seen her in anything lower than a stiletto.

'I don't need you tomorrow,' she said. 'They're with their nan.'

'Oh. No worries.'

A day off! Which would come in handy for Anya Eats Too Much. She itched to check her Instagram DMs.

'So, I'll see you on Monday.'

'Yes, I'll see you then. I hope the girls have a good time with—'

'—wait, I saw your Instagram.' Anya had sent her the handle last weekend, although Aimee hadn't replied to the message.

'Oh, yes, I—'

'And I have an event soon – it's a sort of "meet-Aimee-Morton-thing". For press.' Her tone was grand, and Anya fought to keep her face straight. 'Anyway. It's a big deal, and I'll need it catered. I wondered if you'd be interested.'

Aimee sounded needling and slightly accusatory, but Anya's heart leapt.

'Yes! I'd love to! It's been really exciting, actually, I've had a fair bit of interest already . . .' Aimee looked bored and Anya checked herself. 'What sort of thing would you like?'

'Well, that's the thing. I don't want any of what's on your menu.'

'Oh. Well, that's OK. I can do bespoke menus too.' Aimee looked blank, so Anya added: 'I can personalize it to every event, I mean.'

At this, Aimee gave what presumably passed as a smile.

'That's much better. Can I get my assistant to send you some requirements? It'll be no gluten, obviously. Or wheat. Or dairy, eggs or pineapple.'

'Of course.' What dietary requirement involved no pineapple? Anya also wondered which one of the army of glossy, shellacked harpies she'd seen about the house counted as Aimee's official assistant. 'Of course. That works.'

'Great.' Aimee was drifting back upstairs now, Uggs thwumping on the carpet. 'She'll be in touch.'

'Brilliant. See you on Monday, then.'

But Aimee was on the next landing up now, and didn't say anything in response, and Anya let herself out as she always did, carefully, to avoid attracting Corrie's attention. Outside the smart door, she checked her account again. The dog birthday party host @siobhan.murphy4 said she'd consult the dog's co-parent and let her know. If it came off, plus the catering for Aimee . . . this could make two whole gigs. It wasn't quite a business, but it was a start.

*

Anya spent her day off watching YouTube videos of Microsoft Excel spreadsheets, creating one in order to keep track of her ingredients and costings, and trying to devise dishes that might work for Aimee's specific requirements. This morning, she'd received an email from someone called Tinks, confirming the rules Aimee had set out yesterday, plus an additional one: no macadamia nuts. All other nuts were acceptable.

Anya had shuttled through the library in her head, trying to work out what she could create and how to make sure it still tasted of anything; she scrawled notes for customizations into a smart red notebook purchased in honour of Anya Eats Too Much.

Mid-afternoon, she'd slunk off to the kitchen and made a quick red onion and goat's cheese tart, which she planned to squirrel away in her room and pick at that evening. She cheated with pre-rolled pastry; Claire and Richard were having a dinner party and she didn't want any reason to find herself in the kitchen to meet any of their guests, who – according to Claire – comprised three IT consultants and one of her bridesmaids, a severe woman called Thandie who, at Claire's twenty-first birthday, had given a speech so straight and humourless that Anya could still remember the feeling of despair she felt while she listened to it. ('Claire is twenty-one,' started one line that Anya and her father still regularly quoted at one another, while Georgie looked guilty. 'And that's one year older than twenty.')

By the time the guests arrived, Anya was safely sequestered away in her room, feeling more like Bertha in the attic than ever before, although at least Anya had a crusty tart to chew on, and Tasha to talk to. Her email had proved to be explosive bait; Tasha rarely WhatsApped.

Tasha
Wait, I just woke up and read your email!
Connor??
Strange man from your past??
What are you talking about!

Anya
Ha ha, I knew I'd get you with that
Connor = I bumped into him on the Subway. Turns out
he has a new girlfriend. Seems like there was overlap.
Ran away. Did not linger for details. Taking the emotionally
healthy route of suppressing my humiliation and occasionally
having an evening cry.

Tasha was typing.

Tasha
Oh Anya

She sent a string of red hearts.

I'm so sorry
What a bastard

Anya
Yes
Very horrible

Tasha sent another heart.

Tasha
Tell me about the other stuff now

Anya

Ha ha where to begin

Well, it turns out this other guy from school (Jamie)

is also looking for my 'long lost ex' (Euan)

And he got in touch

So now we're looking for him together

Tomorrow we're going to his old flat in Aberdeen

Tasha

Um wow

Anya

. . .

Do you think I'm weird?

Tasha

Sort of?

I mean, yes

What do you mean 'looking for him'?!

Anya

Well, I don't really know

Yet

Just trying to track him down

With some light field research

. . . yes, I know how that sounded

Tasha

Hahahaha

OK good

Anya

He's nice

I swear

I don't know

It sort of happened the night I saw Connor

He messaged

And then before I knew what I was doing

we were having a drink

And agreeing to become a sort of detective partnership

Tasha

I don't know if I'd watch this show

Jury is out

But also – it could be good for you

A distraction

A very weird distraction

Anya did the teeth-bared emoji in response.

OK I have to get in the shower and get ready for work

But stay safe

And send me a proper email update soon please

xx

Anya

Will do!! X

And now it was Saturday, and she was about to spend the day with Jamie. In Aberdeen. She hadn't known what to wear for a recce to the former home of a man whose face she could no longer quite picture, so pulled on something failsafe: her smartest black jeans, black Converse and a jumper with a swirling turquoise pattern that used to belong to Tasha. Anya had inherited a generous bounty of clothes when Tasha moved to Vancouver, most of which were designed for someone with Tasha's height and/or louder personality, but a few items – like the jumper – made Anya feel ready for whatever the world could throw at her.

She and Jamie communicated a little over the course of the week: logistics, mainly. She'd double- and triple-checked the plans, slightly unable to believe any of it was happening, yet still thrilled by the strangeness of it all. Jamie seemed certain that Euan wasn't at the address in Aberdeen, but also certain it was worth visiting. For now, she'd decided to roll with it.

On my way, he texted now as she fussed with her hair in the bathroom mirror and she felt a little twist of something like nerves somewhere in her chest. Richard's office door was closed and Claire was at yoga, so Anya hovered in the hall, feeling like a child waiting to be picked up from school.

When she received his summons (**I'm outside!**), she pulled the door hurriedly, in a jangle of latches and keys, and got her bag strap tangled around one arm. As Jamie turned around at the end of the street, Anya examined his car. It was red and could do with a wash, although she was pleased to note a Partick Thistle FC bumper sticker. When pulled up next to the kerb, he rolled down the window a crack and she crouched in order to peer in. His recce outfit was black jeans and a blue jumper, with a shirt poking out from underneath.

'Good morning.' He doffed a fake cap. 'Sorry, I told you the windows didn't roll down.'

'Still, way better than a 4X4.'

He patted the side of the dusty car. 'I reckon if we don't go over 40 mph we'll get to Aberdeen and back in one piece.'

'I like those odds.'

He'd shaved; there was a little graze on the side of his chin, and he caught her staring at it.

'So' – she stopped staring – 'are we really going all the way to Aberdeen?'

'Well, I am.' He slung out of the window. 'You're very much invited. But no pressure.'

Anya narrowed her eyes, but she was grinning, 'And how long will it take?'

'It should take us just under three hours.'

'That's a long drive.'

'You can pick the music.'

'I'm a big Bruce Springsteen fan.'

'The Boss it is, then.'

She felt him watching as she walked around the front of the car, swung into the passenger seat, and fastened her seatbelt. The impulsiveness was thrilling; besides, the alternative was spending the day at Hamilton Drive, under Richard and Claire's feet, and something was going on. By the sound of their thunderous arguments this week, Richard's absence remained unexplained (he'd eventually turned up close to 2 a.m., waking Anya up as he stumbled around the hallway outside her room).

The car smelled lightly of air freshener and was a little too warm. She wriggled out of her coat.

'Stick it on the back seat.' He was gripping the key, which was poised in the ignition. 'Ready?' he asked when she'd flung it behind them.

'Think so.'

'Good enough.' He accelerated up the street.

Soon, they were trundling down Great Western Road in

comfortable silence, Anya watching the familiar tableau of pubs and the dry cleaners and the takeaway shops and newsagents pass gently by. They sped up as they approached St George's Cross, where Great Western Road forked into two, one part going up into the muted Victorian blocks of Garnethill and the gleaming glass and sandstone of the city centre beyond, and the other on to the M8 motorway. Jamie glanced in the wing mirror before changing lanes and speeding up and taking them through the junction, to join the throng of cars teeming on to the motorway.

The last time she'd driven out of Glasgow was with Connor, on the day he ended it. He had been irritable on the drive, which in hindsight was probably a sign: muttering about other cars, punching at the buttons on the dashboard, snapping at Anya when she asked how long they had left in the car. He was generally a rather irascible driver; once, on a trip back from Edinburgh, he'd snapped at her for unzipping her jacket ('Anya! I can't hear myself think!!').

Jamie, by comparison, seemed rather relaxed about conversation.

'Sorry, I just wanted to concentrate while I made it on to the motorway.' He dared a side-glance as he slid into the slow lane. 'How was the rest of your week?'

'I launched my catering company and taught two eleven-year-olds how to make an omelette.'

He laughed.

'Who are these lucky children?'

'I babysit them. It's a bit of a long story.'

'How did the omelette turn out?'

'They were disappointed that the eggs didn't produce chickens.'

'I always am too.'

Anya watched the city's outskirts slide by under the smudgy, slate grey sky.

'How was your week?'

He searched for the word.

'Tricky,' he said eventually.

'Tricky how?'

There was a pause while he switched lanes to overtake a vast container lorry.

'Sorry. I hate passing lorries. Well, the other night after I saw you, I had to go see my ex-girlfriend. She was giving me some things back.'

'I'm sorry.'

'Not very fun.'

'How long had you been together?'

'A year. I liked her a lot.'

'What happened?'

Since Connor, Anya had developed a masochist's urge to hear about the ends of other relationships.

'I don't really know.' His brow furrowed and she was a little startled to see a recognizable flash of the teenage Jamie. 'She told me she just wasn't "sure enough". Which I suppose is an important thing to be.' He sighed. 'But it hurts.'

She nodded sympathetically, wondering whether to introduce Connor. She was afraid of being maudlin, or self-absorbed or just boring.

'Sorry . . .' Jamie had clearly mistaken her silence for

something else and flashed her another quick side-glance. 'I can tell I've inadvertently created a funereal atmosphere. I can let you off at the next service station, if you'd like.'

'No!' She laughed, and he joined in. 'Not at all.' She paused, and then added, almost guiltily: 'Actually, I am also recently dumped.'

'Hey! Two losers. What happened?'

'He dumped me outside a petrol station in the car on the way back from his mother's. I don't think he was "sure" about me either. We might pass it on the way there – I'll point it out.'

Jamie exhaled.

'Shit. That is a bad dumping.'

'But a good story.'

He laughed again. She could tell he was a little relieved.

'That's true. Were you living together?'

'We were. We'd been together for four years. Now I sleep on a mattress in my cousin's spare room.' She flinched. 'Sorry, *that* bit was definitely more tragic than funny.'

Jamie shrugged.

'Sounds rough.'

She decided it was overkill at this stage to tell him about Connor and his new girlfriend.

They relaxed back into their comfortable silence, Anya's eyes blurring as the landscape whipped past, generic green fields, motorway-side and unlovely. Jamie occasionally tapped a beat on the steering wheel. He seemed in a cheerful mood.

'So' – he took his eyes off the road for a moment to look at her – 'that was your cousin's house, then, where I picked you up?'

'It was. Claire's.' Anya made a face but Jamie didn't notice.

'She lives so close to Kelvinbridge Academy. It was a bit strange driving past it.'

Anya turned to face him.

'It's even weirder bumping into packs of pupils in the Tesco across the road after school. Oh, and my friend Paddy teaches there now. Which is very weird.'

'You're still friends with Paddy McDonagh?' Jamie sounded delighted. 'You said you didn't see anyone from school!'

'You remember Paddy?'

'Of course. He was so funny. I think we had a few classes together in S3 or S4.' He drummed his fingers on the steering wheel. 'It never felt like he had a lot of time for the rest of us, though, except you. You two were a gang.'

'I think Paddy found school a bit difficult.' Anya remembered some of the taunts and nicknames slung at him and felt sad. 'That's why he left to go to college in sixth form. Which is sort of how I became friends with Euan. And Ciara and all the rest of that lot.'

'Second best.'

'I didn't mean it like that—'

'I'm kidding.' He flashed her a quick smile and she relaxed. 'It's funny, I didn't really spend a lot of time with you and Ciara and Euan's other friends.'

'No, or I suppose we would have hung out more.'

'True.'

'If you don't mind me saying this, you're different to how I remember you. From school.'

'Different how?' He glanced in the rearview mirror and Anya caught his eye quickly, then looked away.

'Well, I remember you seemed kind of aloof.' This time, she saw an unmistakable flash of hurt and regretted it immediately. 'Sorry, I don't mean aloof, so much. More quiet. Quite serious.'

He considered this assessment.

'That sounds about right. I don't think I enjoyed that school all that much either really. I was really glad when Euan turned up.'

'Me too.'

It had started to drizzle and light drops hit the windscreen.

'Did you ever know his family?' she asked.

'No. It never really felt like he had much of one. I know his mother died when he was small, but he never talked about it, really. And I didn't meet his dad. He used to spend a fair amount of time at my house, actually.'

'He always seemed like a bit of a lost boy.'

'Yes. That's a good way of putting it.'

'Do you think we'll find him?' she asked.

'I hope so.'

They drove on in silence again for another fifteen or so minutes, raindrops getting harder, like pebbles on the windscreen, though in the distance Anya could see blue sky.

'I can turn the radio on if you'd like,' Jamie said.

She had a vision of the two of them listening to Heart's loopy love songs in silence, staring at the road ahead, or worse, tuning into an overwrought radio play – about silenced nuns, or a little old lady grieving by the seaside – and felt slightly self-conscious.

'It's up to you. You're the driver.'

'Sorry. I feel a strange responsibility not to bore my

passenger when I'm driving. Speaking of which, there are Twixes in the glove compartment.'

'Nutritious.' But she smiled.

'My car, my snacks. And we should only have' – he glanced at the dashboard – 'about an hour and a half to go?'

'I'm enjoying the view.'

'The motorway is lovely at this time of year.'

He had a slightly lop-sided grin, and she decided she liked it.

By the time they approached the outskirts of Aberdeen, they had left the thick rainclouds somewhere around Stonehaven, and Anya saw a flash of blue behind the granite steeples: the sea. She shuffled a little in her seat so that she could get a better view.

'I've always thought it would be nice to live in a city on the sea,' Jamie said.

'It beats the River Clyde, doesn't it.'

The traffic had thickened as they prepared to pull off the junction that led them into the city centre, and they had slowed a little. Jamie rolled his shirtsleeves up a little higher and turned to Anya.

'Could you pass me a Twix?'

She smiled and obliged. He opened the wrapper neatly and bit into two of the fingers in one mouthful.

'That is a strange way to eat a Twix.'

He chewed and swallowed his mouthful, before he replied.

'I didn't know there was a right way to eat them.'

'One finger at a time. Obviously.'

The pace was picking up again and he rested the choc-olate bar in the cup holder and gave the road his full concentration once more. The Google Maps woman announced in her sing-song voice: 'Continue on for two miles, towards Rosemount.'

'I've never been to Aberdeen,' Anya announced.

'I've actually been a few times. I visited Euan once or twice – I slept on his floor in halls in his first year. And my sister was at university here.'

'Did she cross over with Euan?'

'Yes.' He was concentrating on the sat nav, jabbing at the phone in the holder.

'Was she at Kelvinbridge?'

'She was. Aha!' He straightened up again. 'OK, thirteen minutes it says.' The scenery was more residential now. Anya could no longer see the sea, but she could see plenty of grey stone, Victorian terraces bedecked with bright window boxes, and small independent shops (butchers, fishmongers, a vegan café). This was, clearly, Aberdeen's version of the West End.

'The light's different here,' she said. 'Brighter and purer.'

But he didn't respond and she felt shy, so stayed quiet as they carried on up the straight streets, until finally the Google Maps lady trilled, 'you have arrived at your destination'. Jamie did a few circuits of the block before he spotted a parking space next to a small dry cleaners and manoeuvred them into it.

She watched him close his eyes and massage his eyelids with his fingers, before opening them and blinking a few times.

'Sorry. Driving's tiring.'

'I wouldn't know.' She added: 'Thanks for doing it.'

'Pleasure.' He blinked a few times.

'So.' She scanned the street outside, as though Euan might be standing on the corner. She realized her heart was lightly racing. 'What's the plan?'

'We'll just knock on the door, see where we get to.' He made this sound easy, so she tried to sound game.

'And who's good cop, who's bad cop?'

He smiled.

'I've always seen myself as more of a bad cop.'

'I'm happy with that.'

15

Number 17 Belgrave Terrace was a tall, single-fronted Victorian house with a smart blue door with buzzers for four flats, labelled A, B, 3 and C. The garden path was crazy-paved with thick stone slabs, and there was a small, well-tended rose bush out front. The curtains of the ground floor room were drawn, and Anya resisted the urge to press her nose against the window. Jamie had stopped just shy of the stone doorstep.

'Nice building.' She stepped back again slightly to get a better look at the house. In the second-floor window there was a yellow poster urging the neighbourhood to vote for the SNP candidate for Aberdeen South. 'Which flat was Euan's?'

'He lived in Flat B.' Jamie had also stepped back slightly to squint at the building with interest.

'Well, Detective Kildare.' She gestured towards the buzzer. 'What are you waiting for?'

With a nod, Jamie stepped forward and pressed down on the 'B' buzzer, which raised a blaring, angry note. Anya held her breath, waiting for the scratch of the intercom, nerves prickling.

Nothing happened; Jamie pressed down on the buzzer again, which blared another angry note. Still, no voice called out from the speaker, though they both stared hopefully at it for a few moments.

'Well, that was an anticlimax,' Jamie said eventually. He continued to examine the buzzers, as though a 'Euan' one might appear.

'Which one do you fancy now?'

'Let's go A.'

'Good choice.'

He pressed down on buzzer A, for the ground-floor flat. The bell was closer to them, and Anya heard it chime from inside the flat, listening keenly for the telltale sound of footsteps pacing through the building to answer the call, but none came.

'Third time lucky.' Anya pressed the buzzer marked 'C'.

When there was no answer there either, she pressed '3' without looking at him. To her surprise, a voice sounded.

'Yes?'

The voice sounded tinny and unfriendly, and possibly elderly and male, although she couldn't be certain.

'Hi,' Anya started, 'I wonder if you can help me—'

'I don't want to buy anything.'

'No, I'm not selling anything—'

'Goodbye.'

She shrugged and looked at Jamie. He stepped forward and pressed down on the '3' buzzer again.

The voice was angrier this time, and louder. It was definitely elderly and male.

'I said I didn't want anything—'

'No, we're looking for someone who used to live here—' Jamie started.

'Get off my property or I'm calling the police now.' Jamie opened his mouth, but Anya placed her arm on his and he closed it again. 'You hear me?'

'Sorry.'

The intercom powered off and they both stood very still.

'Well.' Jamie raised an eyebrow. 'The locals are certainly friendly.'

She shrugged, anxious the man upstairs might be listening.

'Come on.' He nodded to the street. 'Let's get out of here in case the old bastard is still watching. We can try the other buzzers again in an hour or so.'

They walked to the end of the path. On the row of houses opposite, she spotted what looked like a bijou café at the end of the block. Outside was a cluster of women in black leggings, goose-down gilets and high-tops, most of them at the helm of large buggies, looking like they were about to depart en masse. She turned to take in the house once more – and could have sworn she saw a curtain twitch in the flat that was once Euan's.

'I swear I saw something!' He gave her a sceptical look, but she pointed. 'In that window. The curtain twitched.'

'It was probably just that cranky old bastard.'

'Maybe.' In her excitement, she had slightly forgotten that Euan himself wouldn't actually be in the flat. She nodded in the direction of the lithe leggings' posse. 'We could go get some lunch at that café while we wait and then try the other doors again?' An idea. 'It's basically a stake-out.'

This earned a grin.

'Good plan.'

'Phew.' She glanced up and down the street. 'I'm starving.'

They crossed the quiet road and homed in on the small

café. There were three tables outside, but the mid-October chill threatened to settle in Anya's bones, so she continued inside to a table next to the window, which gave them a clear view of number 17, with Jamie in a slightly wobbly chair to her right.

Inside, the café was sleek, chic and modern, with sparse wooden tables, white walls bearing framed, abstract artworks by local artists, and a shiny chrome coffee machine, manned by a red-faced, wild-haired barista whose hands were whizzing from milk steamer to coffee grinder and back again, according to some internal order. The eclectic menu was scrawled in chalk on a slate board on the wall: standard posh caff fare – paninis, salads, open sandwiches – plus several Mexican dishes. Anya contemplated the merits of a tuna melt over a burrito.

'What are you getting?' Jamie craned over his shoulder to examine the wall.

'I'm not sure.'

Jamie turned to face Anya just as a plump waiter in his fifties appeared at the table. He wore tartan trousers, a bright red jumper and a name tag that informed them his name was Roger.

'Hello!' he said in a sing-song east coast accent. 'And what can I get for you today?'

Jamie smiled at the man.

'Tuna melt, please.'

The man's eyes lit up.

'Now, you're not from Aberdeen, are you?'

He leaned in as if to get a closer look. Jamie shook his head.

'Glasgow. Sorry.'

'Well, we can't be having Weegies in here. There'll be complaints.' His eyes twinkled. He nodded at Anya. 'You as well, I take it?'

'Afraid so.' Anya smiled. 'My dad's from round here though. Originally.'

The man grinned back.

'We'll let you off then. What can I get you?'

'Same please. And a Coke. Not Diet.'

'Good woman. Any drinks for you, sir?'

'Orange juice. Please.'

'Aye, all right then. It'll be ten minutes or so. We're a bit backed up wi' orders and the ladies out here have just put in for fifteen or so coffees to go.' He gave them another twinkling grin and was backing off when Anya yelped, 'Wait!' He turned, a little startled.

'Sorry, I was just wondering. You didn't by any chance know someone called Euan Carrick? He lived in that house over there' – she pointed at number 17 – 'the second-floor flat. He's a friend of ours who fell off the radar and we're trying to . . . track him down.'

The man mimed a thinking face.

'I don't think so. Not by name anyway. What's he look like?'

'Erm . . . tallish, light hair. Good looking.'

The man shook his head in apology. 'Sorry.'

'No worries.' Anya felt a little embarrassed, worried she'd ruined their automatic rapport. 'Thanks.'

With a nod, the man trotted off behind the counter.

'Good looking, eh?'

She blushed deeply and opened her mouth stupidly, like a goldfish.

He grinned back. 'That was a good idea.'

'Thanks.'

'We'll go back over in an hour or so. I'm sure one of the other neighbours will be more cooperative.'

Anya nodded, hoping her flush had settled.

'So, how did you know about this place?' She tried to imagine Euan on this street, in one of those flats, walking past this coffee shop.

'What, the flat? A friend had been here for a party.'

'But this friend has no idea where he is now?'

'Nope.'

'So, Euan must have stayed in Aberdeen after university.'

'Oh, yes. He did.'

'What did he do? I can't really imagine Euan with a job.'

'Well, at university, he worked in this sandwich shop near their campus. Once, when I stayed with him, he came home from his shift with all this coronation chicken that was about to expire.'

'Sounds disgusting.' She made a face. 'Do you think anyone there would know where he'd got to?'

Jamie considered this.

'Well, it would have been quite a long time ago that he worked there.' He stopped while a different waiter – a spotty, callow redhead who nonetheless looked like the spitting image of Roger – silently placed their drinks on the table. He continued: 'And I'm not sure what it was called.'

Anya pulled her phone from her pocket.

'Well, we can find the campus and then we could google sandwich shops. There can't be that many.'

'Good point.' She tapped 'sandwich shop aberdeen uni', while he continued. 'More recently, I know he worked in a theatre company up here for a bit. Doing lighting and sets and things.'

'Really?'

She weighed this detail, hungry for more. She couldn't remember Euan liking theatre, particularly, although she did remember he'd been quite good at art. Occasionally, on a Friday night, when the light was OK, he'd submit to drawing quick portraits of his friends in the pencil he'd stuck self-consciously behind one ear. He drew her once, on the back of her English jotter; she hadn't thought about that sketch in years.

'So, he lived in this flat' – she gestured at the house with her fork – 'when he was working for this theatre company?'

'Yeah.'

'Do you know what they were called?'

'No idea. And it wasn't like he was an actor.'

'Maybe he's still moonlighting at the sandwich shop and is right now doing the lunchtime shift?'

'And he'll give us a free coronation chicken baguette when we turn up.'

She made a face.

'I'll pass.'

They ate swiftly when the food arrived, occasionally pausing to pull strings of molten cheese from their mouths. On one such occasion, they locked eyes and grinned at one another. She finished hers first and took a satisfied slurp of Coke.

'OK' – Anya scrubbed her chin with a napkin – 'so we'll go back to the house, try those other two doorbells, and then what. Do we try the sandwich shops?'

Jamie considered this.

'Could do,' he said evenly. 'But I don't think he's worked there for years. Might be a bit of a long shot.'

'Unlike the rest of this trip?' But she smiled. 'OK, let's leave the sandwich shop. We don't have any leads on the theatre company?'

'I think there was a production of *The Lion, the Witch and the Wardrobe*, but I don't think that's much to go on.'

Google didn't think so either, although there were three pubs called The Red Lion in the city.

'I'm just going to nip to the loo.' Anya stood up and pushed her chair away. 'Want anything else?'

'All good.' He had taken up her role of watching the house now. 'Thanks.'

The very small toilet was the opposite of the ordered chic of the café floor. It was decorated top-to-toe with Highland cows: on the wallpaper, in framed pictures on the wall, and even one in a tam o'shanter, perched on the top of the cistern. Anya considered giving it a pat for good luck, then remembered where it might have been.

When she reappeared, their table had been cleared and Jamie was standing up and putting his wallet in his back pocket.

'I've sorted the bill.'

'You got the last one!'

'You can buy me a Twix.'

Back on the doorstep for round two, Anya felt emboldened by the sugary Coke. When there was still no answer from Flat B, she stepped forward.

'My turn.' She pressed the buzzer for Flat A.

They heard it chime again, but this time, they heard

another sound: footsteps. Anya did a sharp intake of breath in spite of herself; Jamie leaned forward, towards the intercom, which sounded again.

'Hello?'

'Hi, I'm sorry to bother you. I'm looking for someone.' Jamie spoke loudly and distinctly, like a pensioner yelling into a webcam and Anya bit her lip, trying not to giggle. 'Someone who used to live in this building? Euan Carrick?'

'Euan?' crunched the voice from the speaker, after a moment. 'Aye, I knew him.'

Anya's heart leapt and she elbowed Jamie.

'Hang on,' the voice on the intercom said, 'I'll just come tae the window.'

There was a horrible, metallic rustling sound as they signed off, like someone scraping a set of keys across gravel, and then, a few moments later, the curtains parted, and a woman appeared. She tugged at the window frame until it was halfway open and then kneeled down in order to rest her arms on the sill.

'Hi.' Anya stepped forward and tried to look as friendly as possible.

The woman was probably in her early forties and was dressed in overalls, covered in smears of paint. Her hair was thick and greying and tied on top of her head with a strip of fabric, and she had gold hoops all up both ears, and one coming out of her nose.

'Excuse my appearance,' she said, brightly. 'Been working in the shed out in the garden.' They both blinked. 'I'm a potter.' Anya opened her mouth, and then thought better of it. 'Paint portraits too, sometimes. Can't beat the light out back in the evenings.' She clapped her hands. 'Anyway, you're looking for Euan, are you?'

'Yes, we're friends of his,' Jamie said. 'Old friends. We know he's moved and we're trying to track him down. You don't know where he went, do you?'

The woman appraised him calmly.

'I don't.' She was playing with one of the hoops in her ear, spinning it and spinning it. 'He left in a bit of a hurry, I remember, because the guy who owns the place – Ally – was annoyed about him breaking his contract. I think there was a bit of a tussle over the security deposit, or something. I don't remember all the details.'

'And when exactly was that?' Jamie asked. 'That he moved on. How long ago?'

'Must have been a year ago? Maybe a bit more.'

'And you've never heard from him again?'

'No. Never seen or heard from him since.' She picked a fleck of paint off her knuckles.

'No forwarding address or anything?' Jamie pressed.

'Oh no, nothing like that. I didn't know him all that well, just as someone to say hi to in the corridor. I think he watered the plants for me when I was away visiting my mum in the hospice one weekend.' Anya made a sympathetic face and the woman batted her away. 'Naw, she's long gone. Spiteful old witch.'

Anya blinked fast. The woman considered them both for a few beats and then added: 'What you want wi' him anyway?'

'We're just old friends,' Jamie repeated. His face was inscrutable now. 'We've lost touch and would love to see him again.'

The woman cocked her head to one side.

'Where you from? You local?'

'Glasgow,' Anya said, priming herself for another round of territorial slings and blows.

'We knew him at school,' Jamie added.

The woman nodded.

'Is Ally still the landlord?' Anya asked.

'I think so. He lives down in London, so I don't see him much but all of us who own flats in the building are in touch from time to time.'

'I don't suppose you could pass on his number, could you?' Jamie had leaned forward a little, and the woman appraised him for a few beats.

'Of course.' She smiled and Anya's shoulders relaxed. 'Let me get my phone.' She ducked back inside, and Anya and Jamie exchanged a glance before she popped back out of the window. She stabbed at the phone, peering short-sightedly at the screen.

'Here he is,' she said. 'Ally.'

She paused to check that Jamie was primed with his own phone, and then read out the number.

'Thanks,' he said. 'That's brilliant.'

'No worries.'

There was a polite silence.

'Well, I ought to get back to painting. I'm afraid I don't know any more than what I've told you. Plus' – a mischievous grin – 'you're letting the chill into my house.'

'Sorry!' Anya must have looked anguished because the woman laughed.

'I'm just messing with you.'

'Thank you,' Jamie said. 'You've been really helpful.'

The woman shrugged again.

'Good luck finding him.'

Jamie and Anya both waved as the woman pulled down the window to close it, and then drew the curtains again.

They tried the other buzzers a couple of times, exchanging nervous, slightly self-conscious glances as they waited for an answer. But none came from the others; Anya started to feel a little deflated.

'Shall we—' Jamie pointed to the street and Anya nodded, and they walked back to the car in contemplative silence. Her mind raced: Euan hadn't just vanished from the internet, he'd vanished altogether.

Jamie had unlocked the car and swung himself into the driver's seat, and she followed. Instead of starting the engine, he faced Anya.

'Well.' There was a deep line etched between his brows.

'Sounds a bit weird him leaving in a hurry like that.' She realized she was whispering. 'Do you think he's . . . OK?'

'I wonder.' He still looked deep in thought.

'So, he was there a year ago.'

'If only we'd started sooner.'

A year ago, she was living with Connor, and Euan was nothing but a memory. Jamie had placed the key in the ignition but hadn't turned it on yet.

'Sorry if that was a bit of a waste of time.' He looked rather beaten, his eyes – dark, but with flecks of green and grey – downcast.

'It wasn't! We found out a key clue! Euan vanished into thin air, sort of.'

'Yeah. Although we don't know *where.*'

'True,' she agreed. 'But! We've got the landlord's number.'

'We do.' This seemed to cheer him up a little. 'I'll text him right now.'

She peered over his shoulder as he composed a message.

'I guess we're a real detective duo now.' Anya gave him a side-glance. 'We've got a cold case to uncover. Plus, we had a nice tuna melt.'

'And visited Scotland's largest shrine to the Highland cow.'

'One to tell the grandkids.'

He fixed his phone into the stand on the dashboard and then turned the key in the ignition. The heating roared to life, and Anya held her stiff hands in front of the heating vent.

'So, what do we do next?' It felt like a bit of an anticlimax to go home, but so did driving through Aberdeen in the hope of spotting him.

She had her answer: he had started reversing out of the space and she paused while he navigated the car out. Paddy didn't like to be spoken to when he was reversing. Once he was out, she continued. 'What about school?'

'What? Ask if they've heard from him?' The omniscient sat nav advised it was a right turn at the next street. 'That's not a bad idea.'

'I pop in and see Paddy there a fair bit. I could try the office one day.'

'That would be brilliant.'

Jamie commenced their route in reverse and soon the

city gave way to quiet suburbs. Anya was glad of the car, of the companionable silence broken only by the smart tones of the Google Maps lady, and of the calm of watching the grey slate roofs that ringed the city's outskirts rise and fall with the hills. Jamie put the radio on somewhere near Dundee, a sports show where the announcer read out the day's football scores.

'This reminds me of car trips with my dad. On the way back from an away game.'

'Same.' That was a new smile, more wistful.

She half-listened while the scenery flew past, eyes skittering so fast that she'd occasionally nod off, then wake with a start, hoping he hadn't noticed. When Glasgow eventually arrived on the horizon, she was pleased to see it, feeling a nostalgia – for the Victorian spires in the distance, the familiar landmarks flagged on green roadway signs – that was disproportionate to the time she'd been away.

'So' – she moved in her seat until her body faced his again – 'I'll try the school. What else should we try? What about his dad, have you ever tried to track him down?'

'I've done a fair bit of googling but haven't been able to track him down yet.'

'Maybe he's a good avenue. If we could find him. Did your mum know him?'

'Afraid not.'

'I wonder if mine did. She was very ... involved in school.'

As a teenager, Anya had longed for the sort of distant, disinterested parent who never knew when Sports Day was and had no interest in attending it. Despite the fact that neither Anya nor Georgie had ever brought athletic glory on the family in any way, Irene was always there, gripping two bananas, which she'd press into the girls' hands before the 4 x 100 m relay. She was in the Parent-Teacher Association and often volunteered to help on opening nights of school plays, handing out programmes and ushering people to their rows. Perhaps she'd crossed paths with Euan's dad at some point.

Jamie stole a glance at her.

'I knew you'd be a good partner.' His eyes sparkled, and she was a little disappointed when he returned them to the road, but they were approaching the junction near St George's Cross and the traffic was a little cantankerous now. Jamie glanced over his shoulder and nimbly overtook another car, flashing a grateful palm in the rearview mirror. Eventually, they made it through the junction and beyond.

Obviously, this was all silly and a short-term distraction from the chaos and disappointment of her life. But as Anya settled back in her seat for the home stretch, watching the blur and rush of a Saturday evening in her city, she felt newly purposeful. It was a nice change.

16

Anya curled a long noodle around her wooden spoon and nibbled the end. It was still on the dente side of al dente. She gave the soup – a mixture of coconut milk and ginger and vegetable stock – a final stir and switched it off while the noodles finished up. On a chopping board beside the hob were chopped greens and some crushed cashews to sprinkle on top.

This was a new recipe, which she'd improvised from one she'd found in a weekend supplement (she'd added the ginger and some sugar-snap peas, and noodles instead of rice). She was feeling cheerful this morning, with good reason: she'd received an email that morning – she was being booked to do a fortieth birthday party at a smart address on the south side of the city in three weeks' time.

'Not formal – mainly just family and a few friends,' it read. 'But we're big eaters (!) and there are lots of vegetarians.' Anya had sent back a slightly over-eager message with a few too many thank yous, but she was grateful. Thrilled, in fact; she was no longer a fraud, which meant she now had two reasons to call her mother.

Anya turned the noodles off, drained them and poured them into the soup, then gave the saucepan four slow, methodical stirs anticlockwise. She decanted a portion into one of Claire's deep soup bowls and took it to the table. The ginger was zingy and energizing and welcome.

The phone in Balfron rang just once before Irene picked up.

'Anya! So good to hear from you!'

Anya cringed guiltily.

'How are you?'

'I'm just doing the crossword while your dad persists in that greenhouse. I told him he won't grow anything in late autumn but he won't listen. What are you up to?'

'I've just made a soup – ginger and coconut with noodles and greens.'

'Well, that sounds very . . . different.'

'It's good, actually.' Anya took a pointed slurp. 'Anyway, I'm calling for two reasons. Firstly, I got a job.'

'Anya! That's wonderful! Doing what?'

'Oh no, I mean someone booked me. For a job. A catering job. It's a fortieth near Newton Mearns. In a few weeks. And I'm doing some cooking for Aimee too. Fiona's daughter. She's having a party.'

'Well.' Anya could hear the cogs turning. 'How about that.'

'I posted on my Instagram and they got in touch through that. And Tasha's got someone making me a fancy logo and fine-tuning my website. I'm going to do a test run of some of my dishes on Paddy and Georgie on Friday.'

'I'm thrilled for you, Anya.'

Anya tried not to feel too disappointed that her mother's professed enthusiasm was absent from her tone.

'Anyway, I just wanted to let you know.' She took another slurp of soup. It was a gingery bit and her eyes watered. 'The other thing was – did you ever know Euan Carrick's dad? Euan was in my year at school, he was a—'

she dropped a beat, 'a friend. And I wondered if you knew his father at the time.'

'Oooooooh.' Her mother sounded far more enthusiastic now. 'Something Carrick, then? He was in your year?'

'Yes, only for the last two years. No mother – she died – just a father.'

'Oh, how terribly sad.'

'Yes. Did you know him?'

There was a pause as Irene considered this. 'I don't think so,' she said eventually. 'Or if I did, I don't remember him. Sorry.'

'Never mind. It was a long shot.'

'Why do you ask?'

'Oh, no reason. Just something about school. A reunion. People from my year are trying to get in touch with each other.' She realized too late that this lie would attract too much interest.

'A reunion! What a lovely idea.'

'Mmm.'

'Where will you do it?'

'Not sure yet. We're just seeing who we can track down and a few people are doing it through the parents. Anyway, forget I mentioned it. It's not a big thing.'

'I'm sorry I can't be more useful.' She sounded it, and Anya felt that bittersweetness again.

'That's OK. Really, don't worry. It was just an idea. Anyway, that was all I was ringing about really. I should go. Claire and Richard are cleaning and I suppose I should probably help.'

'Oh, Anya.' But she could hear a smile in her mother's voice now. 'Come and see us again soon.' She paused. 'In fact, I meant to say, Georgie told me what happened after you were here last time. With Connor. I hope you're OK.'

Anya realized she hadn't thought about Connor today.

'I am. Really.' She added, quickly, 'But thank you for checking.'

'Of course. Come and see us soon, anyway.'

'I will. Love you, Mum.'

'I love you, too.'

The rest of Anya's Sunday meandered. She continued to avoid Claire and Richard by holing up in her room to watch an ancient Anthony Bourdain documentary, although as afternoon slipped into Sunday evening, she could hear them arguing. She paused the show and crawled to the door, intrigued, but all she could hear was the buzz of bad tempers. With a sigh, she returned to bed and turned the show back on.

At dinnertime, she tiptoed downstairs for more broth and bumped into Richard in the front hall. He was winding a thick scarf around his long neck. For some reason, this made Anya feel unsettled.

'Where are you off to?'

She'd meant to be casual, but Richard snapped.

'None of your business.'

'Fine,' she said tartly.

He fastened his coat deliberately, then patted down each pocket until he'd located his keys and – without a word – opened the front door and vanished. Anya gave the closed door the finger.

When the clock struck 9 p.m., she was relieved to call it a day. Somewhere in the soupy Sunday hours of 4 p.m. to

6 p.m., she'd made the mistake of checking Connor's Instagram; while there were no clues about his new relationship (he hadn't posted anything since March, when he'd shared a picture of a canned craft beer), she couldn't help but wonder if one of his female followers was his new girlfriend.

She prodded at her phone and noticed her mother had emailed. Anya tapped the notification.

Irene had forwarded on a bulletin, with the subject line: 'Kelvinbridge parents – TEA! And golf at Gleneagles'. Above, her mother had typed a message.

> Well! I don't know if it's anything to do with your friend, but it turns out that a Craig Carrick is down to play golf with a few of the Kelvinbridge Academy parents at Gleneagles . . . next Sunday!

Anya scrolled down through paragraphs about a Christmas lunch, and a picture of someone's newly minted daughter (Anya didn't recognize the names of the parents, although apparently both had gone to her school, and had been in the year above) and there, at the bottom, the relevant paragraph.

> Adil Khan, Fraser Clarke, Craig Carrick, Angus Duncan and Ruaridh Bell are looking for a sixth member for golf at Gleneagles on Sunday 17th October. We'll tee off at midday and finish the day with tea at the clubhouse! First come first served – if you're interested, please email Fraser on fraser.clarke@excelsiorconsultants.com.

Craig Carrick: could that really be Euan's father? It wasn't that unusual a name.

Anya
So – I have what might be a clue

She screenshotted the relevant part of the email and sent Jamie the picture.

> My mum found this email
> Could just be a random Carrick
> But maybe worth a try

He was online and already typing.

Jamie
!
OK
Sounds like we might be going to Gleneagles next weekend

She was pleased to find there was a golf flag emoji and sent this back by way of reply.

> Are you free on Friday
> We could have a drink and discuss a plan?

Anya
Yes!
I'm cooking dinner for Paddy and my
sister but we could meet first

He replied.

Jamie
Perfect – want to come round to mine?

Anya
Sounds good

Jamie
Excellent

Anya really had to stop underestimating her mother.

17

On Tuesday, Anya won her third official customer: the organizer of the dog birthday party had committed. It turned out it was a fifth birthday party, and the centre-piece would be a 'large doggy cake that looks like Luna!' but they would love Anya to make snacks for 'about four-teen human guests'. The afterglow of this success sustained her all week, and good thing too, for Aimee was in overdrive.

Aimee Twins

Hi Anya, I need you to stay late tonight and cook for the girls

I have a dinner with a brand

Anya

OK no problem!

Aimee Twins

Hi Anya

Rachel is sick

They sent her home from school

Can you come round now and watch her

Is urgent

Anya

Of course!

Poor her, I will head round now

Can I bring her anything?

Aimee Twins

No she's vomiting so nothing you can do

Anya

Ah, OK

Hope it's not contagious

Aimee Twins

I wouldn't know. I'm not a doctor Anya.

Aimee Twins

Hi Anya I need you to take the girls to their bowling
party on Thursday night
Springfield Quay
Have a drinks thing
They should be done by 9 pm

Anya

No problem

Aimee Twins

DONT let them have fizzy drinks this time.
Or a burger or any kind of junk food.

When Anya arrived at Springfield Quay – the strobe
lighting and earsplitting pop music an assault on the
senses – both girls were holding cups of Fanta as large as
their faces and were sharing a grab bag of Haribo. They
were dressed in matching pink jeans, one in a yellow jumper,
the other in a blue one. They waved, a little reluctantly.

'Hi girls!' Anya yelled gamely over the din. 'Who won?'

But they didn't seem to be able to hear her over the
music. Beside them on the banquette were four other
girls, slack-jawed from a junk food coma; there was one

other girl up bowling, her pink ball ready on the rack, which she was angling carefully before she pushed the ball off and down the lane. On an opposite banquette sat three mothers. Anya counted three finished bottles of Chablis.

'Are you almost done?'

Rosie and Rachel exchanged a glance.

'Where's our mum?' one of them asked, though Anya noted the tone was more forlorn than hostile.

'She's busy this evening.' Anya felt the mothers eyeing her carefully now. 'Didn't she tell you I was picking you up?'

'No,' said the other twin quietly. 'She didn't.'

'Well' – for some reason, Anya clapped her hands together – 'I am. Are you almost finished? We'll need to get a cab home.'

'We still have two more goes,' they said almost in unison.

'Oh. OK. Well, I can watch.'

Awkwardly, Anya sat down on the end of the banquette, beside the girls, all of whom appraised her snottily. On cue, they all started laughing. She really did not know how Paddy did it.

'Hi,' she half-waved at the women opposite and instantly regretted it. 'I'm Anya. I'm Rosie and Rachel's babysitter.'

The women were all dressed in spray-on jeans and floaty blouses, with the lace-up bowling shoes a ridiculous addition. The friendliest one, who had dark hair that curled around her shoulders, gave her a tight smile.

'I'm picking them up this evening,' Anya continued pointlessly. 'Aimee had a last-minute event. And I'm more of a nanny really.'

The mothers just nodded and then resumed their

exclusive conversation. Anya wondered at what point life stopped feeling like secondary school.

She turned her attention to the bowling: the screen flashed 'ROSIE' and the twin in the blue jumper stood up. Anya reflected that it was a shame she could not always rely on this technology to flag which girl was which.

Rosie's first wild shot went straight into the gutter, while the second hit only a single pin on the edge. Anya glanced at the screen again and saw that this meant Rosie ranked in last, by some distance, and felt guilty that this slightly cheered her up.

When the girl sat back down, Rachel grinned a ghastly grin, her mouth stuffed with Haribo gummies.

'You're *last*.'

'Shut up, Rachel.'

Rachel swallowed her gummies and stood up for her turn. She was a little more successful than her sister, managing two pins the first time and two the second. It was now clear why the women had needed a bottle of wine each.

In this group, Rachel's turn appeared to constitute success, and she now sat a more respectable third place in the leaderboard. Currently in first place was the birthday girl, Samaire, who was wearing a crown and a very frilly party dress.

'I'm better than you,' Rachel said to her sister as she sat down again. 'Just like I am at everything.'

By the time Anya managed to drag them out of there, the bickering and taunts had evolved to physical warfare. There had been scratching and hair-pulling; as Anya tried to separate them, they'd pulled her hair too. After an attempt by Rosie to bite her sister, Anya grabbed them both by the forearm. Mercifully, her Uber was already waiting.

'Get. In,' Anya hissed. 'Rachel – front. Rosie – back.'

To her surprise, the twins obliged automatically, and stopped the bickering too. Rachel even offered what might have been an apologetic flash of the eyes as Anya swung into the back with Rosie. As they crossed the black mirror of the River Clyde, back over to their side of town, she could hear the child's heavy breathing gently subside.

Much to Anya's dismay, the driver was taking a circuitous, stop-start route that led them through all of Glasgow's busiest streets on a Thursday evening. Near Central Station, the car was forced to weave through crowds of lairy revellers, and the girls' eyes were big and wide as they watched the people play. Eventually, as they neared Park Circus, Rosie turned to Anya.

'I'm going to be sick.'

Anya turned out her tote bag on to her lap, but it was too late. With impressive noise, Rosie directed a stream of green, lumpy vomit straight on to the middle seat. The driver whipped round.

Rosie repeated her trick, whimpering a little this time, and Anya spent the rest of the journey mopping up the mess with her tote bag.

The mood was sombre as he parked up.

'You're paying for that.' He pointed at his sodden, smelly back seat.

'Of course. Sorry.' She'd have to speak to Aimee.

After a struggle to wash the vomit out of Rosie's hair in the sink, Anya managed to get the girls to bed and tiptoed back downstairs to sit at the kitchen island and watch the digits on the oven clock tick past. She was glad tomorrow was Friday. She was seeing Jamie before serving her menu up to Paddy and Georgie at Georgie's flat; the sooner she perfected it and got Anya Eats Too Much rolling, the sooner she'd no longer find herself sitting in the soulless chrome quiet of Aimee's kitchen at a quarter past eleven on a Thursday night, the smell of vomit lingering on her knuckles.

When the woman eventually returned, a little drunk, just before midnight, she was unapologetic. Tottering as she removed her stilettos, she thrust a clutch of twenty-pound notes into Anya's hands, spearing her palm with a nail.

'See you tomorrow,' she slurred.

'You're welcome,' Anya muttered as Aimee closed the door in her face. In the glow of the street lamps, Anya was overjoyed to notice Aimee had wildly overpaid her.

Aimee appeared to have no memory of this exchange – nor the inflated pay cheque – when Anya arrived at Park Circus again the next day. It felt too soon to be returning. She had spent the day in Claire's kitchen preparing her food, which she'd be taking to Georgie's via Jamie's later; she was transporting it all in a red coolbag – her first proper business purchase. Tasha's designer was on a third – and hopefully final – draft of the logo, and the website tweaks she'd asked for were 'almost there'. When the logo was ready, Anya was thinking of having it printed on to the side of the bag.

'How much do I owe him for it all?'

They'd had another snatched FaceTime the other evening Anya time, during what was Tasha's lunchbreak.

'Don't worry.' Tasha tossed her mane. 'I've sorted it.'

'Tasha! What does that mean?'

'Just consider me an angel investor.'

'You have to let me pay you back.'

'Sure.'

Miraculously, the twins were subdued after their school-night bowling exploits the previous evening and were mainly interested in watching television. Perhaps it was Stockholm Syndrome, but Anya had started to quite enjoy their favourite show, about a group of tween girls who fought crime after they did their homework. Jamie texted near the end of an episode in which the gang had foiled a plot to kill the mayor of their small town, in time to make it to their middle-school prom.

Jamie
Still on for later?

Anya
Yes!

Jamie
Great
Address is 46A Highburgh Road.
7ish work?

Anya
Sounds good – need to be at my sister's at 8.30 latest

Jamie
Great – see you in a bit

When she was released by Aimee with a dismissive wave (her talons were manicured in blood red today), Anya decided she'd walk the twenty-five-minute trip to Jamie's, lugging the coolbag over one shoulder and over the other, her tote bag – not the one Rosie was sick in – containing a bottle of wine she'd borrowed from Claire's rack and the

walk was long enough to be wearisome. She'd have preferred a taxi but was still on an economy drive; Anya was
relieved when she reached his street, a Victorian terrace
lined with cars, which sloped up towards a warren of residential streets she had walked around countless times. In
fact, she'd probably passed this house nearly every day for
many years: her childhood home was only a few streets
away and the doctor's surgery where her father worked
stood sentry at the end of Jamie's road. And there, on the
corner, was a church where Anya had intermittently
attended Brownies and, once, played a stammering Wise
Man in the nativity play. Georgie had co-starred as a sheep.

Inside her big bag was her tester menu for the fortieth
birthday, where the brief was 'little veggie snacks and small
plates'. Duly, Anya had gone for okra bhajis with a creamy
spinach and artichoke dip; a zesty butter bean salad; courgette and halloumi fritters; an asparagus frittata; and gooey
avocado brownies. She hoped it would impress; even Claire
had been lured into delivering a rare compliment.

'Something smells . . . good,' her cousin had ventured
earlier, a little suspiciously, as she appeared in the kitchen
doorway. She was working from home and was wearing a
pair of professorial spectacles on her nose.

'Oh thanks. I'm cooking for Paddy and Georgie.'

Claire sniffed the air again.

'Lucky them.'

After this unexpectedly civil exchange, Anya had felt a
little guilty about pilfering a bottle of wine, but planned
on replacing it tomorrow, and figured Claire wouldn't
miss it overnight.

The evening was carefully choreographed. She had an

hour to spend at Jamie's and then she would need to go on to see Georgie and Paddy; conveniently, her sister lived only a twenty-minute walk from Jamie's flat. Walking slowly down the pavement in order to peer at the numbers on the doors, she spotted number forty-six. She daubed Carmex across her lips and then squared her shoulders, walked up the front path and pressed the doorbell for A. As she waited for an answer, a strong gust exhaled, blowing her hair across her face. When Jamie appeared at the door, she was picking sticky clumps from her mouth.

'Hello.' Jamie looked like he'd just got in from work: navy suit trousers, a white shirt, rolled up to the sleeves, two top buttons undone. He was clean-shaven again, and his face looked younger and unfamiliar without the stubble. At the sight of her, the grin appeared.

'Hello. You live very close to where I grew up.'

'Really?'

Jamie stepped back and ushered her into a high-ceilinged hallway, which opened on to a huge living room. There were three navy blue, structured sofas arranged around a white rug and a glass coffee table. On top of the coffee table, there was a ringbinder folder and a *Scotsman*. Set into the off-white walls were shelves, lined with a few rows of books – *Catch-22*, several Lonely Planets, a clutch of Narnia books – and a few framed photographs. There was a large flatscreen television in the corner not taken up by a sofa, and an archway leading through to a large, white kitchen with a few chrome gadgets, as well as a large wall clock.

'Wow. Nice flat.' She dropped the coolbag beside one of the sofas and flopped on to it. Sadly, it was as uncomfortable as it looked.

'Thanks. So, where was your house?'

He'd perched himself on the end of one of the other sofas and was smiling that open grin.

'About four streets from here. Victoria Crescent Road?'

'Ah!' He looked delighted. 'I know it well.'

'Do you live by yourself?'

'I do.' He poked the coolbag with his toe. 'Is this the famous meal?'

She'd told him all about the fortieth birthday and the trial run this evening.

'Watch what you're poking. I don't want you to dislodge a brownie.'

'Is there a spare one going?'

She had prepared for this.

'There might be.' She unzipped the bag and extracted a single, squidgy square.

'Really?'

'Of course. I made way too many.'

'Wow.'

He placed it reverently on the pristine counter-top.

'I'll save it for later if that's OK.'

For some reason, she felt a little disappointed, but nodded.

'Of course. I've brought something else for now anyway.'

She pulled Claire's wine out of her tote bag and handed it to Jamie.

'Wow.' He examined the label carefully, a quizzical smile playing about his lips.

'What?' she asked.

'Well, it's just that this is quite an expensive wine.' He laughed, a little uncertainly.

'Oh.' Her blood froze. 'Is it?'

'Yes. It's quite famous.' He made a face. 'Sorry. My mum is into wine.'

But Anya was too busy panicking to tease him.

'I didn't . . . I didn't actually buy it. My cousin gave it to me.'

Jamie looked very amused now.

'Your cousin must really like you.'

He stood up and walked through the archway into the kitchen, and Anya clenched a fist and tried not to worry about what Claire might do to her when she worked out what had happened. He reappeared with a rather complicated-looking corkscrew and started winding it into the bottle.

'Anyway, I'm truly honoured' – Jamie placed a glass in front of her – 'that you'd choose to share it with me.' A pause. 'It's not every Friday you drink a hundred pound wine.'

Anya really, really wished she'd googled the wine label.

'Any time,' she managed weakly, her cheeks hot.

Jamie gave her another dancing glance and poured two modest glasses of wine into the tall, slender glasses, then pushed one towards her. He settled on the sofa to her left, and took took a deep sniff of his wine glass.

'This is what you do, isn't it?' He knocked back a sip and swilled it around his mouth. 'Delicious.' There was still a sparkle in his eyes that she suspected was at her expense. For want of a better solution, she took a swig too.

'Right!' He grinned again. 'To business. Or rather, to Gleneagles.'

'Yes.' She was very pleased to have a distraction from her impending bankruptcy.

'Your mum's a good detective too, it seems.'

'Irene Mackie is a very accomplished woman.' She leaned back on the sofa and tried to relax.

In turn, Jamie leaned forward slightly. 'So, what I'm thinking is that *we* could go to Gleneagles ourselves on Sunday and see if this Craig Carrick has anything to do with Euan. Try and talk to him. What do you think?'

'I'm in, in theory. But' – she frowned and sat up a little – 'we've got no idea what he looks like.'

'True. But we know he tees off at two p.m. And he's in a group of about six men, roughly in their, what, sixties?'

'There can't be that many of them, I suppose.'

'I'm pretty sure golf is all groups of men in their sixties.' Jamie raised a teasing eyebrow. 'But the tee time can help us narrow it down.'

'Will we have to play golf?' Anya could not imagine herself in plus fours.

'I think there's a risk we will.'

'Can we get a golf buggy?'

Anya pictured the pair of them trailing retiree golfers in a buggy, taking it in turns to peer at them through a set of binoculars, trying to ascertain whether any of them looked at all similar to their long-lost friend, Euan Carrick.

'I insist on it.'

'And if we find him – what then?'

Jamie considered this.

'Well, we just tell him we're old friends and we'd love to see Euan. Perhaps he'd be able to give us a number or just pass on a message. Or something.'

'Easy.' Anya took another sip of the wine, which tasted to her like velvet and pound signs. 'This is quite exciting.'

'I can assure you you're the first person in existence to

ever use the word "exciting" about a game of golf. But' – another grin – 'we'll have fun.'

'How shall we get there?'

'Train? I'll look into it. Oh, and speaking of trips, Ally replied.'

She drew a momentary blank and then remembered.

'Ally! The landlord.'

'Afraid he didn't have much for us.'

Jamie extended his phone towards her and she leaned in. He smelled like laundry detergent and expensive shaving gel.

Hi there haven't spoken to him since he ran off. Good luck finding him – if you track him down remind me he owes me money. A

Anya winced.

'Exactly.' He pinned her gaze. 'So. Gleneagles. You in?'

'I guess so.'

He looked disappointed, so she added: 'Sorry. Of course.'

'Good.' Jamie nodded towards the cool bag. 'So, besides brownies, what's on the menu tonight?'

She described her dishes, feeling self-conscious.

'That sounds amazing.'

He sounded awed and she hated that she flushed.

'Well. Hopefully, I don't poison them.'

'Have you ever poisoned anyone?'

'I once tried to make a lasagne which came out all . . . hard. Years ago, now. No one was poisoned, though. Just hungry.'

'I can't cook a thing.'

'People always say that. I bet you're fine at cooking.'

249

'No' – his eyes widened – 'I really mean it.'

'Surely you can follow a recipe.'

'I don't have any recipe books.'

'Have you heard of this thing called the internet?' This earned a wry roll of the eyes. 'But,' she continued, 'if you don't cook, then what do you eat?'

'Have *you* heard of this thing called a microwave?'

'Oh, Jamie. You're what – thirty? You can do better than a microwave meal. Next time, I'll show you how to do an omelette. Like I did with the twins.' She peered through the archway into his kitchen. 'I bet you have all sorts of whizzy, alpha male gadgets in there.'

'Alpha male gadgets?'

'You know. Blenders that pulverize at twice the speed of a normal blender. An espresso machine.'

He laughed.

'I'm not sure how I should feel about this assessment.'

'But you do have an espresso machine, don't you?'

'It was a thirtieth birthday present.'

'From your mum?'

He flashed a guilty smile.

'So,' he said, 'tonight is a dry run. When's the real event?'

'Few weeks' time. I've also been booked to do the menu at a dog's birthday party. The human food, not the dog food.'

'Presumably you will eventually graduate into making dog food.'

'Only the truly talented make it that far.'

He laughed, and she felt pleased. He looked relaxed, one arm slung across the back of the sofa, and she took in a few more details of the living room. On a nearby shelf was a framed photo of a little boy and an even smaller girl sitting on a small wall in a seaside town. The children were in sunshine colours, beaming toothy, unselfconscious smiles. In the middle was a man who looked very like Jamie. He too was smiling.

'Is that you?'

He turned.

'Yes, that's me and my dad and my sister. We were in Largs, I think. My parents used to take us up there in the holidays. I think that was the summer my dad taught me to swim by throwing me in the sea.'

'Nineties' parenting.'

'Very nineties. I can remember a lot of saltwater going up my nose, and then my dad gathering me up and carrying me back to the shore. And my sister just laughing and laughing. She was a much better swimmer than me.'

'How did he die?'

'He had lung cancer.'

'I'm sorry.'

'Thank you.' He stood up and loped to the kitchen, and Anya was worried she'd spoiled the evening, but when he turned around, holding the wine, he looked like himself again. He poured her a little more.

'OK.' He had a mischievous look in his eyes. 'Correct me if I'm wrong, but you seem to have things at least a little bit sorted.' He nodded at the coolbag again. 'Cooking for dogs and everything.'

'What do you mean?'

'Well, all this stuff about wanting to find Euan to help you get a job?'

Anya's face betrayed her; she opened her mouth helplessly and he laughed.

'Sorry – that was mean of me. It's just I was thinking about it, and it doesn't really add up.'

For the second time that evening, she was blushing and hoping Jamie didn't notice.

'OK, fine.' There was no way out of this one. 'I don't want to ask him about this uncle's restaurants. I was curious – it was just nostalgia, really.' She could feel herself starting to babble. 'It was just after Connor and I had broken up and I ended up thinking about him and what could have been,' – she winced – 'Euan and I had this silly teenage thing, you see.'

Jamie waved a dismissive hand.

'I know all about that.'

'Oh.'

'He was my best friend. We did discuss these things.'

'Oh.' She was starting to blush now, and added: 'It's not like I think he's going to see me and fall madly in love with me . . .'

'It's only a little bit like that, right?' He raised his eyebrows but couldn't hold it; his face collapsed again. 'Sorry.'

'Do you think I'm tragic?'

'Not at all,' he said kindly.

'You're lying.'

He laughed.

'No, I'm not. But' – he shifted in his seat. She noticed he looked a little uncomfortable now – 'well, I don't want you to . . . get hurt or anything. I'd feel a bit guilty.'

There was a slightly awkward pause and Anya blushed.

'Oh,' she stammered, 'no, don't worry, it was just a silly thing. I don't actually want to try and rekindle our teenage romance. It's just curiosity, really.'

She wasn't sure she'd made her case, but he looked half-convinced.

'As long as you're sure,' he said, eventually.

Her face was still pink.

'Really. It's not about that. Anyway, now that we're looking for him, he feels less real. He's become sort of frozen in time. If we do find him, I'm imagining we'll find the seventeen-year-old Euan, not an adult version.' She shook her head. 'I'm not explaining it very well.'

There was another pause, and he found her eyes. His expression was gentle, and she relaxed a little.

'We really are getting old.' He grinned, and she laughed, more relieved.

'We are. Very old.' She took a deep breath. 'Where's your bathroom?'

'That old excuse.' She rolled her eyes and he added: 'It's straight across the hall.'

The first door she opened was in fact a bedroom and – after first checking over her shoulder to confirm he hadn't caught her snooping – Anya peeked inside. There were few clues to the man who slept there: a bed made up with a navy-and-white pinstriped duvet; a wooden bedside table; a half-full glass of water; a small Anglepoise lamp. There was a tall, white chest of drawers and a matching wardrobe. The blinds were almost entirely pulled.

Holding her breath, Anya tiptoed back out of the bedroom, closed the door silently, and then tried the second door, which was indeed the bathroom.

It was clean in here, she thought approvingly, although given the state of the rest of the flat, this wasn't much of a surprise. There was a standing bath and a shower, which contained nothing more than a bottle of a fancy brand of man shampoo. There was nothing illuminating in the bathroom cabinet: spare razor heads, a pack of ibuprofen. After making a few faces at herself in the glass, she washed her hands, then returned to the living room.

He was on his phone, scrolling.

'I was just checking the train times to Gleneagles.'

'What time shall we go?'

'There's an eleven fourteen a.m. train on Sunday. The journey takes about an hour, so we could get lunch there and then commence our . . . mission. I'll try and book a tee time too.'

'What do you wear to play golf?' Anya asked.

'Black tie.'

She rolled her eyes again.

'Just wear something warm. We can probably rent golf shoes while we're there.'

'And do you need clubs?'

'I actually have some. Hand-me-down from my dad. I've never used them though – not my thing. He'd be pleased I am, though.'

'Even better reason to go, then.' She'd perched on the end of the sofa. 'What are you doing this evening?'

'Nothing.' He made a face. 'I had someone's leaving do last night, so I definitely need a night in tonight.'

'You don't seem hungover.'

'I'm just about holding it together.'

'Where did you go?'

'Pub round the corner from the office, then some horrible late-night place. Kebab. The works.'

'That is something I do not miss about being in an office.'

'The kebabs?'

'The kebabs. And the weekday hangovers.'

'I'm certainly too old to do it regularly.' He brushed his hand through his hair. 'But I promise, I'll be much more alive on Sunday.'

'I hope so.' She nodded smartly. 'You're driving the golf buggy.'

'I take my duties very seriously.'

'Good.' Their eyes met for a moment and she was disappointed by what she had to say next. 'I'm afraid I should probably go soon. My sister is always on time.'

He nodded.

'Don't worry. My hangover is evolving and I'll soon be incapable of proper conversation.' He stood up and did a rather feline stretch. 'Where does your sister live?'

'She's on Dalcross Street, so not far.'

'Maybe when I'm slouched in front of the telly this evening, I could do some research on our golf buddies.' He gestured for her to go first and she felt slightly self-conscious walking to the door, wriggling into her coat sleeves.

'Save it,' she said. 'Watch some Gogglebox. We can do it together on the train.'

'OK.' She could hear the smile in his voice. 'Good plan.'

He opened his front door and Anya stepped into the corridor, averting her gaze this time when she saw the gilt mirror in the communal hallway. Jamie raised a palm in farewell.

'I'll see you on Sunday then.' That mischievous look again. 'And thanks again for the wine.'

'My pleasure.' At least she sounded serene.

18

It wasn't until Anya was halfway up the stairs of Georgie's building, that she realized she'd left the food at Jamie's.

'You're on time!' Georgie was wrapped in a towel, hair dripping, a dribbly ring of mascara round her eyes. 'Sorry – I went to the gym after work and I was just getting myself sorted.' She peered short-sightedly at Anya. 'I haven't got my contacts in, but you look—'

'Like an off-duty ScotRail conductor?' Anya supplied, miserably. This was a comment Paddy had once made about an outfit she was wearing.

Georgie gave her a strange look. 'I was going to say like something terrible has happened. Are you OK?'

'No. I've done something really stupid. I've forgotten the bloody food.'

Her sister clutched her face and almost dropped her towel; she recovered quickly.

'Oh no!'

'I'm just about to go back for it.'

'Could Claire meet you halfway?'

Anya dropped a beat but recovered quickly.

'She's busy tonight, I think. Something with Richard.' Anya shook her head distractedly. 'Anyway, I should go now. I might make it before Paddy arrives.'

'OK.' Georgie nodded vigorously, and this time the towel wrapped around her head unravelled. 'See you soon.'

'Sorry.' Anya's voice echoed in the stairwell. 'I'll be back as soon as I can.'

The evening was brisk and Anya was pleased that she had to trot, boots slapping against the dark, slightly slick pavements while she fumbled with the zip pocket of her coat, trying to find her phone. She WhatsApped Jamie:

> So, I'm an idiot
> I left the food at your house!
> I'm on my way back
> Please don't eat it

She'd stopped to walk for a few minutes to catch her breath but sped up again. As she rounded a corner, fleet-footed and panting, an older man walking towards her demanded, 'Where's the fire?' but Anya didn't stop even to roll her eyes. She was close now. Jamie hadn't replied to her texts; at least he'd said he was staying in.

When she reached his doorstep, she took a moment to compose herself, combing her hands through her hair and taking a few deep breaths until the panting subsided. She probably looked mad: wild-eyed, hair everywhere, but she couldn't waste any more time. She pressed the buzzer.

The silence seemed to go on forever; when it continued, she pressed it again. And again. On the third go, she swore.

> I'm outside!
> Are you in?

The messages had been delivered but not read. She pressed the call button, instead, feeling a little silly, but the phone rang off. She hung up on Jamie's slightly stilted answerphone message, frustration fizzing in her temples.

She was unsure what to do next. It would be strange of him to pretend he was having a night in when he wasn't; perhaps he'd just popped to the shops. But she couldn't bank on him being minutes when he might be hours. She felt a shudder of frustration – this evening was important, Paddy and Georgie tasting the food, and taking pictures of some of the dishes for the website. She gripped her phone, willing him to reply, but he still hadn't read any of her messages. Her mind swum at the prospect of trying to explain this to Georgie and Paddy.

She lurked there for another ten or so minutes, ringing the bell a few more pointless times, praying he'd appear, until she finally admitted defeat and walked back to her sister's with her tail between her legs.

When Georgie opened the door this time, she was both dressed and made up, eyes ringed with liner, damp hair curling at her temples, and Anya felt even more woeful by comparison.

'I don't—' Anya started, but Georgie ignored her and called out over her shoulder.

'It's her.' She turned back to face Anya, a quizzical eyebrow raised. 'You have some explaining to do.'

'What?' But Georgie had walked off, into the kitchen, and Anya followed, uneasy. In the living room, she spotted Paddy on Georgie's sofa.

'Hi Paddy.' Beside him sat the big red cool bag containing Anya's food. 'Wait – how?'

Georgie had joined Paddy on the sofa. Before their united front, Anya felt teenaged and disgraced.

'Well, it's a weird story actually.' Paddy seemed to be

enjoying this. 'A man on the street handed it to me. He said you'd left it in his flat this evening.'

So Jamie had been out trying to find her! Despite everything, she felt a little pleased.

'Oh.'

'So?' Georgie asked, that eyebrow raised again. 'Who is he?'

'What?' Anya tried, weakly, but playing for time wasn't going to work. They both gave her a look.

'OK, fine, I wasn't at home right before this.'

It wasn't a particularly good starting point for the story, but she didn't really know how to explain. Paddy's eyes glinted.

'So, where were you?' he asked.

'Um.' Her stomach sank. 'OK, the guy is Jamie. Kildare. He's a friend from school – you might remember him, Paddy.' He looked blank, so she continued: 'Anyway, we ended up back in touch because he was trying to find Euan Carrick too.' Anya dared another look at them both; Georgie opened her mouth. 'So,' Anya continued before Georgie could speak, 'we've sort of been hanging out, sharing . . . clues. And he wanted to have a drink this evening to talk about . . . a plan' – Paddy looked confused, and made a noise like he was going to interrupt – 'and so I just nipped there first on my way here and left all the food at his. I'd told him I was going to see you and that you lived nearby' – she looked at Georgie and then looked at her feet again – 'although I'm not sure exactly how he found you.'

'I bumped into him outside the Subway,' Paddy supplied.

So, he'd been running around in search of Anya – she'd wondered why he didn't have his phone.

'At least now we have the food.' There was a muted silence. Paddy and Georgie exchanged a glance and Anya felt her temper flicker. She sank into an armchair opposite them and waited for further inquisition.

'I thought we agreed that the Euan Carrick idea was a bad one,' Georgie started. Paddy frowned, so she added: 'Remember Euan? She suggested looking him up, we told her in no uncertain terms not to do so . . .'

Paddy clicked his fingers.

'Yes! I remember now.' His face changed to one of pity. 'Oh, Anya.'

'It's not like that!' she said, hotly. 'Jamie's also looking for Euan. His dad's just died and he's a bit of a mess about it.' That was a mistake: Paddy's pitying face turned sceptical. 'And he suggested we join forces to try and track him down. Like detectives.'

She'd meant the last part as a joke, to try and nudge the conversation back into her control, but Paddy and Georgie didn't go for it.

'It's harmless, really.' She shouldn't tell them about Aberdeen. Or golf.

'Jamie who?' Georgie asked, eventually.

'Kildare,' Anya repeated. 'Used to hang around with Euan and all that lot.'

Georgie screwed up her face, trying to remember, but she shrugged.

'Don't remember him.'

'He was a bit . . . unknowable in school. But he's changed. He's nice – funny.'

And he had run down the wet pavements of a dark Glasgow to bring her all the food she'd left in his flat.

'But what do you mean *track Euan down*?' Paddy's eyes were narrowed again.

Anya shrugged. 'We've both put out feelers. In a sort of co-ordinated way.'

Georgie shook her head.

'But what does that *mean*?'

'Well' – Anya hesitated – 'last week we went up to Aberdeen, to his old flat.' She said the last part in a rush.

'What?' Paddy asked sharply.

'We just popped up to see if any of the neighbours had a forwarding address for him. Or something.'

'You just popped up to Aberdeen.' Georgie eyed her beadily.

'That's a bit weird, Anya,' Paddy said flatly.

'Well, we also had lunch and stuff,' Anya tried lamely.

'And did you find anything?' Paddy.

'No. It was a bit of a wasted trip.'

'To Aberdeen?' Georgie.

Anya decided she would definitely avoid mentioning Gleneagles.

Paddy narrowed his eyes. 'Is it a sex thing?'

'No!'

He looked unconvinced.

'Not at all. It's purely professional. We're just helping each other.' She heard how it sounded. 'I mean, we're just looking for an old friend. It's a bit unconventional, but there's nothing sinister – *or sexual* – about it.' She added, sulkily: 'I'm an adult, you know. I don't need minding.'

'You do,' said Paddy at the same time as Georgie said, 'Of course, you don't.'

This time Anya folded her arms.

'Look,' Georgie started in earnest. 'We know you're not a baby' – she gave Paddy a hard stare – 'but you've also had a rough couple of months and we just wanted to make sure you weren't doing something . . .'

'Weird,' Paddy supplied. 'Which you are.'

Anya opened her mouth in indignation, then closed it again. Whatever she was doing with Jamie, she had to concede it was a little unorthodox.

'*But* as long as you're fine' – Georgie gave Paddy another look – 'then it's up to you what you do.'

'Thanks,' Anya said, sullenly, and then regretted it. 'Sorry.'

There was another suspended silence.

'And he's definitely not a weirdo.' Georgie.

'No! He's just a regular man. Who was so concerned about you lot having your dinner that he ran around in the dark trying to get it to you.'

Paddy gave her another sceptical look, but Georgie had clearly decided the matter was closed. Or at least, ajar for now. She stood up.

'Are you going to show us said dinner then?'

Anya smiled a small smile.

'Yes, please.' She stood up and took the cool bag from the sofa. Paddy didn't say anything, but he stood up to help, which Anya considered a peace offering. They walked towards the kitchen half of the kitchen-living room.

Georgie's flat was on the first floor of an appealing old

tenement building, which had been modernized inside. The flat was small but perfectly appointed, and the living room area cosy: always warm, plenty of thick rugs and cushions adorning every surface. Sometimes, when Anya felt that peculiar homesickness of adulthood, the longing not for a place so much as for a feeling, of the happiness that used to come more easily, it was Georgie's sofa she'd go to. She'd pitched up often at Georgie's over the past few years, looking for solace. Perhaps she and Connor had not been as happy as she'd believed. Well, obviously he hadn't been, but perhaps she hadn't been either. Acknowledging this felt like a future cautiously opening up ahead of her.

'So, what are we having?' Paddy was practically buzzing; she suspected his severity was at least partly hunger.

She had opened the coolbag to examine the containers. Luckily, everything looked like it had travelled fairly well.

'This one is okra bhajis with a creamy spinach and artichoke dip. We should heat the bhajis up.' She handed the box to Georgie. 'One forty with fan.'

Obediently, Georgie started placing bhajis on an oven tray.

'Then we have a zesty butter bean salad, courgette and halloumi fritters. Actually, let's heat those too.' She pointed at the remaining boxes. 'That's an asparagus frittata, and we have gooey avocado brownies to finish.'

'Wow.' Paddy slung an arm around her shoulder. 'I've forgiven you already.'

She avoided his eyes, but felt better.

For a few moments, they worked together plating up and passing cutlery. Anya took pictures – she wanted some 'action' shots for her website – and Georgie opened a bottle of wine. While the fritters and bhajis heated up, they returned to the sofa and armchair.

'Is Elspeth in?' Anya never relished seeing Georgie's flatmate.

'No, she's at her boyfriend's.'

'Elspeth has a boyfriend?'

'Yes, he's an acupuncturist. Lives in Edinburgh.'

When the oven beeped, Georgie leapt up and Anya followed her, keen to ensure the food was arranged perfectly on Georgie's best plates. They brought it over to the sofas.

'Wait!' Anya held up a palm as Paddy leaned towards a bhaji. 'Please can I take a photo first.'

He leaned back again.

'How do you want them arranged?' Georgie had her head cocked to one side.

'Well, if you could move that magazine' – Georgie obliged – 'and then maybe put the plate so it's covering that stain.' Georgie obliged again. 'There! That looks good.'

Anya captured a few shots of the food, pausing to rearrange the biggest, most even fritter on the plate.

'OK, I've got it.' She'd borrowed her dad's big proper camera for the occasion. Photography was his semi-retirement hobby, and the camera's memory card revealed a few sweet, unspectacular pictures of tomatoes and one of her mother, beaming from the sofa in Balfron, which had made Anya's heart seize up when she saw it.

'Hooray.' Paddy reached for a fritter and Anya watched

anxiously as he took a bite; he screwed up his face in disgust and her stomach plummeted.

'Anya, I'm kidding. This is delicious.'

Georgie made an appreciative noise through a mouthful of butter beans.

'It's great.'

'Thank you!'

After a few more appreciative noises, Paddy said: 'I'm sorry for calling you weird. And I'm not just apologizing because you have — eventually — fed us.'

'It's fine.' She laughed, relieved. 'I mean, it is weird.'

They both gave her a slightly indulgent smile. Everyone was playing nice.

'I did do something bad, though.' They both looked alarmed again, so she added: 'Well, silly.'

Anya made a face and then swallowed hard.

'Don't kill me, but I accidentally drunk one of Claire's bottles of expensive wine.'

'Oh, Anya.' Georgie clutched her face.

'I didn't realize it was so expensive. I thought I could just replace it.'

'How expensive?'

'About a hundred pounds, I think.'

'That's probably one of the ones she was saving for the wedding. They had a few bottles they were going to serve at the top table.'

Anya's stomach dropped. Paddy was trying very hard not to look amused.

'You should replace it.'

'I will. I'll save up to buy her a new one.'

'When did you drink it?' Paddy had a funny look on his face.

'I . . . well, it was the wine I took to Jamie's this evening.'

Paddy nodded.

'She's probably already clocked it.' Georgie sighed.

'I was cooking and I didn't have time to run out and get any.' She chewed her lip. 'Are you mad at me?' This was directed at Georgie.

'No . . . it's just. With Claire. You always manage to do something and then I'm in the middle of it.'

'I know. I'm sorry.'

Unsubtly, Paddy took this as his cue to return to the kitchen for seconds.

'Georgie—'

'It's fine. Worse things happen at sea.'

On cue, Anya snorted. This was one of their mother's favourite sayings. Irene would utter it with feeling, casting a meaningful gaze into the middle distance, as if she had personally witnessed countless terrible – almost unspeakable – things at sea. As far as Anya was aware, the only time her mother had been 'at sea' were the times she'd got the CalMac ferry to her friend Allison's second home in Arran.

'Sorry,' Anya whispered again, earning a smile.

The rest of the meal was also well received and extensively photographed. Paddy's favourite were the fritters; Georgie's the bhaji. Eventually, Anya even relaxed enough to enjoy her own food, which she agreed was good, although might have been better without its multiple detours en route.

Paddy and Georgie washed up while Anya placed three brownies on a plate.

'Thank you so much for being my guinea pigs.'

'It was hardly work.' Paddy stifled a hiccup.

They settled into their seats again, each armed with a brownie.

'Oh, while I remember, I didn't get the job,' Paddy said lightly, picking a crumb from his jumper.

He was pretending not to care, because that was his style.

'Oh, Paddy!' Anya grimaced. 'I'm sorry.'

'It's all right.' He shrugged. 'I'm disappointed – obviously – because I'd really talked myself into wanting it. But it went to an outside hire, apparently, so at least I won't have to sit with the humiliation that Mrs Cricklewood got it over me.'

She nodded understandingly.

'And it would have involved bigger responsibilities, like having to chaperone the S_3 activities field trip to Abernethy in September.' Loyally, Anya made a face. 'Which would definitely have involved abseiling. So maybe it's for the best.'

'There'll be another one.'

'One day. If I didn't get it, it wasn't the right job.' He had said this last part with the air of a guru espousing a deep philosophy, and also the air of someone who'd been saying it to themselves a fair bit since they got the news.

'Exactly. Plenty more jobs in the sea. Or something.'

It was Georgie's cue to say something encouraging, but she missed her beat; curled into the armchair, she was absorbed in her phone, fingers flying, a funny smile on her face.

'Georgie?' Anya poked her sister's chair with a toe. 'What are you doing?'

'What?'

'Who are you texting?' Paddy sounded delighted.

'Um.' There were pink spots high on Georgie's cheekbones, but she looked quite pleased.

'Who?' Anya prompted.

'Remember that night we went to the Loft, and Anya was a mess about Connor?' Georgie stopped briefly to bask in Anya's glare. 'And you dared me to chat to that barman?'

Paddy shrugged.

'Vaguely.'

'Well, he asked me out! We went on a date last week and we're going on another one.'

This was a big deal. Georgie was an unenthusiastic dater.

'Oh my God, you pulled the barman!' Anya said.

'Oh shut up,' Georgie said, but she sounded delighted, and Anya felt a rush of love for her sister.

'What's his name then?' Paddy asked.

'Alex.' She smiled shyly. 'He's coming for dinner.'

Paddy and Anya shrieked.

'Will we get free drinks at the Loft?' Paddy asked, while Anya nodded eagerly.

'Let's not get ahead of ourselves.'

'Do you want me to cook you something for your dinner?' Anya asked.

'Would you actually?' Georgie's eyes were big.

'Of course. It can be payback for . . . well, the tab's pretty big.'

'Oh, shut up,' Georgie said. 'But yes, I would love that. You know I'm a useless cook.'

'Of course. I'll come up with a menu and send it over for your approval. When's the date?'

'Thursday.'

Anya nodded.

'Consider it done.'

Georgie took another bite of brownie. 'I'm especially glad these ended up here after their adventure.'

'Yes, I wouldn't want this Jamie eating our food,' Paddy said.

Fearful of further cross-examination, Anya unfolded her legs and made for the sink, carrying the brownie plate.

Paddy had waited until she returned.

'I will say though, it's a bit of a shame it's not a sex thing, really. He's hot.'

19

Central Glasgow was quiet at this time on a Sunday morning; just the odd taxi driver smoking outside his cab, or twenty-somethings plugged in, hoods up high, quick marching up and down the long streets. Unusually for a mid-October morning in the west of Scotland, it was a glorious day: cold, but still and sunny, the cerulean sky marred by just a few feathery, faraway clouds. Good golf weather, Anya supposed, although she wouldn't know. She scanned the sparse streets near Queen Street Station for Jamie's face.

After his heroics on Friday, she was really looking forward to seeing him. She'd texted ('YOU'RE A LIFESAVER X') when she got home from Georgie's on Friday, a little drunk. Yesterday, she had made an olive oil cake with almond flour and amaretto (a good distraction from the mild hangover lashing her temples), and she had some with her, boxed up and wrapped carefully in greaseproof paper.

He was a few minutes late; Anya tugged at her quilted coat. She hadn't known what on earth to wear to a recon mission at Gleneagles Golf Club and feared that she looked like one of the women in her mother's gardening club in jeans, sensible flat boots, a light red knit and a coat she suspected in fact *belonged* to her mother. She had also, in a misguided moment, cut her own fringe in the mirror with a set of nail scissors. It was definitely lopsided.

Before she could worry again about its asymmetry, she spotted Jamie, who was hurriedly taking the corner of George Square. As he got closer, she noticed that the stubble was growing back, and that he was carrying a set of golf clubs over one shoulder. He didn't yet seem to have noticed her. Feeling self-conscious, she busied herself with her coffee, took a slug and promptly dribbled it down the front of the quilted coat. She was still wiping her chin with the back of her hand when Jamie appeared in front of her, beaming, a hand raised in friendly salute.

'Sorry I'm late.' He swung the golf bag around and placed it on the ground.

'You're not really.' She presented the container. 'And before we go anywhere, please accept these as a token of my appreciation for Friday.'

Quizzical, he took the box and snapped the lid.

'Oh!'

'Thank you so much. It was so kind of you to—'

'Don't' – he waved a dismissive hand – 'sorry I didn't text, I ran out without my phone. Then I realized I didn't know where I was going, so started going back for it – at which point I bumped into a very confused Paddy, coming out of the Subway.'

'Ah. He was definitely confused.'

'Sorry. He definitely didn't remember me. Can I have one of these now? I meant to say, I had the brownie when I got back from my mission and it was superb.'

He fumbled with the container and she noticed he had a thick sticking plaster on his finger.

'Wow.' He took another bite. 'This is really good.'

She was pleased to see the lop-sided grin.

'The secret ingredient is my eternal gratitude. What happened to your hand?'

Jamie raised it carelessly.

'Oh. I sliced it open when I was sharpening a knife yesterday. You'd actually inspired me to attempt to cook. But I ended up with five stitches.'

'Shit!'

'There was a lot of blood.'

Anya imagined Jamie in his very clean kitchen, dribbling blood all over the very white surfaces.

'What were you making?' she asked, curiously.

'Trying to make spag bol for a few people. Safe to say it didn't work out.'

'Did you have anyone to go with you? To A&E?' She'd only thought a little about Jamie's life outside . . . well, her.

'Yes. My friend Elsa came. She's good in a crisis.'

She wondered about Elsa's other characteristics.

He shouldered the golf bag again. 'Anyway, shall we go in? I haven't bought a ticket yet.'

'Yes' – she blinked – 'of course.'

He led the way with those long strides. Queen Street Station was calm and the hush – and the tall, modern vaulted ceilings – reminded Anya of a cathedral. Besides a blue-coated member of staff and a cluster of hearty young men and women in hiking boots, tucking into tinfoil-wrapped breakfast sandwiches, they had most of the concourse to themselves. They stopped near a clutch of empty ticket machines, and he dropped the club bag again.

'That's some serious equipment.' Anya nodded at it.

'I managed to get a tee time! And a reservation at the Dormy, which I'm told does good pizza.'

'Great! I can get the tickets. I owe you by now.'

'I'm not sure. I believe that wine was pretty expensive.'

On cue, Anya squirmed.

She had only seen Claire a couple of times since Friday night: once on the stairs yesterday afternoon, when Claire had told Anya not to wear her shoes indoors; and again in the kitchen in the evening, when Claire had told Anya not to chew so loudly. She'd managed not to snap back, but only because she knew Richard had been sleeping on the sofa. She'd found him there asleep one morning, his phone in his hand. It definitely didn't seem like a good time to mention the wine.

'To tell you the truth, I didn't technically know that wine was so expensive because I stole it from my cousin.'

'Oh dear.' He looked amused. 'I hope she didn't mind.'

Anya grimaced. 'She doesn't know yet. But, she's not my biggest fan as it is, so this will be further confirmation that she's right to prefer my sister.'

'I prefer her too.'

'Oh, ha ha.' But Anya grinned.

As she was buying the tickets, Jamie moseyed off to get a coffee and Anya watched the group of hikers. They all appeared to have paired off into couples, helping their partner locate backpacks and walking sticks and cagoules. Anya remembered the time she and Connor had taken a hiking holiday to the Cairngorms: he'd twisted an ankle on the first day, just as they reached the highest, midway point of their walk, and she'd had to serve as a pair of human crutches for the whole way back down, which had taken twice as long. Still, they'd been loopy about each other then, so loopy that they'd go on a drizzly holiday in the Cairngorms in which one of them came home half-lame and consider it a triumph. Remembering this trip felt like thinking of two people she'd never met before, so she stopped.

'Here you go.' Jamie had reappeared. 'It's platform three. Four minutes. Shall we go get seats?'

'Let's do it.'

They started off in the direction of the platform, Anya's boots making a squeak on the concourse floor.

Their train looked like it would be fairly quiet, the other passengers filing up the platform numbering a few lone travellers and two small groups of ruddy-faced, barrel-chested middle-aged men, several carting their own golf bags, presumably going to Gleneagles, too. Midway down a carriage near the front of the train, she remembered Jamie's kit and turned, but he had already heaved the clubs up the steps and was fitting the bag into the luggage hold near the doors.

Anya slid into the window seat, at a table halfway up the carriage; and Jamie took the seat opposite, knocking her legs under the table as he arranged his.

'Sorry.'

When the whistle blew and the train started drifting out of the station, Jamie raised his eyebrows.

'Here we go, then.'

They both stared out of the window, Anya feeling the thrill of adventure as she watched the train fly past first the modern spires of the city centre and then on to the tangle of suburbs and the greenery beyond. As the scenery became reassuringly uniform, Jamie drew his gaze from the glass and began to fiddle with the dressing on his finger.

'Don't fidget with that!' He blinked, and she added, apologetically, 'It won't heal properly, that's all.'

'Sorry. Automatic.'

'Will you be able to play golf?'

'Not well, but I couldn't before either.'

'Does it hurt?'

'It did at the time.'

'Was there a lot of blood?'

'Lots.'

'That sounds horrible.'

'It's all right. Perhaps my scar will make me look cool and dangerous.'

She snorted, and he looked pleased.

'I remember Euan once split his head open on a radiator at a party.' She had mopped his clammy forehead with a fistful of loo roll.

'Yes, I remember that. I was there too. I think I took him to A&E in the end.'

'Oh, sorry.' She shook her head, feeling silly. 'I didn't realize.'

'Well, as discussed, we didn't really know each other that well.' But he smiled.

'No.' She smiled back. 'Just think, we could have been a three!'

'I think I'd have felt like a third wheel.' The way he tilted his head made Anya feel self-conscious.

'Hardly.'

The train had slowed at a red signal; a few moments later, another train whipped past in the opposite direction.

'So, do you think he's married with two kids by now?'

She'd assumed he'd find that funny too – Euan,

kids – but he didn't respond, although she could see his eyes reflected in the glass.

'Jamie?'

'Sorry' – he shook his head – 'what?'

'Are you OK?'

'I'm great.' He mimed delight but she felt a little wrong-footed and didn't push it. They settled back into silence, Jamie with his head resting against the window again, face angled slightly away from Anya. After half an hour or so, Anya daydreaming about not very much as she watched the green hills roll into blue sky, they began to close in on Gleneagles: she could see the slope of golf courses in the distance.

She waved at Jamie across the table, and he raised a questioning eyebrow.

'It looks like we're almost there.'

'It does.'

'So, what's the plan?'

He smiled and sat up industriously.

'We'll have lunch and then I got a tee time of two thirty, which means we'll be just behind Craig and the rest of them on the course. Hopefully we can at least whittle it down to the right group of golfers, for a start.'

'We were going to look them up!' She wished she hadn't spent the journey staring out of the window.

Jamie nodded.

'I've actually tried Craig already. Not a lot out there. If he's on Facebook, I couldn't find him.'

'Like father, like son.'

'Exactly.' Jamie laughed. 'But we could try the others. A clue about what one of them looks like would be a good start.'

Anya dug out her mother's email.

'Let's split them. You take the top three, I'll take the bottom three.'

Their research produced a LinkedIn profile of a man who looked like the right Ruaridh Bell, and a message on the NextDoor website by a man called Angus Duncan – although not necessarily their one – complaining about a noisy lawnmower.

They both examined Ruaridh Bell's professional history on Anya's phone screen.

'Yet again,' she began, 'I find myself feeling a little creepy.'

'We're in too deep now.'

'Shame the picture's so small.'

'Yes. And that he's bald. Hair would have been a more useful clue.'

He looked pleased when she sniggered.

When the train drew into the station, Jamie climbed out of his seat and stretched, exposing a flash of abdomen that Anya pointedly avoided staring at. She followed him down the carriage, where he retrieved his bag and propped it on the small platform. Everywhere, there were men of a certain age, and billboard adverts for fine Scotch.

'I arranged a cab,' Jamie said, when Anya had finished anxiously patting every pocket on her body to check she had her iPhone.

'Amazing.'

They carried on through the station concourse to a small car park out the front, in which stood a wiry man holding a sign reading: JAMIE KILDARE. The drive was short; as they pulled up the driveway of Gleneagles Hotel – a grand grey lady, a fountain bubbling in the driveway and manicured lawns as far as the eye could see – Anya felt a giddy wave of nerves.

'Thanks, pal,' Jamie said heartily.

Anya's father also used 'pal' when he was trying to appear relaxed with taxi drivers, pub landlords and handymen, and she pressed her lips together, suspecting now was not the time to laugh. As soon as Jamie had taken his golf bag out of the boot, the man accelerated back down the gravel path, dust clouding in his wake.

'I'm kind of nervous,' she said. He was occupied, untangling the handles of the bag. 'Can I help with that?'

'No' – he heaved it on to his shoulder – 'I'm all good. Let's go.'

She tried to keep stride with his long, loping ones. The hotel was imposing, its white-trimmed windows like so many eyes, so Anya looked at her feet instead.

Dormy's, the restaurant they were booked in at, appeared to be a plush holding pen for a menagerie of untamed children and their golf widow mothers, most of whom were sat at a single long table, glasses of Sauvignon filled to the brim, pizza untouched, ignoring their children. They all looked like Aimee, and Anya was fairly certain the twins would be right at home with this crowd, several of whom were drawing in crayon on the linen tablecloths, others mashing pizza into wide-eyed younger siblings' faces, or drizzling ice cream down the emerald banquettes.

Still, the service was efficient, and their pizzas and beers appeared quickly. From their perfectly positioned table, they watched the chaos unfold. As one child darted across the restaurant and almost collided with a waiter, Jamie nodded at the mothers.

'So, which one do you think is Ruaridh's second wife?'

Anya chewed a crust and considered the line-up. Eventually, she settled on a bottle blonde wearing a yellow sleeveless T-shirt that read, 'Eat, sleep, yoga, repeat'.

'Her.' She pointed the crust at the woman.

'Yes.' Jamie nodded. 'Good.'

'This morning, he took the kids while she went to a two-hour Bikram class. Golf is his reward.'

'When they got together he had hair,' he said. 'Not loads, but enough.'

'Oh yeah. He doesn't know it yet, but she's getting him plugs for Christmas. On the joint credit card.'

Jamie cracked up at this and she grinned in reply.

'Which one of those kids do you think will be first to get expelled from their private school?'

He surveyed the candidates.

'Toss up between the one waterboarding a toddler with Fanta, and the one who's definitely stealing a purse from that handbag.'

Sure enough, one of the elder children – Anya put him at about nine – had his sticky little mitt inside what looked like a very expensive crocodile handbag.

'Good shout.'

'How's your pizza?'

'Very good.' Anya had selected some sort of vegetarian extravaganza.

'Could you do better?'

'I'm OK at pizza, actually. But it's quite labour intensive.'

'Easier just to get one delivered.' He tilted his head and, fleetingly, the gesture reminded her of Connor, but it passed. 'You've never worked in food before you started your business?'

'Well, as a teenager I was a waitress, which is sort of where I got into food in the first place.' He had a sweet concentration face, and it emboldened her. 'Fancy events stuff, mainly. Silver service at charity things and galas. Whatever a gala is. Anyway, most people I worked with hated it, but I loved seeing what the chefs created.'

'I think I'd have been with the others on that job.'

'It was fun! Anyway, when I graduated I meandered a little, like everyone does. And I wasn't as good at cooking then as I am now. At the time it felt like more of a hobby. Also, my parents wanted me to get a real job.'

'What do they think now?'

'They still want me to get a real job.'

He smiled.

'Anyway' – she straightened her knife and fork, which she'd placed on her plate – 'what time is it?'

Jamie consulted his watch.

'Time we got going.'

'I'm nervous,' she said again.

'Don't be. We're just two friends here to play a round of golf.'

'That isn't very reassuring.'

They split the bill in a hurry. When Anya stood up to leave the restaurant, she realized she was a little giddy from her lunchtime beers.

'Are you going to be over the limit for driving the golf buggy?'

'It's widely accepted that two beers is the sweet spot for driving a golf buggy.'

They were passing the woman in the yellow yoga T-shirt, who glared at them.

'I think she knows you're looking for her husband,' Jamie said, when they were barely out of earshot. Anya giggled.

They did a quick detour via the reception of the golf clubhouse, while Jamie changed his shoes and ditched his things in a locker. When the door to the men's changing rooms swung open, Jamie emerged in a pair of chinos and a pair of golf shoes that made her snort with laughter again.

'Nice shoes. Wish you'd brought me a pair.'

'Don't worry, we're getting yours next.'

He started walking towards the small reception, where a very bored teenage girl was sitting. At the sight of them both, she raised a heavily pencilled eyebrow. Jamie was also looking at Anya expectantly.

'What size are your feet?' he prompted.

'A five, but I don't need—'

Wordlessly, the girl disappeared under a desk and re-appeared moments later with the shoes.

'Lockers are in the changing room,' the girl said. When Anya reappeared, Jamie looked delighted.

'Shut up.'

'I didn't say a thing.'

Gleneagles was magnificent, a gently sloping green as far as the eye could see, although Anya had already heard rather too many American accents that day for her liking. The sun was blazing, and a light breeze occasionally lifted her hair across her eyes. She hoped the winter sunshine was too weak for her to get sunburned.

Jamie had clocked her expression.

'The King's Golf Course is very famous. Eighteen holes.'

'Oh good, I was hoping there'd be a tour.'

He was about to retort when a member of liveried staff pulled up in a golf buggy – smart and sporty, with plush white seats and a front bonnet printed with the Gleneagles logo.

'Good afternoon, sir.' He stepped out of the buggy. 'This one will be yours.'

Jamie placed a hand on the roof and Anya struggled not to giggle. Everything was suddenly very funny – especially Jamie, who had assumed a face of serious concentration while the teenager ran them through the instructions for how to manoeuvre the machine. Anya didn't even notice when he'd finished.

'Got it?' the liveried man challenged.

She smiled sweetly at him. 'Loud and clear. Thank you.'

With a dubious look in her direction, the man loped off back towards the clubhouse. Anya climbed into the passenger's seat and looked at Jamie expectantly.

'We have to hit a ball first.'

'Oh.' She kept forgetting the golf wasn't just subterfuge.

Jamie placed a ball on the tee, and took a few minutes selecting a particular club from his bag. Eventually, after a few practice strokes, his legs apart and slightly bent – golf really was a sport invented for the middle-aged and generous of girth, Anya reflected – he knocked the ball clean into the sky.

'Did you see where it went?' she asked.

He put a hand over his eyes and surveyed the course.

'Just about.' He lifted his bandaged hand aloft. 'Not bad considering I'm limited by this. Anyway' – he approached the buggy and swung into the driver's seat – 'time to gain some ground.' He paused. 'Unless you fancy having a shot.'

'No.'

Jamie raised a teasing eyebrow.

'You have to do the next hole.'

They bounced at some pace across the green course, the wind whipping her hair, Jamie taking the corners at full pelt, one hand on the steering wheel, the other resting casually on the roof of the car.

'I bet this is how Formula One drivers feel.' They'd just taken another corner fast, the buggy bouncing on the smooth turf. As they rocketed over a hill, Anya clutched the side of the car.

'If I fall out, you're on your own.'

She was slightly relieved when he parked up at the next hole, until Jamie handed her a club.

'Your turn.'

'I wouldn't even know where to start.'

'Hitting it would be a good place.'

He lined the ball up on the tee and then stepped backwards.

'Off you go.'

Her first attempt she struck nothing; the second she caught the club in the grass and winced.

'You're a natural.'

'Watch out, or I'll club you over the head.'

He raised his hands in surrender, a glint in his eye.

'Try again,' he instructed.

The fifth time, she did manage to hit the ball. It travelled about 100 metres ahead of them. Jamie pretended to peer into the far distance and Anya prodded him with the club.

'I hit it, didn't I?'

'Just about.' He'd already climbed into the golf buggy and pressed the pedal. 'Now hurry up, we need to catch them. And your technique has slowed us down.'

'Hey!' She started running after the car; he in turn started zigzagging across the course, so that every time she almost gained on him, she couldn't quite catch up. Eventually, she was laughing too hard to run and sat down on the grass.

He stopped the buggy. He peeked over his shoulder.

'Aren't you getting in?'

But Anya was distracted by a group ahead of them: identikit fellows, in navy trousers and white golf shoes, distinguished only by the different rainbow hues of their polo shirts, poking out from underneath tweedy jackets and waterproof windbreakers. A few of them leaned on golf bags, surveying the scene, others practised their swing, while one of the number hit a ball from the tee. There were two buggies parked up nearby. Even from a relative distance, Anya thought she could see a bald man who could be Ruaridh Bell.

Jamie followed her gaze. She stood up, brushing the grass from her knees and climbed into the passenger seat.

'Do you think that's them?' Jamie had his eyes fixed on the group.

'There's certainly enough of them. And that guy looks like he could be Ruaridh.'

'The slightly pink head is hard to miss.'

'What do we do?' Her stomach was somersaulting now. 'How do we play this?'

'I think we just tell the truth.' Jamie sounded casual. 'Sort of, anyway. We mention your mum, the alumni parents' newsletter . . .'

'How do we bring up Euan, though?'

Jamie considered this.

'We'll improvise something.'

He started to drive the buggy at a trundle, and it was struggling a little to make its way up the slight incline. He turned sharply to the left and parked up. They were about ten metres away from the group, who so far hadn't paid them even a glance.

They both clambered out of the cart and walked up the rest of the incline. One of the men, a stringy chap in a green polo shirt, navy baseball cap and zip-up windbreaker, nodded at them.

'Sorry – too much gassing and not enough golfing,' he chuckled. 'We shan't be long.'

'No worries!' Anya squeaked.

'Lovely day,' Jamie said.

'Isn't it fine.' The man glowed with pleasure.

'I don't suppose you're the Kelvinbridge Academy group, are you?'

Anya tried not to wince at the baldness of Jamie's enquiry, but the man simply beamed.

'Why, absolutely we are.'

Jamie nodded, pleased.

'Her mother gets the parents' newsletter. She mentioned there'd be a group of you up here today.' Jamie stretched out a hand. 'Jamie Kildare. We went to Kelvin-bridge too.'

'You never!' Anya wondered if the man was about to self-combust with delight. 'I'm Angus Duncan.'

A few of his buddies had noticed them and had turned around; Angus beckoned them all over. Slowly, they all trotted down, most of them looking a little bemused.

'This pair are Kelvinbridge too.' He nodded at Jamie and Anya.

'Jamie Kildare.' He smiled fluently; Anya stepped forward too, mimicking his confidence.

'And I'm Anya. Mackie.'

'This is Adil Khan, Fraser Clarke, Craig Carrick and Ruaridh Bell.' They each nodded pleasantly when introduced. They were a mixture of ages – Adil looked only a little older than them, while Fraser was certainly getting on. Anya was pleased to note she had identified Ruaridh correctly. He wore a navy V-neck jumper, which had an aquamarine shirt collar poking out of the top.

But Jamie was more interested in Craig, a tall, stringy man, who didn't remind her much of Euan at all, with his grey hair, rather satisfied face, chinos and thick bottle green jacket. She could feel Jamie's eyes on the man; she hoped Craig hadn't noticed.

'So, when did you finish up at Kelvinbridge?' Adil asked, pleasantly.

'2007,' Anya replied.

'A long time after me,' Fraser said, and they all laughed heartily; Anya and Jamie joining in, a little less heartily. When the laughter tailed off, they all blinked expectantly at each other.

'Lovely day, isn't it.' Anya knew Jamie had already said this, but she couldn't remember her script.

He could, though.

'Now, wait' – Jamie frowned, playing his role – 'was it Craig Carrick, did you say?'

'Aye,' he said evenly. His voice was low and earthy; Anya felt a little self-conscious as he examined them both with big grey eyes, cast in shadow by his navy baseball cap.

'You're not by any chance related to Euan Carrick, are you?' Jamie asked.

'Afraid not.' His tone was starchily polite, and his smile didn't reach his eyes.

Anya's heart sank into her toes, while Jamie continued pointlessly.

'Ah, that's a shame. We were at Kelvinbridge at the same time as him – he was a good friend. We've actually been trying to get in touch with him recently.'

There was a rather awkward pause, in which Angus and Ruaridh glanced between Craig and Jamie, nodding eagerly.

'Ah.' Craig couldn't be bothered to sound interested. 'Well, I'm afraid he's not one of mine.' Another of those smiles that didn't reach his eyes. Jamie looked like he might have been about to say something, but Anya cut in, unable to bear it suddenly.

'Never mind!' A game smile. There was another awkward pause.

'Well' – Angus waved a four iron with intent – 'I guess we'll be getting on so we don't keep you.' On cue, the group started to scatter, with a few mumbles about the 'early sunset'. Craig turned towards the tee again, and

Anya tried very hard not to look at Jamie. Eventually, only Angus remained. He smiled.

'Sorry, Craig keeps himself to himself a bit. He's the newest member of our little golf group. Didn't know him at school, myself – few years after me, I think. Anyway, you're too young to know my lot, I reckon. Catriona and Ross Duncan?'

Jamie and Anya looked politely mystified.

'Och, I thought so. They'd have been a good few years above you both. Both married now – Catriona with two little boys.' They both looked apologetic, so he added: 'Well, it was lovely to meet you all the same. We'll not be keeping you.' He cupped his mouth, and called out, 'Come on boys, you hit your balls so these two can get away.' He bustled away up the hill after the rest of them, Anya and Jamie following a few awkward paces behind.

There was a renewed sense of industry around the tee, and Anya and Jamie watched sheepishly as they waited for Ruaridh's gang to hit their balls. After the last ball was hit, Angus clapped his hands together and said: 'Well, this hole's all yours then.'

'Thank you,' Anya said.

'Lovely to meet you,' he added, with feeling, as he gathered his golf bag. The other polo shirts had lost interest now, although Ruaridh offered a shy salute as he walked off, and Anya felt mean they'd teased him. One by one, they climbed into the two golf buggies and pootled – swerving a little – on to the next hole.

As his car staggered into the distance, Craig turned around and fixed them both with those big grey eyes, and didn't break the gaze until he'd disappeared from sight.

20

Back on the train, Anya slid into her window seat, and Jamie took the one opposite. They'd abandoned the golf after the mission collapsed, returned the buggy to the clubhouse and caught a taxi back to the station, muted all the way, the anti-climax ringing in Anya's ears. As the train pulled out of Gleneagles station, Jamie sighed for the umpteenth time that hour.

'Well, at least we settled one thing.' He was fiddling with his bandage again. 'Golf is really boring.' Anya smiled tightly. 'But driving a golf buggy is quite fun.'

'Seven out of ten,' she said. 'Would probably do again.'

The train was gathering pace, the landscape rushing in reverse, and they both sat in their disappointment for a little while, watching the dusk land on the horizon beyond. She could see Jamie's face reflected in the glass of the window, his dark brows knitted across his forehead.

'I really thought that was going to work.' She fiddled with an earring, the metal smooth between thumb and forefinger. 'I really thought that would turn out to be Euan's dad.'

'Me too.'

'For a wild moment, I almost wondered if Craig was lying. I was so convinced that he was going to be the right person that when he said he wasn't Euan's dad, I didn't really believe him.'

'Yeah.' He wasn't looking at her.

'And did you see the way he watched us as his buggy drove off?'

'No.' He looked at her now. 'What do you mean?'

'I don't know – it was weird. He had his eyes on us until he finally vanished from sight. And he wasn't very friendly.'

Jamie made a non-committal noise.

'I suppose he did seem quite prickly.'

'Maybe I should have made a scene.'

This earned a dull, defeated smile.

'I'd have enjoyed that.'

'Although we might have been escorted off the premises.'

'Banned from golf for life.' But his dark eyes didn't sparkle as she'd hoped they would.

Down the carriage, an advancing inspector called for 'tickets, please' in a sing-song voice and they both fumbled for theirs. Anya placed hers on the table in full view and then continued.

'So what next? I guess I still have to try the school.'

'Yeah.' He didn't sound very enthusiastic. 'I suppose we could try that.'

The ticket inspector appeared at Anya's shoulder and checked both their tickets before bustling away to the next carriage.

'Or – is there anything else obvious we're missing? What about your other leads?'

Jamie shrugged.

'I don't really have any. School is the only place I can think of. And it seems a bit of a long shot.'

His disinterest stung and it showed on her face.

'I'm sorry.' He leaned forward. 'It's just. Well. Maybe this is all getting a little silly.'

'Oh.' Her stomach plummeted. 'But—'

'It was my idea, I know. And it's been . . . fun. But, well, we're not really getting anywhere.'

'Like I said, we could try the school—'

'Yeah,' Jamie interrupted. 'But if Euan's not on Facebook, then I doubt he's bothered to send his old school a forwarding address. I'm not saying we have to give it up, just that at some point we might have to accept defeat. It looks like he's quite good at disappearing.'

She frowned.

'What—'

'Sorry,' he interrupted. 'I just mean, that he clearly doesn't want to be found. So the point of defeat, well, it might be approaching.'

There was something in his expression she couldn't quite decode; she felt a little unsettled. But she nodded and shrugged.

'Of course. We can't do this forever.'

He was right, of course; Euan could, theoretically, be anywhere, and they hadn't really learned anything, besides the fact he once violated the terms of a tenancy, making an enemy of a landlord called Ally in the process, and that he didn't have a father called Craig. If Euan was her star-crossed soulmate, he was making it pretty hard for them to realize their fairytale ending.

She caught Jamie's eye and he smiled a little unconvincingly.

'I'll try the school,' she said quietly. 'One last shot. I know it's probably a non-starter, but we might as well.'

'Of course.' He nodded. 'And we can keep our ears to the ground. I just don't know if it's worth us spending every weekend criss-crossing Scotland in hot pursuit of red herrings.'

This stung too, although it was true.

'Good point.' But she felt small and a little silly, as though he were humouring her.

The train pulled into Queen Street an hour later, the station quiet except for the sound of a man on a mobile floor-cleaner circling the premises, and they'd disembarked in silence.

'Are you getting the Subway?' Anya was determined to resist the siren song of the taxi rank outside.

'Ah, I'm actually going to meet a friend in town for a pint.'

'Oh.'

'So, I'm going this way.' He shouldered the golf bag. 'With hundreds of pounds of iron clubs. *And* everyone will think I like golf.'

She laughed but her heart wasn't in it.

'OK, well – I'll keep you posted about whether I discover anything at school.'

'Great.' A funny half-wave. 'And thanks for being my caddy.'

'Never again.'

This earned one of his trademark lop-sided grins and then he turned and loped off in the direction of the exit, and she turned the opposite way and descended to the Subway station, wondering who he was meeting and why it bothered her.

Though by the time she was turning the key in the door

at 26 Hamilton Drive, bafflement had turned to irritation. He'd started all this, with his grand pitch at Metropolitan; then turning up here in his car; Aberdeen; booking lunch at Gleneagles. And then, just as she was starting to have fun, he'd decided – without a moment's warning – that he was bored of it, thanks all the same. Suddenly, he felt unknowable again, and she didn't like it at all.

She was puzzling over this when, with a start, she noticed Claire. Her cousin was standing in front of the mirror at the end of the hall, wearing a very strange expression on her face.

'Hi Anya.'

Claire's tone was sharp, as always, but her usually angular face was softer, pinker than it usually was. Anya would almost have said Claire had been crying, although Claire was famously stoic. The time she broke her leg in two different places while playing goalie for the Kelvinbridge under-11s hockey A team and didn't cry once was part of their family's lore.

'Are you OK?' Anya stepped towards her. It was dim in the hallway – as ever – and she peered into Claire's face uncertainly. 'You look—'

'I'm fine,' Claire tried, unconvincingly. She cast an eye up and down Anya's ensemble. 'Where have you been?'

'Um.' Now was not the time to confide in Claire. 'Nowhere important. A walk. For a few hours.'

Claire narrowed her eyes, but the fight seemed to have drained from her.

'Well. Fine.' She sniffed. 'If you see Richard, then let me know.'

'Where did he go?'

'If I knew I wouldn't be asking, would I?'

Anya raised her hands in surrender.

'Sorry.'

Claire pressed a hand to her temple.

'No, I'm sorry . . . it's just. Well. We had a . . . disagreement, that's all. Another one.' A short, mirthless laugh. 'Then he left and . . . he hasn't come back.'

Another disagreement; another strange disappearance. Anya examined Claire again.

'When?'

Claire inhaled deeply. When she spoke, her voice was studiously offhand.

'Last night.'

'Claire . . . are you . . . I mean, where's he gone?'

She fixed Anya with a characteristically withering stare.

'Sorry.' Anya moved towards Claire cautiously, like someone approaching a volatile dog, but her cousin remained still. Emboldened, Anya chanced a quick squeeze of her shoulder, and was rewarded with a very small smile. 'Have you . . . have you . . . I mean, do you want me to help you look for him?'

'I've tried everything. All his friends, his parents. No one knows where he is.'

Anya remembered Richard sleeping on the sofa and keeping his phone in a drawer. 'Do you want something to take your mind off it? We could have a drink – in or out? I could cook us something?'

For a second, she thought Claire was going to bite her head off; instead, she smiled gratefully.

'Some food would be nice.'

What a strange day. While Anya cubed aubergine to

throw into a making-it-up-as-she-went-along pasta sauce, Claire sat at the kitchen table, talking more than Anya could ever remember her talking. She tried to make noises in all the right places.

'And I know he's been under a lot of pressure at work recently and the wedding is coming up and he's decided he doesn't like the venue, and our parents keep adding more guests to the reception, which is making everything even more expensive and I *said* I'd pay for it, but that makes him feel *emasculated*, he says, even though living in the house I bought doesn't seem to bother him at all.'

Claire drew breath and Anya stirred the tomatoey gloop on the stove, before placing a lid on the pan, and returned to the kitchen table.

'Sorry,' Claire said, brusquely. 'For going on like this.'

'Don't be daft.'

Claire sipped her wine and closed her eyes for a few seconds. When she opened them, she seemed a little steelier.

'Where have you really been, anyway?'

Anya hesitated. She leaned back against the counter and watched Claire's face carefully.

'You have to promise you won't laugh.'

Claire raised her eyebrows. 'Were you auditioning for *Britain's Got Talent* or something?'

Anya burst out laughing.

'Claire, where on earth did that come from?'

Claire looked a little pleased.

'I don't know. I ended up watching some ancient episode of it on some channel last night when I didn't know where Richard was. I couldn't concentrate on anything better.'

'I was not auditioning for *Britain's Got Talent*.'

'It was a joke.' Claire still sounded pleased. 'So, what were you doing, then?'

To buy some time, Anya turned her back on Claire and stirred the saucepan.

'I don't suppose you remember Euan Carrick?' She still wasn't looking at Claire.

'That boy from school you really fancied.' She sounded matter-of-fact and Anya's stomach did an involuntary swoop. She turned.

'Was I really that obvious?' Georgie had only dimly remembered.

Claire gave her a look.

'Remember, I was at your house every day after school, Anya.'

'Right.' Anya dreaded to imagine what sort of moony, overly candid lovesick moments Claire could recall. 'Well, anyway, I've sort of been looking for him.' She saw something like alarm flash across Claire's face. 'I know, but it wasn't like that. It was a silly idea. I was a bit drunk and down about Connor – I regretted it the next day. But I'd sent a message that ended up in the hands of Jamie Kildare. He was also at school with us—'

Claire nodded. Two out of two; no wonder she was a lawyer.

'Well, anyway, it turned out he had been looking for Euan too. So, we've spent the last few weeks looking for him together. I don't know why – I got all caught up in it, and then today we ended up in Gleneagles.'

'Hence the weird outfit.'

Claire was definitely feeling better.

'*Anyway*' – Anya gave her a don't-push-it look – 'we thought we'd got a good lead, which turned out to be a red herring, but Jamie suddenly wants to give up on the whole thing. And now I feel annoyed about it. He started it.'

Claire weighed this.

'Why do you want to find Euan?'

'Oh, it's just a silly nostalgia thing. Curiosity. I don't know. Maybe I'm getting old.' She'd hoped Claire might smile at this, but instead her cousin just fixed her with a beady stare. 'And I've been quite enjoying having something going on in my life. Which I know is sad, before you say it.'

'Why don't you just get a new job?'

'I have a job, Claire. I'm a childminder – *and* I've started my own catering business.'

'Oh.' Claire looked put-out. 'I didn't know that.'

'It's fine.'

There was a long pause.

'You should have done that ages ago,' Claire said eventually, clearly irritated. 'You're a very good cook.'

'Thank you.' The compliment was surprising.

Claire shrugged.

'But if you have all that going on, you don't need Euan. Or Jamie.'

'I know.' Anya was stirring the bubbling pasta sauce again, steam warming her face. 'It was just . . . fun.'

'Do you fancy him?' Claire asked.

Anya turned again and dribbled sauce from the wooden spoon on to the floor.

'Euan? No . . . well, obviously I used to, but I'm just curious, really—'

'Not Euan. Jamie. Please wipe that up.'

'What? No!'

Anya reached for a cloth. From the kitchen floor, she added: 'It's nothing like that.'

'I see.' Claire arched an eyebrow and fixed Anya with a penetrating stare. After a moment, she added: 'Well, it all sounds like a silly, pointless distraction. No offence.'

Anya said nothing but returned to the table and took her seat next to Claire again, who pointed at Anya's phone.

'It buzzed.'

'Oh.'

'It's Jamie. I saw.'

'Right.'

'Read it, please.'

I'm sorry – was just a bit disappointed by another wasted trip.
We should definitely try the school. X

Anya placed it facedown on the table.

Later, much later, Richard returned, and Anya made herself scarce so that Claire could read him the riot act. They had started in the hallway of the house, then moved downstairs, and then graduated to the top floor – to their bedroom, where Anya could hear too much of what was being said to feel entirely comfortable. Richard had no explanation, he just needed to *think*, to which Claire replied that he could do his *thinking* here in the house that she'd bought for them; it was this, on a loop, so that after a while, Anya could virtually predict what each one's next line would be.

As the argument continued on its pointless, circular

journey, she grew twitchy and distracted. She'd pick up her phone, unlock it and then drop it again. She tried turning on a silly pop-culture myths podcast (this episode was about Tonya Harding), which she could only half-concentrate on, feeling like a teenager playing music in her bedroom while her parents fought.

She hadn't replied to Jamie yet, because she wasn't sure what she really wanted. Certainly, the prize, Euan, felt more and more like a mirage. Even if they did find him – and where? – was she really going to whip out a scrap of ancient lined paper they'd scrawled on fourteen years ago, and see where that took her?

Still, she'd been having fun, though. Much more fun than she'd expected.

'ANYA!'

It was Richard's voice.

With a deep sigh, she called back.

'YES?'

'CAN YOU COME HERE?'

She sighed again and shuffled to the bedroom door. Richard and Claire were standing on the landing, Claire's arms folded and hackles raised. Richard, meanwhile, was dishevelled in a hoodie and tracksuit bottoms and looked very twitchy.

'What's going on?'

'Richard, leave Anya alone—' Claire sounded quietly furious.

'I just wanted to ask, Anya' – his voice was a hiss – 'when you are planning on moving out? I've thought about it and I'm concerned that your presence here is affecting my sleep.'

'What?!'

Richard stepped towards her, and she noticed his beard was unkempt.

'I'm not kicking you out, I just want a date—'

'Shut up, Richard,' Claire interrupted coldly. 'OK? I own the house, and Anya is my cousin. Therefore, I decide how long she stays. And I would suggest that what's affecting your sleep is you sleeping on the sofa. So maybe if you stop being such an arsehole, I'll stop making you sleep there.'

Richard had turned puce.

'Anya' – Claire fixed her with a cool stare – 'you can go back to your room now.'

Wordlessly, Anya stepped backwards and closed the door behind her, her breathing a little heavy. She stayed leaning against the wall and from the hall, heard their feet on the stairs and Richard whining, 'It's not my fault'. Soon, it was silent again; but it was the kind of calm that made her feel edgy and impetuous. She sat cross-legged on her bed and texted Jamie before the feeling passed.

> It's OK – you were right. Let's call it a day. Let me know next time you need a golf caddy. X

21

It appeared that Aimee had done something to her lips over the weekend. When she opened the door on Monday afternoon, Anya was alarmed to discover they were glossy and swollen. So much so, in fact, that it sounded a little like she was slurring her words.

'Cmern.'

Aimee backed away from the door and Anya – assuming this meant, 'come in' – stepped into the hallway. She started unwrapping her scarf. Aimee was scrutinizing her more closely – which was to say, at all.

A little thrown by the attention, Anya started saying, 'How are you—' but Aimee spoke over her.

'Are you free on the 30th?'

'Um . . . I think so.'

'The twins were talking about something you'd made. A soup or something. And I wondered if you'd do their birthday party.' In Aimee's mouth, 'party' now sounded more like 'putty'.

'I'd love to.' Anya drew her eyes away from the pout. 'Where is it?'

'It's here. There's an entertainer coming, about twenty girls. I was just going to do Waitrose but they like your food better, apparently.' Aimee sniffed, seemingly unable to imagine a world in which anything would be preferred to Waitrose, particularly something created by Anya. 'I'll pay you, of course. And there'll be other mums there – we were going to have some cocktails while the girls watch the clown, so it's probably good networking for your little company.'

'Yes.' Anya decided not to let the 'little' sting. 'It would be. Thank you so much.'

'Well, make sure the food is good.' Aimee picked up one of her identikit quilted handbags from the table in the hallway. 'They're doing their homework in the kitchen.'

This was Anya's cue; without another glance in her direction, Aimee clopped off down the hallway in her heels, and Anya hung her coat on the edge of the banister.

The girls couldn't strictly be said to be 'doing' their homework. In fact, Rachel was scribbling on the front of Rosie's jotter with one hand and holding her twin sister off with the other. Rosie, for her part, was pulling on one of Rachel's pigtails.

'Stop that,' Anya said sharply.

Rachel dropped her pencil and Rosie dropped her sister's pigtail. A little taken aback that this had worked, Anya decided to try her luck.

'Your mum has just asked me to cook for your birthday party next week. So, I thought today we could decide what you want to eat.'

The twins exchanged a glance and then both nodded slowly.

'So, why don't you tell me which of the things I've made you that you liked best.' She tore a piece out of Rosie's jotter, and the girl looked a little scandalized. 'And then' – Anya picked up a blunt pencil from the countertop – 'I can make a note to make them.'

The girls exchanged a seemingly telepathic glance, and then said in unison.

'The soup.'

'The ramen?'

Ramen for twenty eleven- and twelve-year olds would be a feat, but maybe she could rent a huge vat to brew it up in.

'Also, the egg thing,' Rosie said. 'That we made that time.'

'The omelette, OK.' Anya tried not to smile.

'And the dip. With the cracker.'

'Red pepper hummus.' Anya had an encyclopaedic memory for her own recipes.

'And the little ball thing. That had rice.'

'Arancini. Yes, I can do those too.'

'Mum's getting us a big cake,' Rosie said. 'But maybe you can make us a small one.'

'I can make you a smaller cake each, how does that sound?'

'What, so we don't have to share?' Rachel looked suspicious. 'Two cakes?'

'Yeah. Just two small ones, so you can each have your own.'

They nodded again, satisfied.

'I don't want a lemon one,' Rosie said. 'Mum always gets us a lemon one.'

'I promise you, there'll be no lemon.'

While the twins watched, Anya wrote: 'TWO CAKES – NO LEMON!!!' on the piece of paper. She then folded it carefully and put it into her jeans pocket.

'Right – do your homework now.' She nodded at the jotters. 'Properly. And I'll make you a snack.'

On Anya's request, Aimee had started ordering her general dogsbody/housekeeper to stock the fridge with a few things; Anya transformed peas and feta into fritters. The twins overcame their initial concerns about the green hue.

'Do you want me to add these to the list?' Anya asked when they'd stopped eating. She noted there were quite a few fritters left.

They exchanged another telepathic look.

'No thank you,' said Rachel.

You couldn't win them all.

She had agreed with Aimee that she could leave fifteen minutes early that evening. Anya was meeting Paddy outside the school, where he was attending a safeguarding event, to go to the cinema. But almost as soon as she stepped out of the house at Park Circus, he messaged.

Paddy
So sorry but this is going to run on
The person leading it was 40 mins late
Have you left yet?

Anya
Oh no!
Yes, literally just left the twins

Paddy
SO sorry
Is it cold outside?

It was cold, windy and drizzly. Anya stamped her feet and willed the bus – three minutes away – to drive more quickly.

Paddy

Shit

Maybe you could go to the school office and

sign in and wait for me there

It should still be open coz of this event this eve

There's a showing an hour later we'd probably still make

She considered this. It probably wasn't worth going back to Claire's first.

Anya

Ok no worries

The bus appeared and Anya tapped her card and settled on a top-deck seat. Condensation rolled down the inside of the windows, and the vehicle lurched out of its stop and on to the congested road ahead, looping towards the school.

The playground looked strange at this time of night, without the blur of tartan skirts and flying footballs aimed at the big perimeter wall. Usually, when Anya visited Paddy, it was lunchtime and the shrieks and yowls echoed. Now, it felt like a stage set in an empty theatre.

She turned towards the main school building, where there were lights on, and headed up the stone steps towards the set of double doors at the top. She carried on inside, straight into reception, where a young man sat in a small office, behind a Plexiglass screen with a small window. He had his legs up on the desk and was watching a football game on the computer screen. When he spotted Anya, he placed his legs under the table hurriedly.

'Can I help you?' He grunted this as though he'd rather do anything but; Anya suspected he'd been forced to work due to Paddy's event running on. Either that, or his team was losing.

'Sorry – hi. I'm a former pupil.' This didn't seem to earn her any points, so she changed tack. 'I'm a friend of Paddy . . . Mr McDonagh's. I'm meeting him here but his event ran on.'

'Uh huh.' The man's eyes flickered to the screen.

'He said I could wait in the school office while he finished up. Can you sign me in?'

The man gave her a look as though this was a great, great imposition, but after a few moments – and with a heavy sigh – he extracted a clipboard from under the desk and slid it across the counter.

'Name there.'

'Thanks.'

She scrawled 'Anya Mackie' and then passed it back to him. He tossed it on to the table.

Anya waited expectantly at the door for him to buzz her through into the main school building. After a moment or so, she turned around.

'Can you?'

She could hear him sigh from all the way across the room.

Feeling a little naughty, Anya wandered corridors that were usually full of students – if she remembered correctly, this was the way to the Geography department – their chatter ricocheting around the halls. She turned right, down another corridor, which led to the school office. Her breath sounded loud in the hush, as did her feet slapping loudly on the linoleum floor.

There was a light on in the office. She rapped on the door and then, without waiting for a reply, stepped inside to find a woman sitting at a desk in front of a computer, in a room wallpapered with bulletin boards covered in school calendars and forms and term dates and timetables. The central heating was on too high.

The woman looked to be in her forties, her dark hair pulled into a tight bun, eyes too big behind large framed glasses that were either very hip or very high prescription. She wore grey trousers and a V-necked jumper and her chair was slightly too low to the ground. She looked a little startled to see someone appear.

'Can I help you?'

'Um, hi,' Anya took another step forward and offered an uncertain wave. 'Sorry, I'm Anya, I'm a friend of Mr McDonagh's – Paddy – and I'm meant to be meeting him after the safeguarding event.'

The woman nodded smartly.

'Erm, but it's freezing outside. So, he said I might be able to wait in here?'

'Oh.' The woman blinked behind the huge wire frames. 'Of course. Take a seat.'

She gestured towards a line of three cushioned chairs that ran along one wall, underneath one of the bulletin boards. Anya took a seat on one of the end chairs, and the woman resumed reading her book. She had a bag of Starburst on the desk in front of her. Without breaking her gaze on her book, she took an orange one from the packet, unwrapped it, and popped it into her mouth. She repeated this with a red, purple, and then another red one.

'Would you like one?'

She had noticed Anya staring.

'Oh' – she didn't really but thought it would be rude to refuse – 'er, sure. Thank you.'

Anya stepped towards the desk.

'Which flavour?'

'Orange, please.'

The woman selected an orange one and passed it to Anya.

'Thank you.' She sat down in the same chair and unwrapped the Starburst.

'I got the raw end of the deal this evening.' The woman placed her book spine-up on the desk in front of her. 'The other ladies said they had plans.'

'Oh no.' Anya tried to dislodge a piece of Starburst that had got stuck in her molar tooth. 'And now the event has run on.'

'They always do.' The woman sighed.

'I used to go to school here, actually,' Anya said.

The woman beamed.

'Did you?'

'Yeah. I left in 2007.' Anya made a face to indicate that she was an ancient crone.

'I've worked here ten years now. I love it.'

Anya smiled.

'I was very happy here.'

This was true, she realized. Anya was lucky enough for school to have been a settled time, when everything followed a plan and whole months would go past before she even noticed they had. Then, life had been punctuated only by the sort of small dramas that – when compared to the blood-red horrors of adult life, of death, grief and heartbreak – barely registered as misfortune. And there was something about those school dramas that had almost felt exhilarating, like she was living properly for the first time.

Many of those feelings had been wrapped up in Euan, at least towards the end: the pair of them taking those first wobbly steps towards adulthood with each other. She had been trying not to think about him – or Jamie – since Sunday. Jamie had responded to her message (**'Golf buddies for life x'**), but after spending a little while trying to think of something clever to say to this, she couldn't. It didn't really require an answer, anyway. And so, as quickly as he'd unexpectedly returned to her life, Jamie had disappeared again. She tried not to feel too disappointed about it.

But now she was in the school office. And although she'd given up on anything serious coming of the Euan idea – it had always seemed foolish to peg even the vaguest of romantic hopes on to someone whose face she couldn't totally remember – she was still gripped by the mystery of it all. Plus, if she did *find* him . . . well, she'd be able to go back to Jamie with something concrete.

She took a deep breath.

'In fact' – she sounded casual: good – 'now that I mention it, I've been trying to organize a school . . . reunion. With a few friends.'

'Oh!' The woman nodded eagerly.

'But I've been struggling to track one of them down. Do you think there's any chance you have a contact for him? Like an email, or a forwarding address, or anything?'

'Well!' The woman was still beaming. 'We do always say it's such a wonderful part of our school – the network of

309

people who stay in touch afterwards. The happiest days, and all that . . .'

Anya smiled politely.

'Anyway' – she beckoned Anya over to her desk. 'I assume you've tried all the alumni groups?'

'Yes – no luck there.'

The woman furrowed her brow.

'What a shame.' She moved her mouse to wake the computer up. 'Well. Let's see what we can do. We can't give out the contact details, I'm afraid – it's a privacy issue – but we can contact them for you.'

'Oh.'

This was a wasted attempt. There was no way she wanted to reach out to Euan like that.

'What's the name, then?'

'Um. It's Euan Carrick.' She felt self-conscious saying it aloud. 'But I'm sorry, I thought you might just be able to pass on an email address or let me know where he's living now.'

The woman wasn't listening.

'And you were class of . . . ?'

'2007. But—'

'Ah yes, here he is! Oh, how nice! Related to Craig Carrick, who was also one of us.'

'Wait – what?'

The woman blinked at her from behind those huge frames.

'Craig Carrick – looks like he went here too.'

After a few beats, Anya realized an answer was expected of her.

'I didn't realize that,' she tried.

'Lovely, isn't it.' The woman beamed at her, and then returned to her computer screen. 'We've got an address on here, where Euan was living when he was a pupil here.' The woman looked stricken. 'But, sorry, I can't give it to you.'

'Oh no, I understand.'

Euan had said his dad had moved away when he finished school anyway.

'And there's no email or anything else on here, I'm afraid.' She sounded dejected. 'I'm sorry.'

'That's OK.'

'We could send a letter out, see if they're still based there?'

'No, no, honestly it's fine – it was just a silly thing. Never mind.' Anya took a few paces backwards, towards the seat by the door again. 'But thank you so much for looking. I really appreciate it.'

'That's no problem at all.' The woman beamed her owly smile again. 'We get a fair number of alumni doing the same. Sorry not to be of more use.'

'Not at all.'

Anya stared at her feet, listening to the sound of the woman sucking on her Starbursts, and wondered why Craig Carrick had lied about having a son.

22

She'd only half-concentrated on the film; Paddy kept telling her off for checking her phone.

'Anya,' he hissed, on the sixth time. 'People are muttering about you. Put it away.'

'Sorry, sorry.'

Next time, she'd cupped her hand to block the glow of the screen and Paddy had elbowed her.

'Ow.'

'*Ssssssh*,' came the noise from behind them.

She couldn't help it. She'd WhatsApped Jamie from her seat in the school office.

> Craig Carrick lied!
> He IS Euan's father

That – surely – was irresistible bait.

But by the time the film was over, he still hadn't read the messages, and she felt a little unsettled. She checked and double-checked and double-double-checked as they descended the escalators, travelling down from the screen on the second topmost floor of the huge multiplex.

'Anya?'

Paddy looked irritated.

'Sorry, what?'

'I asked what you thought of the film.'

She put her phone back in her pocket.

'Sorry.'

'What's with you this evening?'

'Nothing, sorry. I'm just distracted. I thought the film was good.'

'Which of the three minutes that you saw did you enjoy most?'

She was going to try and say something clever but felt something vibrate and seized her pocket. Paddy rolled his eyes.

But it was just a notification – a silly one, from her meditation app, advising her to check in. She put it back in her pocket and noticed he'd started walking down the escalator ahead of her.

She caught him up in the lobby.

'Do you still want a lift?' he asked, tersely.

'Yes, please.'

He'd driven her home, both a little subdued; as they pulled up outside Claire's, Anya grasped to make amends.

'Shall we do something this weekend? We could go to Ashton Lane.'

'That sounds good.'

He allowed her to give him a peck on the cheek.

Jamie had eventually responded the next afternoon. Anya had just collected her phone from her locker after a (rare) yoga class and, for a second, her stomach swooped, but it turned out the message hadn't been worth the wait.

Oh – that's weird. X

She stood rooted in the middle of the small changing

room, frowning at it, while a lithe woman manoeuvred past her to get to her own locker. That was it? Anya felt slightly embarrassed. He clearly wasn't interested; he suddenly felt like a stranger. She showered and walked over to the twins' house, still squirming.

The afternoon at Park Circus passed without note. She'd overseen a 'still life' that the twins had constructed for their art homework (comprising one of Corrie's chew toys; a toilet roll; three bananas; one of Aimee's sillier shoes) but the girls detected her half-interest, and sulkily declared the day's snack – eggy bread with chilli sauce – to be 'rubbish'. This had stung.

By way of distraction as much as nourishment, she made a vast batch of kimchi fried rice when she got home on Wednesday evening, garnished with an egg, sesame seeds and peppery spring onions. It was an old favourite: spicy and satisfying, just the sort of elevated comfort food that put Anya's soul at rest. She was going to take some over to Georgie's tomorrow in time for her date.

As she was scarfing a third serving and feeling rather better about life, Claire appeared in the kitchen. She was still in her work clothes – charcoal trousers and a shirt, her hair pinned back with a barrette.

'Hi Claire. Do you—'

'This arrived for you.' Claire was holding an oblong cardboard box, which she extended towards Anya.

'Oh.' It was quite heavy; she placed it on the table beside her bowl. 'What is it?' This was too stupid a question for Claire to dignify with an answer. 'I mean, when did it come?'

'It was on the doorstep when I got home ten minutes ago.'

Anya tore off a thick piece of Sellotape and unlatched the top of the box. Inside was something wrapped in lots of bubble wrap. She pulled the object out; from the weight of it, it felt like a bottle. She reached into the box for the note.

I believe I owe you one of these. Sorry for dragging us on a wild goose chase. Hopefully see you for a regular drink one of these days. X

With dawning realization and half an eye on Claire, she unpicked the Sellotape and started to unwrap the plastic swaddling cautiously. It was definitely a bottle and opening this specific bottle in front of her cousin might not be wise.

Luckily, her cousin had drifted over to the wok and was nose first in Anya's kimchi fried rice, which gave Anya time to rewrap it and slide it back into the box.

'Do you want some, Claire?' she called out. 'There's plenty.'

'What is it?'

'Kimchi fried rice. With an egg and some spring onions on the chopping board for seasoning. It's good. Spicy.'

'OK. Thank you.'

While Claire loaded a bowl for herself, Anya considered the gift. It felt like a gentle and generous – if you took into account the price of the wine – snub. Hers and Jamie's search really was over; she had a funny melting feeling in her stomach.

Claire sat down, and Anya gathered herself.

'Is Richard around?'

'He isn't.' Claire was eating with gusto.

'Where is he?'

'I don't know, Anya, I'm not his keeper.'

'Right. Sorry.'

'He never tells me where he's going anymore.' Claire was still wolfing the food down and barely looked up.

'I'm sorry,' Anya said, quietly.

Without a word, Claire placed her fork in her now empty bowl and walked to the sink.

Upstairs in her cell, Anya placed the box into the bottom of a suitcase full of summer clothes. She'd return it to the rack when Claire was at work tomorrow. Jamie had saved her bacon: Claire clearly had enough on her plate, without worrying about Anya's sticky fingers.

Thanks for the wine. See you soon. X

After she'd sent this message, she put her phone on Do Not Disturb and placed it facedown on the floor beside her bed.

Anya had finally created some harmony from the chaos of her bedroom, clearing the suitcases and boxes into a corner, and sourcing a small chest of drawers from Gumtree, which she'd collected from an address up the road a couple of weeks ago. The yearbook was still beside her bed, hers and Euan's 'vow' slipped inside the front cover. She placed the book into the suitcase beside the bottle of wine and pulled the zip closed on them both.

The rest of the week trundled past. On Thursday, Rosie fed Corrie three Lindt balls by mistake, so when Anya arrived the dog was vomiting on to Aimee's Uggs. Speaking of dogs, Anya received more details for both the dog's birthday and the fortieth celebration – addresses and specific numbers and the kitchen set-ups available in the respective venues. Tasha had also sent over a final version of the logo, with a promise to send a proper dispatch on life and Loic very soon ('it's got serious, which is less hot,' read the most recent email, dashed off on her way to a boxing class). The new logo was perfect: the broccoli was a lot smaller and the 'A' a lot prouder. Anya had winced a little at the price of getting it printed on to a cool bag – and then gone ahead and done it anyway, remembering that one of Paddy's favourite aphorisms was 'you've got to spend money to make money'. She wasn't sure what it meant when he applied it to working as an English teacher.

On Friday, she was permitted to leave Aimee's an hour early again: the twins' elusive father was in town for the weekend, and he was taking the girls to TGI Fridays. Aimee was doing the handover and had trotted downstairs just as Anya was leaving to meet Georgie and Paddy at The Loft. She was in pink spray-on bodycon.

Anya walked up University Avenue in the mizzle towards Ashton Lane, blinking rain from her eyelashes. The Loft was Anya's apology for ignoring Paddy at the cinema on Monday; it had been agreed in advance that the first two rounds would be on her. Though when she arrived, Georgie was already sipping a free gin and tonic, courtesy of Alex the barman. Anya slid in beside her.

'Hi!' Georgie beamed.

'Hi.' She gave her sister as warm a hug as she could manage from the neighbouring seat. 'Where's Paddy?'

Georgie pointed across the room. The Loft was already full of sparkly-eyed Friday evening customers, although

Paddy was in conversation with two rather dowdy, bespectacled men.

'Colleagues,' she added by way of explanation. 'They spotted him as soon as we came in.'

Anya made a sympathetic face.

'I'll go get him a Negroni.'

Georgie stopped chewing her straw. 'Wait, quickly, before Paddy comes back: are Claire and Richard OK? She sent me a slightly weird text the other night.'

'I don't think so.' Anya felt a skitter of dread. 'They've been fighting a lot. I can't really get to the bottom of it, but she's been very upset a few times. I cooked her dinner once or twice, but she didn't tell me much.'

'Claire's very proud.'

'I know. But it doesn't sound good. I keep finding him sleeping on the sofa, and there was a time he ran off for twenty-four hours.'

'Yes, she told me about that.'

Paddy was forcing his way through the crowd, elbowing past yet another hen party, who were commandeering six tables near the balcony.

'If the Chemistry teachers are coming here, I think this place might be over. Hi, Anya.'

A quick but warm hug.

'I was going to go get you a drink,' Anya said as they separated.

'Wait' – Paddy had a gleam in his eye – 'G, is your man working this evening?'

Georgie started to glow from within.

'He's over there.' She pointed and, in perfect synchronicity, he looked up and beamed.

'Brilliant.' Paddy slid into the booth beside Anya. 'Can you get him to bring me a Negroni? Anya's paying.'

'It isn't table service!'

'Go ask him then. Anya, give her your card. Maybe he'll give you a discount.'

Anya passed her Monzo card to Georgie, who began to shrug her way through the sweaty, excited crowd, feeling the gravitational pull of Alex the barman.

'You get one more drink after that and then my penance is paid,' Anya said. She was still watching the hen party. This evening's 'bride-to-be' looked strangely familiar, although she wasn't quite certain why.

'I'll be the judge of that,' Paddy replied, silkily.

Anya nodded in the direction of the hens. 'Another one. Glasgow really is the new Ibiza.'

Paddy shook his head.

'Such a shame.'

Anya was still watching the bride, who was model tall, and tossing her blonde hair around like a liberated woman in a tampon advert.

'I feel like I know the bride from somewhere.'

Paddy snorted.

'Anya, we know everyone here. We went to university up the road, school down the road, and your parents used to live about ten minutes away.'

Anya sighed.

'Do you think we should move to Mexico?'

Paddy smiled.

'Maybe just Edinburgh.'

Georgie had reappeared, holding three Negronis and a bowl of nuts.

'I bought the Negronis on Anya's card, but the nuts were free.'

'So generous,' but Paddy was smiling. 'Thanks, Georgie. And Anya.' He popped a nut into his mouth and nodded in the direction of the hen party. They were moving a little quicker than the last hen they'd been acquainted with, already tossing a tray of shots down open mouths (all except for one, most likely a younger sister, or cousin, who was perched on a chair, a little distance from the group, looking terrified). 'Anya thinks she knows the bride.'

Georgie peered at the woman – who was now hugging another woman wearing a 'Team Bride' sash – for a moment, and then shrugged.

'Don't think I recognize her.'

Anya shook her head. 'Forget I said it. It'll either come to me or it doesn't matter.'

The three of them cycled through a standard Friday evening repertoire: work (Paddy's, then Anya's, then Georgie's); relationships (only Georgie had one to speak of); the reality TV show Georgie and Paddy were obsessed with, but Anya hadn't watched because when they weren't fighting, Claire and Richard were hogging the telly (a German thriller – generous term – set on an oil rig); Claire and Richard's marital troubles (Paddy was gripped); the prospect of an Easter holiday in April (Paddy was obsessed).

'I've been looking at big farmhouses in France,' he announced. 'And I think I've found the one we should go for. It's got a huge pool, and a shady terrace and is set in the middle of nowhere. It's free on the right week, and I've already found flights.'

'Is it a teacher thing to be this obsessed with holidays in November?'

Paddy gave her a look.

'You try spending all your time with children. Then you'll need—'

But what Paddy had decided she'd need they would never learn, because at that point, the bride-to-be had appeared at their table, and was squealing.

'Oh my God, Anya Mackie!'

It took her a second. But with a start, Anya recognized her: Ciara – Ciara from sixth form, Ciara of those nights on the hill in the park.

Blinking fast, Anya stood up, and got the full measure of her evolution. Ciara's eyebrows were microbladed to perfection, her shoulders sculpted, her skin glowing, and her eyes dancing to the beat of the very inebriated. 'I thought it was you from across the bar!!' she was burbling now.

'Hi Paddy,' she simpered. 'How are you?'

Paddy had not recognized Ciara.

'Oh look at you all!' Ciara clutched Anya's arm. 'You look exactly the same!'

'Oh dear!' Anya managed.

'I know right, I've had a real glow up.' Ciara tossed her blonde hair over her shoulder.

Anya managed: 'You're getting married!!'

Ciara pouted expertly.

'I know.' She extended her ring finger to display a diamond the size of a baby's fist. 'He plays for Kilmarnock. I'm a WAG!'

'Wow!' Anya decided it was very important not to look at Paddy right now. 'That's amazing!'

'I know!'

'Where are you doing it?'

'Traquair House! Near Innerleithen – 270 people.' She leaned in, conspiratorial. 'They're sending someone from the *Daily Record*. Just the online bit, but still.' Ciara gasped, and her hands sprung to her mouth, the diamond catching the light. 'In fact – it's *soooooooo* funny, bumping into you, because you know who I saw there when I was down on Wednesday finalizing the table placements?'

Ciara raised her perfect eyebrows, and Anya wondered if she was meant to guess, but before she could open her mouth, she'd added, in a high-pitched screech:

'Euan Carrick! You remember him from school? In fact, didn't you have a little thing with him—'

Anya experienced the strangest feeling, like time was slowing but also speeding up, and everything was both so quiet you could hear a pin drop, and deafeningly cacophonous. She felt a little like she was going to faint, or start laughing, or both.

When she tuned back in, Ciara was still going.

'He's doing the gardens, working at the *fuck off* hedge maze where we're doing champagne and canapés. Such a coincidence! He didn't seem all that happy to see me, if I'm honest, but I knew him straight away – you don't forget that face, even if you're about to be a happily married woman! In fact, I'm pretty sure that Jimmy was a bit jealous, which is no bad thing really, I've seen the messages he gets from girls on Insta, you know?'

'Yeah,' Anya said weakly, although she didn't.

'Honestly, some of the filth they send! Pictures to his DMs saying all sorts and—'

'Wait, sorry, rewind. So Euan's working at – where was it?'

'Traquair House! It's basically a big castle though. Very in demand, Kristy and John got married there . . . he plays for St Johnstone and—'

'And you spoke to him?'

Ciara frowned.

'Well, yes, for like five minutes. He was cutting a hedge' – she leaned in again – 'topless. And I was like, "Euan!" And he took a bit of warming up but in the end we had a nice chat. Good old days. He's been there a little while now. Bad break up.' Ciara made a solemn face.

Anya almost laughed: if Euan had broken up with someone too, then they were truly both single.

'Anyway!' Ciara squeaked. 'It's *soooooo* nice to see you. I should get back to the hens – we're going back to One Devonshire after this. I think my mum's got me a stripper.'

Ciara pointed at a woman in a very small, very sequined dress, wearing a 'mother-of-the-bride' sash. She was standing on a table.

'She's become a new woman since the divorce.' Ciara sounded proud.

'Congratulations to her. And to you.'

Anya outstretched her arms and felt herself slightly winded by Ciara's large – and rather hard – breasts. They separated, and Ciara offered a last megawatt grin – the teeth were almost as shiny as the diamond – and then cooed 'byeeeeeee' and sashayed off back to her table.

Anya sat down.

'Well?' Georgie demanded .

'Ciara Gilmour,' Anya supplied. 'I was friends with her

that year you were at college.' Paddy frowned. 'She looks so' – Paddy opened his mouth, so Anya added, quickly – 'different. She was a bit of an emo back when we were friends.'

'Typical,' Paddy snorted.

'And she found Euan?' Georgie.

'Yeah.' She took a deep breath and started tapping out a message to Jamie.

I've found him. He's working as a gardener at Traquair House.
Confirmed sighting. X

23

The Botanic Gardens was busy, even on a bitter early November morning, with swarming families on the paths and couples, arm-in-arm, clutching steaming coffees as they walked up the hill that stretched towards the far end of the park. Perched on a bench outside one of the glasshouses, Anya could feel the cold seeping into her jeans.

A man was advancing across the lawn, his strides long and purposeful. Surely, it was Jamie; she set her features to 'casual' and fiddled with her phone, seeing but not reading the screen. Presently he arrived, stubbly and bundled up against the chill. His nose was pink and she realized she'd missed him.

'Hey!' He was slightly breathless, but his eyes were alive.

Jamie had replied almost immediately when she'd messaged from The Loft last night.

Outstanding detective work. Free tomorrow? X

They'd arranged to meet in the Botanics the next morning to discuss everything. Feeling a little giddy with her success, Anya had drunk until her head swam and it was still slightly swimming this morning.

'Hi.' She stood up and he grinned. 'How are you?'

'Good.' He made a muffled clap with gloved hands. 'Cold.'

'It's freezing. Shall we walk?'

She nodded to the road that stretched up the hill, lined by bare trees that looked like scarecrows against the leaden sky. They took five or so paces, and both started simultaneously.

'So—' Anya began.

'Right—' he said.

They broke off and exchanged a smile, and she felt pleased they were a team again.

'You go,' Jamie instructed. 'I want to know everything.'

'OK.'

And so she told him all about Ciara and Euan; the sighting; Traquair House; the hedge maze . . . He nodded, interjecting only to laugh and groan at the appropriate moments.

'So that's where he is. She mentioned something about a bad break up.'

'Oh really?'

A shadow of something crossed Jamie's face moment-arily.

'Uh – yes. Ciara didn't tell me anything more than that though. There's also the matter of Craig Carrick. I texted you about it last week.' This sounded more accusatory than she'd intended it to.

'Ah, yes – Craig.' They were walking quite slowly, Anya's paces matching Jamie's for once, and she'd turned to face him better. He'd cut himself shaving again – right on the jawline – and the graze looked slightly raw; Anya knew he should have stuck to the stubble. 'Sorry, I was a little rubbish about that. Last week was busy.' This was obviously an excuse and he changed his mind about it. 'Well, no. In truth I wasn't sure about it all – after Gleneagles. As I said on the train.'

'I remember.'

'It just felt like we'd never find him. Like we were wasting our time and—' He knew he'd said the wrong thing and was babbling a little. 'But now' – he grinned – 'we have found him. Well, *you* have.'

For some reason, this gave her butterflies.

'It turns out we were just going about it all wrong.' She folded her arms across her chest, and added lightly: 'Instead of going golfing, we just needed to go for a drink. Down the road.'

He laughed, a little more uproariously than Anya felt the joke merited but she appreciated the support.

'So' – she blew on her hands to warm them up – 'what do we now?'

'I was hoping you'd ask that' – she knew what was coming and was grinning too now – 'because I checked, and it'll only take us about an hour and a half to drive there.'

Forty minutes later, they were shooting to Innerleithen like a rocket, going straight from the Botanic Gardens to Jamie's, and climbing into his Nissan. She was glad she'd put on mascara that morning.

'Are you excited?' she asked, as Jamie made a darting overtake. He took a few seconds to respond.

'I am. I'm also a little nervous.' He was drumming his hands on the steering wheel lightly. 'Confronting him after all this time.'

'Confronting?'

'Sorry, wrong word. I just mean seeing. I'm a bit nervous to see him.'

'What if he doesn't recognize us?'

'He will,' Jamie said determinedly. 'Definitely.'

Anya was enjoying clocking the towns they drove through: Hamilton, Wishaw, Carluke, signs for Lanark and Biggar, reminding her of day trips in the car with her parents and Georgie, pilgrimages to forest parks and white sands and weather-beaten picnics. They passed a sign for Traquair House.

'Imagine we get there and it turns out Ciara has mixed him up for someone else.'

This earned an unimpressed look from Jamie, which she met with a mischievous grin.

'I'm just joking.' After a moment or so, she added: 'I just can't believe we're going to see him.'

'Me neither.' Jamie was still drumming on the steering wheel. 'I wonder if he's bald now.'

She laughed. 'Craig was definitely thinning on top. Although Ciara seemed pretty delighted to have seen him. So he's probably still as handsome as ever.'

'No doubt.' He snatched another quick glance at her before returning his eyes to the road. 'We've got about thirty minutes to go, by the way.'

Thirty minutes! She gnawed on her thumbnail.

'So, what do we do when we get there?' she asked. 'What do we say?'

'"Hi, Euan. Been a while."' She rolled her eyes, and he added: 'We just see what happens. Improvising has served us pretty well so far.'

Time felt stretchy in the car, like it was both passing too

quickly and too slowly. Jamie's nervous energy was infectious and Anya could feel it surging through her veins. She was desperate to be there, but at the same time she never wanted to arrive.

Almost exactly thirty minutes later, they did. Traquair was a neat, stately pile, with small windows punctuating its expansive white front. Anya could only see a few other people, mainly doddery, elderly couples wandering towards the grounds from the car park gripping guidebooks and looking rather pleased with themselves. Jamie parked the car, and Anya climbed out to take in the view of the house ahead of her. Moments later, Jamie joined her, bundling himself into his layers again. For a second, Anya had a strange urge to grasp his hand. Instead, she took a step forward, then another, and then it was easy, really. It was a chilly day, thick white clouds low in the sky, though by the time they'd reached the iron gates that guarded the house, Anya had warmed up.

'Do we need to pay to get in?'

Jamie nodded at a sign at the gatehouse, outlining the ticket prices for adults, children and friends of Traquair house.

'I'll get them,' Anya said, as she and Jamie took their places in the short queue at the gatehouse, Anya diverted by a magnificent peacock, sashaying slightly unsteadily across the circular lawn in front of the house. For a Saturday, it seemed fairly quiet, although Anya supposed she wasn't sure how busy stately homes ever were on a Saturday in November.

The couple in front of them departed and they stepped towards the booth, which was occupied by a very pretty young woman with a name-tag that read 'Alishah' and who confirmed that they'd want only grounds tickets, which would cost £12 in total. Anya offered her card.

'Hey,' she'd almost managed to sound off-hand, 'is Euan working today? He works in the gardens I think?'

'Euan?' Alishah was prodding at the chip & pin machine. 'I don't think we have anyone here called Euan.'

'Oh.' Anya replied, pleasantly. Jamie's eyes were like black mirrors. 'Really? It's just a friend of ours mentioned she'd seen him here. He was working in the gardens?'

Alishah frowned.

'We have an Ian?'

'Um . . .'

'Ian's a gardener here.'

'Right.' Anya's stomach lurched. 'Yeah! Maybe that's him.'

Alishah gave Anya a very strange look.

'Wow,' Jamie said, pointedly, steering Anya away from the ticket office. As soon as they were out of earshot, he whispered, 'That was smooth.'

'Maybe she's confused.' Her chest was fluttering. 'Ciara swore she'd seen him! They had a conversation! She couldn't have him mixed up.'

Jamie looked a little unconvinced.

'Come on' – she cast around for a clue – 'let's go to the maze.'

'OK.'

Jamie moved forward purposefully, and Anya struggled to keep up with his strides, though as they came out into the gardens, he pulled up and she almost bumped into him. The lawns were magnificent: green and rolling, and being enjoyed by many more peacocks (and – keeping a respectful distance nearby – a family of ducks). In the distance was the hedge maze, green and tall and imposing.

'This place is amazing,' Anya said, though Jamie didn't seem to be listening.

In the distance, on the east side of the maze, they spotted a man with a hose, spraying down the hedgerows. Jamie set a beeline towards him and Anya followed in his wake, making the ducks scuttle out of her path. Ciara wouldn't have got it wrong, would she? She'd spoken to him – she'd recalled the very details of their conversation. It must have been Alishah who was wrong. Perhaps she was new? Jamie was leaving her behind and she trotted a few steps to catch him.

They were approaching the man from behind. He was tall, lean, dressed in waterproof trousers and a navy T-shirt, fair hair sticking up slightly at the back. She hadn't seen Euan in a decade; it was a tall order to identify him from here. But still, her mouth was dry. Still a little distance away, Jamie had stopped.

'Maybe you should go first,' he said.

'What?'

'You know, you're better at this stuff than I am.'

'Jamie. I've never done anything like this before.' But he looked so uncharacteristically anxious – his brow furrowed and eyebrows knitted – that she softened.

'OK, fine, I'll go first. But you're following me.'

When they were metres away from the man, Anya sighed and then – with a last glance at Jamie, and her stomach ricocheting with anticipation – she stepped forward and tapped his arm. In surprise, he swung around, spraying her entire body with a jet of water and Anya cried out – it was cold – and Euan swore loudly.

It was definitely him. Older, yes, but weren't they all, and she'd know that face anywhere. He was stubbly now and his hair was closer cropped than she remembered, but it was unmistakably Euan. Her stomach was still flipping over, but she felt something else too, like all her senses had been tuned up.

'I'm so sorry,' he'd started to say, and then broke off and, for an awful second, she thought he hadn't recognized her until suddenly, he broke into a baffled grin.

'Is that – is that Anya Mackie?'

His voice was also deeper than she remembered and he was struggling to snatch the earphones from his ears. He'd taken a step back and was observing her. He looked pleased, she supposed, if still very confused. Her clothes were dripping on to her shoes now, and she felt the cold seep of wet cotton clinging to her stomach, but she was smiling too in spite of it.

'Is that you?' he repeated, peering into her face.

'Yeah,' her heart was beating clumsily in her chest and for fear she might faint, she stepped back and swung a clumsy arm to point at Jamie, 'and Jamie! We're here to—'

But before she could say anything more, Jamie stepped forward and socked Euan lightly on the nose.

24

It all happened very fast: Euan sank to his knees, clutching his face, Anya gasped and stumbled backwards, knocking over the hose reel, and landing awkwardly. But she had no time to pay much attention to that because Jamie was standing over Euan, looking a little like he couldn't decide whether to go for a second blow. Euan was examining his nose for (non-existent) blood.

'JAMIE!'

To her surprise, none of the few other visitors in the distance seemed to have noticed the soap opera suddenly unfolding in front of her.

She struggled to her feet, wincing gingerly as she placed weight on her ankle.

'What are you doing?' At Anya's voice, Jamie had straightened up. Sensing his chance, Euan scrambled to his feet, hands raised in surrender.

'Jamie!' she demanded.

'You know.' This was directed at Euan, but the fight had fallen from Jamie's shoulders and he sighed. 'That was pathetic. Sorry.'

'What's going on?' But neither of them were looking at her.

The hose was still going. Slowly – as though any quick movements would attract further, unwanted attention – Euan picked it up and turned it off. This completed, he turned to Jamie expectantly.

'Well?'

Jamie looked momentarily furious again, and then sighed heavily.

'Euan was going out with my sister Iona.' He still wasn't looking at her.

'Wait, what?' Processing this information felt a little like dragging her mind through treacle. 'What do—'

'—He vanished one night with £2,000 of Iona's savings. She hasn't seen him since.'

'I'm going to pay her back,' Euan said quietly. 'I have a job now—'

'It's been a year, Euan.'

He made a noise of protest but Anya cut across him, pinning Jamie's gaze.

'What are you—'

'—I'm sorry, I should have told you, but it never seemed like the right time.'

'What, not even the six-hour round trip to Aberdeen—'

'Wait, you went to Aberdeen?' Euan's eyes were wide. 'Wow.'

They both ignored him.

'Wait' – she had Paddy's voice in her head now – 'did your dad even die?'

Jamie's face flashed with hurt and she regretted this immediately.

'Yes. He did.'

There was an uncomfortable silence. This was all going horribly.

'I'm really sorry to hear that,' Euan said eventually, his gaze on the ground, but Jamie ignored him and there was another long, squirming pause.

'You didn't even text her—' Jamie's voice was low and bitter.

'It was complicated.' Euan's was a whine and Jamie raised an eyebrow. He turned to Anya. 'I'm sorry, I should have told you. But I didn't know how to start and I didn't want you to—'

'To what?' She had the same feeling she'd had at the Loft – like the moment was going too fast and too slowly.

'Well,' Jamie was struggling a little, as if there was something he was trying hard not to say. 'I thought it was up to you, to make your own decision – I knew you . . . well, you used to . . .'

Suddenly, horrified, Anya knew exactly what Jamie was about to say, but Euan was curious.

'Wait.' The penny was dropping and she felt a little sweaty. 'Why were *you* looking for me?' A baffled frown was etching a line between his eyebrows, and she flushed.

'Um.'

She blinked fast under the exposure, unable to look at either of them.

'Anya?' Euan prompted. She was sure she'd sensed the ghost of a smile.

Still unable to look at either of them, she stared at the grass instead. 'I . . . I'd found that stupid note we wrote on the last night of school . . .' She dared a glance at Euan who looked totally blank now. 'About . . .' Was she really going to say this? 'About us, well, us looking each other up . . . at thirty and . . .' He looked mystified; she couldn't bear to continue. 'Forget it, really. It was just a silly half-idea. Never mind. Really.'

Was that it? He couldn't even remember it! In a horrible moment, she saw everything for what it was: a far-fetched notion, silly, infantile, strange . . . She continued to stare at the ground, wary of Euan's eyes on her, during yet another of those long, uncomfortable silences; so much for their reunion. As for Jamie, she couldn't look at him.

Eventually, he spoke.

'I feel you owe me an explanation. At least.'

They were still standing in a triangle, facing one another. Euan stepped aside and for a wild moment Anya thought he was going to run away, but instead he picked up the hose again and started winding it up.

'OK.' He had his back to them when he spoke, but his voice was even. 'Let's go somewhere quiet so I can try and explain everything.'

Jamie turned to Anya. He looked hopeful, but she frowned and his face fell. She wasn't playing friends quite yet.

'Follow me,' Euan said.

Anya tried a step, placing weight on her awkward ankle. It ached but she could walk; still, Jamie had appeared at her shoulder. There were more visitors around now, and Euan led them out of the gardens, threading through the passers-by wandering across the lawns, their snatches of conversation about tea rooms and car parking charges and five more minutes carrying on the breeze. Anya's ankle twinged with each step – but she didn't want to say anything. Whatever was happening was fragile; the merest obstacle could break the spell and she didn't want to end up back in the car, still wondering about what had really happened.

They walked on for another five or ten minutes until eventually Euan stopped on a small bridge, which stretched over a rushing stream.

'If we climb down there' — he pointed to a narrow, uneven stone staircase — 'we could sit beside the water.'

Anya had hoped there'd be somewhere to sit that didn't involve climbing, but with a few missteps the three of them managed it, until they were perching beside the water on three separate rocks. She could hear the stream tickling the cool stones and the thicket of trees smelled green and woody. Jamie stared fixedly at the water, while Euan was picking at some moss on the stone. Anya noticed how filthy Euan's fingernails were.

'You cold?' He'd asked roughly but was already throwing his jacket towards her. She wasn't really but felt awkward refusing.

'Thanks.' It was soft and smelled earthy and worn.

'OK.' Jamie sounded a little impatient. 'Let's hear it then.'

Euan sighed heavily.

'It's hard to—'

'She had the police looking for you.' Jamie was brusque, determined to have his questions answered. 'She thought you were dead at first, until she realized the money was gone, and put two and two together.'

Anya felt a sickness in the pit of her stomach, but said nothing, instead watching them closely. Euan looked pained.

'I know,' he said, finally. 'It was stupid and cruel but I was always going to pay her back.'

Jamie made an impatient noise.

'I was! I've been putting money aside.'

'It wasn't just about the money you took. You haven't once tried to even get in touch with her. Or me.'

This hung in the air, until Euan spoke again.

'I was ashamed,' he said finally.

'You stole from her and then you couldn't even call to explain or break up with her in person. She couldn't work out what she'd done wrong. And neither could I.'

Anya could have sworn Jamie's voice wavered for a moment, but it was just that, a moment, and as if to compensate for dropping his guard, when she next glanced at his face it had darkened to a scowl.

But Euan had noticed too, and it seemed to trigger something in him.

'Well, it wasn't really about her. Or you.' When he spoke he was calm, but was blinking fast.

'What—' Jamie started, but Euan cut across.

'My dad was back and I needed to go fast.'

'Your dad?' It was the first thing Anya had said in a while. Jamie, on the other hand, made a scoffing noise.

'What does *that* mean?'

Euan sighed a deep long sigh and rubbed his left eye socket again. He looked tired.

'It's a bit of a long story' – Jamie opened his mouth indignantly, but Euan raised a cautionary finger – 'which I will tell you. If you just let me get a word in.'

There was something about his tone – that edge of irreverence, despite the seriousness of everything – that collapsed the years. For a moment, they were on top of the hill, staring at the city beneath.

'OK,' Jamie also sounded churlish, teenaged. 'Hurry up then.'

Euan nodded.

'OK then.' He was rolling a stone under his shoe, taking his time. 'But if you can manage it, I'd really rather you didn't interrupt.'

Jamie made an irritated noise, but Anya wanted to hear everything.

'We promise.'

'Thank you, Anya.' There was another flash of that mischievous teenager and then he left another long, unsettling silence, before he added: 'It really starts with my mother, actually.'

He was going to tell this story haltingly; he fidgeted with the stone again.

'After she died, my father went off the rails, drinking and things, which meant that when I was about fifteen, my dad left me with my uncle Craig for good.'

Anya wasn't sure if Euan had noticed her stiffen; if he had, he didn't look up. After another age, he continued.

'Craig had been keeping an eye on me for years anyway . . .' He looked up. 'I presume it was you two that met him? He mentioned a couple of people had turned up in Gleneagles.'

Anya nodded. 'That was us.'

'I don't understand,' Jamie started, but Euan gave him a cautionary look and Jamie muttered, 'Sorry.'

'Anyway, Craig's a shy man. And he really wasn't proud of me for running off.' He gave Jamie a look. 'He was furious, actually. But when it comes down to it, he always looks out for me.'

Anya was sure she was breathing too loudly in the next silence that followed. She could feel Jamie's tension, coiled like a spring, and could tell he was desperate to urge Euan on.

'Anyway' – she sensed Jamie's shoulders relax a little – 'when I . . . left Iona, it was because my dad, my real one, had turned up at my flat, looking for me.' He kicked the stone away and it rolled towards the water. 'I think he wanted money, or something, I don't know. Anyway, I didn't want to see him and I didn't want him knowing where I was. But he didn't like that. He started turning up at the flat drunk and threatening to hurt me. Once he stopped us both when we were leaving my flat—'

'So, you' – Anya regretted speaking immediately – 'um . . .'

'I disappeared, yes. And obviously, I wasn't proud of myself but I needed money to go. And, well, Iona and I weren't happy anyway—'

Jamie started to intervene but Euan qualified: 'Fine, *I* wasn't happy. I know she's your sister but it wasn't going all that well and with my dad throwing his weight around, I wanted to get out of town. I didn't see another way at the time. I know it sounds stupid.'

Anya's mind felt like quicksand. Euan's face was twisted – pain, rage, something – and she and Jamie exchanged another look.

'So, you steal two grand,' Jamie started, 'run out of town and eventually turn up in the Scottish borders, pretending to be a man called Ian?'

'Yes,' Euan said, simply. 'A fresh start. It had been a

difficult few years of odd jobs and broken relationships. Not just with your sister.' He looked flattened.

'Sorry,' Anya couldn't look at him; none of this was turning out as she'd expected. Euan ignored her and continued to address Jamie.

'I really have been saving my wages to pay her back.'

'Right.' Jamie was more awkward than she'd ever seen him. 'Well, that's good.'

'Craig knows where I am, but that's it. And you two now. I didn't want anyone to find me.'

'Has your dad found you here yet?' Jamie's voice finally had an edge of tenderness to it.

'Not yet. I worry he will.'

'Why didn't you tell Iona?' Anya asked quietly. 'Instead of just vanishing.'

'She didn't know anything about my family. I don't really talk about it.' He swallowed. 'And my father has been nothing but grief my entire life. Having him turn up like that made me angry . . . frightened, all of it. I panicked and turned up here and managed to get this job, which I liked. Better than what I was doing in Aberdeen.'

'Why did you come here?' Anya's fingers felt frozen in the cold.

'I came here on a school trip when I was eight. When I was trying to think of where to go, it was the only place I could think of.'

For some reason, this made sense to Anya.

'So. How . . . how is Iona doing?'

Euan asked this so nervously that Jamie softened again.

'She's all right. Ups and downs, mostly about Dad. She'd kill me if she knew I was here.'

'Ah.' Euan gave Jamie a careful look now. 'So you didn't tell her you were looking for me?'

'No. This ... well ... it all got a bit out of hand.' Jamie directed this at Anya. She gave him a very small smile, and he looked relieved. 'I'm sorry about your nose,' he added to Euan.

The water rushed past the banks, clear and shallow. There was a gentle breeze and Anya wrapped Euan's jacket around her more closely.

'Wait, what about you?' With dread, Anya realized Euan meant her. 'What's this note?'

'Oh, don't.' She wondered if this would work. 'It's a really long story.'

'I told you mine.' Euan even had a ghost of a grin now. Anya didn't want to look at either of them.

'Yes, and it's going to sound even sillier now you have.' But they were both watching her expectantly, and she sighed.

'Before you judge me, I had just been dumped ...' They were both watching her, Euan warily, but there was a light smile playing about Jamie's lips, which for some reason made her feel much better. She continued: 'And, well, I found this stupid note we wrote when we were kids. On the last night of school. About how' – oh God, here it came – 'if we were still single at thirty we'd ... find each other. And so, I got it into my head that it might be worth doing it. Not like *that* – but just as friends – and then Jamie ended up hearing I was looking for you and ... Well. As he said, it all got a bit out of hand ...'

She trailed off, her face hot again, and hazarded a look at Euan.

He looked amused, if a little wary.

'Wow.'

This was definitely more mortifying than she'd imagined.

'I . . . I'm afraid I don't remember that at all. Sorry.'

She laughed.

'It's OK. It was a long time ago.'

'So,' he grinned, and for a moment again he looked just like the teenager she'd known, 'what, you're here to call in this contract?'

'No!' She put her face in her hands. 'I don't know. I was just intrigued to find you after all that time. Really.' She pointed at a blinking Jamie. 'It's his fault. It wouldn't have gone anywhere without him. Plus, you were so hard to find. It kind of made it more interesting.' She added, 'And I'd been dumped, and I'd quit my job . . . I was feeling very . . . you know.'

There was a beat as this landed and then both Euan and Jamie grinned cautious grins, and for a second the decades collapsed as she grew redder and redder and closer to nervous giggles.

'Stop it!'

'I don't think I'm the man for you, Anya.' Euan shook his head. 'In case you hadn't heard, I've got a bit of a rubbish romantic record—'

'Yes,' Jamie interrupted. 'Anya – like Iona – is definitely way too good for you.'

'Anyway,' she said hurriedly, shaking her head, desperate to catch the moment before everything shifted to dark again, 'Euan, you don't have to worry.' She shivered again. 'You're under no obligation to ever see me again. Let

343

alone sweep me off my feet and into the distance. But I hoped it would be nice to see you. It's been a while.'

He gave another of those grins that seemed to reach through the decades.

'It has been. I hope it hasn't been too disappointing.'

'It hasn't.' She smiled and he looked grateful. 'It just wasn't really what I expected.'

'Sorry I didn't stay in touch. At university.'

She waved dismissively.

'I didn't either. It was a long time ago.'

After the icebreaker of Anya's humiliation, Jamie and Euan had returned to avoiding eye contact, their half-truce fragile and imperfect. She suspected this was as happy as the ending was going to be.

'Are you both still in Glasgow, then?' Euan was trying to pin Jamie's gaze, but he avoided it carefully, so Anya did the answering for them.

'We both are. Not much has changed.'

Euan nodded, and there was another silence.

'I really am going to pay Iona back,' he said eventually. 'I promise.'

'How long will it take?' Jamie still wouldn't look at him.

'A little while. But I'm getting there.'

'Tell her, will you?' He looked up now, eyes lightly blazing. 'She doesn't expect anything else. But I think she'd like to know you're alive. And planning to do the right thing.'

'Yes. I will.'

Anya really wanted to believe him, although she noticed he didn't look at either of them as he promised it.

'OK.' Jamie spoke evenly, though Anya noticed his shoulders were hunched around his ears. 'Thanks.'

Euan stood up and brushed the moss from his trousers and Anya had that horrible sadness she always got when something was about to end. Euan looked as though he was about to speak, so she got there first.

'Will we all keep in touch?' she asked in a small voice. She knew the answer, but she still felt like she had to ask.

Euan looked at Jamie.

'Depends if he wants to.'

'Depends if he pays her back.' Euan looked as if he was about to gripe, so she spoke.

'Well, maybe we'll see each other again when you're next in Glasgow.'

'Sure.' Euan looked fidgety, eager for this all to end. 'I'll let you know if I'm ever in town.' He paused. 'I should head back to the grounds before someone notices I'm gone.'

Jamie nodded.

'We should start driving back too.'

'It's going to rain.' She pointed dully at the horizon, but Euan and Jamie had already turned around.

Families milled outside the hedge maze, weighing up whether to take it on in the stormy light. Anya observed a brother and sister set off at a run, their mothers tapping their wrists and promising to time them.

The three of them were back lingering near the hose, Euan standing in the puddle of water they'd left behind during the scrap. Anya shrugged out of his jacket and handed it back.

'Thanks for the jacket.'

'Sorry I got you so wet,' he said, though his smile vanished quickly. Jamie still wouldn't meet Euan's eyes but he held out a hand and Euan shook it quickly.

'Nice to see you both,' he said.

Anya tried a wan smile of her own.

'Quite the school reunion.'

'It was. On which note, I presume it was Ciara Gilmour who gave you the final clue you needed.'

'I bumped into her in a bar on Ashton Lane.'

'Ah well. It was overdue anyway.'

A last, uncomfortable silence, before Jamie spoke.

'Sorry again about the punch.'

'It's all right. I deserved it.'

When they were a few metres away, Anya turned around to get a last glimpse of Euan, but he'd already vanished.

25

Jamie swung an arm behind the headrest of Anya's seat
and reversed out of their parking spot. They had walked
back to the car, not speaking but exchanging glances, his
eyes bright and a little glassy, hers wide. The heating was
on but Anya was shivering, her wet clothes sticking to her.

'Do you want it warmer?'

'Yes, please.'

After ten or so minutes on the road, Jamie veered into
a petrol station.

'I'll be quick.' She nodded but he'd already climbed out
of the driver's seat. She listened to the glug of the diesel
filling the tank and then watched as he crossed the fore-
court and went into the shop to pay up. In the queue, he
turned and caught her eye and she looked away immediately, feeling exposed, although she wasn't sure why.

When he returned to the car, he tossed a Twirl on to
her lap.

'In case you're hungry.'

'Always.'

And then they were on the road once more, Jamie
worrying at his chin with the hand that wasn't on the
steering wheel.

'I'm really sorry.' He found her eyes in the mirror for a
moment before he returned them to the road. 'About not
telling you my reasons for wanting to find Euan.'

'Why didn't you?' She watched him.

'I don't know, really,' he said after a pause. He manoeuvred into the inside lane, and she held her breath, but then he continued quietly. 'I suppose at first, you'd told me that lie about Euan and restaurants' – she could automatically feel herself reddening – 'which I didn't really buy, but I felt like it gave me a licence to be a little bit . . . well, economical with the truth.' She smiled, though tried not to; he didn't seem to notice. 'And then when you said what it was actually about I considered telling you everything, but I didn't know if you'd be upset. And' – she took this in, and he continued – 'well, we were having fun.' They looked at each other fast and then turned away, as though they'd seen something they shouldn't. 'I was anyway.'

Anya felt something move in her chest.

'I was,' she said. 'Definitely.'

'Good.' He sounded pleased. 'But I did start to feel guilty again, which is why after Gleneagles I wondered if it would maybe be easier if we just . . . stopped. So, you wouldn't end up going out with him, for a start.'

She laughed, embarrassed.

'Jamie, please. That was *never* going to happen. For so many reasons.' She chewed her thumbnail again. 'No way.'

'OK.'

Another pause.

'I still wish you'd told me.'

'Me too. I'm sorry I didn't.'

She nodded, drawing the curtain on it. 'Are you OK?'

'Yes. I think so.'

'What a horrible thing to have happened.' She shifted in her seat so she was facing him better. 'To Iona. And to you.'

'Yes. It was pretty awful.'

'Had you and Euan been close again, then?'

'Not as close as when we were kids – or those first years of university,' he said evenly. She was watching him closely, observing the way his face crinkled when he thought deeply. 'He was up in Aberdeen the whole time they were together, so I didn't see him – them – all that much. It was a little different – *he* was a little different. Darker somehow, more disillusioned with the world. But we were in touch fairly often, and I liked him feeling like a part of my family. And I would see him a bit. Hear things from Iona.'

'Was it strange when they started going out?'

'At first. Then as I said, I grew to quite like it.' He laughed wryly. 'And then, for obvious reasons, I did not.'

She nodded. 'And how do you feel now?'

The pause was so long, she thought he was ignoring her, but eventually he replied.

'Defeated. Sort of like the anti-climax after a funeral.'

'Are you going to tell your sister you saw him?'

'I will, yes. I already felt uncomfortable doing this without her, but . . .' He didn't seem to have an answer to that thought, so he changed tack. 'Plus, I'd probably better warn her he might get in touch. Not that I'm banking on that.'

'Mmmm.' Anya also wasn't sure if she bought Euan's assurances. 'How do you feel about him now?' she asked, instead of saying this.

Jamie rolled his shoulders and flexed his neck from side to side before he replied.

'Ambivalent,' he said crisply.

'After all that!'

He shrugged.

Anya bit her lip while Jamie changed lanes again, accelerating fast to overtake another car.

'It certainly all makes much more sense now,' she said, once he'd slowed again. 'Why you wanted to find him so much.'

'Yes. Well, I hope you don't think it was a sad, macho power trip.'

'He stole from her! I think it's very justifiable. And he let you down too. Also' – a teasing smile – 'I've never seen anyone hit someone before. It was kind of thrilling. Although I don't think I'm meant to say that. And I'm glad you didn't hit him very hard.'

He laughed now and she felt pleased.

'You definitely won't see me do it again.'

She laughed in exchange.

Neither of them said anything more for a while. Jamie weaved down the roads and Anya closed her eyes. She felt a little sick: the theatrics; the light hangover; the stuffy, clammy heat in the car. Her clothes were finally almost dry but felt sticky.

'How's your ankle?' Jamie asked, as they rejoined the motorway, and civilization.

'Oh, I'm sure it's fine.'

Jamie took his eyes off the road to shoot her a mischievous half-glance.

'I still thought there was a chance that you were going to take one look at Euan and decide you were madly in love with him.'

She squirmed.

'No way. It was all just . . . silly.'

'You can definitely do better.'

As they reached the outskirts of the city, passing the Glasgow's Miles Better sign, the traffic thickened, and she felt strangely wistful, like the feeling at the end of a holiday: watching the last sunset drop over the horizon and realizing, with a sad inevitability, that you didn't read half the books you'd packed, or see half the sights you'd planned to. Today she'd lost the (silly) dream of Euan; but what about Jamie? There was no reason for them to stay in touch but the idea of not seeing him made her head swim a little.

He turned off Great Western Road and wended his way on to Hamilton Drive, proceeding at a crawl until he had parked up outside Claire's house. Automatically, Anya looked towards number 26 and saw a shadowy figure pass across the living room window and felt a prickle of dread at the thought of encountering Richard.

Jamie's hands were resting on his lap and she turned towards him.

'So, case closed, I suppose,' she said.

'Retirement beckons. Time to hang up the badge.'

'Will you let me know if you hear from Euan? Or if your sister does.'

'Definitely – I'll tell you everything.' She gave him a look, so he added: 'Really, this time.'

'OK. Deal.' She patted her pockets for her keys but didn't move. After another few moments, she started, 'I'll go—' and then stopped because he'd also started talking.

'Would you—' he broke off. 'Sorry, what were you going to say?'

'Oh,' she pointed at the door. 'Just that . . . this is me.'

He gave a clumsy salute.

351

'Keep in touch.' She opened the car door. 'Or I might try and find you in ten years.'

He grinned.

'See you, Anya.'

He nodded and she closed the door. She could feel him watching her, and she fumbled the key as she tried to get it into the lock.

26

Sunday

Jamie
Watching a Scandi detective show.
The detective duo reminds me of us.

> **Anya**
> I bet they are better dressed.
> **Anya**
> And better at their jobs.
> **Anya**
> Also better looking.

Jamie
Speak for yourself. X

Tuesday

Jamie sent a picture
They're serving your wine in the restaurant I'm in. Guess how
much a glass costs?

> **Anya**
> Please don't do this to me. Also tell me.

Jamie

£26. Will toast you.

Anya

Are you actually ordering one?!

Jamie

It's good wine.

Anya

Stop showing off. X

Wednesday

Anya

Had a weird dream that Euan was the ringmaster of a circus
that we both had to work at. I was a clown. Can't remember
what you were but you were definitely there. As was my mother.

Anya

Wonder what my subconscious is trying to tell me. X

Jamie

Seems pretty obvious to me. Clown. X

Thursday

Jamie

Since we went to Gleneagles my phone won't
stop advertising golf holidays to me. Shall we?

Anya

Only if I can borrow those shoes?

Jamie

OK. You have to drive the buggy too.

Friday

Anya

Wait, let me get this straight before I make any plans.
It's a Friday evening – you aren't planning to drive
us to the other side of the country, are you? X

Jamie

The night's still young, Anya. X

'Oh, I'm sorry, am I interrupting you?'

Aimee raised a precision-engineered eyebrow and Anya dropped her phone into her pocket. She noted that Aimee was wearing her blue contacts today, which made her eyes look like a Barbie's.

'Sorry, no—'

'Where are the girls?'

'They're getting changed into their football kit.'

It was 5.30 p.m. Despite the dark and the gloom, the girls' passion for playing in the garden was undimmed.

'I see.' Aimee blinked her frightening eyes. 'How's the menu for their birthday coming along?'

The twins' birthday party was in two weeks' time; this weekend – Sunday – was the fortieth, and Anya was nervous and terrified and excited all at once. That evening, she was planning to go to Paddy's to vegetate and hope this might take her mind off everything.

'Yes, I've spoken to them about all their favourites.'

'Good.' Aimee nodded, satisfied, then examined her large Apple watch with the bright pink strap. 'You can go if you want.'

'Are you sure?' Anya looked dubious. 'They'll come in all messy and—'

'Anya, it's not your job to clean.'

Anya was so taken aback by this rare moment of humanity that she laughed, and she could have sworn Aimee looked a little pleased.

'Well, thank you, Aimee.'

'That's fine.' She waved dismissively. 'I'll see you on Monday. Money's in the hall.'

Her heart skipped as she closed the heavy door. She called Paddy.

He picked up after the third ring. 'Yo.'

'Aimee's let me loose already. It's a Friday miracle.'

'Oh great, come over now then. I've just got home.'

'OK. Do we need anything?'

'I've got some oven pizzas?'

'You always have oven pizzas. Posh ones or freezer ones?'

'Posh ones, obviously. I'd say we could order in, but I've spent too much already this month.'

Like many woefully paid teachers, Paddy lived pay cheque to pay cheque, which was to say that he spent most of his salary in the first two weeks after payday, and then spent the subsequent two weeks trying to eke out the remainder through creative accounting, which prioritized fun over the basics. Anya was hardly in a position to judge, or volunteer to pay for dinner.

'No, don't worry. I can always tart them up with some vegetables.'

'Now we're talking. How long will you be?'

It had started spitting lightly; she pulled up the hood of her coat.

'I'm walking now. So, fifteen, twenty minutes?'

'Great. See you soon.'

'Bye.'

As she hung up, a notification appeared at the top of her screen.

Jamie
Assume your weekend feels
empty without a mission. X

Anya
Actually, it feels full of possibility.
Those car journeys were long. X

Jamie
I'd bet the price of a bottle of THE wine
that your plan is to sit on your sofa.

Anya
Incorrect.

Anya
Paddy's sofa.

Anya
Do I win the wine?

Jamie

Depends. Will you come drink it with me tonight? X

Anya was walking up University Avenue now, close to the Hunterian – its columns throwing imposing shadows in the evening light – and stopped on a corner, chewing her lip while she re-read the message. She typed out *'tempting'* but deleted it again, then worried he'd already seen her typing. She couldn't ditch Paddy, even though she really wanted to. This was a surprise.

Anya

Unfortunately, you'd have to take Paddy too.
And he drinks fast.

She hesitated and then typed another message.

Anya

How about tomorrow?

He was there straight away.

Jamie

Can't tomorrow. Another time? X

She worried at her lip. What was he doing tomorrow? She typed again.

Anya

Next Friday?
X

Jamie

I'll hold you to that. X

Paddy was wrapped in a blanket when she arrived.

'It's freezing in here,' he said, by way of greeting, although Anya – a little clammy from her walk – didn't notice. She tossed her coat on an unused exercise bench and followed Paddy into the kitchen.

'No Ivy tonight?'

She'd sounded too pleased and Paddy gave her a look in response.

'I'll put these on for you, shall I?' The pizzas were waiting expectantly on the kitchen counter.

'Thank you,' he said tartly, then dropped the act. 'Sorry. It was a long day.'

'I'm just teasing. What happened?'

'Oh, nothing particularly bad; it's just that parents' evening is coming up. Lots of meetings to discuss how to make it more 'dynamic', to involve the pupils, which is a terrible idea . . .' He moved the chair back to get a better view of Anya, and it made a roar as it dragged across the floor. 'Anyway. How was your day?'

Anya turned on the oven.

'Oh, fine. I couldn't stop worrying about the fortieth on Sunday so I made another practice round of bhajis, which came out a little under-salted.'

Paddy understood the point was to make a sympathetic face, which he did.

'Everything you make will be delicious. It always is. Stop worrying.'

'Thank you.'

While the oven preheated she joined him at the table, which this evening was covered in jotters and last Saturday's *Herald*, spread open to the puzzle page. Paddy was a sudoku wizard, although last week's 'Fiendish' had appeared too fiendish even for him. Anya examined the grid, placed a 3 and then realized there was already a 3 there and scored through the whole thing so hard she tore the paper.

'Oops.'

Paddy put his phone facedown and pointed at the torn paper.

'What did it ever do to you?'

'Sorry. I messed up a three.' Paddy raised an eyebrow, and then she added: 'OK, Jamie asked me to have a drink this evening.'

Anya had relayed the unexpected drama of the weekend at Traquair to Paddy, Georgie and Tasha (via email). Paddy's favourite part had, inevitably, been the dramatic bit. 'I just can't believe the punch!' he'd said on an evening FaceTime. 'I wish I'd seen this.'

'Really?' He raised his eyebrow even further. 'What the hell are you doing here with me, then?'

'What do you mean?'

Paddy looked at her as though she were very stupid.

'Anya, are you joking? He asked you out.'

'No, he didn't.' She couldn't help but smile though.

Paddy gave her the same look.

'He asked you to go for a drink on a Friday. I know you're out of practice but—'

'I know, I know. But—'

'Can I see the messages?'

She hesitated and then presented the exchange for his examination, chewing her lip while he read. After what felt like forever, he handed the phone back.

'You should have gone!'

'Paddy, I wouldn't blow you off to go meet Jamie.'

He shrugged.

'Why not? I don't mind. We're just sitting and eating an oven pizza.'

On cue, the light on the oven turned off, and Anya put the pizzas in and set the timer. When she returned to the table and slid back into her chair, Paddy was primed.

'Next time he asks, you have to say yes.'

'You're more important than a boy!'

Paddy rolled his eyes. 'Don't be intense. I know. Doesn't mean you can't blow me off to go on a date with one.'

'OK.'

But she must have looked dubious because he added: 'Unless you don't want to, obviously.'

'No, I do.' She considered this. 'I like Jamie.' He raised an eyebrow at 'like' and she felt self-conscious and added: 'Not like that.' He raised the eyebrow higher. 'Shut up, I don't know! It's confusing. And we've never had a drink that wasn't something to do with Euan.'

'Well, perhaps now is the time to do so.'

They dispatched the pizzas quickly, dipping the hardened crusts in Hellmann's mayo. Afterwards, they migrated to the living room, picking through the contents of Ivy's make-up collection, which was strewn across the living room table (the room was widely accepted to have the most flattering lighting in the flat), to sit on their respective sofas. As they weren't drinking, it was agreed that they'd watch a proper film, something new, much-decorated and worthy. Paddy fell asleep forty minutes in. Technically, Anya made it to the end, but she had started double-screening midway through and therefore found herself rather nonplussed when the credits rolled. She had been weighing up whether to text Jamie but wasn't sure if she dared. She was still considering it when Paddy started.

'I really shouldn't nap with my contacts in,' he shifted on the sofa. 'What time is it?'

'Nearly midnight,' Anya replied, surprised.

'Ooft. Definitely bedtime. Want to stay?'

'I think I'll walk back. I want to wake up in my own bed.'

'Fair. I'd rather you weren't in my bed either.'

'Ha ha.'

She stood up creakily. Paddy sighed and followed suit.

'Text me when you get home safe?' he said, following her into the hallway.

'Will do.' She wriggled into her coat and pulled on both boots, while he watched dopily.

She gave him a hug and then ducked out the door and trotted quickly down the stone steps and on to the street below. It had recently stopped raining and the pavements were black and slick, and Anya set off at pace, distracted still by the thought of an evening with Jamie that could have been. Would they have enough to talk about without Euan? The thought of seeing him made her feel shy, which was new.

She'd finished the roughly twenty-minute walk through fairly quiet streets back to Claire's before she even realized it. Still, when she turned on to Hamilton Drive she felt the relief in her chest: warm and sedative. She was exhausted; thoughts of Jamie still swimming on the edges of her consciousness.

As she reached Claire's house, Anya could see that all

the lights were on. Confused, she frowned, and then stopped dead: the front door was ajar – and there was a policewoman standing in the doorway of Claire's house. There was no sign of either Claire or Richard, although they were presumably acquainted with the woman if she was standing in front of their open front door.

'Can I help you?' The policewoman was tall and broad and brusque.

'I . . . I live here,' Anya replied stupidly.

The policewoman raised an interested eyebrow.

'Do you?'

'Yes, I'm the, erm, lodger. What's going on?'

Anya stepped forward. Under the warm pool of the hallway light, she could better see the policewoman's face: lined, her expression a little haughty.

'Is Claire OK?' She felt her heart starting to beat in her chest again.

'She's absolutely fine.' Anya found herself eye-to-eye with the policewoman. 'Now, can you just confirm your relationship to the residents?'

'Claire's my cousin.'

'Thank you. I'm afraid there's just been a bit of a domestic disturbance.'

'A disturbance!?'

'Nothing too serious. One of your neighbours called us. We arrived about twenty minutes ago.'

'That sounds pretty serious.'

Anya stepped forward. She noticed the policewoman shift her weight slightly but unmistakably, in order to stop her from entering the house.

'It's really nothing to worry about. My colleague is just

in there talking to your cousin and her husband right now,' the policewoman added, though a little more kindly this time.

'They're not married yet.' The policewoman nodded. 'He didn't—' Anya felt sick. 'He didn't hurt her, did he?'

'No. Nothing like that,' the policewoman said reassuringly. 'As I said, there were some damages done to the property. Some plates, and things. And a computer, which turns out to have been company property and quite valuable.'

Anya had never seen Claire use a computer; it was always Richard who was plugged into various different devices. She felt a shiver of unease.

She was about to ask, when a stringy policeman appeared on the doorstep. Behind them, shuffled Claire. She was as polished as she usually was, except for the barrette in her hair, which was skew-whiff.

'Claire?'

'Hello, Anya. I'm fine, by the way. Sorry about this fuss.'

The policeman stepped forward and looked at Anya.

'I'm afraid there's been a bit of commotion here this evening.' His accent was thick and comforting, although what he said next wasn't. 'Since you're here, would you have five minutes to answer a few questions?'

Anya's mouth was dry.

'Um. Yes. But – is she – Claire, are you really OK?'

'Yes,' she said shortly. 'I'm fine.' A sniff. 'Thank you.'

The policeman gave Anya a 'see?' look, then muttered something to Claire and directed her back down the hall.

'Just a few questions,' the stringy man repeated. The policewoman put a hand on her shoulder, which Anya presumed was supposed to be collegiate, but in the circumstances felt vaguely threatening.

'Your name.'

'Anya. Mackie.'

'And your address.'

Anya frowned.

'Here.'

'And how long have you known the residents?'

Anya blinked.

'Claire is my cousin.' Their faces suggested a better answer was expected of her, and she added: 'So, my whole life, really. She's two years younger than me.'

'And what about the other resident of the property?'

'Richard,' Anya supplied.

'Aye,' said the policeman, a little impatiently.

'I've known him for a few years. Since they started going out, so four years, maybe.' Anya swallowed. 'We don't get on that well, really' – she heard immediately how it sounded – 'I mean, not because he's a bad person, or anything.' They were both eyeing her beadily now. 'Just because he's a bit weird and smug about his boring job in IT.'

The policewoman was scribbling something in her notebook, and Anya felt a jolt of panic. After what felt like an eternity, the woman looked up again.

'And have there ever been any domestic disturbances of this nature before?'

Anya felt a little sweaty.

'Well, they've been fighting a bit recently. But it's been just raised voices really. Mostly they watch Scandinavian detective shows and hoover.'

There was a suspended pause as the policewoman wrote more in her notebook.

'Are they in trouble?'

'It's nothing serious,' said the policeman soothingly, although Anya was not particularly soothed. She was about to say something, but the policewoman was speaking again.

'Thank you for your co-operation, Miss Mackie. You've been very helpful.'

Anya wasn't sure this was true but appreciated the vote of confidence. The policewoman was steering her gently towards the pavement.

'Now, do you have somewhere else you can stay this evening?'

'A boyfriend's house. Or a friend's house?'

'What?'

'We'll need a couple more hours here, I'm afraid,' the woman said, briskly.

A few more hours!

'But why do I have to leave?'

The policewoman shrugged.

'It's procedure.'

'What? But can't I just go up to my room and go straight to bed? I'll be really quiet, I won't listen or anything. I've just had a really long day' – she knew she was fighting a losing battle – 'and I'm so tired and I just left my friend's house to come back here specifically so I could sleep in my own bed.' She paused. 'Please?'

The police exchanged a look.

'I'm afraid we need to discuss a few things with the pair of them, about the destruction of the property. So, we'd really prefer you were somewhere else tonight so you don't get in the way.' The policeman was baring his teeth in what Anya assumed he thought was a sympathetic smile. 'What about a friend, eh? Any nearby? We can drop you somewhere.'

Anya sighed.

'One second, I'll call my sister.'

She stepped off to one side. It was half midnight and Georgie had been out with Alex, so there was a chance she was still awake.

It rang off; she WhatsApped.

> Not an emergency don't panic
> Although Claire and Richard have had a fight
> so the police are here
> And they say I have to stay somewhere else
> So it is a slight emergency, actually
> Gonna call Paddy

The texts only returned one tick – Georgie must have her phone on airplane, which she usually did when she slept – or presumably whenever she had her hands full with Alex. Anya decided she did not wish to pursue this line of thinking.

Paddy slept like the dead; predictably, his phone rang off. Anya listened to his gruff, unfamiliar answerphone message and then cancelled the call. She WhatsApped him too, remembering Paddy had urged her to send a 'home safe' text.

> SORRY IT IS NOT AN EMERGENCY
> I'm totally fine

367

> Basically Claire and Richard have had a fight so police are here
>
> And say I have to stay somewhere else
>
> Can I come back??
>
> I mean you are asleep so prob not

Anya had plenty of friends and acquaintances – she did, right? – but contacting someone at 12.30 a.m. looking for a temporary place to stay called for a very specific type of friend, and she appeared to only have two of them. Tasha would be awake, but there wasn't much she could do from Vancouver.

She turned back to the police.

'I tried my best friend and my sister,' Anya said flatly. 'They're not answering.' She added, accusingly: 'They're probably asleep.'

The coppers seemed unfazed.

'What about your parents?'

'They live out of town,' she supplied quickly.

The policewoman nodded.

'Please can I not just go to bed? I really won't do anything. I'll just go straight to bed.' The policeman shook his head.

'I'm sorry, miss,' he said, not sounding it. 'Your alternative is to sit out here on the kerb for a few hours until we're finished with our questioning.' He gazed into the inky, impenetrable sky and added, theatrically: 'And it looks like it's going to rain again.'

Anya wasn't going to win this and she knew it. A few hours! She was so frustrated – not to mention starting to vaguely panic – that she could scream, but knew this probably wasn't the best way to proceed with Police Scotland.

Instead of obscenities, she clenched the fist that wasn't holding her phone. In her other palm, the handset vibrated, and her heart leapt momentarily. Georgie! Paddy!

Jamie, in fact.

Actually, tomorrow would work. X

She absolutely couldn't just ask to spend the night at Jamie's; she surely had somewhere else she could go. She must do.

'So, what's the plan, miss?' The policeman stepped forwards. 'Can my colleague drive you somewhere?'

Jamie's sofa was objectively better than sitting on the kerb between Glum and Glummer; though perhaps he'd be appalled by the suggestion. Still, she hadn't much of an option.

Impulsively, she tapped out a message.

Anya

Long story but the police are at mine and
I've been told I can't stay here. I've tried everyone

She paused and rephrased this.

My sister and Paddy aren't answering
and the police are still telling me I need
to clear off. I know it's weird but could
I by any chance come to yours?
I promise to make you breakfast. X

He replied immediately.

Jamie

Are you OK?! Definitely, head over – or
can I come and meet you? X

369

She took a deep breath and then – with a nod of decisiveness – she replied.

Anya

THANK YOU

And no, thanks – they're giving me a lift

. . . In a squad car. X

He was typing again.

Jamie

What an entrance. See you soon. X

Address is: 46 Highburgh Road (in case you'd forgotten)

In spite of everything, she smiled. The stringy policeman was standing with his arms crossed and chest puffed out, as if he were doing a feeble impression of a bouncer.

'OK,' Anya said, a little sullenly. 'I have somewhere I can go.'

The policewoman nodded smartly.

'Great. I'll give you a lift.'

'Thank you.' She hesitated. 'Wait. Can I come back tomorrow?'

'Oh yes,' said the man. 'Tomorrow will be fine.'

It was a Friday night and as soon as they hit Great Western Road, the city was alive. From the window, Anya could see punters pouring out of pubs, the embers of their cigarettes glowing in the dark, and unsteady groups veering down the pavements, one or other of their party occasionally straying into the road, shrieking, unmoved by the sight of a police vehicle. Anya was gripped with a sudden fear someone she knew would see her in the back of the squad car and assume the worst.

Mercifully, within fifteen minutes of sliding about the back seats as the policewoman took the corners, Anya was ducking out of the car.

'Thanks for the lift.' She hesitated. 'And . . . you're sure I can come back tomorrow?'

The woman nodded, clearly already tired of Anya, and this situation.

'Yes.'

'OK. Thanks.'

Anya stepped backwards and the policewoman rolled up the passenger window, nodded at Anya through the glass and accelerated back up the street.

It was raining a little. There was a set of five steps that ran up to his building, which Anya faced down now, breath heavy again. She became suddenly very conscious that she was in the clothes she'd rolled into to pick up the twins, so many hours ago: jeans, a nondescript jumper and a pair of slip-on trainers, which had an unfortunate and undeniably 'orthopaedic' look to them.

On the bottom step she spotted Jamie's face at the window, his dark eyes visible even in the darkness of the street. He grinned and her heart rate doubled.

27

'Insomniac,' Jamie offered, noticing Anya's interest in his impressive collection of herbal teas, and Anya recalibrated his permanently bruised eyes.

'Do they help?'

'Not really.' He smiled. 'But it's something to drink when I'm staring at the ceiling at four a.m.'

She was leaning against the counter, watching him potter around in a T-shirt and tracksuit trousers and odd socks that had made Anya smile when she spotted them at the door. It was the most undone he'd ever been and she liked the slight vulnerability, and how delighted he'd looked when he opened the door.

'Speaking of, what can I get you? I've got some wine, although I always think it's dangerous to start drinking wine at' – he glanced at the kitchen wall clock – 'one a.m.'

'Agreed.' She felt nervous.

'I've also got Laphroaig.'

He stretched into a bottom corner cupboard and presented a two-thirds full bottle, and the sight of the amber liquid made Anya feel warm.

'That would be nice.'

He nodded and poured a dram into two crystal glasses. Anya took one and walked towards the sink and added a splash of water.

'Sorry. My dad hates it when I do that.'

'Sacrilege.'

In the living room, he joined her on the sofa, angled towards her. He smelled clean, like laundry that had dried outdoors.

'So' – he massaged one shoulder, and fixed her gaze – 'what happened with your cousin?'

Anya recalled the latest events at 26 Hamilton Drive – the dour policewoman and her stringy sidekick, a sheepish Claire, the off-stage, menacing presence of Richard.

'Do you know what they were fighting about?'

'I have no idea. The police wouldn't tell me much except that it wasn't particularly serious and had involved some "smashed plates, raised voices and a damaged computer".' She'd WhatsApped Claire on the way over, but the message was stuck on one tick. Anya had tried not to see this as alarming. 'Although that sounds quite serious to me.'

Jamie grimaced sympathetically and she felt pleased to have him.

'They'd definitely been having . . . issues,' she continued, swirling the whisky in her glass. 'But a plate-flinging, computer-smashing brawl is out of character for Claire. And Richard, to be fair. He's pretty weedy.' She paused. 'And creepy.'

'What's their relationship like usually?'

'Well, until all this happened, I would have assumed it was cold, clinical and utterly lacking in passion. The idea of them having sex is about as erotic as buying loo roll.'

To Anya, the word 'sex' hung like a baited hook and she immediately wished she hadn't said it, although he was smiling playfully. After a steeling sip of whisky, she added:

'Thanks for letting me stay. I was otherwise going to be very stuck.'

'Pleasure. If you remember, I invited you earlier.'

She matched his mischievous grin.

'I'm afraid I'd never stand up Paddy.'

'Noted.'

She raised her eyebrows and he mimicked her, so she rolled her eyes and he smiled.

'Although I note you're not sitting on his sofa right now.'

Anya laughed.

'He's a very heavy sleeper. As is my sister, Georgie.'

'I'll take third place.'

She grinned.

'Thanks again.'

There was a pause and he sat up a little on the sofa, slightly more alert.

'So,' he started. 'I have news, actually.'

'What?'

'Euan *did* get in touch with Iona. Today. He sent her an email to apologize and transferred her £200. A sort of down payment, apparently.'

'What!' She swivelled to better face him. 'Why didn't you tell me?'

'Sorry.' He raised his palms in play surrender. 'It only happened this afternoon. And' – he pinned her gaze – 'I wanted to tell you in person.'

There was a crackling pause but Anya was too impatient for details.

'I can't believe he did it.' She recalled Euan's squirming indignation. 'Did he mention you'd been up to see him?'

Jamie shook his head.

'He didn't. Although I told her, so she knows.'

She took this in.

'So, he wanted some credit for doing it all by himself?'

Jamie shrugged.

'Maybe.'

'Have you seen the email?'

'Yeah.' He wriggled to dislodge his phone and now their legs stayed touching. 'Here.' Up this close, peering at his phone screen, she could feel the heat from his chest.

From: ecrrck@gmail.com
To: iona.kildare@gmail.com
Re: Sorry

Iona,

I've long owed you this message, but for lots of reasons I didn't feel ready to send it. I'm so sorry. For everything. For leaving, for not explaining and definitely for stealing. The truth is complicated and I'm not ready to explain it yet but perhaps you'll know it soon. £200 coming today. Will repay the rest of it as soon as I can. I promise – I hope that still means something to you.

E

'Wow.'

They exchanged a glance, his brows low and dark and knitted.

'Not exactly a grovelling apology.' He pinned her gaze again.

'No.' She considered this. Anya imagined Euan sending

375

the email, hunched over a laptop somewhere, phrasing and rephrasing the sentences. Or maybe he'd dashed it off, eager not to be made to think about his own misdeeds for too long. 'But we must have got through to him. A bit. What did Iona think of it all?'

Jamie hesitated.

'She was surprised,' he said eventually. 'Pleased, obviously. About the money. She said it was a bit strange to hear from him, even though I'd warned her he might. I think it made her feel a bit unsettled. She'd spent a long time trying not to think about him.'

'Understandable. How did she feel about you tracking him down?'

A guilty smile.

'She was pretty furious at first. But then I think she understood. I think I understand a bit better now too. Why I wanted to find him so much.'

'Quarter-life crisis?'

He laughed.

'Is that what yours was?'

'Touché.'

'Unfortunately, I think I'm too old to call it that. But an early thirties version. I missed him, but it wasn't really him I missed.'

'I think they just call it nostalgia.'

Anya felt an unmistakeable – and slightly terrifying – charge when their eyes met this time.

'Be more happy!' She wasn't ready, not yet. 'You saved the day. She got an apology and is getting the money.' On instruction, he nodded and looked pleased, and she added: 'That's much better.'

'I had help, of course.'

'You did.'

She was feeling a little giddy, so she took another sip of the whisky. Even watered down, it tasted almost too peaty and her eyes felt rheumy and warm. She must have made a face because Jamie laughed: 'Not a fan?'

'Sorry. I know it's very good. I *want* to like it. It just always tastes too much like whisky.'

'I think that's the point.'

He laughed again at her guilty grimace.

'Can I get you something else?'

'No thank you.'

'Food?'

She fixed him with a glint.

'Are you going to prepare me a midnight snack?'

'Of course not,' he replied silkily. 'I was going to suggest you made it.' She affected indignation, and he added: 'Well, you're the one who needs a roof over your head.'

He pinned her gaze again and she felt the charge once more, rattling, thrilling and a little terrifying all at the same time. She contemplated her move.

'How many strikes before I'm out again?' She was pleased with this.

He raised an eyebrow, and examined the liquid in his glass, playing for time.

'One more,' he started, 'and the sofa is no longer available.' Their faces were already close but edged closer, and his voice dropped to a whisper. 'Although I suppose there could be somewhere else you could sleep.'

Even Anya – rusty as she was – knew what she was supposed to say to this.

'I didn't come all this way to sleep on the sofa.'

'Good.'

The kiss was the kind of urgent one that seemed impatient for what was surely coming next, their hands and mouths moving fast, and Anya only just had the presence of mind to put her whisky glass safely on the coffee table before she started unbuttoning Jamie's shirt.

28

Paddy

OMG Anya

What happened at Claire's???

Also, assuming you stayed with G and didn't have

to walk the streets of the west end

Georgie

No, wait, she didn't I thought she was with you!!!

Anya where are you???

Anya

Anya!! Answer!!

You're stressing me out

Paddy

Anya!

Georgie

ANYA

I've called her like six times

Paddy

Ffs Anya

Oh wait SHE'S TYPING

Anya

SORRY SORRY SORRY I AM ALIVE

DON'T PANIC

I'm at Jamie's
DO NOT LAUGH
And it's not like that
Well actually it is exactly like that
Anyway you two were asleep and he
texted and I had nowhere else to go

Georgie
Um WHAT have I missed

Paddy
👀

Anya
It has been an eventful 12 hours
Can we go for a walk
Still not sure if I'm allowed back to Claire's
I've texted her but haven't heard anything back

Georgie
I've texted too – nothing yet
Shall we meet at Kelvingrove Museum?

Anya
Oooh yes!

Paddy
Perfect
11?

Anya
Sounds good
I apologize in advance for my appearance
I'm in yesterday's clothes and make-up

Anya placed her phone down on the table.

'Paddy and my sister are suitably horrified they slept through my distress texts at midnight last night.'

'Uh oh.'

Jamie had his back to her while he washed the cafetière up at the sink, but she could hear the grin in his voice. While he pottered, she observed him, noting that his hair was sticking up at the back. He was barefoot, long feet sticking out from under the bottom of checked pyjama trousers, and her chest did a skittering thing it had been doing a lot for the last twelve hours.

'The WhatsApps have been coming thick and fast.'

He placed the clean cafetière on the countertop, filled and turned on the kettle, then turned to face her.

'Does this mean I'm in their good books already? And I barely had to lift a finger.'

She raised a playful eyebrow, which he returned, before carrying two mugs to the table. Anya selected the bigger one.

'Have you heard anything from Claire?'

'Nothing yet.' She'd texted three times; the messages were at least delivering now. 'But the policewoman said I could go back this morning, so I'm just going to assume I can.'

The prospect of returning was making her feel anxious, but she was trying to ignore it. She also felt a little sticky from sleeping in her make-up and her outfit – yesterday's jumper and a pair of Jamie's ballooning jogging bottoms – wasn't helping. She pulled the sleeves of her jumper down over both hands, fiddling with the cuffs, as Jamie finished tipping coffee into the cafetière and joined her at the table.

'I'm going to go meet Paddy and Georgie at the Kelvingrove in a bit.' She was disappointed to be leaving.

'What are you doing later?'

'Well. It slightly depends on if I'm allowed back into Claire's house.' She swallowed another yowl of anxiety. 'But in theory, I'm practising my cooking.'

'I thought you were really good at cooking.'

'I *am*.' She was still fighting with the cuffs of the jumper. 'I'm doing my first catering event tomorrow and so I just want to practise my menu for the thousandth time.'

'Oh, yes, of course. Dog birthday party?'

'A fortieth. The dog's event is next week.'

'Of course. Hottest ticket in town.'

She laughed impatiently. The kettle sounded like it was about to blast off and Jamie stood up again to decant the water into the cafetière.

'I presume you need a sous-chef?'

He placed the cafetière on the table.

'What, really?'

'I mean, I wouldn't get too excited. Last time I tried to cook I ended up in A&E.' She snorted appreciatively. 'But as long as it doesn't involve too much chopping, then I reckon I could handle it.'

'Everyone has to start somewhere.' She took a sip of coffee, smiling as she watched him over the rim of her mug. 'I'd love you to come round. The only issue is if Claire and Richard are still involved in World War Three.'

'So why don't you come and cook here instead.'

Her stomach swooped.

'Deal.' She nodded, unable to keep the pleasure out of her voice. 'As long as you promise no A&E visits. I'm terrible with blood.'

He placed his hand on his chest, grinning. 'You have my solemn word that if I slice a hand open and need five stitches, I'll go there all on my own.'

She laughed again and dribbled coffee down her front.

'Very smooth.' Jamie passed her a tea towel.

'I'm going to need to borrow another jumper now.' She dabbed at the coffee. 'And pour myself some more coffee.'

'I'll get the jumper.'

He reappeared a few minutes later with a different sweatshirt, soft and worn. She examined it more closely.

'Is that a Kelvinbridge Academy sweatshirt?'

'There are very few women I can lend it to – and believe me, Anya, I've tried.'

She rolled her eyes again and shrugged into it, feeling his eyes on her.

'Well, it's definitely nostalgic.'

And then they were kissing, insistently, her arms around his neck, he pinning her gently against the kitchen counter. When they broke off, Jamie wore his most dashing, inviting grin.

'I have to go!' Anya laughed regretfully.

'Do you really?'

'Yes.'

'Oh, fine.'

He kissed her again – hard – and they drew apart, grinning.

'Want a shower before you go?' he asked.

'Will you judge me if I say no?'

'I will think you are revolting and never invite you back.'
He managed a straight face for half a second.

'Phew, because I don't think I have time.' The clock
said 10.30 a.m. 'But I want it on record that I *want* to have
a shower.'

'Sure you do.'

She stood up and he joined her, wrapping his arms
around her waist and kissing her hard. When they separated his eyes were dancing again.

'You definitely need a shower.'

'Is that Kelvinbridge Academy PE kit?'

Georgie was waiting on the steps of the Kelvingrove
Museum, holding three takeaway coffees. There was a
confident breeze and her sister's hair was flying wildly
with each gust, her nose a little pink in the chill. Anya
shuffled up the steps as quickly as she could, eyes watering
a little in the wind.

'Pass it over. Please.'

Georgie handed the coffee over and tied her hair back,
and Anya took a sip.

'Thank you. And yes. It is. I spilt a different coffee all
over my other jumper.' She paused. 'And this is the only
thing that Jamie had.'

'Yes, what—'

'I'll explain everything when Paddy arrives.'

'He's there.' Georgie pointed to Paddy, who was walking up the sweeping driveway towards the museum's stone
steps, clutching his coat lapels in the breeze. His ears
looked cold.

'I can't tell if he's in a good or bad mood,' Georgie mused. 'What do you think?'

'His ears look a little cross.'

Paddy took the last few steps at a trot. Georgie passed him the last coffee.

'Thanks G. Oh, Anya.' He appraised her outfit sadly. 'What happened?'

'Shut up.' Paddy would not ruin the thrill of last night, even if he did look particularly wholesome this morning, clean-shaved, his hair lightly gelled. 'Neither of you can criticize me, actually, as you weren't around during my hour of need.' Georgie's eyes were huge, but Anya couldn't resist sticking the knife in a little further. 'If I'd had somewhere else to go, I wouldn't be wearing someone else's old school sweatshirt.'

Paddy snorted.

'You also wouldn't have slept with Jamie. Which I'm assuming you did.'

'I did.'

He grinned in response. Simultaneously, Georgie and Paddy made a 'told-you-so' face at one another, which would usually have annoyed her, but on this occasion did not.

'Shall we go inside?' Paddy prodded her. 'It's freezing. And I want to hear everything.'

Like the Necropolis high on the hill above the city, the Kelvingrove was a place they'd been coming since they were children and the museum had a familiar comforting smell of artefacts and school trips. Sometimes, when Anya couldn't sleep, she'd draw it in her mind's eye, mapping out its floors and stone staircases and familiar exhibitions. Without conferring, they automatically started in the Scottish wildlife wing.

Her voice dropped to a low, respectful museum hush, Anya completed the story, with a few looping tangents and backtracks and pauses for Paddy or Georgie's 'Wait, *what*?' She enjoyed the thrill of being the ringmaster.

'And just to check' – Georgie glanced between Anya and Paddy – 'we're happy about this, right? Jamie is nice.'

'Well, I think so.' Anya squirmed a little. 'I mean, it's only been one evening. And I'm a little out of practice.'

'Hey, you had all those weird road trips,' Paddy supplied.

'Well. Yes. But those were different.'

'I can't keep up with all your men.'

'And Euan is . . . ?' Georgie was staring at her closely.

'Definitely not a thing. Very much not.'

'Good.'

'Yes.' Thinking about Euan still made her feel something, although that something wasn't romantic so much as wistful and a little sad. 'That was never going to work out.'

They were in the vicinity of Sir Roger, a vast elephant who always attracted a crowd and, as usual, they stopped a respectful distance away in order to admire him. Their silent pilgrimage completed, they wandered towards the thick stone steps that led up to the next floor.

'I'm tired,' Anya announced, when they'd got halfway up the stairs.

'No wonder,' Georgie replied from three steps up.

'Shut up. Can we go sit down for a bit?'

'I know you've dressed like someone who's given up, but

386

you can't sit on the floor of the museum.' She made another face at Paddy, who compensated by slowing to a crawl.

'Not here – a bench or something.'

The others continued to walk, although Georgie slowed down too.

'We haven't talked about Claire yet.' Georgie looked grave. 'I've texted her so many times but haven't heard anything.'

'Me neither,' Anya said. They were winding their way down one of the picture galleries now. It was low-lit and quiet, the only other signs of life the odd murmur from another visitor. Paddy had pulled up in front of a macabre still life.

'Maybe she's in prison and has already used her one call,' he said.

'Paddy, it's not funny!' Georgie whipped round. 'Poor Claire.'

'I'm sorry G.' He sounded it. 'Obviously it's not funny. Well. It's only a bit funny.'

Georgie whipped round again.

'I'm sure she's fine,' Anya said quickly. She wasn't sure, in fact she felt a little sick, but thankfully her sister had read her mind.

'We'll take you back after this and see how she's doing.'

Anya squeezed her tired eyes together.

'Thanks.'

They mooched around the museum at a snail's pace a little longer, Anya leaning into the familiarity, and trying not to think about what she might find at Claire's. As she was starting to feel very ready to leave the place, it started to pick up, the families arriving with pushchairs and rucksacks, and clusters of bookish students with long skirts and identical tote bags printed with the name of a small, independent bookshop.

'Shall we head?' Anya asked, and Paddy and Georgie both nodded assent.

They exited on to University Avenue, its grand trees like scarecrows silhouetted against the grey November sky. It would take twenty minutes to walk to Claire's.

'Maybe Richard will move out,' Anya said hopefully, as they made their way up the avenue, damp leaves underfoot.

Paddy snorted.

'Yeah, and if you can get Claire to move out too, then you'd be laughing.'

29

Anya had half-expected a police cordon or new locks, but the street was empty and she slid the key into the door and opened it without any trouble. When she paused on the threshold, Georgie prodded her on the back.

'Come on.'

Reluctantly, Anya stepped into the hall. The house beyond the front door was dark and hushed. Anya felt Paddy bringing up the rear.

'This really is so much nicer than I expected.' He sounded disappointed.

'You've been here before,' Anya said. 'You helped me move in.'

'I know but I was too busy trying not to make eye contact with Claire to really notice the surroundings.'

'Claire?' Georgie called out in a clear, high voice. 'It's Georgie.'

'And Anya,' Anya added in a smaller voice.

'Don't tell her I'm here,' Paddy muttered. 'She'll stay hiding.'

They advanced towards the staircase. It was still dim, Claire's graphic objects casting odd shadows. There was a loud creak and they all froze, but no voice – or person – appeared.

'Claire?' Georgie called out again, a little more uncertain

now. Anya and Georgie exchanged a glance, with matching fear in their eyes.

'It sounds like they're both out,' Paddy said flatly. He had spotted a Scandinavian lamp and was examining it closely.

Anya directed her instructions at her sister.

'Will you check upstairs and I'll go down?'

Georgie nodded and they split, leaving Paddy to covet Claire's fixtures and fittings.

Downstairs was also empty, the kitchen as clean and pristine as usual, welcome daylight pouring in from the back door, and no sign of splintered crockery anywhere. There was a single mug in the sink, which Anya recognized as Claire's preferred coffee mug, big and flat and rather prone to letting the heat out.

'No one upstairs.' Georgie and Paddy had appeared in the doorway.

'Maybe they've disappeared and left Anya the house,' Paddy said. He opened the fridge and then closed it again.

'Should we call the police?' Georgie looked anxious. 'Or Richard?'

'I'd rather call the police,' Anya said. 'Or . . . do we try Auntie Sal?'

'I don't want to worry her.' Georgie's eyes were huge.

'OK, I'll text Richard,' Anya said.

Their only text exchange since she'd moved in had been Richard asking whether she had a single first-class stamp.

She typed.

Hi Richard, I'm back at the house. Where are you two?

'Sent.'

Georgie looked relieved.

'You know, they might have just made up and gone for a walk,' Paddy shrugged. He had stopped poking through the fridge. 'Or for lunch.'

'Maybe.' Georgie didn't sound convinced.

'Do you want us to wait with you until they come back?' Paddy asked.

'No – it's OK, honestly. I'll be fine.' She didn't mean it. 'I was going to do some cooking with Jamie later for tomorrow.' Both Paddy and Georgie's eyes lit up, and she felt shy. 'I'm meant to be going to his but I'll obviously cancel if Claire needs me.'

'I'm going to text Mum,' Georgie said.

'Don't text Mum. That's worse than texting Auntie Sal. She'll just flap.'

Georgie ignored her.

'Claire's read my messages! She hadn't before.'

Immediately, Anya felt slightly calmer.

'OK, so that's progress.' Paddy nodded, reassuringly. 'Look, you can't do anything except wait. And Anya, if you want us to stay, we will.'

'No, it's OK. As you said – we can't do anything. Might as well try and keep busy.'

Georgie looked a little unconvinced at this, but eventually, she nodded.

'OK. I'm meant to go and see Alex this afternoon. But I'll be nearby. We're going to the cinema.'

'I'm going home to do some parents' evening prep.' Paddy swung an arm around Anya's shoulders and she put her grateful, tired head on his shoulder. 'So, I'll also be nearby. And bored. So let me know if you need me.'

'And you'll keep us posted?' Georgie asked.

Anya nodded. 'Definitely.' She bit hard on her thumbnail to quiet her anxiety as she walked them both up to the doorway.

'Bye.' Paddy kissed the top of her head. 'Call me later.'

'Let us know if you need us,' Georgie muttered into her hair for the umpteenth time as they hugged farewell.

She closed the door and the hush felt loud, the house creepier than it ever was when Richard stalked the hallways. Anya still couldn't shake the paranoia that one or both of them had been hiding. After a few moments listening to the echoes and gurgles of the empty house, she pulled her trainers back on and slammed the door behind her.

She made deliberately slow work of a trip to the supermarket around the corner, willing Claire and Richard to appear while she was out, but when she returned the house was still empty and unwelcoming.

'Hello?'

Nothing.

'Claire?'

More nothing.

'I'm just going to take a shower,' she added pointlessly.

She took her time in the bathroom on the top landing, enjoying the feeling of the warm water on her skin, the feeling of sloughing off all the tension and anxiety and nervous energy. Wrapped in a towel in her bedroom, she texted Jamie.

Anya

Still no Claire. What time shall I come round? X

Jamie

6? Just laundering my sous-chef's whites. X

It was 4 p.m. now. She'd left the food in the hall, and some of it could do with refrigerating. After a little deliberation, Anya pulled on jeans and a black silk shirt, outlined her eyes with mascara and pulled her damp hair into a ponytail. She took the first step of stairs at a jump, collected the Tesco bags, trotted down the second set, and screamed.

Claire was standing in the kitchen, holding Anya's most rustic and Italian cookbook in one slender arm. She was dressed in a chic, long, black dress, her hair neat, barrette in place again, but she looked exhausted. Her eyes were puffy and shrunken. At the sight of Anya, she closed the book.

'Claire! You gave me a fright.'

'Sorry.' Claire's voice was stiff. 'I got back about ten minutes ago.' She pointed at the book. 'The spaghetti puttanesca looks delicious.'

Anya moved to her. 'Are you OK?' She gestured at the kettle. 'Can I make you a cup of tea, or something?'

Claire shook her head dismissively.

'What about something to eat – have you eaten?'

Claire shook her head dismissively again.

'No. Thank you.'

Cautiously, Anya sank back into a kitchen chair and took a deep breath before she asked: 'Are you going to tell me what happened? Last night? They wouldn't let me stay.'

Anya remembered the sight of her cousin in the doorway, sullen, and knew Claire was remembering it too.

'Sorry,' Claire said primly. 'There was a . . . disagreement.'

'I know.' Anya frowned. 'What happened?' She paused, then added: 'I was so worried. Georgie too.'

Just for a second, Claire looked furious and then her

393

face crumpled and to Anya's surprise, her cousin started crying, tears coming thick and fast, mouth red and open. 'Sorry,' she kept saying, still standing stiffly by the oven as Anya leapt up and put an arm around her shoulder, guiding her back to the kitchen table. Claire's sobs continued but eventually she composed herself enough to speak, in rushed gulps like she was coming up for air.

'Richard is having an affair.' A gurgling sob. 'She's twenty-one.'

'What?' It seemed extraordinary that there were two people in the world who'd consider having sex with Richard. Claire sniffed.

'She works at the escape room where he had his last birthday party. It's been going on for months, apparently.'

The image of Richard chatting up some student in the strip lit insides of an escape room – and her falling for it – made Anya feel nauseated.

'Claire, I'm so sorry' – she reached for her cousin's hand and was allowed to grasp it – 'how did you find out?'

'Her texts were coming up on the iPad. I was doing a sudoku.'

Anya winced.

'How long have you known?'

'Since last night.' Claire wiped snot from her nose with the cuff of her cardigan and Anya politely pretended not to notice. 'He'd been being weird for weeks. Which I'm sure you'd noticed.'

Anya made a diplomatic noise and Claire returned an impatient one.

'Anyway. Last night he told me everything.' She sniffed again. 'I snapped.'

'Oh Claire. No wonder.'

She shrugged one shoulder and said nothing.

'Are you sure I can't get you anything? A glass of water?'

There was a pause and then Claire said, in a voice a little closer to her normal one: 'I'd prefer a glass of wine.'

'Oh.' Anya stood up. 'Of course.'

'There's some in the fridge.'

Anya moved to the fridge and retrieved a half-open bottle of Chablis and poured Claire a generous measure. She took a grateful gulp.

'You're welcome to have some.'

'Ah . . . I'll wait. I think. Well. I'm meant to be going out in a bit, but I'll cancel.'

Claire raised both eyebrows.

'Jamie?'

'Actually, yes.'

Claire did a half-smile and nodded.

'Don't worry, I'll be fine.'

'No, Claire, I'll cancel. I'm not leaving you alone.'

'You can invite him round here, if you'd like.'

She considered this. She felt mean leaving Claire, whatever she said. Plus, Anya would be prepared to bet that Jamie had all his blokey mod-cons and not a single baking tray.

'No,' she said decisively. 'I'll cancel him tonight and stay here. I could cook you dinner and maybe we could watch a film. Or' – inspiration! – 'I'll play Scrabble with you.'

This earned a reluctant smile.

'Anya, that's very sweet. But you having someone round isn't going to change the fact that Richard is having an affair with a twenty-one-year old junior supervisor at an escape room near Motherwell.'

'Fair point.' Still, Anya hesitated. 'If you're sure it's fine' – she paused – 'then I'll text him and suggest it.'

Claire waved dismissively.

'Do it.'

> **Anya**
> OK, so change of plans: Claire is back and seems OK-ish. Slightly long story. Do you mind coming here? I don't want to leave her. X

> **Jamie**
> Of course not. What time?

> **Anya**
> Shall we stick with 6 pm?

> **Jamie**
> See you there. X

> **Anya**
> X

'He'll be round at six.' A pause. 'Thanks, Claire.'

Her cousin said nothing. The shopping was still in its bags, so Anya moved deftly back and forth between the fridge until it was all offloaded. When she was finished, she returned to the table, and Claire's eyes flickered with acknowledgement.

'So. Is the . . . wedding—'

Claire pinched her nose.

'Off. He's picked her. Not that I'd have him back now, anyway.'

Anya winced.

'Oh Claire.' Anya squeezed her cousin's shoulder gingerly. 'I'd have thrown more than a plate in that situation.'

Her cousin looked a little pleased with herself.

'They were his grandmother's plates. Very sentimentally valuable. Although' – she sniffed again – 'I probably shouldn't have touched the computer.'

'What exactly did you *do* to it?'

'I poured a glass of the Chablis I'm drinking into the hard drive.'

'Wow.'

'Yes. Well. I was angry. Unfortunately, the computer I damaged was very valuable and belongs to a company he'd been doing some work for. The information contained on the hard drive was very important.'

Oh God.

'Are they ... pressing charges?' The words sounded too dramatic for an afternoon in Claire's kitchen.

'I'm not sure. I've offered to buy them a new computer.'

'OK.'

'And I've taken Richard's keys away. The police agreed with me on that one.'

But the bravado vanished as quickly as it had appeared; Claire took another gulp of wine and squeezed her eyes shut before she opened them again. 'I'm so embarrassed,' she whispered. 'I'm going to have to tell everyone.'

She looked so desperate and Anya felt wretched.

'Richard should be embarrassed,' she tried. 'Not you.' Claire looked unconvinced, so Anya added: 'I can help, if you want. I can do the family side, anyway. With Georgie.'

Claire offered a watery smile.

'Thanks.'

'Of course. Speaking of Georgie, do you mind if I let her know you're OK?'

Claire looked downcast again.

'I won't tell her everything yet,' Anya said. 'If you're not ready. Just that you're back and you're fine. You know how she gets.'

Claire nodded and dabbed at her nose again with her cardigan.

'Yes, OK. That's fine.'

> **Anya**
> Claire fine
> Bit upset – will explain
> But she's back

Georgie
Oh THANK GOD

Paddy
Where was she????

> **Anya**
> Tell you later – just with her now

Paddy
Hope she's OK
(Really)

Georgie
Send her my love xxxxxx

Anya placed her phone facedown on the table.

'Georgie sends her love.' She decided not to mention

Paddy. 'Do you want some food? I've got snacks in the fridge. I made them yesterday but they should be OK.'

'Yes please.' Claire's shoulders were sloped in defeat. 'If you have enough.'

'I definitely have enough.' She opened the fridge. 'I've got baba ganoush and some crostini so far, though we'll be making more bits later.'

The wall clock read 4.30 p.m. She wasn't quite sure how the collision of Jamie and Claire was going to work, but she was going to have to improvise. She prepared a plate with two of the prettiest, most uniform burgers and a big dollop of dip and four crostini breadsticks and presented it to Claire.

'Thank you.' She started nibbling at a dry breadstick.

'You're meant to have it with the dip,' Anya started and Claire gave her a look. 'Never mind. Have it how you like.'

But with her next mouthful, Claire dipped the bread-stick in the baba ganoush.

'This is very nice,' she said. 'Thank you.'

She sounded so formal that Anya laughed.

'Thank *you*, Claire.'

'What time is Jamie coming round?' She nibbled delicately on a crostini.

'Six p.m.' Anya replied. 'So quite soon.'

'Don't worry.' Claire nodded smartly. 'I'll disappear upstairs.'

'No! Claire, you don't have to do that.'

'Don't be stupid, Anya,' she sounded far more like the normal Claire when she said that, 'you live here too. Anyway, I've got plenty to do. Caterers of my own to cancel, photographers . . .' She wiped a stray tear away and Anya squeezed her hand.

399

'Well let me help with some of it. Whatever you need. I've got this job in the morning, but I should be home by about three p.m. We can divide up the jobs together.' She squeezed Claire's shoulder. 'Shotgun the worst ones.'

Claire took a heavy breath.

'Thank you.'

She finished the rest of her plate in silence before heading to the fridge to pour a little more wine into the glass.

'Have fun with Jamie.'

'Thanks.'

'I take it this is a date.'

'I think so.'

Claire managed a small smile.

'I see. Well, I have this' – she raised the glass aloft – 'and some anti-wedmin to do. Wedmin.' She paused. 'I despise that word.'

Anya smiled.

'It's not even really a word.'

Claire nodded.

'Thanks again for the food.'

'My pleasure.'

Claire stood and Anya dared a hug, which was, if not warmly received, at the very least received.

'Thank you.' Anya watched her cousin disappear up the stairs, her tread heavy and defeated, and her heart snagged for Claire. It was awful to see her this miserable; she'd give anything to have her brusque, assured and superior instead.

Twenty minutes before Jamie was due to arrive, Anya felt distracted and a little skittish with date nerves. To calm herself down, she opened and closed all the cupboards in the kitchen, tried to read an *Economist* that Claire had left on the table, then wiped down the surfaces with a damp cloth – living with Claire had really changed her – until the doorbell rang and her heart rate doubled again.

Rinsing her hands under the tap quickly, she legged it up the stairs and towards the front door. A tall figure stood, obscured behind the blurred glass. With a deep breath, stomach somersaulting, Anya opened the door. To Richard.

'Anya!' Richard's tone was chummy, as though he were pleased to see her. 'I'm just popping in.'

Automatically, Anya closed the door a little, so that it was just her head poking out of the frame.

'You know you're not meant to be here, Richard.' She was trying to sound firm but her voice had a wavering edge.

'I'll only be a minute,' Richard was casual although he stepped forward another pace. 'I just wanted to get some clothes.'

'She doesn't want you in the house. She took away your keys. And it's not your house.'

Richard was attempting an impression of a man caught in a misunderstanding, but was growing undone by his reddening face.

'No, Anya, it's OK.' Richard clenched his jaw in what he presumably thought was a conciliatory smile.

'No Richard. It isn't. I know what happened.'

He clenched his jaw tighter.

'It's my right to get my things.'

'No, it isn't.' The blood was roaring in her ears now. 'And if you try, I'll call the police.'

Richard's face was really red now; his mouth twisted into an expression of pure rage, and for all Anya's bravado and charge, she was also quite concerned that he might try and force his way in – until she saw Jamie advancing up the front path behind him. She tried to catch his eye but Jamie had already clocked the situation. Richard, however, had not yet noticed she had back-up.

'Listen—' he started spitting but Jamie stepped forward.

'Excuse me' – his pleasantness clearly disarmed Richard – 'I think you'd better leave now.'

'Who the hell are you?' Richard asked, incredulously.

'*He's* invited here,' Anya said pointedly.

'Listen, Anya – just get out of the way, OK?' He moved closer, making to open the door and automatically, Anya flinched, taking a step back into the hallway.

'Hey,' Jamie said calmly, stepping in front of Richard, who gave him a look of pure loathing, and then stopped like he'd been shot.

Claire was standing in the hallway, silhouette elegant in the dim light. She was still holding the glass of wine, though it was empty now.

'I told you you weren't to come back here, Richard.'

'Claire, I just need some—'

'Get. Out.' In the half-light, Anya could see Claire's face was icily calm. 'Or I will call the police.'

There was a pause.

'You're being unreasonable—'

'GET. OUT!'

Anya held her breath and exchanged a nervous look with Jamie. Richard hesitated but after a moment, all the fight seemed to drain from him, and with his shoulder slumped, he retreated, avoiding eye contact as he shuffled down the steps. To Anya's surprise, he climbed into an unfamiliar car a few houses up the street. The new girlfriend must have driven him here; Anya really hoped Claire hadn't noticed, but her cousin was impassive, her posture perfect.

'Are you OK?' Jamie was still hovering in the doorway.

'Completely fine,' Claire replied calmly. 'Come on in, Jamie.'

He walked through the open door. He was holding a bottle of wine.

'Hey,' Anya whispered.

They exchanged a quick kiss on the lips, Anya feeling pleased and shy in front of Claire.

'I sent him ahead so I could really make an entrance.' The corner of Jamie's eyes crinkled.

'You must be Claire.'

'Yes. Sorry. I was supposed to be upstairs pretending I wasn't here.'

Anya laughed.

'Claire, you don't—'

But her cousin was disappearing into the shadows again, up the stairs towards her bedroom.

'See you later, Anya,' she called out.

'Claire – do come and join us if you change your mind.'

But her cousin didn't reply; Jamie and Anya exchanged a glance. As she led him downstairs, her legs felt like helium.

'Thanks for the back up. Do you want a drink?' They were standing in the kitchen now, and Jamie ignored her and wrapped his arms around her waist; they stood locked in each other for a long moment. He tasted like mouth-wash. She decided she liked this.

'So, Richard seems like a great guy.' Jamie sat down at the table. Anya laughed guiltily.

'Last night, Claire learned he is having an affair with a twenty-one-year old he met at an escape room where he was celebrating his fortieth birthday.' She paused. 'Every time I hear that it sounds more ridiculous.'

Jamie whistled.

'Shit.'

'I know. The wedding is no more. Poor Claire.'

'Oh Christ. Are you sure it's OK I'm here?'

'I offered to cancel or go to yours several times. She insisted. I think she might want company without having to actually have company. I'll go up and check on her in a little while.'

'Good plan.' Jamie nodded. 'So' – he cast around the kitchen for clues – 'what exactly are we cooking?'

'I'm cooking. You're helping.'

He laughed.

'Fine, I know my place.'

'As you should.' She moved towards the countertop and Jamie followed. 'The courgette and halloumi fritters are the hardest things to get right. So, I'd like to have another go at them before tomorrow. And we need to make the brownies.'

Despite his valiant-ish efforts, it became quickly apparent that Jamie was a useless sous-chef. He chopped everything unevenly, got distracted and kept eating ingredients. Anya, however, very much enjoyed barking instructions at him.

'Raw halloumi isn't that nice.' He popped a wonky cube into his mouth.

'That's why I'm cooking it.'

He grinned and popped another piece into his mouth. 'Sorry. I'll stop now.'

While Anya drizzled oil into her huge wok, Jamie made his way around the kitchen, opening drawers and cupboards in search of a corkscrew and glasses.

'Corkscrew is there.' She pointed at a drawer beside the sink. 'Glasses up there.'

'Thanks.'

Items secured, he opened the wine and sniffed the cork and she snorted at him.

'Hey, you get food. Let me have wine.'

She put him in charge of the wok and fritters – after very careful instructions – and set to dribbling the brownie mixture into a tray.

'Am I the worst student you've ever had?' He'd just dropped the spatula.

'Much worse than the twins,' she said lightly. 'So yes.'

As soon as the brownies were in the oven, she manoeuvred him away from the wok with a nudge of the hips; he kissed her.

'Go sit at the table.' She grinned. 'These will be a while.'

While the brownies made the kitchen smell sweet and sugary, they divided the fritters.

'So' – Jamie licked his fingers – 'what's so hard about them?'

'Having an amateur as a sous-chef.' She raised her eyebrows. 'But mainly just frying them so everything gets gooey but also crispy. If that makes sense.'

He took another bite.

'Taste good to me. My compliments to the sous-chef.'

She smiled.

'I think I've cracked them though. Now to do it again tomorrow. For real.'

They cleared up together, Jamie colliding regularly with her in the unfamiliar kitchen, occasionally looping an arm around her waist to further derail them. When they'd finished, she squeezed the cloth in the sink, and he crouched in front of the Perspex door of the oven.

'They'll be another forty minutes I think.' She pointed upstairs. 'I'm going to check on Claire. Try not to break anything.'

'I promise to try.' She could only see the back of his head, but she could tell he was pleased with that one.

Anya tiptoed up the stairs, feeling like an interloper. All was quiet and gloomy; in the living room, a pillow and a duvet remained on the sofa, vestiges of Richard. Anya recalled the evening she'd found him hiding his phone in the drawer in the hallway, picking up the switched-off handset, its black mirror betraying no clues to his misdeeds. Richard's fortieth had been ages ago; she couldn't believe he'd been lying all that time.

She knocked lightly on Claire's bedroom door but there was no answer, so Anya crept forward and into the room, to discover Claire sprawled across the bed, fast asleep, an iPad lying beside her. Barely daring to breathe, Anya moved the iPad to the bedside table and tiptoed backwards. On the other bedside table – Richard's side – there was a strange plastic form: on closer inspection, Anya determined this was his Invisalign. With a grimace, she stepped backwards out of the room, pausing in the doorway. She'd never been in Claire's room before. It was fairly spartan; besides the bed there was just an old oak dresser, an oval standing mirror with a small crack and a bookshelf packed with serious looking books. It had the charmlessness of an austere guesthouse; she gladly closed the door behind her.

Jamie was reading *The Economist* when she returned, but he pushed it aside when he heard her footsteps. Seeing his face light up when she appeared made her feel brand new again.

'How is she?' he asked.

'Sleeping.'

'Sounds like she needed it.'

She'd had an idea earlier.

'Do you fancy a walk?'

A big open smile.

'Sounds good.'

Even wrapped in coats and scarves, it was chilly on the climb to the top of the hill in Kelvingrove Park, and Anya was glad of Jamie's arm around her waist. It was dark now and the park was mostly empty and very quiet, the trees casting long shadows in the glow of the street lamps. A dog walker appeared on the near horizon, spaniel zigzagging up the path.

'I always feel like the worst thing about having a dog would be the night walks,' Jamie whispered straight after the pair of them had passed.

'I've just taken you on a night walk.'

'Yes, but that's different.'

'Don't worry, we're almost there anyway.'

After a few more minutes of walking in companionable silence, Anya veered off the road and on to the grass, leading Jamie with long, wobbly strides, her footing a little uncertain in the dark. Finally, when they reached the spot she remembered, she sat down and he followed suit. Ahead of them, the illuminated spires of the university and the city beyond stretched out ahead of them, warm and twinkly in the dark. Jamie arranged his arm around her and she smiled.

'So, I used to sit here all the time with Euan when we were at school.' In the dark, his eyes looked bright and deep. She continued: 'We'd drink whisky I'd nicked from my dad, mixed with apple juice or Fanta or something else to disguise the taste. And then eventually you'd text and he'd go and meet you instead and I'd pretend not to care.'

Jamie laughed.

'The good old days.'

She gave him a look.

'We know what happens when we get too nostalgic.'

'We do.'

The kiss was long and hopeful, and felt like the future and not the past.

Acknowledgements

Firstly, an enormous thank you to my agent Hannah, who, as ever, remained a cool, calm champion who was so generous and patient every time I had what I think are known, technically, as Second Book Jitters. Your insights and instincts are always spot on. Thank you, too, to everyone at Northbank for your ongoing support and wisdom – here's to many more years working together.

To the brilliant team at Michael Joseph, I don't know where I'd be without your hive mind (let's face it, probably still weeping over an early draft). My editor, Rebecca: thank you for your smart, honest and incisive edits that made this book immeasurably better, and for always being a kind and reassuring voice on the end of an email or Zoom call. Clare and Madeleine, thank you too for reading my many drafts, fixing my many plot holes and believing in the book the whole way through: I'm so grateful. Thank you, too, to my publicity dream team of Sriya and Courtney, who masterminded so many ways to get the book out there (I promise to get better at social media). And thank you to the patient editorial team of Emma Henderson and Riana Dixon for guiding me through the final stages of the publishing process, and to Kay Halsey for your keen subbing eye.

Mum, Dad, Toby, Georgia and Molly: I do hope this book pays a suitable tribute to the Glasgow years (the best years). I'm so pleased that some of those happy days could inspire this story.

Lastly, thanks to those ex-boyfriends who dumped me in the inventive ways that informed the book (as journalists always say: life is copy), and to all the friends who scraped me up off the floor afterwards. And the biggest thank you as ever goes to Samuel, who was always my plan A.